Praise for

"Top 10 Romance of 2012." (and 2015)
– Booklist, *The Night Is Mine (Hot Point)*

"One of our favorite authors."
–RT Book Reviews

"Suzanne Brockmann fans will love this."
–Booklist, *Wait Until Dark*

"A rousing mix of romance and military action thrills…Buchman blends tender feelings with military politics to keep readers riveted."
-Publishers Weekly

"Buchman continues to serve up nonstop action that will keep readers on the edge of their seats."
– Library Journal Xpress

"The Night Stalkers is a series you'll want to read, in order or not."
– Kirkus Reviews

"A must read for fans of military romantic suspense… "
– Fresh Fiction

Praise for the Firehawks series:

"Buchman again pens an excellent read!"
-RT Book Reviews, *Full Blaze*

"*Full Blaze* hits it out of the park."
-Reading Reality, *Full Blaze*

"*Full Blaze* has it all;
suspense, hot-hot romance
and as much edge-of-the-seat
excitement you could possible ask for."
-Fresh Fiction, *Full Blaze*

"It's wonderful fun!"
-Reading Reality, *Flash of Fire*

"Buchman writes with beauty and passion.
The flames of passion burn brightly in this
meticulously researched, hard-hitting, and
suspenseful contemporary."
- Publishers Weekly, starred review, *Pure Heat*

"If you are looking for an action packed
romantic read...*Pure Heat* is one you
will want to pick up."
–Fresh Fiction, *Pure Heat*

Wild Fire

a Firehawks romance

by

M. L. Buchman

Sign up for M. L. Buchman's newsletter and
discover more by this author at:
www.mlbuchman.com

Cover images:
Sky, Clouds, Fire And Smoke © Livingsee
Healthy Young Guy Posing Near A Wall © Isn5000
Forest Fire In Night © Photosky
Pulaski Fire Ax © Jerimy Colbert
Erickson Helicopter © UDSA by Lance Cheung

Buchman Bookworks

Other works by M. L. Buchman:

Acknowledgement

My *thanks for the* kind assistance of Erickson, Inc. can never be properly expressed. My appreciation goes to: Susan Blandholm the Sr. Director of Marketing and Strategy at Erickson, Inc. who arranged everything so patiently and Erick Nodland for both his service and a ride in his Bell LongRanger.

However, it is Chief Flight Instructor Randy Erwin's generous sharing of his time and knowledge—and his *vast* patience with my naive questions—without whom this book would not have been possible. The mistakes are mine; everything that's right is his. Thanks again, Randy!

Chapter 1

*G*ordon. *Hit the hotspot* at your two o'clock."

"*Perfect,*" Gordon Finchley mumbled to himself. The call came from Mark Henderson, the Incident Commander-Air, the moment after Gordon carved his MD 530 helicopter the other way toward a flaming hotspot at eleven o'clock and hit the release on his load of water.

Two hundred gallons spilled down out of his helo's belly tank and punched the cluster of burning alders square in the heart. He glanced back as he continued his turn and the flames were now hidden in the cloud of steam, which meant it was a good hit.

"Die, you dog!" He yelled it at the flames like…Austin Powers…yelling at something. He really had to work on his macho. Or maybe just give it up as a lost cause.

"I have the other one, Mark," Vanessa called up to the ICA from her own MD 530. Her touch of an Italian accent still completely slayed Gordon…and any other guy who met her. Because her "Italian" was more than just her voice.

Gordon twisted his bird enough sideways to watch her, which

was always a pleasure, in the air or on the ground. Vanessa Donatella flew her tiny, four-seater helicopter the same way she looked: smooth, beautiful, and just a little bit delicate. Her water attack was also dead on. It punched down the second spot fire, which had been ignited by an ember cast far ahead of the main fire.

The two of them were fighting their aerial battle beyond the head of the wildfire—he and Vanessa were making sure that nothing sparked to life ahead of the line of defense. He could just make out the Mount Hood Aviation smokejumpers suited up in flame-resistant yellow Nomex, defending a ridgeline. The heavy hitters of the main airshow, MHA's three Firehawks and a Twin 212 helicopter, were attacking the primary fire, ducking in and around the columns of smoke and flame to deliver their loads where the smokejumpers most needed them.

He twisted back to straight flight, popped up high enough to clear the leading edge of the flames, then ducked through the thin veil of smoke and dove down over the burning bank at the lake's shore. He could feel the wash of radiated heat through the large windshield that gave him such a great view—a nearly unbroken sweep of acrylic starting below his feet on the rudder pedals, then sweeping above his head.

It became much cooler once he punched out over the open lake.

Gordon slid to a hover with his skids just ten feet over the water—low enough to unreel his snorkel hose and let the pump head dip below the lake's surface. It would be forty seconds until he had two hundred more gallons aboard.

Vanessa slid her helo down close beside him and dunked her own hose.

Their helos were identical except for the large identifying numbers on the side. The MD 530 was as small as a helicopter could be and still have four seats. Last season they'd switched from dipping buckets dangling on longlines to belly tanks attached between the skids. There was an art to steering the swinging buckets to their target that Gordon could get nostalgic about, but the tank was certainly more convenient.

Their helos were painted with the MHA colors: gloss black with red-and-orange flames running down the sides. The effect was a bit ruined by the big windshields that made up the whole nose of the aircraft, but Gordon would take the visibility any day.

"Nice hit," he offered. The pilots kept a second radio tuned to a private frequency so that they could coordinate among themselves without interfering with the ICA's commands to the airshow. It also allowed them to chat in these brief quiet moments. In the background was a third radio tuned to the ground team. Thankfully, there weren't any fixed-wing aircraft attacking the fire or there'd be a fourth radio running. When flying solo, it could be harder to fight the radios than the fire.

"You too. It is such a pity that you hit the wrong fire." He could feel Vanessa's warmth in her tease.

"Even a couple seconds more warning would have worked. If I didn't know better, I'd think Mark was doing it on purpose."

"Whine. Whine. Whine."

They shared a smile across the hundred feet that separated them. It was a real bummer that it hadn't worked out between them. After months of silent but—he eventually discovered—mutual attraction, they'd gotten together. Only to have nothing come of it. Making love to someone as beautiful and gentle as Vanessa was a joy, but there'd been no spark. They'd talked about it, tried again, and still nothing. Despite his typical awkwardness around stunning women (most women really) and Vanessa's natural shyness—or perhaps because of the combination—they'd come out of it as close friends. Friends without benefits, which was still a pity, but good friends.

His water tank gauge reached full and he lifted aloft as he reeled in his hose. Vanessa would be about ten seconds behind him.

Together they flew over the flaming bank that sloped steeply up from the lake. No point in fighting that fire, it would burn down to the shore and then there would be nowhere else for it to go. It was simply one flank of the main fire. The head itself was a long burn running south toward a community of homes at the other end of the lake—*that* they had to defend.

Henderson gave him enough lead time to pick his path this time. His whine to Vanessa had some basis. Messing with a pilot didn't sound like Henderson at all, but lately there'd definitely been something going on.

Gordon shrugged to himself.

He was never big on worrying about what came next. After three years of flying for the man, Gordon knew that whatever Henderson's game was, it would show up only when he was good and ready to reveal it. But another part of him—the one that had told his father precisely where he could ram a hot branding iron the day he'd left the family ranch for the last time—decided that if Henderson kept it up, Gordon might need to buy a branding iron of his own.

For now, only the fire mattered. It was getting even more aggressive and it took a punch from both of their birds to kill the next flare-up.

"I'm back to base for fuel," Vanessa announced on the command frequency.

"Roger," Henderson called down from his spotter plane three thousand feet above the fire. "Gordon, fly twice as fast."

Typical. "Sure thing, boss man." He flipped a finger aloft, then wiggled his cyclic control side to side to wave at Vanessa by rocking his helicopter. She returned the gesture and peeled off to the northwest. By pure chance, this fire was less than a ten-minute flight from MHA's base on the eastern foothills of Mt. Hood. The eleven-thousand-foot volcanic mountain was a shining beacon of glaringly bright glaciers, even in late September. The midmorning sun was blinding off the high slopes. In moments, Vanessa was a black dot against that white background. She'd be back in under half an hour and then it would be his turn.

Below him was a land of brown and green, heavy on the

brown. Eastern Oregon had none of the green lushness that everyone associated with the Oregon Coast and the Willamette Valley. Out here, Ponderosa pine grew far enough apart for grass to grow tall between them. And now, late in the season, the grass was all dried to a dark gold and carried fire fast and hard. The pine and western juniper weren't in much better shape. Several seasons of drought had taken their toll. The hundred-foot grand firs and the fifty-foot alder were all as dry as bone and lit off like Roman candles.

Gordon climbed an extra fifty feet, crossing the worst of it. He remembered back in his rookie year with MHA when Jeannie had a tree blow up directly under her. The superheated sap had cooked off and sent a big chunk of treetop an extra hundred feet aloft. It had knocked out her rear rotor over the New Tillamook Burn Fire. She'd managed to find a clearing the same size as her helo's rotor blades and somehow set down safely in it. Gordon had seen it and still wasn't sure how she'd stuck that landing.

He kept up the hustle: lake, climb over fire, hit the latest flare-up, climb back over, and dive down for more water. Occasionally one of the big helos would be tanking at the same moment he was. He'd always liked his little MD. The Firehawks— the firefighting version of the Black Hawk helicopters—could carry a thousand gallons to his two hundred, and they were damn fast in flight, but they had none of the finesse of his MD. They didn't get up close and personal with the fire. They flew higher and could knock crown fires out of trees. He flew lower and could put out your campfire without messing up the rest of the campsite…well, not too much.

He harassed his best friend Mickey at one point in his Twin 212 as they tankered together. Two-twelves were midsized helos, halfway between his own MD and the big Firehawks—the modern version of the Vietnam-era UH-1 Hueys. It made for a good spread of capabilities on the team, but it didn't mean he had to let Mickey fly easy just because of that.

"Hey buddy, you actually getting any work done?"

"More than you, Finchley."

"Believe that when I see it. Honeymoon over yet?"

"Not even close!" Mickey sounded pretty damned pleased.

"You better be saying that, hubbie" Robin cut in as she hovered her big Firehawk *Oh-one* down over the water.

Gordon was glad for Mickey. His easygoing friend had fallen for Robin, the brash, hard-edged blonde, the moment she'd hit camp at the beginning of the year. They were an unlikely couple from the outside, but it looked like it was working for them. They'd hooked up on day one, married last month, and showed no signs of the heat easing—of course, anything involving Robin Harrow would be fiery hot. Gordon wasn't jealous, he really wasn't. MHA's lead pilot was a primal force and would have run right over any lesser man than Mickey. Way too out there for Gordon. The quiet Vanessa had seemed about perfect for him, except instead of fire between them, there hadn't even been ignition.

Not being jealous was one thing. But when they were in camp during those rare quiet moments of the busy fire season, Mickey paid much more attention to Robin than to his old still-single pal. Gordon supposed it only made sense, but he was all the happier about finding a friend in Vanessa to fill that unexpected void.

Up over the fire, they headed for their respective targets.

The real battle, the make-or-break on the fire, was going to happen in the next thirty minutes. Gordon checked his fuel. Yes, he'd be good for that long and Vanessa would be back in another ten.

The wildfire would soon be slamming up against the fire break that the smokies had punched through the trees. Flames were climbing two hundred feet into the air in a thick pall of smoke gone dark gray with all of the ash that the heat was carrying aloft.

With a single load, Gordon managed to hit three separate flare-ups behind the smokies' line. He could see the soot-stained smokie team below, clearing brush and scraping soil by hand even though the main flames were less than a hundred feet away. They had inch-and-a-half hoses charged up and were spraying down their own line.

Gordon swung for the lake, climbed through the smoke, and dove—

Something slammed into his windshield straight in front of his face.

He flinched and jerked.

Wrong shape and color for a bird.

Mechanical!

A hobby drone. A big one. Four rotors and a camera.

It star-cracked his acrylic windshield, then slid upward.

He didn't have a moment to plead with the fates before he felt his MD jolt.

Perfect—the drone slid straight into his engine's air intake.

Not a chance that his Allison 250 turboshaft engine would just chew up the plastic and spit it out the exhaust. Even if it did, the battery was like throwing a brick into the turbine.

The primary compressor, spinning at fifty thousand RPM, choked on the three-pound drone.

A horrendous grinding noise sounded close above his head.

Red lights flared, starting with "Engine Out" at the upper left of his console and a high warning tone in his headset.

Other indicators flared to life, but he ignored them. With the engine failed, nothing else really mattered.

Gordon eased down on the collective and twisted the throttle to the fuel cutoff position. The grinding sound slowed but grew rapidly worse—his engine wasn't just dead, it was shredding itself. He slammed a foot on the right pedal as the nose torqued to the left.

"Mayday! Mayday! Mayday!" At least he still had electrical power to the radios. "Hobby drone strike, straight into my engine. Going down."

The radio fired up with questions, but Gordon was in the death zone and didn't have time to listen. A lift-failure emergency in a helicopter below fifty feet or over four hundred was generally survivable. The range in between those two altitudes cut life expectancy a lot more than he wanted to think about at the moment. He was currently in heavy smoke, descending down through the one-fifty mark.

It was little comfort knowing that the FAA would slap the drone owner's wrist if they could find him. Of course, if this went as badly as Gordon was expecting, MHA would go after the asshole for a million-dollar helo and the cost of one funeral.

"God damn it! And I was in such a good mood." There, that sounded more like Vin Diesel than Austin Powers. Truly sad—he was going to have to die to get it right. Though he couldn't place what movie the line was from.

The smoke wrapped around him and visibility left altogether. He fought for best auto-rotate speed, but at the rate he was falling, there wasn't a whole lot of time to get there.

He'd started flying fifteen years ago on his family's ranch, spent the last three years with MHA, and this was his first real-life crash landing. All the practice in the world didn't count for shit.

His palms were sweating against the slick plastic of the controls. The cabin was filling with smoke, but he couldn't take his hands off the controls to close the vent to the outside.

With his right shoulder, he nudged up the release lever on the pilot-side door. It swung open two inches and stabilized just like it was supposed to. The additional airflow helped the smoke flow through the cabin faster, but it still burnt his eyes and his throat. As a firefighter, he supposed that it was no surprise that death smelled like hot wood smoke.

His visibility was under twenty feet, and the smoke was taking on a distinctly orange glow. At sixty miles an hour, that gave him absolutely no lead time for maneuvering.

He wrestled east for the water.

The first treetop that slapped against his windshield was brilliant orange with flame. Lodgepole pine.

The next one, Douglas fir, snagged his left skid, jerking him sharply to the side before he was past it. If the one that slammed into his right-side pilot's window, white fir, made him scream, he didn't have time to realize it.

The next one, too buried in flames to recognize, ripped the door off entirely.

Gordon's instincts did what they could, with the controls now gone useless. One tree after another battered his helo: Ponderosa, western juniper—he ricocheted off the side of a massive Doug fir harder than being tossed by a bucking bronc.

The ends of rotor blades snapped off.

Then more of them.

The other skid snagged and twisted him the other direction, which saved him from the next flaming tree coming in through the missing door and killing him.

He realized that he was falling, treetop to treetop, down the steep bank toward the water.

His broken helicopter smashed through the last of the flaming line in a slow tumble thirty feet above the water.

With one final effort, he stomped on the right pedal and shoved the cyclic left.

No rotors. No effect.

That's when he remembered where the movie line was from. It wasn't Vin Diesel at all. It was John Goodman playing the hapless Al Yackey in the firefighting movie *Always*.

"No offense, John," he spoke his final words aloud to his dead helicopter. "But I'd rather die as Vin Diesel."

He plunged into the water upside down.

* * *

Five minutes earlier, Ripley Vaughan flew into sight of the firefight and eased her Erickson Aircrane to a hover.

"Wow!" "That's a mess!" Brad and Janet White, her married copilot and crew chief, did one of their synchro-speaking things.

They were right. It was.

The Black, the area already burned by the wildfire, ranged across five hundred acres. No cleanup had been done, there were spot fires dotted all over the Black, and the fire's flanks were eating sideways into the trees in addition to the main head of the fire driving toward a community. It could be the textbook definition of zero percent contained.

Ripley could see the hard slash of a smokejumper defense line across the rugged hills, cleared of trees and brush. It looked so small against the towering wall of fire bearing down on them, but then it always did from altitude. And there was a heavy airshow going on. The battle of this wildfire was about to be engaged big time.

They needed help.

But without a contract, she wouldn't be insured *or* paid if she fought on this fire...unless.

"Are those aircraft painted black?"

Brad pulled out a small pair of binoculars. "Yep! With flames and all."

That meant it was Mount Hood Aviation, their new outfit.

Ripley watched the airshow for another thirty seconds and could see the smooth coordination of the attack effort. She'd been flying her big Aircrane helicopter to fire for a couple of years, but had never imagined she'd get the chance to fly for Mount Hood Aviation. They had the best reputation in the business. Their for-hire smokejumping team was right on par with the Forest Service's Missoula, Montana Zulies, but *nobody* had the renown of their helicopter team.

Back at Erickson's Medford airfield in southern Oregon, Randy had called her into his office.

"I've got a rest-of-season contract request here."

Ripley hadn't particularly cared where she went, as long as it kept her flying.

"For some reason, it came through with your name on it. Something going on here I don't know about?" He sounded some kinda pissed about it. Upsetting a chief pilot with his years of experience was never a good idea—especially not when he signed her paychecks. Randy's cheerful demeanor and the easy smile that normally showed through his white beard were completely missing. Now she could see a flash of that kick-ass retired Army Chief Warrant that was typically hidden away. Word was that he'd graduated top of his Army flight class and hadn't slowed down for an instant during his years with the 2/10 Air Cav, not that the stories ever came from him.

"Unless it's for dancing," Ripley eyed the paperwork Randy was waving at her, "I can't imagine why it would be for me."

With her crew being named Brad and Janet—and Janet looking like a young Susan Sarandon, it was inevitable that their crew would learn "The Time Warp" dance from *The Rocky Horror Picture Show*…and then get known for it. But she hadn't been shopping for someplace else to be; she liked flying for Erickson more than she had liked anything else since she'd left the Navy.

Randy had tossed over the paperwork and Ripley had glanced down at it. She didn't spot her name anywhere. It was a contract for "your best pilot" from Mount Hood Aviation.

His scowl changed to his usual cheery smile. "Man's gotta have some fun. A couple pilots here are as good as you, but I don't have any that are better. You want to fly with MHA for what's left of the season, it's yours. You've earned it. But…" and he'd aimed a finger out toward the landing apron where her helicopter baked under the Medford late-summer heat. That former-military voice came out again, "You better bring my bird back in one piece. Yourself too, while you're at it."

She'd promised she would and then signed it on the spot. It was only later that she thought to ask Brad and Janet, but they were game as always.

The three of them with their Aircrane were supposed to be transiting to MHA's base today but now had stumbled on their new outfit in a full-on firefight.

"Janet, let's scoop up some water. Brad, find me this fire's Air

Attack frequency because I can't fly into a restricted Fire Traffic Area without permission."

There was a lake down below that she could see the other helos were using. It was just long enough that she could use the sea snorkel instead of the pond snorkel. The latter would require hovering and pumping. The sea snorkel was designed to let her fill her tanks on the fly. She could lower the snorkel's long strut to drag the tip below the surface and use the force of her own flying speed to fill the tanks. It was much quicker.

She flew down over the south end of Rock Creek Reservoir.

"Snorkel in five," she called out. Ripley could run the controls from her left side command seat, but since she had her crew chief aboard for the transit, Ripley let her have something to do. Her real duties would be on the ground once they arrived, but it was a chance for Janet to get a little control time in her log book.

"In five," Janet called back. She sat in the observer's seat directly behind Ripley, facing backward. That seat was positioned so that a pilot could control the helo during finicky winching jobs, like when they were assembling transmission towers. Not really needed for firefighting, but it gave her crew chief somewhere to sit and be a part of the firefight.

Ripley flew down until her big helo's wheels were just ten feet above the water. Once they slowed to thirty knots, Janet lowered the sea snorkel's strut into the water. Their speed alone would cause the water to shoot into the two submerged openings on the pipe, each the size of her palm. The water would blow upward like a thirty-five-mile-an-hour firehose. In forty seconds and just over half a mile, they could load up twenty-five hundred gallons of water, a dozen large hot tubs' worth, and be heading for the fire.

She flew along the line of the burning shore as it curved around from east to north. Rock Creek entered at the northern tip of the reservoir, providing her with an excellent gap in the trees for her climb out.

Brad found the frequency.

MHA's communications blasted into Ripley's headset.

"Did anyone see where he went down?" The voice was nearly frantic.

"All aircraft," a powerful male voice called out over the airwaves. "Climb and pull back. There was a civilian drone over the fire. It's already taken out one of our birds, we don't want to lose another. We need to evacuate. Keep an eye out for Gordon, but continue retreat."

Ripley had been on a number of fires where all of the air attack—helicopters, fixed-wing tankers, and command aircraft—had to pull back because someone had spotted a stupid civilian drone. There wasn't a firefighter aloft who hadn't thought about the dangers. But…

Ripley pressed the button on the back of the cyclic control with the tip of her index finger and transmitted. "If it already hit someone, then it's out of the sky. The chances of two simultaneous idiots on the same fire seems pretty low."

"Identify!" The ICA snapped out the command.

"This is Erickson Aircrane *Diana*—Oh shit!"

Ripley saw the body floating directly in her path. It was too late to avoid by climbing or raising the sea snorkel's strut.

* * *

Gordon had been floating on his back, watching the sky. It was amazing how pretty the sky was when you'd suddenly been given a reprieve from certain death. Even the fire still raging along the shore was a wonder of smoke and light as it swirled aloft.

He wanted to feel sad about the loss of his helo, but it was hard. His MD 530 had seen him through hell and given its own life to save his. He'd managed to release his seat harness and swim free before the helo hit the bottom of the reservoir. That first breath of air had been so clear and so sharp that he'd never forget it, not for as long as he lived.

A low thrumming echoed through the water, a heavy bass beat that only a helicopter could create, a big one like a Firehawk.

He opened his eyes and lifted his head to see if they'd come for him.

From less than a hundred feet away, he looked straight into the face of a beautiful helicopter pilot.

If there were moments he was never going to forget, the next three seconds were clogged with them.

The pilot sat almost fully exposed by the curved windshield of the helicopter. Gorgeous. Her straight black hair fell past her shoulders. Her skin was the color of mid-roast coffee with just that perfect amount of cream. Her dark glasses and pilot's helmet with mic boom added to the image. Hot professional female pilot.

The next impression was how huge the approaching helicopter was—and because it was so close, it seemed twice its normal size. Instead of the vicious sleekness of a Black Hawk, it had a bulbous nose and was brilliant orange like the Muppet Beaker, who always looked as alarmed as Gordon was starting to feel.

The last impression, more memorable than anything else— except perhaps that knockout pilot now looking almost directly down at him—was the long white boom that the Aircrane was slicing through the water.

Straight toward him!

There wasn't time to react. Hell, there wasn't even time to blink.

Gordon braced himself to be chopped in two.

* * *

There wasn't time to even swing aside.

Ripley did the only thing she could think of. She rammed the cyclic forward and heaved up on the collective, dumping every bit of nearly ten thousand horsepower into the massive rotor.

The result was like doing a forward wheelie on a motorcycle by slamming on just the front brake.

Her helicopter nosed down hard and lifted its behind high in the air. Hopefully lifting the snorkel up and out of the water with it.

Brad squawked in surprise as he was slammed forward against his safety harness.

Ripley held the attitude for as long as she dared, then yanked back on the cyclic, pulling the joystick between her knees all the way into her lap. The nose of the helo splashed against the lake water. It wasn't rated for water landings—meaning it would sink like a stone if she tried—but that wasn't what she was worried about.

Her main rotor was seventy feet across and reached well ahead of the helicopter. If it even touched the water, the blades were going to shatter. They'd crash into the water and utterly destroy forty million dollars' worth of helicopter and probably kill them all as well—a surefire way to upset Randy back at Erickson.

The Aircrane answered her brutal control maneuvers and she managed to tip the blades back up while they were still inches from the water. The downdraft blew a wall of spray across her windshield, completely blinding her until Brad hit the wipers. Pulling up, then plunging the rear boom deep back into the water. She could feel the drag, but yanking up the collective turned out to be enough to compensate—just barely.

"Did I miss him?"

"Miss who?" Brad managed to squeak out.

* * *

It had all happened in slow motion for Gordon.

The big white boom heading straight for him, slicing a bow wake to either side.

Then, as the helicopter passed directly over him, it nosed

down. The boom lifted from the water. At the bottom, the broad white wedge of a yard-across hydrofoil wing rose out of the water as well. It sailed over his chest with inches to spare, inundating him with spilled water and tumbling him with the wake it had created before rising out of the water.

When he had stopped floundering about and could see again, the helicopter was splashing its nose into the reservoir and the massive flying wedge of the snorkel's boom drove back into the water not a dozen yards past him.

It was only after the huge Aircrane helicopter recovered enough to not crash into the water that he tried to breathe again.

That nearly choked him, as if he needed another near-death experience today, when he inhaled all of the water that must have gotten into his mouth as it hung open in shock.

He was dizzy and barely still afloat before he managed to get his lungs clear enough to think.

By the time he did, the world was a wall of noise. The massive helicopter was hovering directly over him, once again beating him with downdraft and spray. This time he had the common sense to keep his mouth closed. The twin turboshaft engines were screaming with a brain-piercing shriek just a few meters over his head. The rear wheels were actually submerged into the lake to either side of him.

The construction-orange helo, that he could now see in intimate but more casual detail, was an Erickson Aircrane—the tractor trailer combination of the skies. Its "tractor" looked like some normal, large helicopter that had been sawed off right behind the cockpit. Behind that, the open-space "trailer" beneath which he floated, was defined by a thin spine that supported the two engines trying to deafen him, a massive six-bladed rotor trying to blow him back under the water, and two arching legs to support the rear wheels. In the big open space between legs and spine hung the twenty-foot long, ten-foot high, angular water tank used for firefighting.

A rear access door to the cockpit swung open and a brunette

was waving him forward. He managed to swim over until he could hang onto the ladder.

"He's alive," the woman called out toward the pilot.

"You sure?" Gordon asked because he couldn't tell.

"I'm sure. Now crawl on up here."

Since he was certified as being alive, he did. The metal rungs were little more than thick rebar welded to the back of the cockpit's hull, but being once more inside a helicopter was worth the effort.

At least he was fairly sure it was…it took all he had to climb those few rungs and drag himself through the door. He lay panting on the floor.

"Well," he said to no one in particular, "that was a hell of a thing."

"What kind of an idiot are you to be floating in the middle of a lake during a firefight?" The pilot was facing forward but sounded some kind of pissed.

Clearly no sense of humor to pick up on his *Galaxy Quest* joke. Too bad. Gorgeous pilots in massive helicopters were supposed to have a great sense of humor as well.

He decided that lack was okay with him as long as the helicopter kept climbing farther away from the water. The brunette who'd helped him aboard waved toward the only open bit of deck, which he was already sprawled on. The cockpit was tall, but otherwise not much bigger than his MD—his former MD, now sunk at the bottom of the lake.

There were the two forward pilot seats with the broad console in front of them, which came partway back between the seats. Hard against the back of the pilot's seat was the aft-facing seat of the woman who had helped him aboard. He sat up, facing sideways on the steel deck behind the copilot with his feet in the small stairwell for the door at the back of the cockpit. Leaning back against the sidewall, he looked straight across at the cute brunette in the observer seat.

She handed him a headset. He dragged it on and sighed

with relief from the noise abatement. By looking up, he could see the pilot in profile.

"Well?" The pilot sounded just as pissed over the headset. Gordon took a moment to appreciate the sight. If the pilot had been pretty, seen straight on as he'd floated in the water and she'd been on the verge of cutting him in two, she was a stunner in profile.

"I'm a pilot type person," he finally found his voice and managed to resist the need to cough out more lake water.

"Were you flying the goddamn drone?"

Gordon had to think about that for a moment. Either he was in shock, or the pilot's looks were distracting him. She struck him as the sort of woman who would be very likely to distract him—badly. Maybe it was a combination of both.

"No," he managed. "I'm the type of pilot who was *hit* by the goddamn drone."

"Oh."

"Oh?" Now it was his turn to be amused.

"You okay?"

"Well," Gordon tried to figure that out but his mind wouldn't quite connect to flexing and bending to check for injuries. "Someone said I was alive, so I guess so."

* * *

"Janet, check him out."

"He's already checking you out," Janet quipped.

Great! Exactly what Ripley didn't need. She hit the transmit key as she climbed back aloft.

"ICA, as I was saying before, this is Erickson Aircrane *Diana Prince*. I'd like to report that we are heavy by one pilot." She clicked off the mic switch. "What's your name?"

There was a long pause before he said, "*Diana Prince?*"

She glanced back at him to see if he was shocky and needed immediate medical, knowing that Brad would continue her climb. But he was looking at her clear-eyed. Kneeling beside him, Janet shrugged—no obvious injuries.

"That's my aircraft. Erickson Aircranes all have names," she did her best to remain calm, but her nerves were still shaking after how close she'd come to killing him then downing her entire crew. He was average build, blond, and nice looking without being the overly handsome jerk-type she usually fell for.

"I get that," he had a good voice too. "Just thinking about that maneuver you used to save my life. Haven't met a whole lot of pilots who could do that. Pretty sure I couldn't have. Wonder Woman isn't just the name of your aircraft."

He actually knew that Diana Prince was Wonder Woman's secret identity name. Ripley had always liked flying with a secret identity of Wonder Woman. She tried not to be too pleased… and failed. Then she tried to not let it show, and expected that she failed at that as well. The guy had a great smile. She faced forward once more.

"Your name?"

"Gordon. Gordon Finchley."

She keyed the mic again. "*Diana Prince* to ICA. You looking for a Gordon Gordon Finchley?"

She heard Gordon's half laugh over the intercom. More proof that he wasn't being shocky.

"You found him? What's his status?"

"Well, he'd dripping water all over my cockpit, but otherwise appears to be intact."

"Gordon," the ICA's voice sounded a little strained. "Don't do that again."

Ripley keyed the mic and nodded toward Gordon without turning.

"Didn't know that crashing was against the rules, Mark. But I promise to never do it again now that you've told me. I swear, Mr. Henderson, sir." She could practically hear Gordon saluting. "By the way, your helo, though there's not much left of her after the drone and then battering her way through the trees, is in about thirty feet of water off the easternmost curve of the shore."

"Glad you're in one piece. *Diana Prince*, once you have water, I could use you on the west end of the line. Steve was able to track the hobby drone pilot with our *legal* drone and you were right, he was a solo idiot. Started yelling at the fireman who found him for destroying his drone and wanting someone to pay for it. Sheriff is taking care of that. Just wait until he gets the insurance company's bill." The ICA delivered it in two breaths, and if there was any emotion behind his pilot being alive, he managed to hide it well.

"You good?" Ripley called back to Gordon over the intercom.

"I've had my bath for the week, even got my clothes washed in the bargain. So, yeah, I'm good."

"Roger," she keyed the mic and called in, mimicking Gordon's tone to hide her own laugh. "*Diana Prince* is on the way, Mr. Henderson, sir."

And then the desire to laugh whooshed out of her as if it had never been.

Gordon had said the ICA was Mark…Henderson. She'd heard that Major Mark Henderson of the Night Stalkers had retired to fight fires and that his wife Major Emily Beale had gone with him. Could there be two Mark Hendersons?

"Hey, Gordon," she called over the on-board intercom. "You have a pilot name of Emily in your outfit?"

"Emily Beale? Sure. Our chief pilot and trainer. Never seen anything like her. She's about the only other one that could have pulled off that maneuver you did back there. I think she and Mark were in the military somewhere." The sound of worship was clear in his voice.

That was one of the problems: everyone who talked about them spoke that way. Ripley didn't generally doubt her own skills, but Henderson and Beale were spoken of as the top two helicopter pilots in the history of the US Army's 160th SOAR. The Night Stalkers, as they called themselves, were the very best helo pilots in any Army. Or Navy. She'd considered trying to cross over, but they required a minimum of five years flying before applying and she'd been headed out of the military by then.

She glanced back and saw that Gordon had rested his head against the side wall and had closed his eyes. It was nice to see that his easy bravado had been just that. It would be far more worrisome if he had a true devil-may-care attitude. But at the moment, he looked exhausted and more than a little stressed. So, at least one of Henderson's pilots wasn't superhuman, which meant she had some slim chance of fitting in. She was impressed that he'd held it together at all through such a bad crash.

Ripley focused on lining up where Mark wanted her. She came in low from the west and ended up in a line behind three Firehawks. The fire had hit the leading edge of the firebreak that the smokies had slashed through the trees. Unable to move forward, the fire was piling up on itself, building a towering wall along the entire length of the clearing. It looked as if the wave of fire was about to break, falling forward to crash down upon the smokies from above.

The Firehawks slid into a nice neat line and laid down clouds of water in long, six-second spills. As soon as each bird finished its drop, it would peel away, up and east toward the water. Then the next one opened up. Military precision in a civilian outfit.

Aircranes tended to fly alone. A major fire could have an entire airshow going, and there'd be only one Aircrane.

Well, she was here to show them what one could do.

The three Firehawks had dumped three thousand gallons between them.

Ripley shifted another twenty feet upwind of their drop line to compensate for the increased fire intensity as she approached the middle of the line—bigger fires generated bigger winds, which shuffled the water drop sideways. Sixty knots speed and a hundred and fifty feet up. She flew along the fire's leading edge, no more than a rotor width from the flame tops. There she unleashed her drop for a fifty-yard overlap with the last of the Firehawks and a setting for moderate coverage. She let it run. And run. And run.

Twenty-five hundred gallons laid down on the fire in a long, clean line.

"Damn! But that's a lot of water. That's one of the sexiest things I've ever seen."

It wasn't Henderson, so it must be one of the pilots. No, it wasn't over the radio, it was over the intercom. Gordon. He was twisted around and looking out the curved bubble of Janet's aft controller position.

"Damn straight!" Ripley didn't get to watch her own drops, except occasionally on video, but it was an amazing feeling to make such a difference with each pass of her helicopter.

As soon as she headed back toward the water, an MD 530 zipped up close to her port side. A moment later, it had climbed over her and come up to the starboard. The little helicopters had always made her twitchy. She was a Big Iron gal herself: Seahawks for the Navy and now the Aircrane—the first weighed ten tons fully loaded and her Aircrane could pick that up without breaking a sweat. An MD 530 weighed a ton and a half all in.

"Damn it! Why do they even have one of those? They aren't good for much more than watering the plants."

"Well," Gordon said. "They occasionally do a fine job of clearing the skies of little drones."

Crap! Be rude to the guy twice in two minutes. Usually she was smoother than that with members of the opposite sex. Maybe she was still shaky from almost cutting him in half. "Okay. Well, let me know if there are any other ways I can insult you."

"Sure thing," he agreed complacently. "Could you open a second radio on…" and he called out a frequency.

Pilot chatter came in loud and clear. She'd need to get the rest of the frequencies soon. Brad set it so that the ICA's calls would automatically mute the pilot's channel.

"Gordon?" A woman asked. "Are you really okay?" Her voice was soft and smooth with an Italian accent.

"I'm fine, Vanessa. Just wet, shook up, and damn glad to be alive."

Between the Italian accent and sexy name, if she was beautiful, Ripley would hate her just on general principles.

"Oh, thank goodness." Then, with a waggle of wings, the little MD 530 turned to go back to the fire.

Despite its simplicity, the brief exchange had been so intimate that it was almost embarrassing to listen to.

Ripley hadn't been that intimate with anyone since, well, Chief Petty Officer Weasel Williams. Lieutenant Ripley Vaughan, a much younger and more naive version of herself, had left the Navy three years ago because she'd fallen in love with an enlisted man. An enlisted man who'd left her two days from the altar… for the wedding caterer. It was the last time she'd let herself be so trusting. Or trusting at all really.

But having someone to care about her the way Vanessa cared about Gordon would be…nice.

Ripley wished she wasn't such a romantic.

It was all her parents' fault, especially her Senegalese mother. There was no way that a girl who had been raised by a theater drama professor, who wrote romance novels on the side, could be anything but a romantic. Her mixed-race Oklahoman father had taken his one-eighth Cherokee heritage as a calling to become a cultural archaeologist for the local tribes—Ripley had inherited her straight dark hair from him. He too was always bringing home legends of true love, lasting from the time of the creation myths.

Ripley ran another drag of the sea snorkel alongside the burning lake shore—glad to see nobody floating out in the middle of the lake this time. The Firehawks had left her a clear path, settling in a line as they dunked their hoses and ran their pumps.

"Damn, that's bloody awesome!" A female pilot on the helicopter frequency, but without any hint of an Italian accent. Australian this time. How many women were in this outfit? Usually, when Ripley showed up, it increased the total to one.

"How much water, how fast?" A man asked.

"Twenty-six hundred and fifty gallons. Forty seconds," Ripley answered as she finished the run and pulled back aloft. Though even in the S-64F she could only carry over twenty-five hundred if she was at a low altitude and had burned most of her fuel, decreasing her total load. Didn't mean that she had to tell anyone that.

"Mommy, I want one," the Aussie called out. The Firehawks would still have fifteen more seconds to pump aboard their measly thousand gallons while she was already flying back to the fire.

* * *

Gordon just sat back and listened to the on-going firefight. It was strange to be sitting here with nothing to do as the flight volleyed back and forth between water and fire. They finally got a retardant tanker truck and a dip tank set up. The Firehawks switched over to dumping retardant by snorkeling their loads out of a "pumpkin," which looked like a kiddie pool on steroids kept full of the red goo by the tanker.

The retardant was laid down in broad sweeps where the fire wasn't—over the smokies' slash pile, along the flanks, and finally the tail. Each swath coated an area of unburned trees and grass with a sticky red solution of phosphates and sulfates that made it so that no oxygen could reach the wood—no oxygen, no fire. The red let the pilots and ICA see where they'd already dropped.

The problem was that the fire had flared up so hot and fast that it constantly threatened to jump the narrow lines of defense. Twice the flank outran how fast they could lay down the retardant. Then it skipped over and started a fresh fire with new flanks and a new head. More retardant was laid down around that.

Vanessa stayed on water and hit spot fires.

That left the lake wide open for Ripley and her Aircrane to gather massive loads of water and hit the fire directly wherever the ground team needed it to be cooled down. The smokies' line was now being tested by the main head, and the wildfire was definitely in no mood to stop.

Ripley battered away at it, slapping it down out of the crown in one section, only to have it flare up in the next. Several times she had to jump over to killing spot fires when Vanessa's MD and Mickey's 212 were overwhelmed by the number of embers falling and sparking downwind, closer to the community. The hundred homes at the southeast corner were nestled right into the trees. If the fire got loose, they didn't stand a chance. When she flew over it, she could see the rural fire engines wetting down some of the closer houses while the police with their flashing lights were fighting the challenges of a reluctant evacuation.

The battle became a blur. Heat, noise, flame, and the intense chatter on the radios. Everyone wanted attention. Everyone wanted all the resources put to their section of the blaze.

Gordon could see the real advantage of a copilot. It wasn't that they were needed to fly the aircraft. Even a monster aircraft like the Aircrane could probably be handled by a single pilot, but a copilot sure helped handle the radios.

"You take the Vs," Ripley had called out to Brad. He muted her from the two VHF radios that were for talking to the ICA and the air-to-air comm for the helicopters. It let her focus on the FM radios in her coordination with the ground team. Much more rational than trying to pick your instructions out of four or five lines of simultaneous chatter.

They were definitely in it now. The battle was deeply engaged and everyone was doing something…except him.

He hadn't merely watched a firefight since he'd been a kid growing up in Red Butte, Wyoming. A scrub fire had swept over the prairie and a helicopter had flown over to dump water on it before it overran the highway. He'd rushed out on his pony to watch. It had been a simple task for the UH-1 Huey, flying with a bucket on a longline, dipping water out of the lazy waters of the North Platte River…and he'd been hooked. Such a simple thing had shaped his whole life.

And now what was he supposed to do? No helo. MHA didn't have a spare million-dollar aircraft sitting around. His own would be a complete write-off: shattered engine, bent frame, and all.

Yet he felt as if he was sitting once more on his pony watching the helicopter work up and down the distant fireline. His world had just changed…but he had no idea how. He could only hope it was for the better. Crashing once in a flying career was definitely once too many.

Chapter 2

Ripley was fine as long as they were fighting the fire. The MHA crew quickly shifted their patterns for the Aircrane's slower flying speed but massive capabilities. She could feel the Incident Commander-Air Henderson—safer to think of him that way rather than Major Mark Henderson—learning as well. Her Aircrane rapidly took the "heavy" role. Wherever the ICA needed the hardest punch, he sent in Ripley and her crew.

She liked that he called them by name. It was usually "Tanker 753, Coverage 4, 100 percent drop" and a set of grid coordinates. She'd expected a retired major to be an over-controlling military officer type. Instead Henderson used her first name from the very first call and simply gave her the coordinates. He let her choose the coverage and drop, assuming that she just might know the capabilities of a helo she'd been flying to fire for three years better than he did.

It also let her learn her fellow pilots' names. Jeannie was the cheery Australian. Two guys, Vern and Mickey, had almost identical accents (the non-accent of the Pacific Northwest), though the former was nearly Oklahoma slow-spoken and the latter sounded like he was everyone's best buddy. Mickey was also being teased about his recent marriage to Robin—yet another woman pilot—who had that flat, military tone down.

And there was Major Emily Beale (retired). Ripley didn't hear her voice often as she was flying copilot to Vern, but whenever she did speak, the air went silent and everyone else listened. She didn't talk about the fire itself; Emily was all about the flying. "Ten feet too close to the flames on that last run." "Your drop is starting twenty feet earlier than you think it is." No one asked how she knew what they were actually thinking, but neither did anyone refute it.

Soon enough, Ripley was the target of her guidance.

"What was your coverage setting on that last run?"

"Five," Ripley replied carefully. She knew it had been a bit heavy, but better too heavy than too light.

"It would have been the right call on the head, but it was a waste of water on dousing the flank. Try one point of coverage for each ten feet of flame height above the treetops. Make it a Four on the next run; we could have used the extra hundred feet of line."

"She's uncanny," Janet observed after they did that next run. That wasn't a formula Ripley had ever heard before and it wasn't bad.

"You've got no idea!" Gordon assured them. "I think she came out of the psy-corp; you know, the mind readers that the military swears they don't have."

Ripley kept listening and wondered if he wasn't more rather than less accurate. Emily often seemed to know what the pilot was thinking long before the pilot did.

When it was time to refuel, Gordon guided them back to Mount Hood Aviation's base.

The grass runway was perched at four thousand feet up the side of the dormant volcano. Mount Hood towered eleven thousand feet in the air and was glacier-capped. The base itself wasn't much to talk about. The east side of the north-south strip was a solid mass of classic Oregon forest—Douglas fir, larch, and spruce crowded shoulder-to-shoulder and much of it towering a hundred feet or more. Much of the Doug fir cracked two hundred. Unlike the area they were firefighting in, twenty miles away and three thousand feet lower, this was old forest.

The road down the mountain lay to the west. There was a parking lot crowded with typical firefighter vehicles: a few very hot sports cars, several beater vehicles, and a lot of battered pickups. There were a trio of big buildings that had definitely seen better days, and a two-story wooden, fire lookout-style tower overlooking the field.

"Land over by the fuel and service trucks," Gordon said. They were parked close by the base of the tower.

"Place doesn't look like much," Ripley noted the green tinge growing on the north side of buildings as she settled *Diana Prince* down onto the field.

"Don't worry," he assured her. "It isn't any better inside. It was a boys' camp for decades. Then abandoned for a while."

"That must be when it got its homey feel."

"Exactly," she could hear the smile in Gordon's voice. "Mount Hood Aviation turned it into a smokejumper base several decades back, and the helos about a decade ago. Until Mark and Emily came along, they were known for their smokies and Carly, the best fire behavior analyst anywhere."

"Now you're known for being the top heli-aviation firefighting team running." Rough camps didn't faze her. Helispots were as often as not in some farmer's field or carved into a meadow; easy accommodations were often scarce near wildfires.

Gordon didn't even bother acknowledging. He must take it for granted. Arrogance or just acknowledgement of fact? Ripley couldn't tell.

A slender Asian woman walked up to the cockpit's aft-facing door as the fuel driver clipped on the grounding wire and began fueling the bird.

Ripley clambered out of her seat and almost tripped over Gordon.

"Sorry," he opened the rear door and climbed down to make way for her. His one-piece flightsuit made of tan, fire-resistant Nomex fit him well. He wasn't powerfully built, but there wasn't a wasted ounce anywhere on him either. The butt of his flightsuit was the only part that hadn't dried out. She resisted the moment.

Janet didn't. "Crapped your pants something awful, flyboy."

Gordon slapped a hand against his backside, then pulled it away and shook it. "Wetter on the inside."

Ripley kept her smile to herself, as well as any comments about how nicely it clung to him.

When she climbed down beside him, she was surprised that he was only a few inches taller than she was. He had seemed bigger somehow after surviving what he did and doing it so well. Standing beside her, he was more of a…comfortable size.

"Hi, I'm Brenna," the Asian woman held out her hand. She had a strong handshake and enough energy in her lean frame to make Ripley wonder how she held it in—it practically vibrated off her. "Need anything special, air filters okay and so on?" She shouted over the high whine of the turboshafts, still loud despite Brad throttling them all the way down to idle.

"I have my own crew chief," she waved Janet down to the field grass. "She takes care of my aircraft."

"Perfect!" Brenna wasn't the least put off. "Frankly, Denise and I are Airframe and Powerplant certified, but we only just got our Erickson training last week. Denise has it down, of course, because she's totally awesome, but it's something I wouldn't want to depend on just me right out of the chute—you know what I mean. Hi," she shook Janet's hand as she reached the ground but never gave her a chance to speak, "you need anything, I'm your gal. Denise is six months pregnant and wants me fully up to speed on your aircraft before she has to stand down." And with that she was gone around the front the helicopter.

Ripley didn't need to signal Janet to follow Brenna.

"She any good?" Ripley asked Gordon.

"If she hadn't been, Denise would have beaten her into shape faster than a dented skin panel." He patted a metal panel of her helicopter's hull to make his point. "And there aren't *any* mechanics out there as good as Denise."

Again, that sound of utter worship. Either all of the women in Mount Hood Aviation were close relatives of Supergirl, or Gordon thought all women were fantastic. If it was the second, then it made Gordon sound like a charming, if naive goof. If it was the first, maybe Ripley should hightail it back to Medford before she had the chance of being found out.

"Well," Ripley waved toward the old camp buildings, which did have a comfortable, lived-in feel despite their age. "Here you are, safe and sound."

"I'd like to keep riding along, if you don't mind. Don't have anything else to do and I hate to miss a fire. Also, I'm used to flying solo and it's interesting to watch the different dynamics of a full crew."

Brenna zipped by with Janet in tow. The two women were both talking a mile a minute, and Ripley understood maybe one word in four. She knew a lot about the helicopters she flew, but mechanic-ese was a language of its own, far stranger than the Elizabethan English of Shakespeare or the merry musicals of Gilbert and Sullivan—which she'd heard since birth, and probably before. It was a vote of confidence on Brenna's skills that she spoke it so fluently.

And Gordon talked "pilot" just as clearly. Ripley could judge his skills by what he did and didn't say. For being non-military (for that much was obvious), his skill level was probably about the same as hers. He was a good match for her.

And what the hell are you thinking, Rip? A good match for *what?* For…two pilots flying in the same outfit. That's what. He'd rallied after a near-death experience, which she knew was damn hard to do. That was very easy to respect as well.

Gordon stood at ease, awaiting her decision. He acted as

if he'd be fine with whatever she said. *Just happy to be here, ma'am.* His accent definitely had some cowboy in it. Not her own Oklahoma, more Colorado or maybe even Wyoming. She was half tempted to leave him on the ground to see how he reacted. Sounded kind of bitch manipulative, which answered that question for her.

The next time Janet zipped by, Ripley told her to rig the extra jump seat.

* * *

Maybe Gordon should have stayed behind. At first he'd thought Ripley was distracting in profile. Standing next to her on the ground had revealed much more to admire. Even the heavy flightsuit couldn't mask her fine figure. She was neither delicate like Vanessa nor powerful like Robin. She wasn't Denise-short or Emily-tall. She was like the best of each, right in the green on the engine readout.

He didn't even know her last name yet! If he was looking to get all stupid about a woman, he'd long since learned that the best answer for him was distance. A lot of it.

Instead, he was now sitting in the jump seat, tight in between *Diana Prince's* pilot's and copilot's seats and just a foot aft. It offered him a magnificent view forward. An easy glance over his shoulder and he could watch Janet and the water drop through the predominately clear rear wall of the Aircrane's odd, chopped-off cockpit.

It also gave him an over-the-shoulder view of Ripley from a foot away. She flew much the way it had made him feel to stand beside her. "Careful" and "steady" emanated from her. The Aircrane never felt as if it was hurrying under her control, but on drop after drop he came to appreciate her near perfect efficiency. No wasted motion. No wasted energy. The rocksteady flight of the whole operation—even the Firehawks looked flighty compared to the Aircrane's staid presence.

"Why is Emily speaking less to me than to others?" Ripley asked as they were once again skimming water off the lake. "Is it because I'm the newbie?"

"No," Gordon thought about it. "She doesn't play favorites with anyone. In fact, we've checked among ourselves and we're each and every one fairly convinced that she has it in for us personally. Maybe you're just that good. Did you ever consider that?"

Ripley didn't answer and it was hard to read her expression when all he could see around the edge of her helmet was the outer half inch of nose, cheek, and chin, and a fall of luxuriant black hair that he kept wanting to touch.

"Nope," she finally said after lifting off the end of the lake and swinging back toward the fire. "Not buying it. Come up with another reason."

"Because she's preparing you to be inducted into the International League of Oddly Amazing Damsel Fire Pilots. Which is LOAD-FiPs for short."

"So you're calling me odd." Then she started working on the radio with the smokie team holding the outside line. They had a D-9 dozer cutting a new firebreak line, and he could see that it had strayed a little too close to the flames. Ripley swung the *Diana Prince* in to cool down the area.

No, he'd been calling her amazing, but couldn't quite bring himself to say it directly. It was obvious why Emily wasn't critiquing her. She fit her craft perfectly. Emily had spent hours and hours with each pilot, improving their skills. At first he'd thought she was going to throw him out of the outfit for being hopeless, but she hadn't. Instead she'd kept after him, not until he was merely a better pilot, but rather until his skills matched his aircraft and he was getting the maximum potential out of the MD 530.

Ripley was already doing that.

She was a woman designed to sweep all others away because she was so perfectly…what? Herself. He didn't even know her, but somehow he knew it was true. It was a remarkably attractive trait, beyond the dark eyes and barely lighter skin.

Again he looked at that exposed half inch of her profile. It amused him that his own dad would whip his behind but good for even looking at a black woman. And she probably had a big handsome boyfriend like Mark Henderson who would wipe the skies with him for even looking.

So, he forced his attention back to the fire.

"Well, sports fans," Gordon spoke up over the intercom to distract himself. "In the right corner, we have the home team. Six hundred and fifty acres of the sweetest blaze you can imagine. It started as a little campfire minding its own business, but then it saw its chance this morning to become a big contender. In the fire world, that kind of opportunity only comes along once in a lifetime, and this sparky little flame made its bid for immortality in the annals of fire history despite growing up in such a remote area."

He heard a giggle, but it didn't sound like Ripley.

He glanced back and Janet was giggling.

Brad picked up the theme, "The visiting team started the game two hundred acres already engulfed…"

"…before the home team was even called," Janet picked up. "But despite their late start, bets are heavy in favor of the visiting squad."

"The smokies and helos of Mount Hood Aviation have an unbroken win-loss record," Gordon put in. "Going back—"

"Until," Janet cut him off, "someone dumped a helicopter in the lake."

"It was hot," Gordon declared in his own defense and pointed out a log in the water to make sure Ripley saw it and wouldn't clip it with her snorkel's boom. "I needed a swim."

Ripley nodded and stayed well clear of both the log and the conversation.

"One for the home team," Brad declared.

"But…" Gordon drew it out to get back control of his story.

"The fire wasn't ready for the ringer that MHA had warming up in the bull pen."

"Is this boxing or baseball?" Ripley's tone was as dry as the forest.

"Football," Brad announced.

"Badminton," Janet declared.

"Firefighting MHA style," Gordon shut them down. "And that's exactly why Emily isn't messing with you. Bringing in a ringer, you've got to let them do what they do best."

"Oorah!" Brad declared.

"You were never a Marine," Ripley corrected him.

And to distract himself from just how fine this particular ringer was, Gordon continued the play-by-play of his mangled sports commentary as they chased the fire back and forth over the hillside.

It was late afternoon by the time the fire was dead enough to turn over to the engine crews. The smokejumpers stayed behind to help complete the containment. They'd only lost one structure…and it was so selective that it would be hard to prove that it wasn't intentional on MHA's part.

A single spark found its way to the outermost garage of the nearby community. It had lodged in a large woodpile stacked under the garage's eaves, always a bad idea, and two loads of water dumped by Vanessa's MD 530 hadn't been able to save it. The kicker was that the garage had belonged to the drone pilot. He'd been busy riding to jail for punching the policeman when he was informed that there would be a $1.3 million dollar bill for a new MD 530 helicopter. That was on top of the $27,500 FAA fine for violating the TFR by flying a drone into the Temporary Flight Restrictions airspace of a wildfire. Now he needed a new garage and pickup as well.

"Where should I put it?" It took Gordon a moment to understand Ripley was asking him. They had reached the base while his mind had wandered off.

"Well, *my* spot isn't being used."

"So nice of you to trash a helicopter to open it up for me."

"Least I could do to welcome the newest lady to the team."

Ripley laughed easily. "You're just that kind of a thoughtful guy."

Gordon shrugged and then realized she wouldn't be able to see that. "I suppose so." Or he'd at least like her to think so. "See the big oak just north of midfield? Park there with your rotor toward the tree."

She slid easily into place, and took up a huge amount of space.

When Vanessa came in moments later, she had to shuffle a couple dozen meters farther downfield than usual as the Aircrane's rotor was over three times bigger than his MD's had been.

Gordon glanced side to side from the strange perspective. He sat a story in the air. In his MD, he had sat down into the bird, not climbed up into it like the Aircrane. Now, in one direction he looked down on the top of Vanessa's slowing rotor disk and Mickey's Twin 212 wasn't that much bigger.

In the other direction, the three Firehawks were dropping down to the field. Even with the taller landing gear necessary to accommodate the underslung belly tanks, he still looked down at them, his head still a little higher than their rotor disks. At the far end of the lineup, the two smokejumper delivery planes had been parked hours ago. Now they looked normal instead of oversized.

Mark was, as always, the last out of the sky. He landed the Beech King Air twin-engine spotter plane without even a bump. Again Gordon was looking down at him.

It was an uncomfortable perspective.

"Thanks for the ride, Captain Vaughan," he'd spotted her name on the log book that Brad was filling out. "But I'll stick with my little MD in the future."

"Is my *Diana Prince* too much machine for you?"

No, he thought. *But pilot Wonder Woman definitely was.* He was thinking any number of inappropriate thoughts about the pretty pilot with the coffee-colored skin. "Let's just say that it's a very different view of the fire. I'm more of a spot fire kind of guy. I leave the main fire to you and the Firehawks."

"Chicken!" Brad declared as Janet made "Buck-buck-bu-caw!" noises.

"You're always welcome back, Gordon," Ripley Vaughan turned and smiled at him, "whenever you want to try a grown-up helicopter again." Gordon could only manage a nod because she had one hell of a nice smile.

"Uh, thanks." It was lame, but it was all he could think to say. Mr. Hopeless-around-women Finchley was coming to the fore and he finally took his own advice to get some distance before he could screw things up.

Even though there wasn't anything going on to *screw up,* he reminded himself.

He slipped out of the jump seat, folded it aside, and headed out of the helo fast.

When he stepped to the ground, it was like a hard jolt. This had been his parking spot for three fire seasons. Now…it wasn't. He had no helicopter. MHA didn't have an open seat anywhere else either. No copilot slots either. When Robin had joined the team at the start of the season, she'd taken over Emily's seat aboard Firehawk *Oh-one.* Now even Emily Beale was flying copilot for others.

Everyone on the field had a purpose: pilots, mechanics, even the cooks. Which left Gordon nowhere.

He didn't want to leave here. These were his friends. This was family! He was totally fu—

"Gordon!" Vanessa raced over from her parked and shutdown MD. She didn't pause until she had her arms around him.

He wrapped his arms around her and buried his face in her hair. *Thank god for a friend.* With her holding him tightly, all of the day's fears exploded to life.

Falling out of the sky.

Plunging through fire to crash into the lake.

The sea snorkel slicing straight toward him.

And now the fear that, with no ride, he'd end up having to look elsewhere for a new contract. That there'd be no place for him here at Mount Hood Aviation. What would he do without these people?

He held her tightly as she stroked a hand up and down his back and, for only the second time in his life, he let the shakes come.

* * *

Ripley sat in the cockpit and looked down at the scene playing out so near. Vanessa wasn't pretty, she was gorgeous. She'd spent all day flying to fire, and still her hair floated behind her as she ran up to Gordon. Her figure should be in a magazine, not a flightsuit.

And the way Gordon held her was like a knife to the heart.

You only met him today. Decent and funny guy, taken long before you came around. Telling herself all that didn't help how it felt.

He'd looked at Ripley…like she was an attractive woman, which she already knew. It had seemed like there was more behind it and, dammit, she'd let herself feel it and enjoy the attention. That would teach her. She'd just have to hang on and wait for another handsome jerk to come along. Them she always did fine with. If not fine, at least the course of the relationship would be completely predictable.

But her mind was stuck on the man in the model's embrace. His easy banter after a near-death experience had made her want to laugh more than she had in a long time. Brad and Janet's antics could always make her smile, but Gordon had made her laugh any number of times. During a firefight!

He'd done a splendidly ridiculous job with his sportscaster's running commentary, lightening that particularly dismal stretch that typically occurred through the second third of battling a wildfire—when there was no hope of beating "the beast"—until at long last turning the corner and the Visiting Squad of firefighters were actually beating the Home Team fire.

He'd let her hope for more. It had been a long time since she'd hoped for anything.

Ripley had thought she was fine with that. She loved flying. Fighting wildfire was challenging and kept her in the air. But the taste of hope was something she wasn't ready for and it was strange, almost bitter on her tongue. The last place she'd belonged, really belonged...she didn't know. Even in Muskogee, Oklahoma as a kid, her deeply academic family life in a land of wheat and hogs had made her a misfit far and wide. Something that hadn't ended with the Naval Academy. She—

"Come on!" someone called into the cockpit loud enough to shock her out of the dark hole she'd crawled into. She was alone. Brad and Janet were gone. Some outer part of her had kept functioning through shutting down the aircraft, even if her inner part hadn't.

Out the window, Ripley could see that they had even already attached the stabilizer lines to the tips of the rotor blades and tied them back to the aircraft to keep the rotor from turning over the engine if the wind caught it wrong. That meant they were completely done with preparing her bird for takeoff at a moment's notice. The only thing left was the fuel truck she could see working down the line. How long had she been sitting here?

"Ripley?" It was Gordon Finchley's voice.

She turned. He was standing with just shoulders and head exposed in the high doorway of her Aircrane.

"You okay?"

"Never been better. Just admiring the stunning view," she waved a hand toward the buildings on the far side of the airfield.

"Not the greatest, I know. You hungry? We're all going to The Doghouse."

"Famished. But why does that sound even worse than this place?"

"The Doghouse actually is great. Trust me. I know you don't

have a vehicle here, so do you and your crew want a ride? I don't think there's too much crap in my pickup. No rabid schnauzers anyway. Can't much guarantee what else you'll find."

"Uh…sure," she answered before she remembered the lovely Vanessa. And then felt too awkward to ask if they'd all fit. He'd offered, she'd accepted. "I once dated a guy who had a rabid schnauzer. Well, maybe not rabid, but tricky not to step on in the dark."

"I'm already jealous."

And that had her studying him again as they crossed the field. Maybe he was just being funny, because someone with Vanessa couldn't be jealous of anything.

Soon they were all crowded into the same pickup. Gordon's was an old black Toyota Tundra with the front right quarter panel mashed in.

"Ran it off the road and into a tree last winter while getting firewood to a friend's cabin I'd rented." He drove and Vanessa sat in front.

That left Ripley and Brad in the back with random and miscellaneous garbage (a large Fritos bag and a half dozen Starbucks cups along with other normal floor detritus, and a worn denim jacket on the back seat that probably looked damned good on him, accenting the cowboy vibe).

"Brenna, she will be bringing your wife down with her," Vanessa had half twisted around to talk to Brad. Her voice in real life was even more pleasant than on the air. "Once they have all of the services done on all of the helicopters." That hint of Italian was ever so charming. It had to be an act that—

Ripley wanted to smack herself for being so rude.

"Sounds good," Brad said as if speaking to just another woman.

Did marriage do that, make even stunning women like Vanessa of no further interest? It probably did if you were as good a guy as Brad was. Whereas Gordon was starting to piss her off. Had she really misread that he was flirting with her during the flight? She didn't think so. Was he the sort of guy who couldn't help himself around women? Too much like her ex, Petty Officer Weasel Williams, for comfort.

It was a half hour down to the town of Hood River. Gordon and Vanessa did a tag team tour guide thing all the way to town.

"This is called the Fruit Loop, just like the cereal, except this is real fruit. Thousands of acres of apple, cherry, peach, pear. You name, they've got it." After that she heard about one word in four.

Fires did that to her. Since leaving Medford in southern Oregon this morning, she'd been in the seat for over ten hours and she always remained in some kind of a hyper-alert state while flying. Afterward, she mentally crashed. Thankfully, Brad carried the conversation and, as Ripley was sitting directly behind Gordon, it only took leaning her head against the window to be out of his sightlines in the rear view mirrors.

She could certainly do worse for the last of the summer and the fall. MHA was *the* top team out there, and with Emily Beale and Mark Henderson driving them, it wasn't hard to understand why. She'd expected to find big egos to go with it, but at least Gordon had been pleasant. Of course they hadn't been flying together as pilot and copilot—maybe that's when his inner control freak came out. Early on she'd flown with plenty of pilots who wouldn't give her an hour of stick time in a hundred. Personally, she chose to make sure that Brad and Janet both had plenty of control time. Janet was one of the few pilot-qualified crew chiefs out there. She'd lose them all the sooner when they were promoted to pilot-in-command positions, but it would be her training that got them there.

The Doghouse, when they arrived, was even less impressive than MHA's base. The ramshackle structure on the outer fringes of the town of Hood River should have collapsed in the last strong breeze, something for which the Columbia Gorge was notorious. The battered sign hadn't been painted in years and the large windows were tinted so that you couldn't see in. Firefighting vehicles already took up a whole section of the lot—clearly marked by "Firefighters are *hot!*" bumper stickers and the like.

Great, they were taking her to a strip joint—classic pilot outing.

"Maybe I'll just walk into town and find a pub."

Gordon snagged her arm. "Wonder Woman won't find a better one anywhere in town."

"It is true," Vanessa said softly from Ripley's other side. Meekness, too? Someone give her a break.

She let them drag her through the front door.

Instead of thumping music, there was country and western playing—good CW, Little Big Town, and as background rather than blast. The space was brightly lit with the sun streaming in through the large, tinted windows. And the walls, even the ceiling, were covered with pictures of doghouses. Big ones, little ones, cartoon ones, photos of ones, even papier-mâché ones…nothing but hundreds—thousands—of doghouses. A long oak bar ran down one side with a dozen beer taps, all Oregon microbrews by the look. The tiny galley kitchen at the end of the bar was filling the room with luscious burger and fries type of smells.

"Holy shit!"

"Told you so!" Gordon sounded very pleased at having surprised her.

"No, I mean holy shit this is a dive, but as long as we're here anyway…"

He grinned at her tease and tugged her—by her arm that she was shocked he still held—toward the tables. A group of them had been pulled into a line all along one wall. Someone must have called from the base to say they were coming because the other tables were crowded with patrons. Some locals, a bunch of overly fit men and women in their twenties who were probably here for the windsurfing in the Gorge, and the long MHA table.

Gordon even held her chair for her.

If he gave her one more mixed signal…

Then he sat next to her as Vanessa sat with Brad and another pilot further down the table.

She was going to have to...

"Ripley Vaughan," Gordon said in a different tone.

She turned from watching Vanessa introduce Brad to a woman with dark hair that sported a red stripe. Jeannie of the cheery Australian accent—just about how Ripley had pictured her. Ripley turned back to Gordon, wishing she had cue cards for what in the hell was going on.

"This is Mark Henderson and Emily Beale."

Then she looked across the table at the couple they were directly across from...nothing like she'd expected. Mark Henderson was tall, even sitting down, broad-shouldered, and handsome as hell. He had an easy smile below the mirrored Ray-Bans that he still wore indoors and held out a welcoming hand which she shook cautiously—the strong grip he might give any person, but no crusher proving a point.

Emily Beale was the shocker. She was a trim blonde with brilliant blue eyes and an absolutely deadpan expression. The Ice Queen. That's how the rumors had tagged her and Ripley could immediately see why.

"Nice flying," was all Emily said in way of greeting. Her handshake was as brief and abrupt as she was.

Ripley waited for more.

Gordon and Mark laughed together.

"What?"

Gordon leaned in close as if to whisper, but still spoke loudly enough to be easily heard by the others, "That's your cue to take a bow."

Ripley looked at him. Had he lost his mind?

"That's Emily's version of planting a gold star on your forehead, or at least your term paper," Gordon informed her.

"Enough, you two," Emily said it softly and the two men looked as if someone had just cracked a whip. Even her Mr. Macho husband listened when Emily spoke.

"Ripley," Emily addressed her directly. "Randy said you were the best he had."

"More than he told *me*," Ripley muttered and Emily offered an enigmatic smile.

"You also come very highly recommended by Rear Admiral James Parker."

"You spoke to…" Ripley caught herself from repeating the obvious, which was better than she usually managed.

"Emily," Mark laid a casual arm along the back of Emily's chair, "used to cook for him at dinner parties before she went military."

Ripley ignored him. "I didn't even know that the admiral knew who I was."

"Two Distinguished Service Medals and a Silver Star, trust me James remembered you quite well when I asked. Wasn't very pleased when you quit."

Please don't ask why I quit, Ripley begged silently. There was some dirty laundry she'd rather have stay in the hamper, permanently.

"Is that good?" Gordon whispered. "Two whatevers and a Silver Star?"

"Civilians," Mark sighed, saving her explaining. "Only two medals higher than the Distinguished Service. You might have heard of one of those; it's called the Medal of Honor."

"You *won* all that?" Gordon looked shocked.

"No," Ripley did her best not to echo Mark's sigh. "I didn't *win* any medals. No one does. I *received* them."

"The Medal of Honor," Mark continued as if neither of them had spoken. "That one requires an Act of Congress and a presentation by the President. But we could ask Peter if he'd make an exception."

"Peter?" Ripley managed in a squeak. "You're on a first-name basis with the Commander-in-Chief?"

Mark hooked a thumb at Emily. "Her, not me. We just refer to him that way to not attract undue attention. They grew up together."

Ripley's head was spinning and she hadn't even ordered a

beer yet. A cheery redhead was working her way down the table. Maybe she'd just order ice tea.

Gordon looked at her in surprise. "Shit! Two Distinguished whatevers and a Silver Star. You weren't kidding about being Wonder Woman."

Emily actually laughed aloud, causing heads to turn all up and down the table.

"What?" Ripley snapped at Emily. She'd had enough of the games going on around her.

"Your helicopter: *Diana Prince.* I get it now."

"About time!" Mark offered. "Knew that one the second she flew over the horizon."

"You're the one who grew up on comic books, not me."

"Not even Wonder Woman?"

Emily shook her head and Mark groaned like he'd just been stabbed. But there was a merry glint in Emily's eye that had Ripley guessing otherwise. So the woman did have a sense of humor; it was just buried behind one of the most terrifying facades Ripley had ever seen. She'd met a few Night Stalkers over the years, which was how she'd heard stories of—

"Wait a minute. You recruited me specifically? Why?"

Mark instantly sobered.

Ripley's side glance told her that all of this was news to Gordon.

Emily turned to the waitress. "Hi, Amy." And she placed her order.

When it was Ripley's turn she chose the simple expedient of holding up two fingers having no idea what Emily had just said. She'd been recruited…to a firefighting outfit. Why would they check her out all the way back to Admiral Parker?

After the waitress moved on, she turned back to Emily. But Emily didn't give her a chance to speak.

"Let us see how we get on first," Emily laid it down on the table like a decree. "We can discuss other matters later."

"But…" She was cut off by another group of people arriving at the table.

A handsome, broad-shouldered man with an easy smile sat beside Mark, across from Gordon. Next to him, a tough-looking white-blonde with a choppy haircut and a leather bomber jacket despite the warm day kicked out a chair, then crash-landed into it. To Gordon's other side sat Brenna, the mechanic, and Janet.

"Aren't you going to save a seat for your girlfriend?" Ripley asked Gordon.

* * *

Gordon had to scratch his head at that one. "I don't have a girlfriend."

"Oh, give me a break," Ripley rolled her eyes. "Wait, fiancée? Wife? What is she?"

"Who are you talking about?"

"Vanessa."

"Vanessa?" He was definitely missing something.

Ripley was shifting from a little sad, something he'd been puzzling at during her long silence on the drive down, to kinda pissed. He'd wager that if she was ever angry, she'd be lethal.

"Ow! Shit!" Someone had just kicked him under the table, hard. He spotted Mickey's smile.

"Dude, you and Vanessa? Secret's out. You two have been pretty circumspect…" he shared a lascivious grin with Robin.

There'd been nothing circumspect about the two of them.

"…but everyone knows."

"Knows what?" He glanced down the table. Vanessa and Jeannie were chatting away as if everything was normal. But Cal and now Vern were shifting their attention in his direction. "Knows what?"

"Why you hiding it, boy?" Mark faced him squarely across the table.

"I'm not hiding anything."

"You mean you two aren't…" Ripley tapered off.

"Aren't *what?*" Gordon was slowly connecting the pieces, but apparently too slowly for the crowd. Maybe it was nearly being killed twice that was slowing him down. It *had* been a long day.

"Lovers, Gordon. You two aren't lovers?" She looked as if the words pained her.

"I wish!" Okay, not his most tactful answer. Especially not to the attractive woman sitting so close beside him. "Uh…we were. Briefly. It didn't work out."

"Wait a second!" Mickey boomed out. "I practically gave her to you."

Robin spun on him.

"What I meant was…"

"No, explain that one," Robin faced him. "I've got to hear how you *gave* a woman to Gordon."

Gordon was half tempted to let Mickey cook on his own fire, but they'd been best friends for a long time.

"He told me not to be charming," Gordon said it softly. At Ripley's whispered *what?* he repeated it louder. "Said I should just be myself."

"That's all I did," Mickey raised his hands in surrender. "It was the day you hit base, Robin. That very morning when the team split to the two different fires."

She inspected her husband through narrowed eyes. "No. It isn't. I know you, Mickey Hamilton. You were gunning for her yourself."

He sighed. "I was. And getting nowhere."

"Making me second choice."

"No! Why do you think I stopped trying and gave her to Gordon? One look at you, honey and—"

"I'd shut up now if I were you, Mickey." Mark said softly.

"I didn't mean *give*. I meant…" Mickey finally shut up. Robin cuffed him on the back of the head and then pulled his head down and kissed his temple.

"You two really aren't?" Brenna looked at him strangely.

"No. It didn't work."

"Sure looks like it worked," Ripley said softly and several

of the others began nodding. Was that why he'd landed in a relationship dead zone ever since the spring? Because everyone had thought he and Vanessa were together so they wouldn't even consider him or introduce him to someone or...

"Shit, does everyone think that I've been an asshole all season every time I got near another woman?" At their several nods, he banged his head down on the table to a rattle of silverware.

"Pretty much, yep!" Mickey was back in his merry mood. His cross-table slap on Gordon's back only served to ram his nose harder into the table.

Gordon didn't raise his head but he did raise a middle finger, which earned him a laugh from the group.

"Can't a single guy just be good friends with a single woman?" At the silence, he looked back up. The guys were shaking their heads no. The women were looking puzzled.

Even Ripley was staring at him with a narrowed expression he couldn't read.

"Actually, there is a way..." Brenna tapered off.

"Thank you!" Gordon burst out. "At least there's someone on my side. That's all we are. Really good friends. It's just how it worked out."

Robin actually looked to be on the verge of mush-crying, which she never did. "You told me, Mickey," she reached over and took her husband's hand. "That first day you told me that Gordon was too sweet."

"Yeah," Gordon groaned. "He said, 'Finchley's just like Tweety Bird. Don't pay him any mind.' I think that's a direct quote."

Robin leaned forward to reach around her husband and brushed a hand down his cheek. "He's right, you know."

Gordon put his forehead back down on the table. Yeah, he knew. He'd been told that a lot of times over the years. "You're so nice!" "You're such a sweetie pie!" And on and on and on. Always just right before they dumped his ass. As if he didn't have enough character to hold onto a woman. Yeah, totally macho.

And now Henderson was going to dump his contract because he had no bird to fly.

At least his luck was holding consistent: Ripley was sitting right beside him to witness it all. Nothing felt as good as crash-and-burning twice in the same day. If he could fold up and disappear, he would.

* * *

Ripley had a lot to think about as Gordon drove back to the MHA camp. The headlights sliced through the deepening twilight, leading them like a train on a predetermined track to…somewhere. Somehow it was just the two of them. Vanessa caught a ride with Janet and Brenna; Brad and Vern had hit it off as well, bonding over their sports car passion.

The silence between them was oddly comfortable and, at the moment, Ripley really appreciated that.

Gordon's mixed signals…hadn't been mixed signals. Which meant he was attracted to her, and her random thoughts about him through the day perhaps hadn't been so random.

But she thought that his friends underestimated him. Four years in the Navy and she'd seen some awful things. Good friends, waving before jumping into their aircraft, only to never come back. Whoever said flying a Seahawk off an aircraft carrier was the safest kind of flying there was had never been in the Navy. If the bad guys didn't get you, the weather did. And if the weather didn't, the ocean might. Even the salt air was a lethal enemy, corroding out some crucial part when you were at your farthest point from the carrier. A landing missed by a dozen feet onto a heaving deck meant a sixty-foot fall into freezing ocean or getting in the way of a jet trying to trap on a wire.

She'd been lucky: in four years at sea she'd only lost a crew chief, a lucky shot straight to the face by a pirate far below. She'd put a missile into his boat, six dead and no regrets, but it had been too late for Canter.

And each of those returning Navy crews, if they made it back, were altered forever. Many never flew again. Reassigned to desk jobs, some even to landside because they couldn't face the waves again after watching chance take their mate, but leave them alive. Or even after a crash with no fatalities, sometimes they couldn't stand back up through the fear.

Others came back unchanged, or apparently so. It would only show in brief flashes that they hid ever so carefully. A false front covering over their hidden-hell fears.

But Gordon fell into a different category. He'd nearly died, acknowledged it to himself and others (Mark and Emily had gotten a detailed description out of him over the rest of dinner), yet he'd helped her on the fire. That, she knew, took a deep kind of strength that few others saw. Mark and Emily did, of course, perhaps Robin too, who was surprisingly gentle under her brash exterior, but none of the others. To them he was just...

"Gordon?"

"Uh-huh?" He answered as if their shared silence for the drive back to the base hadn't been anything unusual.

"You did really good today. You know that, don't you?"

"Sure, dumping my lack of love life out on the table for all to see. I'm completely rocking it. Not bad for my swan song."

"Your what?"

"My last day with MHA. You know they're going to cut loose my contract tomorrow, at least for this season. They don't have another helo for me to fly. Henderson confirmed it would take months to replace it. I'm gone."

"No," Ripley sat up as they pulled into the base parking lot. "That can't be right."

Gordon parked and turned off the truck, but made no move to get out. "Trust me, Ripley. I wish it wasn't so, but I don't see any other way around it that makes sense. Not from their point of view."

Ripley tried to think of a solution, but she didn't need another pilot. Nor did any of the other craft.

He clambered out of the truck and came around to hold her

door open for her. Another thing that her ex-fiancé had never thought to do for her. She stepped out onto the gravel, which crunched underfoot. The cool night had settled over the camp and she pulled her jacket more tightly around her shoulders. The stars above had conquered the night sky; there was no light pollution here. The Milky Way was a white band. Cygnus the Swan soared high in the sky.

"This can't be right," she repeated though she wasn't sure why. She was intensely aware of Gordon standing close beside her.

"Trust me, Wonder Woman, there are a lot of reasons I wish it wasn't so," his voice was a soft caress.

The air seemed to warm between them, wrapped in a cocoon of cool mountain air.

"Come on. Let's grab your gear and I'll show you to where you'll be bunking."

Ripley stumbled and almost fell despite the small penlight Gordon clicked on and aimed at the ground so that she could see where she was stepping. She'd been leaning forward… expecting…and then he'd turned on the penlight and walked away from her without looking back.

He led her across the field, her feet catching in the tall grass to either side of the mown runway.

By the time they reached *Diana Prince* and she'd snagged her duffle, her brain caught up with what had just happened.

"You know something, Gordon Finchley?"

"Not a thing, Wonder Woman Vaughan."

"There's such a thing as being too sweet."

"You think?"

"I *know.*" She hadn't eviscerated her fiancé when he'd cheated on her two days from the altar; she'd just walked away. She should have shot him in the balls.

"Huh!" It was a thoughtful sound. In the little bit of backwash from the penlight, she could see him looking at the sky. "Well, if this is my last day here, there's something I'll really regret if I don't do it."

"What's that?"

He clicked off the penlight and he became a dark outline against the starry sky.

Gordon's hand slid around her waist and pulled her forward against him in a strong, abrupt move. He paused for an instant. If she was going to resist…but the moment for protests slipped by with no surprise attached to it. Her body pressing against his was the most natural thing in the world.

And his kiss.

Great Hera! There wasn't a thing tentative, sweet, or Tweety Bird-like about Gordon Finchley's kiss. He held her tightly, not grabbing ass or digging his hand into her hair to control her. He simply snugged their bodies together and laid one on her. A damn good one. It was filled with need, frustration, and—

Then, before she could tell what else or completely melt against him, he jolted back.

"Sorry. Should have asked first. But you're just so goddamn attractive, Ripley. Watching you fly this big ugly bug-beast," he thumped a hand against the helicopter close beside them. "It's unreal."

About ten things tried to register at once, but the one that came out of her mouth was, "How dare you call *Diana Prince* an ugly bug-beast!"

He froze for a long moment, then burst out laughing. It was a good sound in the dark of the night. "I kiss you goodbye before I have a chance to say hello. I do it on the first day I've ever met you. And the thing you're upset about is I insulted your helicopter?"

"Yes," Ripley grabbed for some degree of sanity, laughing at her own ludicrous response. "Now take it back."

His chuckle was soft. "I really need to get a life." Then his tone became very formal, "I apologize to you ladies *both*. One of the most capable helicopters I've ever seen and her fair mistress of whom I now have taken quite indecent advantage."

His shadow sketched a deep, apologetic bow against the stars.

"C'mon. Your room is this way," his hand brushed hers as her took her duffle bag from her nerveless fingers then headed back across the field.

Ripley almost pulled him back into the darkness to take some more indecent advantage of her, but thought better of it and followed along instead. She knew so little about him. And if he was truly going to be gone—one-night stands were no higher on her list than meaningless sex. Of course imagining sex with Gordon to be meaningless was quite a stretch of the imagination.

Chapter 3

His bunk was just two doors down from Ripley's quarters—though he kept assuring himself that wasn't why he couldn't get to sleep. Gordon eventually wandered out to the radio shack that sat atop the wooden lookout tower. It was unmanned at night; TJ kept a radio and his cell phone close by his bed so that he wouldn't miss any fire calls. It made the tower a quiet place to sit and watch the field.

Gordon often did that. He liked looking down at the shadows of the sleeping helicopters and up at the shining stars. In the quiet of the night, the tower was always a soothing place to be. Most heli-bases were just some corner of a much larger airfield. Erickson at Medford, Columbia at Aurora, Evergreen had been in McMinnville before they went under. Mount Hood Aviation was the only outfit he'd heard of that maintained their own private airfield.

Nowhere else was he going to find such peace—or such people. Maybe, if he was lucky, they'd want him back next season. Yeah, lucky like running into a drone, losing a helicopter, and…

he couldn't bear to consider what Ripley must think of him after he'd grabbed and kissed her.

In the hours since he'd shown Ripley to her door, the thin crescent moon had risen. Tall trees left the whole field in shadow, including the helicopters parked along the edge of the forest. Pale, cool light shone upon the low buildings and his own perch.

The radio tower was set up like a classic fire lookout tower. A ten-foot-square cabin with counter space on three sides and a couple of squeaky chairs. A stack of old radio gear was collecting dust below the counter, and their newest radio (which could outperform all of the others combined) perched on the counter above them. The third wall had the door and a narrow cot for whoever was on radio watch. A narrow walkway wrapped around the outside of the cab.

Gordon didn't want to sleep tonight. He didn't want to miss a moment of it, which was just as well since he couldn't get to sleep anyway.

Thinking didn't seem to be of any real priority either. He just put a chair out on the walkway, propped his boot heels on the lower rung of the safety rail, and watched the night. Bats flitted by and he heard a great horned owl calling *Who*-Who!-*who-who* for a mate, somewhere off in the distance. He'd been working it for weeks now, often keeping Gordon awake when he was in camp.

"Good luck with that, buddy."

The owl kept calling. There was no response.

After what might have been hours, a tentative *Who-who?* sounded from the far side of the field. The call echoed back and forth between them for a while. Then there was a great flapping of wings and he caught sight of the massive girl bird flying from somewhere beyond the parking lot to the west over to the towering trees in the east.

"You show off!" The male Great Horned Owl didn't make any argument from his now happy perch in the thick forest.

Gordon looked at the cluster of picnic tables by the dining

hall where so many meals had been shared: both the cheery celebrations and the ragged moments before collapse after a particularly tough firefight. Birthdays, weddings. Mickey and Robin had been wed right at the base of this very tower. Emily had gotten herself ordained at some place online. Jeannie and Gordon had stood for the bride and groom.

It had all happened so fast that Gordon had felt it was his best-man's duty to point that out. They'd sat right here in the heat of a midsummer's night and hashed it out. Mickey had insisted, "When it's this right, you simply know it. Then your job is to just hold on as tight as you can and never let go." Four months from first meeting to married.

Gordon couldn't even imagine what that was like. He'd known Vanessa for two years before they kissed for the first time, for all the good it had done them.

He resisted the urge to bang his forehead on the tower's railing, instead watching the constellation Cygnus the Swan continue her slow dive down to the horizon. At some point he must have dozed off.

The sky now was pale blue and filling with a warm yellow.

And Mark Henderson was standing on the walkway, leaning on the rail, mirrored shades in place. Betsy, who'd been MHA's cook since forever, must be awake because he was holding a big MHA mug of coffee.

"Hey."

"Hey yourself." Mark made a real show of enjoying his coffee.

Gordon could see the steam rising in the morning air. His tired body felt a hard stab of coffee envy. If coffee was up, that meant that breakfast would be on soon. A good last meal.

Mark wasn't saying a word, just watching the morning. The first birds were already awake and at work. Stellar jays flitted up to perch a moment on the rail and see if he or Mark had food yet—just coffee—they were gone. Then they were back the next moment to see if food had somehow magically appeared in the past ten seconds. A turkey vulture soared high in the morning light, his identity marked by the spread "fingertips" of his outer wing feathers.

"I'm going to miss all this."

"You going somewhere?"

Gordon looked at Mark.

Mark kept watching the morning.

"Don't see a spare MD sitting around for me to fly."

"That's true," Mark sipped his coffee.

Gordon figured keeping his mouth shut was good advice from last night. He also considered mugging Henderson for his coffee, but that was a no-win scenario as Mark was a retired Army pilot and could probably kill him with a look. So Gordon stayed in his chair, leaning back with his feet on the rail.

"Tell me about *Diana Prince*," Mark said after a while.

"Wonder Woman?"

"Her too. But tell me about the helo first," he tipped his cup to where the bright orange Erickson Aircrane was parked in the tree shadow across the field.

"Impressive," Gordon wasn't sure what Mark was looking for. "Has a really solid feel to it. Ripley says that it is dead reliable, sort of like you'd expect. That's how it acted on the fire too. You know there's one named *Incredible Hulk?*"

Mark nodded.

"Well, it's kind of like that. I can see where it could be useful laying down big lines of retardant, but its ability to slap a big fire down out of the crown and back onto the ground where it can be fought is its real strength."

They talked yesterday's fire tactics back and forth for a while. Mark had a different view up above the fire; a view that Gordon had often thought about. Circling a thousand feet or so above the fire, the Incident Commander-Air would see the various helicopters and the smokies as chess pieces in the wildland firefighting game.

"I used to fly our ranch's little helicopter," Gordon was trying to find a way to explain the muddled images in his head. "Dad had a Korean War vintage Bell 47. I'd go up to find the strays… ranches need a lot of land per head of cattle in central Wyoming. It's rugged Front Range territory. But it wasn't enough to find them, because if you went about it wrong, you'd spook them into places they'd never come back from. The way to attack a fire always seemed like that to me. Herding the fire this way and that, but sometimes you want the horses and sometimes a couple hands on ATV four-wheelers. A guy on a dirt bike is good in the right situation; the bad ones you just have to slog out on foot. If conditions were just right, you brought down the helo and herded them about with a bit of fear and wind. Can't run them hard though…cattle overheat real easily and then their meat gets tougher, earns you a lower grade at market." And Gordon could remember the painful weals left by his father's belt to drive home that lesson.

Mark nodded. "Battle tactics is how I always think of it. I commanded a couple of attack birds, a heavy lifter, and a flock of Little Birds—seriously armed versions of your MD. If I had the wrong element in the wrong place, some raghead could slip out the side of the box we were trying to build around them while Rangers or Delta were busy kicking down the doors."

Gordon added that to his thinking and saw how it might fit, but he still thought of fire more as an unruly herd.

"You've flown the 212 with Mickey."

It wasn't a question, so Gordon just shrugged a yes that Mark didn't bother looking around to see.

"I want you up with Vern a bit. Get the feel of a Firehawk."

Gordon tried to get his mind around that. "I'm…what?"

Mark stood up from leaning on the rail, raised his coffee mug in a salute, and walked away.

"So I've still…" he tapered off because there was suddenly no one listening to him. *Still got a contract? Doing what?* Going for a ride. But *why* was the question.

Gordon was still trying to puzzle out what was going on when he noticed something was wrong with the sunrise. He'd seen so many from this vantage point that he knew something was wrong, even if his brain couldn't identify what.

The grass airstrip was empty, as was the sky. Across the field, the line of MHA's wildland firefighting helicopters and airplanes were all lined up quietly—the Aircrane all out of proportion with the other aircraft, but that wasn't the issue.

Diana Prince. Ripley Vaughan. If Henderson was sending him up to learn the Firehawk, maybe he'd be around to—

"To get your imagination way ahead of reality as usual, Gordon." Like some fantasy image of falling out of the sky and landing in the lap of a pretty lady had anything to do with reality for the likes of one Gordon Finchley. Even though it had actually happened, he'd gone out of his way last night to scare her off but good.

But, for just a moment, he'd *needed.* Desperately. It had flooded over him. He'd needed...someone. To help him celebrate being alive. To bury his fears in. To...

Yeah, he'd put signed, sealed, and do *not* deliver on that one. They hadn't exchanged a word between the kiss and saying, " 'Nite," at her door. That was *all* he'd said, because he was just that suave of a guy. Which was one word more than she'd said to him.

Shit!

He rose to stand at the rail and kept checking the field to avoid seeing if she was crossing from bunkhouse to dining hall behind him. A glance back anyway. The bunk house, parachute loft, equipment shed, and dining hall—the four main buildings of the MHA headquarters—were just coming awake. A few early risers were already headed to breakfast across the driveway that ran from the tower and out between the buildings, but none of them were dark-skinned beauties. He should go grab breakfast and stake out a corner. She'd have to put in an appearance at some point.

But he didn't move. Something was itching at him still.

He turned back to the flight line. Behind the aircraft, the

towering heights of the Douglas fir trees were swaying lightly in the westerly breeze, guarding the airfield in staid silence. The only evidence of life anywhere on the field were the three mechanics, Denise, Brenna, and Janet, working down the line of aircraft making sure that they were ready for whatever was coming. Actually, they were at the far end of the line working on one of the service trucks—another pulled up close.

"Hey, Gordon."

"TJ. Didn't hear you coming up. Thought you'd still be sleeping, Old Man," Gordon teased the base's manager and radioman. He noted with disgust that TJ had a half-empty mug of Betsy's coffee.

"Worth waking to watch the morning," something they often did together. Gordon liked the idea that he and TJ could keep doing that in the future.

"Sure is," TJ made a loud show of slurping his coffee. "I see we've got a new helo on my field. That's one ugly-ass bird."

"Don't let Ripley hear you say that. She'll make you kowtow three times to Hera's statue for giving offense."

"She a looker, huh?"

"You're old enough to be her father, TJ. Maybe her grandfather, so forget about it." He'd been one of the founding smokejumpers for Mount Hood a long time back. He'd been retired to the base after a hard fire and a busted ankle that had left him with a lifelong limp.

"You're never past looking, son."

"She's old enough to fly just fine." Somehow he didn't like the idea of anyone looking at Ripley. Jealousy wasn't his style—especially not with a woman he wasn't even dating. But still he felt it.

"So?" TJ leaned on the rail beside him. "Give."

Gordon couldn't suppress his grin. "No, TJ, the pilot isn't a 'looker.' We're talking way better than that. Serious eye candy."

TJ turned to look at him and snorted out a laugh.

* * *

Ripley considered dumping the mug of coffee she'd brought for Gordon over his head. He'd looked so damn lonely up there in the tower that she'd tracked down the kitchen and grabbed two mugs.

The older man was looking at her over Gordon's shoulder, his eyes bright with merriment. She did hold two mugs. Maybe she should dump one on each of them.

"Shit!" Gordon's curse was abrupt and sharp. "TJ, what's wrong with the sunrise?"

"Huh?" TJ looked to the east.

Ripley wondered how something could be wrong with a sunrise.

"There," Gordon was pointing to the treetops across the field. "Dark where it should be light. Almost a third of the line. Usually the sun hits the high treetops all together this time of year."

"Cloud?" TJ asked.

But Ripley could see that wasn't the cause, the sky was achingly blue.

"The land is rough to the east, but it isn't high. Something is blocking the light, something we can't see."

Gordon spun and squeaked in surprise. Five-ten of turbo-charged male actually squeaked in surprise at seeing her there. He had to be turbocharged, because he'd certainly fired up her body and her imagination last night. She was really sad that he would be leaving today and was even regretting a little that she hadn't stayed in the hall long enough to find out which room was his.

"Vanessa!" Gordon practically shouted in Ripley's face.

"No. I'm Ripley."

Gordon pointed over her shoulder and shouted again.

Ripley turned to look at the same time Vanessa turned on the grass below.

"Get aloft. I need eyes to the east."

"I was going to get breakfast. I can bring some to you."

"Aloft! Fast!" Gordon shouted and Vanessa bolted after only a moment's hesitation.

Damn it! She even ran beautifully. And fast. Gorgeous *athletic* woman. Were she and Gordon really just friends? How did something like that happen? There were guys she liked, just liked, but there was always that little sizzle there even if it would never be acted on.

It was an agonizing three minutes for Vanessa to reach her helo and fire it up. At some point Gordon took the coffee from Ripley's hand and mumbled a thanks.

This was a totally different man from the one she'd met yesterday. He wasn't the shaken firefighter covering his nerves with humor, nor that embarrassed beta male pounding his forehead on a restaurant table. This was the one who had delivered a searing kiss last night that she'd been unable to account for in the seemingly mild man. If she was Wonder Woman, maybe he was Doctor Jekyll and Mr. Amazing.

"Come on. Come on. Come on," he egged Vanessa to hurry from across the field.

"Vanessa headed aloft," she called on TJ's radio as her skids eased off the ground.

The cranking helo had acted like Prospero's call, beckoning a ship to beach upon his remote isle. Pilots wandered out of the dining hall with their coffee. Some of the smokejumpers—most still in their fouled Nomex gear, testifying to quite how late they'd come off the line last night—raced out of the bunkhouse, then stumbled to a halt and looked up at the tower and its silent alarm.

The MD 530 cleared the treetops and slid to a hover there for five long heartbeats before the radio squawked to life.

"TJ, please tell me there is a Prescribed Fire today."

"No. I repeat, *no* planned burn."

Five more heartbeats.

"Ten acres involved," Vanessa's voice was suddenly firefighter crisp on the radio. "Smoke will be visible at camp in minutes.

The westerly winds have been sending the smoke east. The fire, it is already in the crown. I estimate fifteen minutes until the flames reach the camp."

TJ spun and reached inside the tower cab. He slapped down a hand and the alarm just over her head blasted to life, making her jump and spill her coffee, which had thankfully cooled as she'd stood and waited.

Gordon set his coffee mug on the rail, then rushed to the side of the tower facing the camp.

"Get aloft! We need everything aloft!" The crowd broke and ran.

He turned to look at her for one long second. Asking some question? Trying to tell her something? Too little time either way. Gordon raced down the stairs.

She planted her mug on the railing beside his and was just a step behind him.

Chapter 4

The screaming fire alarm chased them toward the barracks. Gordon moved in front of Ripley to make way against the tide of firefighters streaming out of the bunkhouse. Neither of them were wearing their Nomex flightsuits. In fact, Ripley was wearing an eye-popping fire shirt that had done almost as much for awakening Gordon's pulse rate as the fire had.

Most big forest fires had a t-shirt made for them. It wasn't what her t-shirt said that stood out, so to speak. It was the way the brilliant red material emphasized the parts that did stand out. Her curves were neither slender nor generous, but they were damned fine ones. It also had a woman's V-neck, a rarity for fire shirts, which were mostly cut for guys, and revealed a splendid expanse of her perfect skin. A statement made all the stronger by her shorts. Damn but the woman had legs.

Of course in the category of not blowing it, calling her "serious eye candy" had been a big step in the wrong direction.

He wove a path through the thinning crowd, taking the opportunity of body-checking Mickey into a wall for the hell of it, and she followed in his wake to their doors. Mickey's second grunt as Ripley must have done the same only made him like her all the more.

Thirty seconds later he had his flightsuit on and was back in the hall with his PG bag. Unlike a smokejumper, who might live out of his personal gear bag for a couple of days, his had one change of clothes and he'd shoved in his laptop, no time for more. He grabbed his helmet and bolted.

Ripley was back in the hall at the same moment he was. The contrast from tight t-shirt and splendidly short shorts to powerful woman in a Nomex flightsuit made his mouth go dry—especially because he now knew what she was wearing under that flightsuit. This wasn't Ripley. In a moment, she *had* changed into Wonder Woman.

"Where the hell is your golden lasso, lady?"

She grinned as she slapped the duffle she had slung over one shoulder. "Why? You looking to get all tied up?"

Gordon grinned over at her as they sprinted side by side down the now-empty hallway. "Is that an offer?"

"Just remember, no man can tell a lie while bound by Wonder Woman's magic lasso."

"Okay, rain check then."

"Buck-buck-bu-caw!" She repeated Janet's chicken call from yesterday.

"Around a woman like you? Damn straight!" Ripley's laugh broke loose as they raced into the sunlight and broke into a dead run across the field toward their respective birds.

Ripley made a whirling motion over her head.

Gordon saw Brad in *Diana Prince's* cockpit nod his head. In moments the high whine of the auxiliary power unit on the Aircrane screamed to life.

"Go get 'em, Ripley!"

"Give me an M41A Pulse Rifle and I've got it covered."

"Deal! I'll get you one as soon as they're invented."

She offered her laugh of acknowledgement that he'd understood the reference before veering off toward her door. Ellen Ripley, the Sigourney Weaver heroine of all of the *Alien* movies, had forged into her second movie battle bearing one of those with an over-under flamethrower and grenade launcher. It was easy to imagine Ripley Vaughan toting one just like it.

Gordon slammed up to Firehawk *Oh-three* and snapped his gear onto the rear cargo net at the back of the cabin. Vern already had the rotor turning.

"You don't look like Emily," Vern greeted him as he opened the copilot's door.

"Ain't nobody on the planet looks as good as her. Not even her, because she's just that damn good looking." Emily Beale was the ultimate definition of the cool blonde.

"That's because we're all unique," Emily Beale was standing about a foot behind him. Her chill gaze said exactly what she thought of him. "At least we women are."

"Shit!" Gordon jolted. "What is it with you women sneaking up on me today?"

Emily didn't say a word, simply reached past him to take her helmet off the copilot seat. She waved him inward.

Vern grinned at him as he climbed in. "So who the hell are you?"

"Your new copilot," he wished the heat would get out of his face already.

"No shit? You ever flown in a Firehawk, Gordon?"

"Henderson's orders and nope. Never."

"Oh great!" Vern shoved a checklist into his hands. "Step 9. Read."

Gordon read aloud as he buckled in. He winced when Emily slammed the big cargo bay door shut before she sprinted off toward Mickey's helo. *Better him than me.* He glanced toward the big, ugly Aircrane for a moment. Maybe now there *was* a pilot on base who looked as good as Emily Beale. Totally different—as Emily had just reminded him—but amazing nonetheless.

* * *

Ripley donned her helmet and helped finish the startup procedures, then eased aloft moments ahead of Gordon in Firehawk *Oh-three.*

When she cleared the treetops, Vanessa was nowhere to be seen. Probably off somewhere charming some water into her tanks. As Ripley was the next one aloft, she called in a report.

"Confirm fire is one mile out and climbing the face of the ridge here. Flames strong in the crown. Ten acres are now closer to fifteen. Concur fire arrival at airfield in fifteen minutes minus. Strong on the minus."

The base was in absolute mayhem; very efficient mayhem. She saw Janet climbing into a truck and getting it moving off the field. Mark Henderson's Beech King Air command plane ripped down the runway, scattering the smokejumpers running toward their planes from the parachute loft where they'd grabbed their gear off the speed racks. A forklift raced across the field close behind them, transporting a pallet of gear for the jump plane.

"We're dry," Brad reminded her.

"Right." No time to get her firefighting tank loaded from one of the base's pressure systems. "Find me some water."

"Janet said to head southwest," Brad didn't even hesitate. Her team was on it.

As Ripley climbed up over the flames, she saw that the fifteen minutes was definitely minus, more like ten minutes plus.

* * *

Vern did a half dozen adjustments too fast for Gordon to follow on an unfamiliar aircraft, then jerked them aloft still only two-thirds through the checklist.

"Hey!"

"Look behind us," Vern kept climbing under the Aircrane.

Gordon took a moment to turn. The forest to the west was no longer dark. Far back in the core, deep in the undergrowth, there was an evil red glow.

Fire!

"Oh shit!"

"That's your cue."

"Roger that." Gordon keyed the mic, "All personnel! Active fire in the trees west. Clear the base and get the hell out of there. Repeat: Evacuate the base immediately!"

Vern shot them ahead—climbing over the other two Firehawks still spinning up their rotors—pouring on speed to the south toward the lake and a load of water.

TJ was racing out of the tower. The second smokejumper plane had its big engines cranking to life with brief plumes of black smoke—the first one was already rolling down the runway. Helos were climbing out in a haphazard fashion barely within the margins of safety.

"Carly, talk to me," Henderson called over the command frequency to the FBAN. Carly was called the Fire Witch because she was the best Fire Behavior Analyst in the business. She flew in Firehawk *Oh-one* with Robin Harrow.

"I'm barely airborne yet. Could you just calm down for… Oh shit!"

Gordon glanced at Vern. "Why doesn't that sound good?"

Vern was just shaking his head. "Don't think I've ever heard her swear before." Vern exchanged a little speed for altitude so that they could see over the treetops and the ridgeline to the west.

"Oh," Gordon suddenly felt a strange calmness wash over him. "That explains it." This was no little burn; it was already a fire with an attitude. The fire's head stretched twice the width of the runway's length and was slow-climbing the ridge—straight toward them. The smoke was a dangerous wall, thick with black ash, now blocking any hint of the low sun.

The fire had caught in a drought-riddled stand of timber in Mt. Hood's rain shadow. Probably a ground smolder started by the lightning that had swept through a couple nights ago. It must have built heat over time until it exploded forth with no real warning. The ridge face was now a roaring inferno—an area the size of a dozen football fields was filled with two-hundred-foot Douglas fir and larch looking more like flaming torches than trees.

The big retardant truck raced out the base's road, close behind the fuel truck.

"Badger Lake," he and Vern said in unison. Vern climbed them up over Mickey in his Twin 212 and banked hard for the south.

* * *

"It's called Badger Lake," Brad informed her.

"Great. I've never actually seen a badger in the wild. Let's hang out here for a bit and see if we can spot one." Ripley figured that she needed something to laugh about this morning. "Let's go with the sea snorkel. I have control."

"Roger," Brad was peering ahead. "No bodies in the water, this time."

"Better not be. Gordon lands in there again, I just *might* cut him in two." *Eye candy indeed!* His searing kiss, which had cost her much of a night's sleep, had been because she was *eye candy*? He was definitely going to pay for that one.

Filling her tank took most of the length of the lake because of how close the trees pushed in along all the shores. She carved her way back aloft. Hard. While she'd been making her run, several other helos had hovered in and dipped their hoses. Two minutes to the lake, thirty seconds to tank, two minutes back. Not a lot of runs to try and save the base.

"Looks like Janet found the best spot for us."

"That's my gal, just doin' her dance."

And that was all the excuse Brad needed to break into a quick rendition of "The Time Warp" from *The Rocky Horror Picture Show*. It didn't work as well without Janet aboard and he gave up after only a verse or two. When he trailed off, Ripley felt bad about being too preoccupied to join him. She'd been watching Gordon come up alongside her in Vern's *Oh-three*.

It was painted, like all of MHA's aircraft, in glossy black with red-and-orange flames streaming back from the nose. A big "03" in flaming letters was emblazoned on the side of the tail. *Diana Prince* would look darned silly in such a paint job. Good thing they were just a seasonal hire.

"Hey, did you see a fire anywhere around here?" Gordon called her on the air-to-air frequency as he caught up to her.

She glanced across the few hundred feet and could see him clearly.

"Sure. I think there's a small one up ahead somewhere."

"Okay. I think we'll go hit it." He waved. "Been real nice chatting, *Wonder Woman*. Gotta go. You're welcome to follow… when you can."

She took her hand off the collective for a moment to give him the finger, pressed up against the acrylic windshield so that he couldn't miss it.

And he stuck his tongue out at her as Vern pulled away. She could tank faster than him with her sea snorkel, but he could fly faster. She looked ahead to the fire. They needed retardant in the big trees, but all they had was water.

"Hit the leading edge," Mark called. "All flights, overlapping drops. Try to smack down the crown fire."

Fat chance. The crown fire covered several acres, all driving against the leading edge of the several-thousand-foot-wide head. Another few hundred feet through the trees and the fire would be threatening the base itself. *Oh-three's* drop was dead on, the white water showering down along several hundred feet of the fire.

Ripley lined up her load to begin at the end of his drop zone.

Brad had already dialed in a Six—heavy coverage that would dump the water fast instead of long.

"Now," she called out as she hit the emergency release button.

The load hit the edge of the fire and it spilled long and clean.

"Damn but that machine holds a lot of water," Jeannie called in an awed voice from where Firehawk *Oh-two* flew next in line.

With her hands occupied on the collective and cyclic, Ripley couldn't pat the helicopter on the dashboard. "Good girl," she whispered instead. "You show them who knows how to kick ass."

As she circled away and headed for the two-minute flight back to the lake, she watched the other fliers. Two more Firehawks, a pair of Twin 212s, and Vanessa's MD 530—just as neat and cute as the woman was.

Ripley really had to cut that out. She'd seen Vanessa on the fire yesterday and she was a damned fine pilot, darting her tiny helo right up to spot fires but never breaking stride to douse them.

The flight swept across in a tight formation: clean, low, and moving fast. It was as precise a drop pattern as she'd ever seen. However rude their awakening had been and the stress of the fire about to overrun their base, any doubts she'd had about their purported skills being the stuff of rumor and exaggeration were dropped squarely on the fire, just as they had been on yesterday's. Mount Hood Aviation deserved their sterling reputation.

The Firehawks had almost twice her speed, so they were back at the lake before she was. These guys even tankered up in nice neat formations. Which worked for her because that left her a clear lane down the length of the lake again. Ripley ran the snorkel out as they cruised past the hovering Firehawks without slowing.

"Now that is cool as shit." It was Robin this time, from the command seat of Firehawk *Oh-one*.

Ripley liked impressing MHA's lead pilot. She would *not* think of the other impression that Gordon had made on her last night. And how she could still feel...

The end of the lake arrived very abruptly and she had to claw aloft to clear the trees.

* * *

"Where can I get me one of those?" Gordon asked aloud over *Oh-three's* intercom.

"Are you talking about the snorkel or the pilot?" Vern replied back over the intercom.

"The pilot, of course!" Then he flinched and looked behind him, but they were alone in the big helicopter. No woman present to criticize his descent into a "guy" moment.

Vern laughed along as Gordon had hoped. "Or are you planning to jump type to the Aircrane before I even have you fully trained in the fine art and wonders of my Firehawk?"

"No," Gordon reeled in the pump hose as Vern headed aloft. "I like the feel of the Firehawk better. It's got way more balls than my little MD, that's for sure. But the Aircrane is a beast of a machine, unlike her pilot. I don't have to fly her to be impressed."

Vern glanced over, but didn't say a word.

Well, that sure as hell had come out all wrong.

He should have said fly *Diana Prince* or the Aircrane, not "fly her." Though he'd meant the helicopter, any attempt to fix that was going to be a dismal failure. *Mouth shut, Gordon.*

They were regaining speed and fighting for altitude to clear the ridge between Badger Lake and the camp with an extra four-plus tons of water. The power of the Aircrane simply took it aloft, climbing far faster than the Firehawk.

"She's making it look easy, even with over ten tons of water aboard," Gordon sought a subject change.

Vern went one better, "So you and Vanessa? Just good friends? How can you be just friends with a woman who looks like that?"

"Careful or I'll tell your wife." That should have worked. Vern's six-month pregnant wife was also their head mechanic. Denise might be just five-five with blond hair down to her butt, but she was about as dangerous as Emily Beale.

"But Vanessa?" Vern just wasn't going to let it go and there was no point arguing. Every one of them had lusted after her at one point or another, but she'd never really hooked up with anyone.

So Gordon told the truth, "I don't know, man. I just don't know. But it's true." Gordon shrugged his confusion. "What with

Mickey hooking up with Robin this spring, I guess Vanessa's natural shyness combined with my natural awkwardness just worked." ...out of bed.

Vern didn't argue the point on Gordon's awkwardness around women, which Gordon kind of wished he had.

Then all other thoughts died as the fire crested back into view. Their first attack had done almost nothing to slow the monster. Now it loomed close above their base.

"One shot?" Vern's voice cracked.

That was all they were going to get. It would be laughable if not for the hole in his chest. When a fire had turned into a wildfire, dumping water on it was no better than throwing money at it. They needed an attack plan, dozer lines, retardant, and firebreaks. None of that could happen in under an hour—they had a hundred feet and maybe three minutes. Their home was a goner and it hurt to watch.

The base itself had gone from organized hurry to utter mayhem. Fuel, service, and retardant trucks were racing out through the parking lot that was full of POVs—personally owned vehicles. The forklift was rushing pallets of parachutes, tools, and food supplies onto a big flatbed truck, but there wouldn't even be time to tie them down. The base was emptying fast.

And he couldn't blame them. The timber was so dry that it was little more than two-hundred-foot-tall kindling to the monster flames that now climbed the hill.

The airfield itself should have been a natural firebreak.

The fire had other ideas. It had started its own weather system, sucking fresh, cool air in at the base in a desperate need for more oxygen. The inrushing air then fanned the flames, heating as it rose, and gathering clouds of burning debris. The light westerly winds weren't a match for the growing fire system, and it was spewing the debris out onto MHA's base.

One of the service trucks was still close by the forest line. That truck had a container on its flatbed—Denise's shop. It had almost everything needed to keep their fleet aloft, from hydraulic oil to air filters to replacement rotor blades strapped on the roof of the service pod.

"Denise," Mark called. "Get the hell out of there."

Gordon could feel Vern freeze through the controls. Gordon tried shaking them, and Vern didn't respond. Hard to blame the guy, he was looking at a two-hundred-foot wall of flame leaning over his pregnant wife.

Gordon shook the controls again, harder, a clear signal for the other pilot to let go.

Vern did.

Perfect! Now Gordon had command of an aircraft he'd never flown before.

"Stalled," Denise called up, "now it's dead. Might be a loose battery terminal or starter wire, I was in the middle of servicing this vehicle. Give me a second." And even as Gordon prepared himself to make the run down the fire line, he saw Denise clamber awkwardly down and circle around to pop the hood.

"God damn it!" Mark sounded seriously pissed.

It was enough to make Vern whimper, his hands clenched white in his lap.

"It goes south," Gordon told him, "I'm going to dive us in there and you grab her. Clear?"

"Clear," Vern choked out.

Of course the chances of them surviving the maneuver with Gordon at the controls was not good, but he wasn't going to worry about that at the moment. The stick took a lot more motion to control than his little MD. And where the MD's rudder pedals were as light as a bicycle going downhill, the Firehawk's were more like kick pedals on a rock and roll bass drum set. He could feel the aggressive power of the repurposed Sikorsky Black Hawk.

"*Diana Prince*," Mark called out. "I need a salvo opposite that truck."

Gordon eased back on the cyclic to hover in the chaotic winds near the fire's leading edge. There might be need for his load as well, depending on how well Ripley hit the mark.

She flew the Aircrane forward and down until she was barely above the flames. At the last second she twisted fully sideways and unleashed her drop all at once. Her tank had a narrow fore-to-aft opening, but it was almost twenty feet long. By turning and flying sideways she turned her narrow drop into a sweeping wall of water.

Unleashed in a salvo, dropped all at once, it wasn't a water-fall—it was a twelve-ton hammer blow.

The water turned white as it hit and mixed with the air, but over a cement truck's worth of solid water slammed into the burning trees close beside the service truck. It was such an impact that it snapped off several of the tree tops. The water streamed down in a heavy flood, temporarily putting out the fire nearest to Denise.

"Now that's not something you see every day," Gordon whispered to himself in awe. It was an amazing display of power.

"Well done," Emily called out on the radio from Mickey's Twin 212. Another piece of high praise for Ripley.

Something had shifted since he'd crashed the helicopter. It was an uncomfortable feeling to know that Emily had been flying in his present seat only yesterday. Gordon supposed that it was a compliment that he was here instead of out on his ass as he'd expected. He still felt like an imposter, especially with the unfamiliar feel of the Firehawk's controls still in his hands.

Down on the field, Denise reached into the truck and it fired off. She slammed the hood and climbed back in. Gordon wondered if Vern's heart had stopped completely while he watched. But all that mattered was that Denise got the service truck moving.

As was the fire.

The width of the runway had forced it back down to ground level, igniting the grass strip gone late summer-brown. It began creeping across the field—actually more racing than creeping.

"Firehawks," Mark called. "Soak the grass, in a line."

Gordon was still in the lead so he dove down, below the

heights of the burning trees, and flew as close as he dared to the camp side of the airfield. Vern's attention was still all on his wife.

Denise raced by in front of him, the last big vehicle off the field, through the parking lot, and onto the road down the mountain.

Gordon planned to drench the grass far enough over that a falling tree couldn't cross the line.

He was halfway down the runway when the fire made his efforts pointless.

Firehawk *Oh-three* was flying down a tunnel of clear, calm air. But the wall of smoke, ash, and ember had tipped over in a great arc above him to touch down upon the buildings. A cloud of embers swirled down in a rain of reds and golds. Despite his racing speed, the view seemed to pass him by in a slow motion panorama.

Betsy's dining hall, from which he'd eaten a thousand meals, caught on the roof.

The small helos doused one side of the roof, the other side caught.

The plywood wall of the ancient bunkhouse went up next.

The parachute loft had its big barn doors left open. A whorl of embers slid through the open door, catching even as they hit.

Gordon pulled up, twisted, arced so that the last of his thousand-gallon load would be slung sideways through the doors, but it wasn't enough.

As he circled up, climbing north and west for safety, the rest of the helos followed. Loads of water dumped on old structures only served to cave in the roofs. Walls disappeared in vibrant sheets of flame. The new fire created a counter-draft that sucked the grass fire across the wet line.

The last to catch was the wooden control tower. How many hundreds of sunrises had he watched from that perch? For just a moment before it disappeared into a sheet of flame, he spotted two white objects side by side on the railing—his and Ripley's unfinished coffee was probably boiled to steam even as the mugs were shattered by the intense heat—then gone in a swirl of flame and smoke.

Once well clear, he slid to a hover to watch.

The wall of fire crossed the runway, racing the steady shower of embers to see which could ignite disaster first. Soon their cars in the parking lot were involved.

Gordon circled higher, helpless to do more than watch. There wasn't even time to get another load of water.

The first car the fire reached was Denise's prized 1973 Fiat Spyder. It was engulfed in moments.

"Ooo. That's gonna piss *her* off," Gordon tried to make it a tease.

"I'll buy her a new one," Vern whispered. He wasn't watching the parking lot. "There. She's clear. Past the first turn in the road. I'm going to kill her next time I see her."

"No, you're gonna hug the crap out of her for being alive. You want control?"

Vern looked down at his hands still clenched bloodless white in his lap and just shook his head. "That was a good passage, Gordon. Don't know if I could have done much better."

"Maybe just a little better?"

"Yeah, maybe," Vern managed a breath, if not a laugh, and a weak smile. "Thanks, buddy."

They both turned to watch the unfolding spectacle. The gasoline tank in the Fiat finally melted through and exploded like a bomb. Henderson's immaculate quad-cab Ford, parked next to the Fiat, blew moments later—eliciting an uncomfortable laugh from both of them. Mark loved that truck and it was funny that fire had taken it out from under their boss…but it was also horrible. Gordon's own beater Toyota Tundra pickup went next. That, at least, was no major loss.

Then he saw what lay just beyond them—

"Get clear!" Gordon yelled into the mic. "I repeat, all aircraft get clear. Betsy's propane tank. Behind the dining hall!" It was engulfed in flames.

Helicopters scattered in every direction.

Mickey almost rammed him—would have if Gordon hadn't somehow felt him coming and yanked up on the collective. Hard to blame Mickey, he'd been hovering directly over the tank.

The tank's pressure relief valve opened and released a gout of flame a couple hundred feet high right through the airspace Mickey had occupied moments earlier. The fire was superheating the tank, which would eventually rupture. But that process never had a chance to finish.

Mickey's big Goldwing motorcycle, which everyone always gave him shit about for being so "old fart" cushy, got caught in the detonation of Vern's gorgeous Corvette. The shock wave must have caught the motorcycle's big wind-guard cowling like a sail. The explosion lofted the nine-hundred-pound motorcycle twenty feet into the air and then dropped it onto the propane tank.

The explosion of the ruptured tank sent a fireball up several hundred feet. The parts of the dining hall that didn't simply disappear were blown back onto the burning runway. The closer vehicles were tumbled aside. Everything in the lot had its windows blown out by the shock wave and many more were instantly on fire from the shower of liquid propane.

Then the shock wave slammed into them. In an instant he went from hovering to pouring on power but still flying backward. Then the shock wave was past, but his speed against the wind wasn't. He and the other helos were suddenly diving toward each other through the much stiller air, straight into the center of the towering flames. Evasive maneuvers were chaotic, but no one collided. He watched Vanessa be tumbled through a sideways roll, but she managed to regain control before she was tossed down into the flames.

Car metal and roof shingles pinged off the side of the Firehawk. Gordon cringed and waited for the red lights of engine failure to light once more, but nothing came on. The gods had been with him this time.

He eased up even higher, only at the last moment remembering to check for proper clearance himself.

* * *

Ripley hovered high to the south. She'd been well clear after dumping her load to protect the mechanic. A momentary hover to make sure the mechanic made it out clean had turned into a front row spectator seat as the camp was obliterated.

"Holy shit!" Was Brad's judgment. Ripley could practically hear Janet saying those same words even though she'd been driving one of the first trucks off the mountain. Their synchro-speaking was either charming or nauseating, depending on Ripley's mood. At the moment she could only agree.

"Well," she tried to think of something to say as she looked down at the airbase that had just been erased off the map. She checked the dashboard clock. "Lucky number—exactly thirteen minutes since we were sent aloft. Our contract didn't technically start until today, so I think we're good for getting in the Guinness Book for the shortest firefighting contract in the history of heli-aviation."

Brad nodded but didn't laugh.

There was a stunned-puppy silence on the radio as well and she supposed that it was hard to blame the MHA pilots. Their home had just been erased...actually, pretty much everything was still on fire, but there was no question about there being anything left when this was done. She'd witnessed homes going up, and once a whole section of a town. But a firebase was personal. It was supposed to be *her* firebase; not anymore. It was only chance that she'd been too distracted by Gordon's kiss last night to unpack her gear and had been able to recover everything in the few seconds they'd had. All she'd lost was a sneaker that had escaped under the bunk as she pulled on her flight boots. Ducking to grab it would have taken an extra few seconds she wasn't willing to risk. Until she hit a store, she had boots and sandals only.

These people had lost everything. A wildland firefighter lived a gypsy life, traveling wherever the fire burned. Seniority only made matters worse, because that qualified you for the off-season southern hemisphere work.

Though, as she wasn't tied to anyone or anything, Ripley didn't much care as long as she was flying. She liked flying with Brad and Janet, but crew rotations didn't place the three of them together all that often. It was usually just whoever she was paired up with that month that created some form of temporary social circle.

The various helos had come to a stop wherever they were—different altitudes, different distances from the camp. Their neat lines of practiced precision were shattered.

She gave it another thirty seconds. Still nothing from the ICA.

"Well," she keyed the mic. "That's certainly a hell of a greeting you gave us. Anything west of here that we don't want burned up?" The fire was still on the move.

That finally evoked a response. Gordon's Firehawk *Oh-three* made a slow one-eighty twist. A few of the other helos eventually did the same as the fire began rebuilding in the trees to the west of the airfield.

"In a couple of miles," Gordon said in little more than a mumble. "Historic lodge, a lot of tourists, only one road out. On the slopes above the lodge sits the only year-round ski area in the country. If the fire climbs high enough, we won't have much of a ski team at the next Olympics."

She appreciated the gallows humor. But another bout of dead air followed.

No response from the ICA. Mark Henderson hadn't struck her as a person prone to being surprised by much of anything.

"*Merda!*" Vanessa called in that lovely Italian accent of hers. "I think my secret stash of chocolate and graham crackers has now been baked. And the marshmallows, they will be all together melted."

Ripley decided that maybe she could get to like the woman despite herself.

There was still nothing from the ICA.

* * *

Gordon looked over at Vern, who wasn't enough out of shock to notice anything peculiar.

Emily wasn't speaking either.

He spotted her. She was in Mickey's 212, hovering nearby. He saw Mickey say something, but Emily held up a finger to silence him. She was waiting for something.

For twenty seconds, silence reigned despite Ripley's and Vanessa's attempt at levity.

Finally, Gordon couldn't stand it anymore and keyed his mic, "This is Firehawk *Oh-three*. Re-tank White River and Mineral Creek. Follow my lead. We're going to need a good set line well before Route 35. Before Mineral Creek too. National Forest road NF-48 should be our cutoff. We have a fire to fight. Let's go!"

Gordon could just see Emily nod to herself—could feel her now watching him. He shoved the cyclic forward and racked up on the collective to gain some speed. The massive power of the Firehawk sent him shooting away from the disaster of their base.

In moments, Mark's strange silence ended as he began rattling out the exact set line for the smokejumpers who were still on their planes circling aloft. He acted as if nothing out of the ordinary had happened.

Gordon thought about that a bit as the others lined up behind him. It had been as if…

"A test," his voice came out as little better than a croak. That was when he became aware of the burning in his eyes, and it wasn't from fire smoke.

He turned to Vern.

"We just lost our goddamn home, and Mark and Emily are using it as a *test?*" His voice kept rising until it echoed about the Firehawk's cabin.

He tried to control it.

He really tried. No one yelled at Emily Beale, ever. Not if they wanted to remain among the living. The only thing that kept him from blistering the airwaves at her was Mark's continuing stream of instructions.

Vern blinked at him in surprise. "I guess so," he wiped at his face. "I almost lost my wife. Kind of puts everything else in perspective."

"You're right. We didn't lose any people. But we sure as *hell* lost everything else." There wasn't a person in the entire team who hadn't just lost a vehicle, possessions, photo albums... everything. The small personal gear bag in the back of the helo now constituted his worldly possessions. There was no secret stash at a friend's and definitely not at his parents' place—he'd left with the clothes on his back, his meager savings, and his pilot's license stuffed in his pocket. Whatever instinct had caused him to grab his laptop this morning was all that had saved his address book, some photos, and his collection of science fiction movies.

Vern slowly came back to life. He switched his own display to engine readouts, leaving Gordon as the pilot-in-command.

"In the Coast Guard," Vern's voice was finally steady, "we constantly trained to remain focused during high-stress situations. I could have done it, but I'm damn glad you were here to do it for me so that I didn't have to reach that deep. Maybe Emily wanted to teach the civilian pilots that lesson."

"This isn't the goddamn military, Vern!"

Vern didn't lash back, which made Gordon feel completely awful. He'd had to watch his wife and unborn child almost die. Another twenty seconds and nothing could have saved them—not even their Firehawk.

"Beale to Firehawk *Oh-three*."

"Go ahead!" It came out as a vicious snarl, a sound he barely recognized in his own voice.

"Pilot, are you safe to fly?"

He looked at the radio, out at Mickey's helicopter close alongside, and back to the radio. Then he looked over at Vern.

"How the hell does she know I'm so fucking pissed at her?"

"Got me, buddy. She's spooky. Always has been."

"Pilot," she'd said. Not "Gordon."

"Self assess," she'd meant.

Hurt. Angry. Feeling stupid about six ways to Christmas.

But there was a fire and it was still on the move. There were people who'd be in a lot of trouble very soon if MHA didn't perform.

Emily would take him off the controls—maybe kick his ass out of MHA if he relinquished them. But that wasn't why she and Mark had selected him to fly copilot in one of MHA's primary aircraft. He was the pilot-in-command, at the moment, of twenty million dollars of premier wildland firefighting equipment.

"I'm fine!" It still came out as a snarl, but it was true. He scanned the instrument panel for the first time in far too long; everything was nominal…and the pilot was getting there. "I'm fine." It came out a little closer to rational.

"Good." That's all she said, then she was gone. Spooky didn't begin to explain Emily Beale.

The line of flight was ragged as they all hunted for places to tank up over the wandering creeks. He found a spot he'd used with his MD on a local arson fire a few years back. It was big enough for the Firehawk, so he headed down.

He could see the *Diana Prince* hovering uncertainly. There were a lot of trees and three separate creeks in the broad valley just south of Route 35. A lot to choose from, and most of it bad. But if you knew where to go…

"*Wonder Woman*," it felt strange calling her that—too impersonal. He took a deep breath to calm his voice further. "Ripley," which somehow felt *too* personal, "this is *Oh-three*. There should be a big enough opening for you about five hundred yards south-southeast of my position."

She slid that way, then doubled-clicked an acknowledgement and descended out of sight behind the scattered trees between them. When she climbed back aloft, the twenty-foot long hose of the pond snorkel suction pump dangled below the Aircrane like a loose wire. He supposed she'd have to leave it down until the next time she landed. Just as well; there were no lakes this high on the side of Mount Hood for her fancy sea snorkel.

When Gordon saw how fast the fire was moving toward the firebreak, he suggested that Vanessa could be better off helping the smokejumpers than chasing spot fires. She soon had a longline with a grabber rigged off her cargo hook—a standard logger rig for when the fires weren't keeping MHA busy. As the smokies dropped trees, she'd lower the line. Twin pincers would snap around a section of tree that the smokies had chainsawed into one-ton pieces so that the MD could carry it. Vanessa would lift the tree away from the fire line, give it a quick swing to the other side of the firebreak, and then trigger the release midair, heaving it deep into the woods on the other side. It sped up the work on the firebreak by a huge factor while Mickey chased most of the spot fires.

It didn't take long to kill the fire—at least not as fires went. It had flared hot, but hadn't had time to grow past five hundred acres before the full, coordinated might of MHA descended on it. They'd killed it long before it reach a thousand. A fire this size would normally have a couple of ground teams and a helo or three assigned to it, and could be killed in a couple of days.

With twenty smokejumpers and six helos, it took less than eight hours before the fire just laid down and died. Denise had set up a refueling and service helispot in the Timberline Lodge's parking lot and—after Vern hugged, then yelled at her—was letting Brenna and Janet do most of the servicing. All of the lodge's high-paying patrons had set up chairs to watch the show while the bar provided outdoor food and drink service. The lodge had also shoved breakfast into the pilots whenever they were down for refueling.

They had the beast contained before the first standard ground crews arrived. With the smokies on the fire, they didn't even need an interagency hotshot crew. In a few hours, they'd be able to pull out as well. Then a standard Type 3 wildfire team and a couple of engines could mop it up and make sure it stayed dead.

Soon, with no specific call, all of the helos were hovering once more above the devastation that had been MHA's base.

Nothing had survived.

Not one building, not a single vehicle.

There wasn't even a question of going down and looking for any personal belongings among the char—the propane tank for the hot water system had erased the bunkhouse. What the forest fire hadn't taken out, the propane and vehicle gas tank explosions had.

The Black, as the area behind a wildfire was called, covered a narrow swath: barely wider than the runway was long and just over two miles from start to finish. Under a thousand acres, it wouldn't even be a blip in the fire season that was projected to reach sixty thousand fires and seven million acres burned. In 2015, fire had eaten over ten million acres.

But this hundred acres was their home.

"It's like the fire got tired of us beating it down and came right after us," Gordon mumbled as much to himself as to Vern.

Vern nodded.

Gordon thought of his years spent here. The women. The good friends. The good times. He looked for the two white coffee mugs on the radio tower's railing, but they were gone despite the charred timbers of the tower still remaining upright. How different might this morning have been if not for the fire?

He sighed and twisted the helicopter to look at the untouched wilderness around Timberline Lodge. They'd killed it, but the cost had been so high.

What he wanted right now was a hot shower and one of Betsy's burgers with all the fixings. What he was going to get right now was squat. He didn't even want to land here.

"Flight, this is Henderson. Reassemble at Ken Jernstedt Airfield, two-five miles north at town of Hood River."

That gave Gordon an idea.

"Vern," he said over the intercom, "Take control."

"Roger, have control." Vern had left him to fly the entire fire.

Instead of taking back command once he'd shaken off the terror, he had taught Gordon how to get the most out of the Firehawk. It had been something to distract them both from all that had happened beyond the windscreen…until now.

Gordon pulled out his cell phone. One advantage to a helicopter: even over the wilderness, the extra altitude was typically enough to reach a cell tower. Two bars, good enough.

He made a quick call.

Vern simply nodded his head, which felt good, as if at least something was returning to normal.

Chapter 5

Ripley followed Gordon into Jernstedt Airfield. She'd done that a lot during the firefight, following Firehawk *Oh-three*.

Robin and Jeannie flew just a little wild for her taste and the lower maneuverability of her big Aircrane. Ex-military stood out all over the way Robin carved turns, and Jeannie in *Oh-two* looked more like she was dancing across the sky than anything else. When they descended, it wasn't some calm lowering of altitude—they were all steep dive and hard pull-out. Gordon, on the other hand, flew with a smooth steadiness of action that might be a percent or two less efficient, but it was far easier on the aircraft and the pilot.

She liked that about him. Rather than trying to match the others, he remained himself. After the first hour she could pick him out miles away just by how he moved across the sky.

Henderson had picked up on it quickly enough and had paired them together for attack patterns against the fire. The fire had reached close enough to the creek that her slower flying speed back and forth to the fire was less critical. Even the slower pond snorkel still picked up two thousand gallons as fast as the Firehawk could pick up the seven hundred that it could manage at this altitude.

Jernstedt Airfield had a single east-west paved surface with no control tower, just the standard, open Unicom frequency—announce yourself and pay attention. There were twenty-odd private planes at tie-downs and a half-dozen lines of hangars: one cluster to the south at midfield, and another to the northwest corner where Henderson directed them. The area all around was cultivated fields and fruit orchards. No towering Douglas firs blocking sightlines like around MHA...like *had been* around MHA.

Word must have spread about the destruction of Mount Hood Aviation's base and apparently that was important to the locals.

The airport hands had cleared a whole section of the northwest parking area for their helos. Before she was even shut down, mechanics had the helos tied down, and local fuel trucks were hitting the birds. As she stepped out onto the runway, another local tossed her a water bottle, a cold one thank god, that she pressed against her forehead and cheeks. No matter how they'd twisted and turned through the firefight, she seemed to only have two positions: facing full-on into the sun and facing straight into the heat blast of the fire. If her skin was as light as Gordon's, she would be bright pink at the moment.

Jernstedt was just like a hundred other airfields. The sun re-radiating off the vast spread of sun-bleached asphalt. The whiff of av-gas, bright and biting on the hot air. Thankfully, the air was dry—not New Mexico desert, but comfortable.

The two MHA mechanics were waiting. Denise had a service cart and wore a tool belt, low on her hips to accommodate her pregnancy. Brenna had her shoulder-length black hair back in a ponytail, her similar tool-laden attire made her look like some fierce Asian warrior of old.

Ripley wondered if there even would be a crew after today's loss.

One of the pilots who she'd barely met rushed over from his

Firehawk, Vern from *Oh-Three*. He towered at least a foot over Denise and wrapped her into a hard hug. They simply clung to each other. Other similar scenes were playing out around the airfield.

Oddly, Gordon and Vanessa were not among them. They sought each other out, but their hug was brief. It wasn't cold, but it was quick. If anything was the final proof that they weren't a couple, Ripley supposed that was it. They were just steadying each other was all.

Hell, Ripley herself was feeling off-balance from witnessing the destruction and it wasn't even her base.

Brenna came striding over. "Hi, I think they're going to be a while. Vern is a worrier. Janet," she put a hand on Brad's arm as he searched the crowd, "is at the gas station with her service truck, but should be here any minute."

Brad thanked her and climbed back into the cockpit.

Vern wasn't showing any sign of releasing his wife—she was the one patting him consolingly on the back.

"Anything immediate or should I leave it for Janet?"

Ripley decided that her first greeting had been a little abrupt yesterday, telling Brenna to keep her hands off *Diana Prince*. "Nothing to report. You can go ahead if you're ready to."

"I heard that," Brenna said cheerfully.

"What?"

"You're nice, but I could still hear, 'Don't touch my precious Aircrane until Janet is here to watch you.' Am I right?" Her smile was bright.

Ripley shrugged, "Caught. Sorry."

"No worries. Don't you just love that phrase. *No worries.* I picked that up from Jeannie. It's an Australian saying that covers a whole lot of issues. I like it. Really, no offense taken. I'll wait for your crew chief." Brenna headed over to Vern and Denise, poked Vern in the ribs sharply enough to make him let go of his wife. Then she and Denise began working their way down the line of helicopters.

This was Ripley's first chance to observe the whole crew. She'd met about half of them last night at the pub, but now everyone was here except the smokejumpers. The ratio of women working for MHA was even higher than she'd thought. Four pilots, two mechanics, and several more ground personnel.

"You," Robin Harrow strode up to Mark Henderson and fisted him in the gut—her hard punch only elicited a laugh—"are an asshole." Robin made Ripley think of a G.I. Jane action figure. The rough chop of her fluffy, white-blond hair looked like it had been done with the K-BAR military knife she wore strapped to her thigh. She didn't walk, she tromped. Fist on hips, she glared up at Henderson.

Mark merely grinned down at her from behind his mirrored shades.

"Fifty-three seconds of stone dead silence," she snapped out. No question about her military background, not if she was willing to face Henderson head-on. "What kind of an ICA are you?"

"One just waiting for someone to step up to the line," he turned to Gordon, who had just walked over from checking on Vern. "Took you less than a minute, Gordon. Not too shabby."

Ripley nodded to herself. It had been a test, in the middle of a messy and very personal fire. And once again, Gordon had proved himself to be more than most others saw.

"*You're* the one who's the goddamn ICA!" Robin's fury exploded when she too connected that fact.

"And you're the lead pilot of Firehawk *Oh-one*," Henderson's voice had taken on a hard, military snap. "That means something. So act like it. ICA commands the attack; the *Oh-one* pilot leads the team. Your team was in shock. Next time do something about it."

Robin blinked only once, then nodded to show that she'd heard and learned the lesson.

"You're still an asshole," she snarled it out.

"Granted," Mark agreed easily.

And that was it, they were done. Apparently Robin was wholly unflappable.

Ripley would have made some joke and then totally crumbled inside.

Then Mark turned back to face Gordon, who stood between herself and Vanessa. "Nice job on the radio, you three. Hell of a hard moment and you all found a way through. Helped the others too."

"Uh, thanks," Gordon mumbled out for all three of them. Ripley exchanged a look with Vanessa and by mutual agreement they both kept their silence, but damn, a compliment like that from Mark felt amazing.

Henderson was as formidable in a good mood as he was in a bad one.

A silence descended over the group once more and had them turning to the south to stare up toward their former camp on the flanks of the towering Mount Hood. It rose eleven thousand feet and they were nearly at sea level here. It looked shining and serene. She could barely pick out the small smudge of the fire's smoky remnants.

Down safely, they were apparently at a loss for what to do next.

"Well, so the morning sucked." Ripley offered in her cheeriest tone. "What's on the schedule for this afternoon?"

Nervous laughter swept through the group.

The pilots all looked toward Mark and then, after finding no satisfaction there, toward Robin who started to look worried despite her having just faced down Mark.

"Oh," Gordon said casually, "I've got that covered." And he waved toward a small flock of minivans that were rolling up to them.

The shapely redheaded waitress from last night at The Doghouse jumped out of the lead vehicle and rushed over. She slid up between Gordon and Vanessa and hugged them both tightly against her. Both hugged her back, but she kept a hand around Gordon's waist.

"Oh. My. God!" The redhead effused. "I can't believe you guys were burned out. How did that happen? That's just so wrong. Was it arson? No. That's right. I heard the fire examiner on the scanner. Lightning strike. Mother Nature must have it so in for you guys. Is everyone okay? Gerald has the grill fired up. This one's on us. Come on!" And she was dragging Gordon by the hand toward the first van without waiting for an answer to anything.

"What is it with this guy and women?"

"Oh, Gordon. He is just such a sweetheart," Vanessa answered.

Ripley had meant that question for herself, but Vanessa had been standing close enough to hear. Then Ripley turned to face the tall Italian woman. Her accent said mostly raised in the US by Italian immigrant parents. There was an easy, if soft, joy about her that Ripley suspected came straight from those parents. Ripley had been born and raised in Oklahoma by a couple of her favorite lunatics on the planet. It felt like the beginning of a bond.

"Really. He is." Vanessa must have read the skepticism on Ripley's face. Vanessa climbed onto the rear bench seat of the second van and slid over to the window. At a loss for what else to do, Ripley slid in beside her.

Ripley's first assessment was confirmed: group dynamics here were incomprehensible to the outsider. Maybe to the insider as well.

Jeannie, the Aussie brunette with a fire-red streak down the back, and a big man with a big camera around his neck took the front bench.

Mark climbed in shotgun in their van, Emily had taken shotgun in the other one.

"So, what's with Gordon and the redhead?" Ripley hadn't really meant to ask that.

"Amy is just like that," Vanessa answered. "Especially with Gordon—"

"For reasons that none of the rest of us can understand," the big man turned to smile back at them, "I mean why not me? I'm *way* better looking." Then he grunted as Jeannie elbowed him in the gut.

"Hey!" He complained. "It's true. Cute women can't help themselves around me," then he leaned over to kiss Jeannie. This had to be Cal Jackson, Mr. Cover of *National Geographic*, the number one wildfire photographer in the business. She'd heard he was flying with MHA but hadn't heard he'd married in.

"Amy, she is happily married to Gerald the cook," Vanessa explained.

"Which still doesn't explain why you're not with him," Ripley continued talking to Vanessa.

Cal twisted around to look at Vanessa. "You're not a couple?"

"No."

"Duh," was Jeannie's comment as the van rolled out of the airport. They drove out through orchards of apple and peach trees.

"No," Cal protested. "I'd know if you and Gordon broke up."

"Did he ever tell you that we were together in the first place?" Vanessa teased him, which caused raised eyebrows from Jeannie and Cal. Even Mark glanced back from the front seat in surprise as Vanessa continued, "Wait, he could not have done this, because all of you were in Alaska on another fire while he and I were in the Washington Cascade Mountains earlier in the season. And still no one has explained why you were so slow to return from that fire. What made that so?"

Ripley noticed the expressions shift on Jeannie's and Cal's faces to one of careful silence. They both glanced forward at Mark, who turned around to the front as if he hadn't heard a thing. Ripley had no idea how to read their reactions.

"Some big secret," Vanessa leaned close and whispered softly.

"Oh," Ripley whispered back, not knowing what else to say. For a distraction, she watched out the window. The orchards gave way to suburbia, but the town was small enough that it only lasted a half-dozen blocks before they were winding through the tree-lined streets of the town.

"It must be my Oklahoma upbringing, but I'll never get used to how green Oregon is."

"Oklahoma always seemed so stark to me," Vanessa answered. "I was born in Dolceacqua, Italy, and we move to Seattle while I am eight. My little sister Graziella is still there—Seattle, not Italy—working as a restaurant hostess. I'm the adventurous sister; she's the pretty one."

That had Ripley twisting around to look at her in surprise.

"Oh, I know. But seriously, she is. She has married this amazing Mexican who cooks Italian like it is nobody's business. He is from Idaho. My parents are still upset that I am not married but my little sister is."

Ripley had had friends for years who she knew less about than she already knew about Vanessa. A quick glance back from Jeannie and Cal marked how unusual this was for Vanessa. Was she seeking Ripley's approval for some reason? If she was trying to draw out Ripley, she was doing a lousy job of it.

Vanessa looked a little surprised and flustered at all she'd just revealed, so Ripley decided to help her out.

"An Idaho Mexican who cooks Italian has married your prettier sister in Seattle. Moral of the story: Welcome to America." Ripley couldn't think of what else to say.

"Yes," Vanessa shrugged with no hint of how bizarre a summary that had been. Then did her best to hide her sudden nerves with one of her model-worthy smiles.

Ripley briefly rested a hand on her arm in sympathy and Vanessa's smile turned more natural. Ripley actually felt a little sorry for Gordon that it *hadn't* worked out with Vanessa; she appeared to be as nice and sincere as she was beautiful.

And a part of herself that Ripley didn't recognize at all was secretly glad that it hadn't—Gordon was still available.

The vans pulled up in front of The Doghouse, which looked no more structurally sound than it had the day before.

* * *

"I must tell you the truth."

Gordon could hear Vanessa chatting easily with Ripley as he walked across The Doghouse's gravel parking lot toward them.

He was actually quite surprised that Ripley wasn't overshadowed by Vanessa. Ripley's beauty wasn't slap-in-your-face (or other body region) intense like Vanessa's. There was an impossibly engaging freshness to Vanessa, like a colt inspecting the meadow in wonder on its first day past the corral.

Ripley was more like the grand bay mare, steady and stunning.

"I will rather eat a good burger any day," Vanessa continued. "Better than one of my brother-in-law Manuel's fancy meals. My parents say that it is far too American of me." Her shrug was both eloquent and elegant.

Gordon fell in beside them, wanting to hear what Ripley's preference would be. She'd barely opened her mouth when Henderson's phone rang.

"MHA. Henderson."

His grunted "uh-huhs" stopped all conversation, but didn't tell Gordon anything. They also were enough to stop everyone's progress toward The Doghouse.

Except Ripley. She kept moving until Gordon rested a hand on her arm. She stopped and studied him, again that owlish inspection from his face to his hand and back.

What was so surprising about it was that she didn't appear bothered by it. She was making it funny.

He could feel the slender strength of her arm through the Nomex flightsuit. Could remember how it had felt to hold her, even for a moment.

Then she glanced over at Vanessa. There was one of those quiet moments that sometimes happened between women. A long silence that wasn't merely silence, like they had telepathy or something. Then they exchanged nods.

Gordon wondered what the hell.

Another of Henderson's "uh-huhs" punctuated it even more clearly.

Ripley turned back to him and looked him up and down as if searching for a flaw. Well, he had plenty of those, starting with how long he'd been touching her arm. He pulled his hand back.

"You—" she began.

"Shit!" Henderson stuffed his phone in his pocket. His eyes were unreadable behind his mirrored shades, but his scowl was deep.

For twenty seconds he stared off into the middle distance and Gordon simply waited along with everyone else.

"Harrow!" Henderson snapped it out, even though she was less than ten feet away.

"Henderson!" She snapped it right back, then frowned—not earning the smile she'd obviously been going for. "Okay, hit me."

"Tell Amy and Gerald we have one hour, max."

Robin nodded, then understanding she was dismissed, headed inside.

"You three, with me." And he turned off and strode across the parking lot.

"Shit!" Gordon already knew what had just happened.

"What?" Vanessa and Ripley asked in near Brad-and-Janet-like unison.

"I hate it when I'm right. Why did he even let me get my hopes up?"

"What hopes?" Vanessa asked, but he could see that Ripley wasn't surprised.

"Wildland firefighter is a gypsy life," Ripley shrugged as if losing so much today wasn't already enough. She shoved her sunglasses upward into her hair.

"Right about what?" Vanessa asked again.

Gordon just hunched his shoulders against the oncoming disaster and followed after Henderson to the far corner of the parking lot.

Another van rolled up, this time Brenna, Brad, and Janet climbed out with a few others.

Henderson turned, "You, Ripley, do you speak for your people?"

"Contractually, yes."

He nodded, then pointed at Brenna. Somehow the impact of his gesture had her turning to look over at him. He waved her over, letting the others continue inside.

"Aw crap! A mechanic too?" Gordon couldn't believe it. Firing him made sense. Letting go of Ripley and Vanessa maybe a little, but not their second mechanic. "That's wrong, Mark, you can't cut her. Sure, the losses today were hard, but you'll need someone to cover for Denise soon. She's not going to get less pregnant."

Vanessa went wide-eyed as she put the pieces together, but Mark remained silent.

Gordon kicked at the gravel while Brenna crossed the parking lot to join them.

"Hey gang. Looks like a funeral over here. Whose is it?"

"I am thinking it is ours," Vanessa told her softly—sad acceptance clear in her voice.

Brenna looked shocked and took a hold of Vanessa's hand for mutual support.

Face it like a man! his father had said to him more times than Gordon could remember. It was his answer to everything, especially one of his brutal harangues. Gordon had never measured up to his father's standards and his father made sure that everyone within earshot knew it.

Mount Hood Aviation was the only place he'd ever fit in. Well, this once, he *would* face it like a man. Gordon looked up and faced Mark squarely. He was going to lose Vanessa, Brenna, and Ripley all in the next moment. The last hurt deeply though he knew her so little. Of them all, only Ripley was acting as if it was no more than she'd expected.

"Bring it on, Mark. Enough dancing about."

Mark offered a grim smile and a nod. "That was the owner of Mount Hood Aviation."

Gordon didn't bother responding.

"I want to remind you four that your work for MHA is covered by a non-disclosure agreement."

"What's to hide so much that you need an NDA?" Ripley asked. "Did you sign it?"

"In the packet back at Erickson. I assume Randy sent in a copy."

Again Henderson did that nod thing of his. "Just wanted to remind you all of that. The rest of the team—"

"Will miss us," Gordon couldn't stomach it any longer. It felt as if his father was once more preparing to tell him he wasn't good enough. His father liked the long, pompous setup as much as, apparently, Mark did. "We're all fired. Fine! We done here?"

Mark just grinned at him.

Not once in his life had Gordon ever punched a man. Never even raised his fist in anger since he was a seven-year-old boy. His father had thrashed him but good for that transgression.

Gordon unleashed a strike at Henderson's face, mirrored shades and all.

Henderson didn't even blink. He brushed it aside, somehow grabbed Gordon's wrist, and with a twist had Gordon groveling on the sharp gravel of the parking lot. Pain shrieked up his shoulder and shouted out his throat.

"Sorry. Sorry," Mark let go and helped him back up. "Didn't expect that from you and my old training kicked in."

Gordon rubbed at his shoulder and winced against the aftershocks of pain. Henderson had moved so damn fast.

"You okay?" Ripley touched his shoulder gently.

"Fine!" Not even close. "We done?" He looked back at Henderson.

"Your choice. You can walk if you want. MHA will pick up your contract next year if you're still interested. Or, you can stop assuming shit and listen."

Gordon rubbed at his shoulder again, accidentally running his hand over Ripley's where it rested there. She didn't pull away. He squeezed it briefly against his shoulder and then wished he hadn't when a fresh round of pain roared out of the stressed joint.

"We're listening," Ripley said softly. "But it was a reasonable assumption. You already told Gordon you wouldn't be replacing his MD anytime soon. That gives you too many pilots. Add to that the major financial hit today of your base burning. Time to cut costs: a pilot who lost his helicopter, a second mechanic. No great surprise you'd cut my and Vanessa's contracts as well. It's okay, I'm used to not belonging anywhere."

Gordon almost took Mark's offer to turn and walk away. But something about the sadness in Ripley's voice held him in place. She hadn't struck him as a sad person, but now he was seeing through her protective shield to a deeper layer, and he didn't like what he saw. Women as amazing as her weren't supposed to sound as if they hurt so badly inside.

He stayed where he was and nodded for Mark to continue.

"It's late in the season here," Mark remained unreadable after Ripley's statement, but at least the smugness was gone. "The fires are tapering off and the other outfits can handle whatever is coming. Our southern clients are already on fire and begging for our help, so the US Forest Service has released us."

"What southern clients?" Ripley asked.

But Gordon knew that the rest of the team had wintered the last few years in different places. Honduras, Australia, he'd once overheard Cal say something to Jeannie about Indonesia—but nobody talked much about any of them. Maybe…he didn't want to get his hopes up again…but just maybe.

"The question at this point is simple," Mark answered without answering the question. "You're either all the way in. Or you're out. We pay you an end-of-season bonus, subcontract you to Columbia Helicopters for as long as they need you, and we'll see you in the spring."

* * *

"What does 'all the way in' mean?" Ripley was having a hard time concentrating. Gordon's hand was still holding hers against his shoulder. It was as if he was so focused on Henderson, he'd forgotten his hand on hers.

"If—and it's still a big if—what our owner expects to happen happens, Australia will only be the first stop. Should that occur, the NDA will come into effect. You will not be asked to do anything more dangerous than fighting fire, at least we hope."

"Which means?" Ripley prompted him again.

"That non-disclosure agreement is no standard document. Anything you do or say will not be discussed except with other senior MHA personnel. Right now that includes all of our pilots other than you three, plus Denise. And I mean *no one* else. Not to judges, police, or in some dumb-ass old-age-reveal-all book like the ex-SEAL guys keep writing despite their oaths. No one. Nowhere. Ever. That's all the information I have at the moment. Decide now."

Gordon barked out a laugh. "Couldn't have told me that before you wrenched my arm out of my socket?"

Henderson shrugged.

"I'm in if Gordon is," Vanessa said softly.

Ripley looked around Gordon at her.

"I trust him," Vanessa read Ripley's question and explained. "He is very smart about things like this."

"Well," Brenna said. "I'm in either way. Been dying to find out what kind of shit Denise has been getting into. Just about my best friend and she doesn't say squat about how she and Vern hooked up. Nothing on where they were last winter or those two weeks this spring either…though I know it was nasty. I saw the inventory list of parts replaced on Firehawk *Oh-one* and it was a damned long list. I'm so in."

Mark's expression would have quelled any lesser woman.

Gordon looked at Ripley with those bright blue eyes, and she enjoyed the moment as he squeezed her fingers just a little, then finally let go. Brenna and Vanessa were still holding onto each other as if they too were suspended in the moment. *Freeze the action stage left. Now the action starts center stage.*

Ripley could see that Gordon had made his decision but wasn't going to speak until she'd made hers.

"Why me?" She turned to Mark and decided that it was a question she'd also have to ask Gordon at the first opportunity on a very different topic.

"Impeccable record both firefighting and Navy. Discreet to a fault. Has a team that is equally highly recommended." He rattled them off in fast order rather than making it up as he went along.

"It wasn't by chance that you contracted me and the *Diana Prince* while Brad and Janet were on the same rotation I was."

Mark didn't bother nodding, which told her that answer clearly enough.

"You need the Aircrane."

That earned her an indifferent shrug.

Only partly? That meant he'd recruited…her. That made it a very different question. She was being asked to take a blind risk by someone who clearly knew a great deal about her. Had they investigated her parents as well? Not that it would tell them much. As much as she loved her folks, she'd never fit in with the pair of quiet academics living in eastern Oklahoma. They were to be found in the library; she was usually out in the neighbor's barn learning how to ride a horse or drive a tractor.

In the Navy, she'd still been the outsider. The Navy was the most gender-integrated branch of the service, all of twenty percent women. She'd also been the very first woman to be combat-rated in the Seahawk, and pilot gender ratios were still massively male. The Navy might have rules, but it didn't mean that the old boys' club didn't totally suck.

By the time she'd been bilked out of having a wedding and started flying for Erickson, she knew how to be an outsider. Shut up and fly. It's what she did. Now she was being asked to fly blind.

"You're asking a hell of a lot, Henderson."

His nod solidly confirmed her assessment.

"Blind faith after two days flying."

"Not quite the way I'd planned it, but the Southern Hemisphere timeline has moved up." He crossed his arms and waited.

She didn't know Mark. There was no questioning his integrity or reputation, but still, she didn't know him.

She'd also seen something that even Henderson hadn't. He was pushing Gordon, specifically testing him for some reason. Henderson might have been surprised, but Gordon had struck out at just about the moment that she'd expected him to.

Maybe she knew Gordon a little better than she thought she did.

Vanessa clearly knew him very well and worshipped him, trusting him to make the decision for her—that he would protect her against all comers. And she knew the man a bit as well. The one who had kissed Ripley, bragged about how she was "serious eye candy," and then been horrified to see that she'd overheard. No, horrified perhaps that he'd even said it in the first place. She reminded herself that she had a lot of questions to ask Mr. Gordon Finchley. But there was one question she didn't need to ask.

She looked at Henderson and pulled her own shades down out of her hair until they shielded her eyes once again—they weren't mirrored, but they'd have to do.

Then, without saying a word, she nodded.

Chapter 6

*T*he *fast hour for* lunch at The Doghouse had been mostly quiet as MHA's crew still processed the loss at their base. Ripley had some of her own thinking to do as well…like what the hell was MHA up to? Not that her prime rib dip sandwich had offered any answers.

Then it had been back to Jernstedt and a half-hour flight to Portland International Airport.

A pair of Antonov An-124s had landed at about the same time they did, and for the last few hours the entire MHA helicopter and maintenance crew had been left to mill around while their helicopters and equipment were loaded. Apparently the smokies and other support staff were not included in whatever was coming. Which said even more that this wasn't just firefighting.

"Damn, but those are big planes." Ripley didn't need to turn to see who said it—they all had said it many times as late afternoon shifted to evening. The work lights were kicked on inside the planes as darkness fell, making them seem even larger.

The Ukrainian cargo jets hulked in a remote corner of

Portland Airport. They completely dominated a 747 that was parked nearby. They were the largest model of cargo jets built except for the single enlarged version of the An-225.

When the fire season in Australia went suddenly out of control, Erickson would hire an Antonov An-124 to deliver two Aircranes Down Under in just twenty-four hours, rather than waiting for the far cheaper trip by freighter. She'd flown one of them last year going to Australia, then come back by passenger jet and had to wait a month for her helicopter to make it home by boat. Two Antonovs together was something she'd never seen before.

They were so big that it didn't take much to put her Aircrane aboard. Remove the main and rear rotor blades. Remove the tall wheels and shocks to lower it onto a small hydraulic carriage. Then it simply rolled aboard.

The Antonovs looked terribly Russian. Side by side they appeared to glower at her. Their massive nose cones were pivoted high in the air so it looked like they were devouring serpents ready to swallow her helicopter and then her. Clearly she'd seen the *Alien* movie and its sequels too many times growing up. Her parents, two closet science fiction buffs, had met in the line for that movie. Apparently she'd been conceived hours before they went to the sequel's opening night, perhaps germinating the embryo during the film itself. The Ripley moniker had been inevitable.

Ripley never actually minded that. There were worse fates than being named for an action heroine and constantly being told she could do anything. Going military hadn't been what they had in mind, but they had let her go with a mixture of tears, fears, and cheers.

Still, the two Antonovs were alarmingly reminiscent of the sharp maw of the monster in *Alien* and she felt as if she were indeed about to be swallowed.

To fit Firehawk *Oh-three* and Vanessa's MD 530 inside along with *Diana Prince*, all they had to do was fold the main rotors and drain the fuel. The cargo bay was simply that big. The other

Antonov swallowed the other two Firehawks, the 212, and the two service pods without so much as a squeeze. They loaded up a launch trailer that was too small to even be a factor in the monstrous cargo bay. But it was big enough to…

That finally gave her pause. She grabbed Gordon's sleeve the next time he walked by. There was little enough for them to do while the loadmasters made sure that everything was placed exactly where they wanted it and chained down.

"I recognize that trailer. That belongs to a ScanEagle drone."

"Sure. Steve flies it for us," Gordon nodded toward a spare airplane tire lying on its side in the shadow of the hangar. They moved over and sat on it, which left their feet dangling above the pavement.

She felt like a little girl again, beating her heels on the hard rubber.

"The drone is incredibly useful on a fire," Gordon explained. "Steve sends us direct feeds of the fire in both visible and infrared light. It's great. Have him make sure that you're set up for it."

"How many civilian outfits have a million-dollar military drone to fight fire?"

"Actually, he has a couple of them."

"Gordon."

"What?"

"Are you being dense on purpose?"

"Am I…what?"

Ripley wished they weren't sitting in deep shadow so that she could see him more clearly.

"About what?"

"What *are* you thinking about?"

"Kissing you the last time we were together in the dark." She'd swear that his voice dropped most of an octave as if he was trying to be smoothly sexy like some Eurotrash jetsetter.

"I get why Mickey told you to just be yourself."

"Why doesn't that sound good?" Gordon spoke in his normal voice.

"You're a nice guy, Gordon. Just go with that."

"Does it get me another kiss?"

"Put that thought on hold." Ripley wasn't sure if she was ready for another one of those from him. "At least until you explain that drone."

"What's to expla…" Gordon trailed to a stop. "Oh."

"Henderson said that whatever this other thing is, it wasn't fighting fire. Add a military-grade drone and what do you have?"

Gordon was silent a long time before he whispered, "Damned if I know."

Vern came out of the hangar munching on a sandwich and Gordon called him over.

"Buddy. tell me about the kind of shit you guys got into this spring."

Vern, still in the wash of the hangar's light, froze. "You guys talk to Henderson yet?" He said it in a whisper. Ripley didn't know whether to shiver or laugh.

"For all the good it did us. He was all mysterious."

Vern nodded. "That's how it starts. Just pray to hell that it stays that way." Then he was gone as if the *Alien* monster was after him now too.

Gordon was silent as he stared after his rapidly departing friend.

"Well, that certainly cleared up everything," Ripley finally broke in on his silence before the pressure inside her could build to a scary point.

"Clear as mud," Gordon agreed.

Ripley sighed. She should have kept her mouth shut and gone for the kiss.

* * *

Gordon figured that the right solution was maybe to do what he'd done last night. To hell with being decent and considerate. To hell with the consequences. Just grab Ripley and—

Vanessa rushed by, then stumbled to a halt when she spotted

him and Ripley sitting on the tire. She looked even more flustered than he felt.

"I—" it came out as more of a croak than a word. Then she rushed off into the darkness.

"Vanessa?" he twisted around and called after her.

As far as he could see, she kept right on going.

He jumped off the tire and pointed at Ripley, "You just remember where we were," as if they'd been interrupted in the middle of foreplay.

If he stopped to try and explain his way out of that one, he'd lose track of Vanessa in the dark. He cursed to himself and raced after her. Thankfully she'd stumbled to a halt just fifty yards further on at a perimeter fence around the back of the hangar.

"Hey, what's wrong?" He managed to find her arm and rest a hand on it. She spun into him and held on more tightly than even after he'd survived the crash and gotten the shakes. The only other time the shakes had happened was the day that he'd permanently burned his bridges with his family and walked away. He'd been alone for that one. If she was feeling that awful, then what in the hell could he possibly do for her?

"Kiss me."

"What?" Certainly not an option he'd expected. "We talked about this. We agreed there was nothing there."

"Just stop with the talking and kiss me."

He thought of Ripley and the kiss he'd been hoping for, when Vanessa locked her arms around his neck and pulled him into a kiss. A deep, tongue-twisting, electrifying one with full-on body contact. It reminded him of every moment of making love to her. And of all the fantasies that had come before that and, sadly, not been fulfilled in feeling even if they had been physically.

As wild as the kiss was…there was still nothing there for her. He could tell, he'd been kissed by eager women before. Perhaps not as thoroughly, but this kiss faded away strangely and far too fast for how it had started.

He also had the feeling that he was kissing the wrong woman, but he caught up with that thought less quickly than she did. Being kissed by a gorgeous woman that he liked so much wasn't exactly helping his thinking.

She eased back a half breath and then rested her forehead against his and began cursing softly in Italian. At least he assumed they were curses: beautiful in sound, harsh with an edge of desperation.

"What's going on, V.?" Something he'd called her at only the most intimate moments.

She kept cursing, but she didn't let go.

"Vanessa?"

"I am having thoughts. They are not thoughts that I know what to do with, Gordon."

Speaking of clear as mud. "Care to give me hint?"

There was a long silence before she shook her head no.

"Am I supposed to guess?"

Again the pause and the head shake.

"You'll let me know if there's anything I can do?"

She nodded. A couple of times. Then stood up, brushed her lips briefly across his, and walked back toward the planes. He followed more slowly, but still didn't know what to think by the time he'd returned to Ripley's side.

"Is she okay?" Ripley asked him in barely a whisper when he stopped close by. Together they watched Vanessa hesitate for a long time before going into the hangar and coming back out with a sandwich, but she didn't it eat. It looked as if she was trying very hard to pretend everything was normal, but Gordon still didn't know what had upset her so much.

"I'm not sure. I don't think so." He scratched his head, but that didn't help anything.

"What's wrong?"

"Don't think she knows either," he tried scratching his head with his other hand, but that just felt awkward.

"What did she say?"

"Not much. She just sort of kissed the crap out of me, then

went on her way." He supposed he shouldn't be revealing that. Whatever was going on was Vanessa's business and he probably shouldn't be sharing it around.

"And?"

"And what?"

* * *

Ripley wondered if there could be a more frustrating man.

Yes, was the answer. There had been at least one and she'd been engaged to him—an event she didn't plan on repeating anytime soon, like ever. Ellen Ripley never fell in love in any of the installments in the *Alien* movie series and that worked fine for Ripley Vaughan.

"Gordon."

"Uh huh?" He simply stood there, half in and half out of the light shining from the hangar, like a conflicted Hamlet not knowing which way to turn.

"She kissed the crap out of you, and…?"

"Oh, she began cursing in Italian."

Ripley had rather thought that *she* was the one who was supposed to be kissing Gordon, but that possibility was getting further away instead of closer.

"It was like…" he paused while a jet roared down the runway. They were far enough away that it didn't really interrupt a conversation, but it seemed to distract him.

"It was like what?" Ripley couldn't help herself. It seemed much more voyeuristic than her norm, but she asked anyway.

"Do you have any brothers or sisters?"

"No. Only child. You?"

"Couple big brothers, running the ranch now, as much as Dad will let them. And a sister just a year ahead of me. Vanessa tried, really put her heart and body into that kiss."

Ripley hated her.

"And it was kind of like I figure kissing Mary would be. Just…

off. Wrong." He sat back down on the tire beside her. "Something is really bothering her."

Maybe Ripley didn't hate her so much. What would an all-out kiss with Gordon be like? She'd actually had a preview of that last night, however brief.

And she'd bet that he had an amazing gentle side.

She slid off the plane tire. She thought she'd find some common sense when her feet hit the ground. It was supposed to work that way in metaphors. Since it didn't, she turned to face him. Ripley rested a hand on either of his thighs and leaned in.

"Let's see what this does for you," and she brushed her lips against his.

Heat didn't scorch through her and make her pulse pound so hard that it had driven all words from her body like last night. Instead, it was soft, gentle, luscious.

He rested his hands on her hips, but used his grip only to keep them both in place as the kiss heated and deepened. It might still be summer, but it was the warm kiss to keep her company on a cold winter's night.

She sighed when it drifted to an end, an almost indistinguishable moment.

"That," Gordon declared, "was seriously nice."

It was. Two such fantastic yet totally different kisses should not be possible from the same man. Which Ripley figured meant that, in her own way, she was in as deep trouble as Vanessa, whatever her problem might be.

Chapter 7

Aboard their Antonov, almost everyone slept on the first leg from Portland to Hawaii—everyone except Gordon.

The Antonov had two pressurized cabins tucked high in the fuselage. A small one forward of the wings for the pilots and the larger passenger cabin aft of the wing.

The latter was split into two sections. The forward part, probably for the stewardesses when there were any, had two sets of three lumpy seats facing either side of a small table, making it impossible to stretch out your legs without tangling them with someone else's. The only saving grace on the long flight was that there were two of these booth setups and they only had seven people on this plane. The aft part was a long section of regular airplane seating that could take eighty people. However, any padding in the too-close-together chairs had been flattened out long ago and Gordon couldn't get comfortable anywhere.

They'd started the day with losing their home and fighting a fire. And they'd finished it with flying half an hour to Portland and loading onto the planes. So everyone was sufficiently exhausted to sleep, except him.

Vanessa had found a spot by the hull, pulled a blanket over herself, and leaned into the heavy white sound insulation that had been taped on the walls and ceiling. It was like the cabin was a white, Quonset hut-shaped tent that had seen a hundred too many camping trips.

"Perfect! A padded cell at last," he muttered to no one at all.

Vanessa had gone to sleep faster than was possible, either hiding or emotionally exhausted, and Gordon couldn't tell which. Denise and Vern, Brad and Janet, Ripley and himself made up the rest of the flight. The Ukrainian crew were in the cockpit and forward flight crew area, separated from the passenger cabin by an unpressurized void. Everyone else was in the other aircraft. He knew that Robin, Mickey, and Mark would be playing poker—probably for the entire flight if past experience was anything to go by—so Gordon was just as glad he wasn't over there. It would be fun, but they were all much better players than he was and being here saved him a lot of money. It made this plane a very quiet place to be. Which was okay with him.

He raided the cooler—the sum total of in-flight service. There was a kitchen, but the pilots had warned them that none of it was working right now. The An-124 was built almost entirely of Russian parts. However, Russia and the Ukraine were now on terrible terms, so keeping the planes flying was more and more of a challenge. Even aside from that, the refrigerator was low on the list of essential maintenance. Gordon found a ham sandwich on whole wheat and what he hoped was a Coke despite the Cyrillic writing. Sitting down and thinking things out wasn't his usual style, but it had been a busy day filled with changes.

Not being fired and shipped back to the family ranch was a blessing of such magnitude that he couldn't quite wrap his head around it. He had been so certain that he'd be homeless... He laughed softly. He'd been right, just not in the way he'd expected.

Almost to the minute of when he thought he'd be shown the door, they'd *all* become homeless.

And the wonder of Ripley's kiss—even Vanessa had never kissed him so tenderly. Ripley's kiss had left a trail of fire that still lurked somewhere inside him like a burn gone deep into the soil.

He no longer served a purpose at MHA that he could see, even with Emily staying behind. Surprising everyone—except her husband—she had begged off in Portland at the last moment, going to join their two children up at Mark's parents' ranch in Montana.

"Australia and other places," that Emily carefully hadn't named, "are too rough for a three-year-old and a five-month-old, even with a nanny's help." But that hadn't been all of it. The children had left for the ranch in the nanny's care two days before the fire, as if Emily had been planning on leaving the MHA team all along.

She'd been at the airfield, but it had been strange to watch the massive cargo doors close and leave her on the outside. Emily Beale had hired him three years before. He didn't like this change. He didn't like it one bit.

Her and Mark's parting had been almost painful to watch. Enough so that Gordon wondered that Mark hadn't stepped off the plane at the last moment.

Gordon went to the airtight pressure hatch and stared out through the round glass portal that looked down on the cargo bay. There was little to see. It was night out over the Pacific and there were no lights in the cargo area. The helicopters slept in the darkness little knowing that they'd be waking up tomorrow and going to work on another continent in another hemisphere.

The odd thing about that was—"Hey!" He'd heard that—

"What?" Ripley asked from close by his elbow.

Gordon almost jumped through the glass portal in shock. "What the hell? Thought you were asleep." He managed to keep it down to a whisper as a glance showed that they were the only ones awake in the cabin. Which gave him some other ideas as well.

"Gordon." He could hear the eye roll in her voice as if she too could hear the sudden change in his thinking.

Yeah, being this close and looking into those dark eyes gave him lots of ideas. Being in a small white cabin at thirty-five thousand feet with five other fliers…not so much.

He leaned back. Except the passenger cabin was inside the top curve of the massive round hull, giving it a steep curve outward. He hit his head, then shoulders against the padding, but there was no wall to support him. It surprised him enough that he sat abruptly and landed on the foot of a bench seat wide enough to double as a bunk on what looked like a pile of some pilot's laundry. When he tried to stand up again, he was too far back under the curve of the hull and merely rammed his head into the padding, which dropped him back on his butt again.

He stayed where he was.

Ripley leaned casually against the hatchway door, her arms folded beneath her breasts, and smiled at him in amusement.

He always wanted to correct women who stood with their arms crossed that way. It might *feel* like closed-off body language to them, but to a guy it mostly emphasized the curves of their breasts above their folded arms, making it even harder *not* to stare. Especially when they were as nice as Ripley's.

He did manage to keep his eyes on hers, which wasn't as hard as it might be on another woman. There was a dark depth to Ripley's eyes that a man could easily tumble into and be lost.

"So," Ripley's lips moved like…

Gordon shook his head a little to clear it and pay attention to her words. What was going on? He was never like this around a woman.

"What cat crawled up your behind?"

"What?"

"Your face," she pointed at it, "isn't very good at hiding what you're thinking."

Gordon reached up to try and wipe whatever expression it was off his face because what he was thinking had far more to do with getting Ripley undressed than with what he'd been thinking the moment before she arrived. But as he raised his arm, he jammed an elbow against one of the door latches. He clutched his elbow and tried speaking without moving.

Ripley waited with a soft smile that must be her idea of being maddening.

"I just remembered that Australia was predicting a below-average fire season."

"I heard that too," Ripley shrugged in a very nice way. "We're just the first wave of protection in case it goes bad fast." The movement caused her bra to lift and define how—

"No," he focused on her narrowing eyes again. "We aren't. I've been slowly connecting the pieces. It's usually your outfit, Erickson, that sends the Aircranes Down Under." He pointed through the darkened portal. "Why is MHA renting an Aircrane, a seriously expensive aircraft, and then taking it there ourselves? Someone knew this was happening, whatever this is. The Antonovs are very spendy aircraft too, especially to move us around with the Erickson. We can slip our whole outfit into a single C-17, but not your aircraft. Two Antonovs makes this a million-dollar flight. Whatever justifies that is way bigger than a fire."

Ripley's look of concern had grown as he spoke until it furrowed her brow. "The way I see it..."

* * *

Ripley kept her arms clenched tight around her waist because the way she was seeing things was utterly ridiculous and she had to find some way to hold herself together. At the moment, the Antonov's doorframe was the only thing keeping her upright.

"You're right, of course." There was something going on. And it was in grave danger of upsetting her entire system.

What sort of a guy kissed her the way he did and then didn't follow up on it when they were the only two awake? And why had his report of kissing Vanessa, and it being somehow wrong, made her suddenly all weak in the knees for him? Ripley Vaughan didn't get weak in the knees for any man.

That was a hard-learned lesson. There was something about her that didn't attract trustworthy men. She should have known that about Chief Petty Officer Weasel Williams before she left the Navy to marry him. Troll Boy in high school. Idiot Instructor at Annapolis, and all of the other anti-superheroes of her life: Twisted Tommy, Needy Nick, and Poor Paul—secretly voted the worst kisser in Muskogee High despite being a truly decent guy.

Gordon was still nursing his banged elbow, sitting on the foot of the narrow bunk he'd collapsed backward on.

Ripley's blindness to relationships was worse than Juliet not seeing disaster climbing over her balcony railing in the handsome Romeo. She never saw the male-shaped disasters coming, always found herself in the middle of them, and was the last one aware of the total train wreck of the looming end-of-line, until the dagger had been driven in deep or the train derailed or wherever the metaphor had gone to. Her mother would be horrified.

Yet Ripley *saw* Gordon. She saw his attraction. She saw the conflicted man, caught between being decent and then morphing one moment to the next into a strong, splendidly needy male. She tried to decide which one she liked better and decided that it was a toss-up; they both had their place.

But, Rip, you like both of him.

Huh!

She did.

A glance back showed that the line of sight was such that, of the sleepers, she could see only feet and someone's knee from her current position.

Watching herself from a detached distance, Ripley pushed off the door hatch and stepped over to the still-seated Gordon. He continued talking about the Australian fire season as she straddled him to sit in his lap. The wide bench forced her legs to slide up around his waist. The seat was low enough that his knees were higher than his lap and she slid down them, abruptly achieving much more intimacy than she'd intended.

So abruptly that she tried to apologize…

But the other Gordon suddenly appeared. He stopped awkwardly in the middle of the word "bushfire" as wildfires were called in Australia.

His eyes questioned her action even as his arms slid around her waist and pulled her in tightly.

Ripley didn't like that question. Didn't want to try to answer it. Two days ago she'd been in her normal space: mostly alone for three years and happily reviewing a new contract. Now she was gearing up to sleep with a guy she barely knew.

Well, not sleep with him, there wasn't that much privacy here but…

His kiss cut off the runaway cascade of her thoughts. It started as the pleasant testing man, and rapidly escalated. One firefighter-strong hand had snaked into the back pocket of her jeans to pull her hard against him. His other hand scooped up to her breast.

She braced herself for the inevitable pinch of pain, but instead, it was a cup and caress completely at odds with the escalating force of the kiss itself. The contrast further emphasized both the intensity and the gentleness.

One of them groaned into the kiss, and she was fairly sure that it wasn't her. She wasn't a moaner…and her voice was much higher.

He shifted down to nuzzle her neck and she ran her hands into his blond hair. It was so fine that it almost wasn't there, a caress against her palms. Had she ever had a blond lover? At the moment, as Gordon continued to investigate her neck with nose and tongue, she couldn't even *picture* any of her prior lovers.

Lovers.

She and Gordon were going to be lovers. Not now. Not in this crowded noisy aircraft cabin over the deep Pacific Ocean, despite his hand somehow now being inside her shirt and teasing along the edges of her bra. But they would be. She wasn't comfortable with that bit of knowledge…but she was really, really looking forward to it anyway.

"It had better be soon," she managed in a voice so husky with need that she barely recognized it as her own. His fingertips were driving her crazy. No matter how she arched her chest against them, he kept the pressure light and gentle.

"Oh please, yes," Gordon whispered into the ear he was nibbling on as if he knew exactly what she was talking about.

* * *

Never in his life had Gordon needed someone the way he needed Ripley Vaughan. With her breast cupped against his palm, he could do anything.

He knew that was an utterly ridiculous cause-and-effect combination, but somehow it was true. He'd never felt so powerful as he did holding Ripley. Now that he could slow down enough to appreciate her, he could feel her lithe strength. Her skin seemed warmer and richer than any other woman's had before. The richness of coffee didn't stop at the color of her skin; she was more powerfully female than any woman he'd ever held.

"You know," he had to speak, otherwise the fact that he couldn't have her right here and now would kill him. "Wonder Woman doesn't begin it cover it with you."

"Oh?" She used the pressure of his hand in her back pocket to leverage her hips more tightly against him. Maybe she really was trying to kill him. "Why is that?"

"For one," Gordon managed, "I'm trying to figure out what Wonder Woman sees in me."

"You mean you're *wondering* what I see in you?"

"Sure thing…*woman*." He could feel her soft laugh ripple up the length of her body against his, but only being voiced as a happy sigh.

"I'll be damned if I know," she whispered against his lips and they descended into another kiss.

Gordon decided that his first assessment had been completely correct. She was trying to kill him.

When they had frustrated one another past reason, they finally slid apart. There was a blanket on the narrow bunk and they lay down there together. Ripley rested her head on his chest and draped a leg over his hips, the only way the two of them would fit there.

He brushed the smooth slickness of her shoulder-length hair with his cheek and held her as she fell asleep.

Did every single thing with Ripley have to be new? He'd never slept with a woman without first making love to her. Despite his various forays into the wonderland of single women at The Doghouse and other firefighter bars, he typically knew something about their past. People like Mickey, before Robin, or Akbar—MHA's lead smokejumper now temporarily assigned to Columbia Helicopters—before Laura, they swept women up just by being handsome and charming. Then they bedded them and often as not cast them aside.

Gordon wondered if he'd talked more women into his bed or into avoiding his bed. He might spend hours in a bar chatting with a woman, thinking there was a connection building there, only to get a goodnight handshake. That's when he often heard just how "sweet" he was. Damn word should be stricken from the English language.

He didn't feel that way around Ripley. He felt avaricious and that wasn't something he recognized in himself. It made him want to swagger a little, or perhaps a lot…a mannerism that epitomized his father. Max Finchley Sr. had walked his land like he was a king, or a god. And Gordon's two older brothers were little better. Even Mary was often held up as an example of Gordon's failure to qualify in his father's eye. Of course she herself was a force to be reckoned with, riding hard on the rodeo circuit and doing well in national-level prize money. She seemed to make a point of rubbing his nose in that too at every opportunity. Gordon had always been the black sheep, content to ride his horse or fly the ranch helo.

"Thinking awfully hard there, Gordon," her voice was the mumble of someone only half awake.

"Thought you were asleep," he whispered back to Ripley.

"Not with the way your thoughts are buzzing. Your pulse rate," she tapped a lazy finger against his chest close by her nose, "has been climbing too."

Gordon blew out a long slow breath. He didn't think about his family often, but it was never a good thing when he did. "Sorry."

"Anything you want to talk about?"

"My family? No. The less said the better. What about yours?"

"You never saw two people so close. Like Vern and Denise maybe, but they're both gentler sorts. Mom is from Senegal, where family is the most important thing there is. Dad was a crazy mix, but he'd latched onto the one-eighth Cherokee as a cultural historian—for him, heritage adds even more to family."

"Then what are you doing out here in the world?"

Ripley sighed against his chest, "Because I don't fit in for crap. Love them to death, but they aren't my type of people. Family isn't for people like me. Not ever. No interest."

Gordon nearly cracked his nose on the top of her head when he tried to look down at where she still lay perfectly relaxed upon his chest.

"What?" She must have felt his surprise.

"You're not making any sense there, Wonder Woman."

"She didn't have family either. Well, except for a lot of Amazons on Paradise Island, but I've never been tempted to swing that way." There was a long silence; she was most of the way back to sleep before she mumbled once more. "I like men—Diana Prince is never really clear on that point."

"But you come from a great family and you don't want that for yourself?"

She shook her head, but kept her peace.

Gordon stared at the low ceiling and listened to the plane's roar. This time the silence lasted long enough that he could feel Ripley finally fall asleep.

He'd come from a train wreck of a family, and yet there was little he wanted more in his life. He wanted to feel that closeness. He wanted to be like Mark and Emily were with their kids. To care so much about a woman that, like Vern, he'd be paralyzed by fear at the thought of harm coming to her. Gordon wanted so much!

If only he wasn't one of those guys who always thought too much. He wished he could simply...be. Be content with the what he had, but another layer always ticked away in the back of his mind.

When he flew, he was always aware of everything happening around him. How it all fit together. He'd always imagined that was Mark's view from farther aloft.

Holding Ripley, it was only too easy to imagine them being anything but temporary. Together they'd...

Prove what an idiot he was. His stupid planning self was running away with him just as it had with Vanessa, and Tabby before that. And Sue in college, Danielle in high school, and...crap!

Then he nuzzled Ripley's hair again. This was different though. Maybe just because he'd had so much practice at fooling himself over the years. But there was one piece of the puzzle he'd never been able to picture completely over the years: how a woman would want to be with him for all that time. Somehow in his idle daydreams of family, he'd always stood to the outside.

He could picture himself with Ripley so easily that it made him feel a little intrusive—as if he was shoving his way into a fantasy he'd never belonged in before.

Gordon smiled to himself. For just a moment he imagined what it would be like if for once he was right and there was the possibility of a future with this amazing woman. That, he decided, was a thought worthy of Wonder Woman herself.

Chapter 8

This trip was a rude shock to Ripley's system and they hadn't even landed in Hawaii for refueling yet. She'd made the trip enough times to know that the long flight and the time change would just make a jumble of everything for a few days. She was okay with that.

Waking up in Gordon's arms was a far more disconcerting thing. And as she lay there listening to him sleep—and thoroughly enjoying the sensation—she wondered what had just happened to her life.

She'd spent the whole season flying to fire—six days on and one day off per US Forest Service regulations. She'd had a total of one date…which hadn't survived dinner well enough to even justify dessert. Mostly she'd hung out with the other pilots and talked fire. On her day off she did laundry, slept, and checked to see if there were any new science fiction movies or local theater Shakespeare productions. Her parents had definitely given her a split personality.

Like the one that had her lying in Gordon's arms.

She eased away slowly, then watched to see if she'd woken him. He curled into the spot she'd just left and continued to sleep.

Then she turned and almost slammed into Vanessa, who stood stock still, clearly watching them both for some time. She blinked hard several times before her eyes focused.

"Sorry," Vanessa blushed fiercely. "I was staring, wasn't I? I—" but nothing further came out. She turned and bolted away through the cabin; her hurried steps fading away quickly due to the steady background of the four roaring jet engines.

Ripley debated for only a moment before following. Past the sleeping couples sprawled in their seats. Janet blinked at Ripley's rapid progress and then followed softly, leaving Brad asleep. She really didn't need another person. But by the time the two of them were passing Denise, she too was up and on her feet.

"Is Vanessa okay?" Denise asked in that pseudo-whisper that was louder than the backwash of the jet engines, but too soft to wake anyone.

Ripley shrugged, shook her head, looked at the two determined women, shrugged again, and turned to go find Vanessa.

It wasn't hard.

The passenger cabin ran only thirty meters from the front pressure door to the tail. At the far back of the cabin—past the rows of three hard-worn blue airplane seats to either side of the windowless cabin lit by a longline of failing fluorescents—was a small service area.

Vanessa had come to a halt at the very rear. Her faced pressed to the tiny round window in the rearmost exit door. There were a few small benches for the occasional flight attendants. The three of them sat quietly and waited.

After a long time, Vanessa turned, her eyes widening when she saw all three of them. She glanced up the aisle leading back to the forward part of the cabin longingly.

"Don't even think about it," Denise warned. "I'm too pregnant to be chasing you up and down the plane."

Vanessa nodded, but still didn't sit.

"Did you suddenly discover you're pregnant or something?" Janet asked.

Ripley always wondered how Janet did that, asking the bluntest questions with such charm that it was impossible to take offense.

Vanessa only shook her head.

"Well, then what's up, girlfriend?" As far as Ripley knew, these were the first words that Janet had said to Vanessa, but that never slowed her down either.

But Vanessa didn't turn to her, she kept facing Ripley. "I am sorry I was doing the staring at you."

Ripley shrugged, "You're not the only one that's surprised by my behavior." She tapped her own chest.

"Slut!" Janet teased her.

"You don't even know what I was doing."

"Don't need to, not if it was with Gordon. He's a sweetie."

Ripley decided the closest route to sanity was to ignore Janet.

"I was only wishing," again Vanessa blushed, then she finally sat on the last remaining seat in the cramped stewardess area, "that I could have made Gordon look as happy as he did when he is holding you. And that I could have looked happy like you too."

Now it was Ripley's turn to feel somewhat flummoxed. *Did she look that way in Gordon's arms? She certainly felt—* It didn't matter.

"I'm not the one who's upset."

Vanessa raised her fine-fingered hands for a long moment, then dropped them to her lap again.

"You were going to protest that you're not upset. But it didn't work." Ripley didn't make it a question.

Vanessa didn't argue.

"So?" Janet reached out and poked Vanessa's knee. "Give."

"I don't know. I kissed Gordon yesterday—I'm sorry about that, I really am." She rested her hand on Ripley's for a moment and squeezed before withdrawing. "I should not have done the intruding."

Ripley discovered that Vanessa was a very easy woman to forgive and did so.

"He is such a nice man. I look at the two of you and I do not understand why it is not me. Why am I not the one so happy in his arms? He is the man who should be right for me." Vanessa hid her face in her hands.

Ripley scooted closer so that she could slip a hand around Vanessa's waist and looked at Denise and Janet in some panic. She had no idea what to do next as the shudders rolled up Vanessa's spine beneath her hand. Ripley lived in a man's firefighting world and upset women were outside of her normal experience.

And she especially didn't know what to do with Vanessa's statement. Had she really been that happy to be sleeping with Gordon? Happiness with a man was something that she had even less experience with. Even in the good times, Weasel had been at most…comfortable. Had she really been so desperate as to settle for comfortable?

Apparently so. It had taken a man like Gordon to put that into perspective. It didn't seem fair that she had to wait until her thirties to get some perspective about men.

That's when Ripley remembered Brenna's comment at The Doghouse, that there was one way that men and women could be as close as Gordon and Vanessa were and still not be attracted. Well, two ways, but they clearly weren't brother and sister.

That meant…

"Oh, honey," Ripley didn't know where that came from as she leaned over to kiss the woman's brow. Some deep part of her suddenly wanted to mother Vanessa. That she was at most five years Vanessa's senior didn't matter.

She looked desperately at Denise and Janet, but neither of them had been there. Ripley could see it so clearly now. She and Gordon, and Vanessa and Brenna standing in The Doghouse parking lot with Mark Henderson. Vanessa and Brenna had been holding hands in mutual support. But what if it was more than that?

Brenna was Denise's assistant. Denise was likely to know her preferences.

And that was when Ripley finally understood the whole problem. Vanessa might have been holding Brenna's hand in mutual support, but Brenna definitely had been doing more than that. She'd been seeing if she was right with her guess from the night before.

Being gay could definitely be a reason for Vanessa to find no fire with Gordon—especially not if his inner alpha male stepped out of hiding. Based on Ripley's own limited experience, holding a beautiful woman in his arms was enough to make that happen every time.

But if Vanessa didn't know that about herself, any attraction to Brenna would definitely be giving her trouble.

"Is there a reason that you're on this plane and Brenna is flying on the other one?" Ripley asked Vanessa the question before she could stop herself.

Denise gasped as the pieces fit together for her.

Vanessa kept her head down, but her nod was clear despite the forward slide of her hair hiding her face. "She was really nice. Just asked a question… I suppose that I wasn't ready to hear it."

Ripley didn't know what to say. Denise obviously didn't either.

Janet came through without even an eye blink, "Brenna's hot, girlfriend. You should definitely go for it."

That jolted Vanessa into looking up at them. "But I'm—"

"Female and single," Janet stated merrily before Vanessa had a chance to complete her thought. "Hell, if I were single, I might go for her myself, but Brad would only get depressed if I did. Besides, I'm a guy kind of gal. So, it's gonna have to be you."

The strident tone of the engines shifted, easing back as the Antonov began its descent into Honolulu International.

"Huh," was all Vanessa finally managed, but the look of severe distress was gone. "That is a thought I am still not ready for… but it is a thought."

"And you!"

Ripley flinched at the force of Janet's sudden attention.

"High five, Wonder Woman!" Janet held up a hand and Ripley felt obliged to slap it.

Denise did the same.

Vanessa leaned her shoulder into Ripley's, "I told you he is a good man. I like to know that you are a good woman."

If Ripley had trouble forming friendships with men, that was nothing compared to forming them with women. The Navy was intensely competitive between pilots, all striving for the cherry assignments—the few female pilots not exempted. And flying the Aircrane, her only female friend had been Janet because there weren't any others aloft at Erickson.

In a day of startling revelations, she decided that she rather liked this latest one. *Against all odds, Ripley Vaughan has just found two more female friends.* How cool was that.

When the seatbelt sign flicked on, they buckled in where they were and spent the descent chatting about nothing in particular.

Chapter 9

G*ordon couldn't figure out* what had changed during the flight.

Vanessa's smile was most of the way back when they clambered out into Hawaii's thick and humid air. It wasn't particularly hot, still an hour to dawn, but the pine-washed clarity of Oregon air had been replaced by the thick sea salt-and-palm atmosphere of the tropical island. He wanted shorts and a t-shirt, but the one change of clothes in his personal gear bag were jeans and long-sleeved shirt just as he was wearing now.

Where Vanessa was cheerier, Ripley was more subdued and thoughtful. He could feel her eyes tracking him as the two crews stretched their legs while staying clear of the refueling teams pumping seventy-five thousand gallons of Jet A from the underground pipelines up into each aircraft. Their helicopters were such a light load for the massive Antonovs, far more air than weight, that they'd be able to make the hop to Australia in one more flight.

Gordon approached Ripley a few times, but she veered off

sharply each time. Finally getting the message, he wandered over to see how the folks on the other Antonov were faring.

"I'm up almost two hundred," Robin greeted him. "Henderson is down fifty. I love playing poker with these guys." She patted Mickey's cheek.

Gordon looked at Mickey, who grimaced. "Well, at least most of it stayed in the family."

"All mine, sucker," Robin clamped a hand over her jeans pocket.

Mickey swept her into a deep kiss…and Robin caught his fingers halfway into her pocket. She twisted them hard enough for Mickey to grunt in pain, but kept her other hand clamped behind his neck so that he couldn't break the kiss. Mickey gave up on the money and focused on the winning tactic, which caused Robin to melt against him.

Gordon now had a taste of what that felt like. And he definitely wanted more.

"Gordon," Mark slapped him on the shoulder. Moments later he somehow ended up in the other Antonov with Mark. By the time he heard the engines cycling back to life, it was too late to switch back to his own plane. He looked around and only Mickey and Robin were in the cabin with him and Mark.

Vanessa, who he'd really meant to make some time to talk to, was on the other plane. As was Ripley, who he definitely wanted to talk to. Even Brenna had switched aircraft along with the rest of team. Apparently he was on the unpopular aircraft…or had Mark engineered something?

The Antonov eased onto the runway and then opened up its four massive engines. With only the light load of the helicopters, they accelerated and pulled aloft quickly. Now it was just the four of them sitting on the bench seats at one of the tables.

Betsy, TJ, Chutes, and the rest of the ground team had stayed with the smokejumpers. Smokies were the ultimate deep wilderness fire specialists, used very rarely outside the US, Canada, and Russia. They jumped in when the fire started far from any other resources, such as roads. Though more than half the time the MHA smokies were delivered by the far less dangerous helitack method, using longlines and winches if there was no convenient clearing to land the helicopters in. Certainly no call for them in Australia.

Australian bushfires occurred in two main varieties. There were the forest fires, typically occurring in the more heavily populated areas. And there were the fires that swept across the dry Outback, typically burning through grasses and other low plants, but at incredible speed. In that type of fire, the wind could drive flames along at ninety or a hundred kilometers an hour, which would overrun any ground team. Australian fires were fought much more from the air than American ones because it was often the only viable option.

Gordon knew all of this intellectually, but he'd never actually been Down Under.

And that's where Henderson started with him, discussing the nature of fighting bushfire over cups of burnt coffee and stale donuts in the upper cabin of the lead Antonov. Mickey and Robin sat beside them, quietly sparring over who got the last jelly-filled one.

Wasn't it enough that Mark was always pushing him while he was piloting? Had he now isolated him on this aircraft for some reason? At least Robin and Mickey were still around.

Robin grabbed a deck of cards to decide the matter of the donut, Mickey held up his hands in defeat. She grinned in triumph. While she had both hands occupied slipping the cards back into the box, Mickey grabbed the donut in question. Mickey, who Gordon had always thought was a very savvy man, raced away down the aisle crowing in triumph. Robin was hot on his tracks.

"No question how that's going to end," Mark grunted out.

"Not much," Gordon agreed, envying them a bit. The woman he was wanting hot steamy sex with was flying a half dozen kilometers behind them.

"What about you?"

Gordon looked at him, "What about me? Are you actually asking who I'm having sex with?"

"The who is obvious and no I wasn't."

"Well I'm not," Gordon wasn't sure why he'd admitted that.

Mark looked at him like he was an idiot.

"Crap, Mark. I've known the woman for two days."

"I'm still not asking. Feel free to stop sharing anytime you want."

Gordon opened his mouth to protest that Mark was just messing with him for the hell of it, then thought better of it and shut the hell up. He bit down on a powdered donut. The confectioner's sugar caught wrong on an inhale, and when he tried to cough it back out, he ended up creating a powder cloud out his mouth and nose. A sip of the burnt coffee didn't help at all.

Mark simply waited until he was done with trying to throttle himself.

Gordon finally nodded for him to talk, unsure of his own ability to do so.

Then Mark smiled, "Should I bet fifty against the two of you making it to three days before climbing into the sack?"

Gordon gave him the finger and Mark laughed.

"Seriously," Mark sobered between one breath and the next, "tell me what we could have done to save the MHA camp."

Gordon felt it like a slap, not from Mark, but rather to his heart. "Before or after it started? Before, we could have cleared a lot of the ground fuels. Parked out the last hundred meters so that there was no underbrush to burn and no dead branches on the tree trunks to take the fire up into the crown."

"How about after it started?"

That stumped him. Gordon thought about what he could recall of the various aerial tactics. There hadn't been time to deploy any ground forces.

Mark waited passively.

"Is this another one of your goddamn lessons? I'm getting tired of those, you know."

Mark shrugged, not answering the question. "I've been puzzling at that all night."

"You've been playing poker all night."

"A man can do a lot of thinking while doing that."

"Which is your lame excuse for losing fifty bucks to Robin?"

Mark shrugged. It was a *yes* this time if Gordon was reading him right.

Gordon sighed. "I had a few ideas, I guess. Evacuate immediately. Most of ten minutes went by while we were getting to that point. Maybe if we'd concentrated on dousing the base itself: buildings, cars, propane tanks. Let the field burn, it wouldn't have been a loss, just a free mowing job."

"I reached pretty much the same conclusion. Did you think of that during or after?"

Gordon tried to recall the jumble of images from the moment he'd spotted the irregular shadow of sunrise along the treetops. He'd known. In that first instant he'd known they were about to lose the base. Even before Vanessa went aloft and TJ hit the fire alarm. So why had he hesitated? Because it wasn't his place? Because he was just a pilot without an aircraft?

"You were the first to figure it out," Mark stated. "I saw the same thing but didn't understand it until we were aloft, and some of it I only understood as I was busy losing fifty dollars building Robin's confidence so I could sweep her up next time. You've consistently been ahead of everyone; I can point to a dozen incidents where that's true. Spotting the fire yesterday morning. Getting everyone moving to protect Timberline Lodge. This spring at the Leavenworth, Washington, fires you kicked ass as well."

"You weren't even there."

"No, I was in the Yukon, Alaska, and Korea."

Mark waited a beat for that to sink in, which was good because it took Gordon a moment to remember how to breathe. Korea. Not South Korea, but Korea. As much as admitting to fighting a fire in North Korea. And Brenna's comment about the repairs to Firehawk *Oh-one…* They hadn't flown *to* fire, Robin had flown *into* it. Something truly serious would have to go down for that to be necessary. Not just Robin—Robin and Mickey. They'd come through a literal trial by fire together. No wonder their bond was so certain, so deep.

"Doesn't mean that I didn't get reports from the Leavenworth fire chief," Mark prompted. "His daughter Candace, the leader of the hotshot crew, had some good things to say on top of that."

Gordon remembered that they'd both proven to be the real deal on the fire.

"MHA only hires the best people."

"Which always made me wonder how I got in. Vern, Robin, Mickey, Jeannie: you've got a long list of unreal pilots. Carly and Steve—the best fire behavior analyst in the business teamed up with a former lead smokie turned drone pilot. What the hell am I doing here?"

"Carly sees fire, but that's all she sees. Steve is the perfect complement to her, providing her with even more information about the behavior, but she's not a pilot. She doesn't really understand what we can do and who is best at doing it."

Gordon toyed with his half-eaten donut, not willing to risk another bite just yet as he could still feel the powder burn from sneezing it back out. Mark was training him. That was no longer a question…but he couldn't figure out for what. Maybe simply trying to prepare him for whatever their upcoming adventure might be.

Mark had taken up the deck of cards that Robin had abandoned in a scatter on the table before chasing after Mickey. He turned them into an orderly pile, then began shuffling them.

"I'm not playing poker against you." He'd be broke in an hour. Mark kept shuffling.

"Seriously! Not a goddamn chance." Maybe half an hour.

Mark dealt out ten cards and thumped the rest of the deck on the table. "How about Gin Rummy?"

Gordon laughed. At himself. At Mark. At this crazy whole

situation, including sleeping with Ripley and the shock of waking up alone. "Sure."

"Five hundred points."

Gordon picked up his hand.

"Twenty bucks a game just to make it interesting."

Gordon sighed and drew a card that matched absolutely nothing in his hand. He set it down and Mark snatched it up.

Chapter 10

Gordon had been right; they didn't rush to a fire as soon as they were on the ground.

They'd landed at Cairns International airport at the northeast corner of Australia after more than twenty hours in transit. Unlike the first leg, Ripley hadn't slept a wink on the much longer Hawaii-Australia flight. By some chance, most of the other plane's MHA crew came over to join them and the passenger area of the second Antonov had turned into a party zone.

It wasn't until they were aloft that she missed Gordon. She'd asked around and Jeannie had seen him with Mickey on the other aircraft. Ripley felt bad about that. She'd avoided him on the ground because she'd needed some time to process Vanessa's encouragement. The others' too, but it was Vanessa's feelings about Gordon that had the greatest impact. And Ripley knew that even being in Gordon's presence shut down her ability to think. Whenever he was nearby, all she wanted to do was feel. His conscious caring combined with his unthinking power was a heady tonic that evaporated anything as trivial as her own thoughts.

But she hadn't meant to make him feel unwelcome near her. No! While walking back and forth trying to clear her head in the darkness of the Hawaiian night, she'd decided that she really did want him close.

For once in her carefully built life, she wanted to break out. Take a chance.

Even the Weasel had been carefully thought out. How long was a woman's career in the military anyway? There was no way to be a military couple and raise a child. There was…a whole boatload of crap that she now saw that Weasel had fed her until she'd bought in. She wasn't even planning to have kids, but somehow that hadn't shot down his sales pitch. He'd been so convincing until the moment she caught him butt-fucking the caterer, still in her cook's apron, her slacks around her ankles and holding onto the kitchen sink to press herself back against him.

Ripley hadn't even been surprised. Hurt, yes. Surprised…no.

Gordon, however, didn't fit into any structure she'd ever had and surprised her all the time. And he kept doing it in a good way.

He wasn't some tall, macho jerk. He was a nice guy—a genuinely nice one. Definitely outside her experience.

Her contract was temporary. She'd be gone after the fire season. So nothing long term and she didn't *do* short term, not much anyway.

But no man had ever made her melt at the lightest touch the way Gordon did.

Ripley's attempts to get off by herself during the flight were stymied at every turn. At the front of the main cabin seating area, Denise and Jeannie talked about the former's pregnancy in soft tones. Brad, Janet, Brenna, and Vanessa were having a giggling conversation in the far back seats. Brenna and Vanessa were sitting apart, across from each other, but they looked comfortable together, which was a start. Carly and Steve, along with Cal, were lounging at one of the kitchen tables, puzzling over why Emily wasn't with them.

"Two kids."

"Heard that's why she left the military in the first place."

"They've got a nanny."

"Fire seasons are hell. Maybe she wasn't seeing enough of her kids."

"What about Mark?"

Shrugs exchanged.

"Never saw a guy who so loves carrying his kids around."

When Ripley expressed disbelief, they all started talking at once.

"Seriously." "He's completely goofy around his kids." "He's so cute with them."

"Yeah, he almost becomes human," Cal laughed, but Carly and Steve were nodding. He projected such pure hardass that it was hard to imagine.

The talk shifted to fires after that and Ripley was soon enjoying their three drastically different views of fire: the behavior analyst, the smokie turned drone pilot, and the hotshot turned award-winning photographer. With her own piloting view, all they were lacking was the Incident Commander-Air.

The rest of the flight had passed as quickly and almost as pleasantly as sleeping in Gordon's arms.

Within an hour of landing at Cairns, their birds were refueled and ready.

Again she'd missed Gordon. And not because she was trying to avoid him this time. As soon as her helicopter had been safely unloaded, she'd gone looking for him, leaving the remounting of the blades to be overseen by Brad and Janet.

But Gordon had already gone. "Off somewhere with Mark," Robin had waved somewhere vaguely toward the west end of the airfield. And Ripley had been left with nothing to do but return to watch her crew remount and test the blades.

As soon as they were set up, they'd then flown a hundred and fifty kilometers through the pre-dawn light, north to Cooktown Airport, and landed.

It was a bewildering place to come to. A single asphalt strip surrounded by green grass and low trees. The six helicopters of the MHA flight increased the airport's number of aircraft to ten. It didn't look like much of a fire zone to Ripley's weary eyes. But it was certainly an out-of-the-way location.

They'd all been trucked over to a nice hotel, a very nice one, in the center of the small town. Another disorienting moment. Firefighters often camped near their helicopters. When they got a hotel, it was generally clean but had little else going for it.

Ripley kept blinking to bring it into focus, but it didn't change. Cool tile floors, a ceiling fan, nice chairs, a pretty view of trees and a slice of the ocean less than a block away. There was a sitting area beside a small river (that she immediately blocked by closing the curtains), and a big bed with fresh sheets.

It had been over thirty-six hours since she'd awakened to be called "serious eye candy" just moments before a firefight. Two hours asleep in Gordon's arms hadn't begun to cover the sleep deficit. She should at least shower and wash off the long flight…and the buzzing energy that necking with Gordon had instilled in her body. Her decision to lie down for a moment was a bad one. Her face-plant into the pillow was the last thing she remembered.

* * *

Gordon looked at the motel door and debated his next action when his knock wasn't answered. The sun was still low over the ocean, the bright and pleasant morning an affront to his senses. Which was about the only part of him still operating.

Five games to three, he'd only lost forty dollars to Mark. Having barely enough cash on him to settle the bet, Gordon begged off. He'd pay Mark later…in Australian dollars. That would save him about twelve dollars due to the exchange rate. He would argue that it was only fair as they hadn't started the game until after they were over international waters.

He could go back to the desk and get a room of his own.

Or he could use the card that he'd talked out of the desk clerk beneath Mark's amused expression.

He'd woken up alone on the Antonov only shortly before landing. Ripley had been distant while they'd been on the ground in Hawaii. Gordon of old would have accepted that, getting his own room and leaving any future follow-up to her choice.

But it couldn't be over. Not with the way she felt against him. Not with the way she'd slid into his lap and kissed him like they'd been together far longer than two days.

Nope.

He swiped the card and eased the door open.

Ripley lay sprawled on the bed, fully clothed, even her shoes.

He took a step into the room and nearly fell over Ripley's duffel bag. He shoved it aside, dropped his small PG bag on top of it, and looked at her again.

You've come this far, pal. Don't stop now.

Gordon pushed the door shut behind him, casting Ripley into dark shadow. But his eyes slowly adapted to her dark outline on the light sheets. He eased forward, encountering no other obstacles until he stood directly over her. If she was going to sleep, she should at least be comfortable.

Sitting on the bed, he eased off one of her boots and then the other. Then socks. Her feet were warm to the touch and he held onto them, appreciating the intimacy of the moment. He considered feeling bad for the voyeurism, but she was the one who had slid into his lap on the plane and then lay down beside him. It was only a few moments of rationalized justification before he slipped off her jeans as well. Then he folded back the side of the covers she wasn't sprawled over and lifted her gently onto the sheets and re-covered her before he could do something indecent about her long legs.

He stripped down to his underwear and climbed into the side of the bed she had occupied. Her warmth had penetrated the covers and he could feel the remnants of her body heat as he lay there refusing to give in to the urge to jump her.

Ripley stirred. The mattress flexed as she rolled over.

Gordon stared at the ceiling and tried to remember the weight loading table for a Firehawk operating at four thousand feet on a ninety degree day.

Ripley's roll bumped her against him. She didn't stop, or even hesitate. Instead she continued the roll until she was snuggled up tight against him in a space no bigger than the narrow bench seat on the Antonov. Except this time the leg she threw over him was bare and smooth against his own skin. When he brushed a hand from her knee to her hip, she purred—a happy hum deep in her throat.

"Some lousy lover you are," her mumble in his ear was almost incoherent with sleep. Her breath tickled his cheek. "You get me half naked and stop?"

"You were asleep."

"Nothing but excuses."

Gordon opened his mouth to protest his innocence. Then closed it. He wasn't in the mood to be innocent. Was it inappropriate to take advantage of an exhausted woman? Badly. As she began lazily sliding her hand up and down his chest utterly electrifying his body? Not so much.

"'Scuses," she mumbled, headed back toward sleep.

Final question: was it fair that she'd banished any thoughts of sleep for him and then she'd get to sleep? Absolutely not.

He rolled into her, guiding her leg so that it stayed over his hip. With her pants off, it was an easy matter to slide his hand up under her shirt and release her bra. He brushed his hand beneath it and slid his hand around to her breast. Firm but full, and so soft that he felt like a cad touching her with his callused hands.

"You're supposed to be kissing me while you do that."

"Awfully controlling for a woman who's still asleep."

"Okay," and she lay back. "I'll just sleep. Not a word. Go ahead. Do your worst."

"Not a word?" Gordon teased her.

There was just enough light from the edges of the curtain to see her now that his eyes had adapted. She mimed locking her lips and throwing away the key. Then she flopped back loosely as if she were a dead woman.

Gordon had always tried to be a gentle, caring lover. But Ripley's teasing passivity awoke something inside him. Hell, Ripley "Wonder Woman" Vaughan gave him thoughts of just what he could do for the right woman. And if ever there was a right woman…

Stop thinking, Gordon.

And he did.

Instead, he felt. He ran his hand over the perfect round of her breast, down over her ribs and flat stomach and back. The room was warm enough that he had no qualms about brushing the covers down or her shirt up. She was a dark shadow upon the white sheets. His white hand a photographic outline against her skin.

Ripley lay still and let him explore. From time to time she shivered despite the warmth of the room. The first had been when he kissed one of those perfect breasts. Again as his hand ran up the inside of her thigh, brushing lightly over her white panties and continuing past to explore the curves of hip, waist, breast, shoulder, cheek.

There was nothing submissive in her giving. She might have intended it to be so, perhaps as a tease. But her short, sharp breaths gave her away. As did the mad speed of her heart when he lay an ear between her breasts. She slid a hand into his hair to hold him there, but her heart rate didn't slow though he lay a long while fascinated by the double-tap sound.

It wasn't enough to know the magnificent curves of her front and he coaxed her into rolling over. He did it by teasing her with light touches until she growled in frustration trying to get more pressure from his touch. As she over-balanced onto her stomach, he now had a different view of the woman. Without beautiful breasts to distract him, he could see the curving outline of strong shoulders, slim waist, and full hips.

In the past, when in shadowed rooms, his lovers' outlines had merged into the sheets, blurring their edges. Ripley's darkness revealed her exquisitely against the light sheets. It made her impossibly real, as if she was more defined, more herself than any woman he'd ever had before.

As he ran his hands over the marvel that was Ripley, learning her body, he could feel the tense knots in her muscles. He massaged them as he investigated, working his way down her body. Several times she tried to roll over, but he straddled her legs to keep her facedown beneath him.

Unable to stand it any longer, he scooped a hand under her hips and she drove down against his palm, pinning it to the sheet with a soft cry.

It undid him. All of his investigation and teasing was suddenly meaningless. That soft cry of desperate need shattered something inside of him. He reached over the side of the bed and found his pants. He dug out one of the condoms he'd thought to buy while he and Mark were running errands in Cairns.

He rolled Ripley onto her back and, the moment he finished removing their underwear and he'd sheathed himself, she wrapped her legs about his hips and was pulling on his shoulders.

There was no gentleness left in him. And Ripley asked for none.

* * *

Ripley clutched at Gordon's shoulders, pulling her chest up against his. Never had she so needed a man to be inside her.

Their bodies came together in one long smooth slide that carried him all the way in. It wasn't an invasion, as it sometimes felt when a man entered past the threshold of her outer skin. Even when completely welcome, it always had been a strange sensation to have part of a man's body inside of her.

Not this time.

Gordon's entry was like a completeness finally come true; one she'd never even suspected existed.

She clenched her legs tightly, convulsively about his hips.

She didn't need him deeper, he'd already done that. She needed him to never go away. Her peak slammed into her harder than any prior experience. Her first solo flight in a helicopter, her first carrier landing, her first firefight…all paled.

Tears would come later, she knew. For now all she could do was cling and experience. But Gordon wasn't done, far from it. He had one hand planted firmly on the bed and the other arm tight about her, holding her aloft so that her only connection was with him. She floated in some impossible free fall space, pinned by her arms and her legs, yes, but the power of his hold on her dominated her thoughts.

No one had ever held her so.

When Gordon arched into his final release, his tight grasp seemed to carry her aloft. And there, ever so safe in his arms, for the first time in her life, a second release slammed through her. She arched into it not caring if it would kill her or maim her for life, for it was so powerful she didn't doubt that it could. The waves rippled through them both for a glorious, timeless forever.

He didn't collapse down upon her, a weight she would have gladly welcomed. Instead Gordon rocked back onto his heels so that he knelt on the mattress. She was still wrapped around him, still not touching anything other than his body. Floating.

Ripley clung there, not wanting to return to Earth. She finally received the kiss she'd asked for, long, slow, deep…jarred but not interrupted by occasional aftershocks making it only all the sweeter.

When she lay her head on his shoulder, the tears began to flow.

"Hey, lover," Gordon's voice was a whisper. "Are you okay?"

She could only nod. Her voice was still somewhere far away. She nodded again. It wasn't just the release that she was crying for, though it had been more than amazing enough for her to do so. It was something deeper, but she didn't want to think about it.

Instead she just let herself hold and be held. The tears would take care of themselves.

Chapter 11

A phone rang incessantly somewhere in the distance. Gordon flailed out a hand and elicited a grunt from Ripley when his elbow found her shoulder.

"Sorry," he grabbed the phone and grunted into it.

"Lunch, thirty minutes," Mark spoke in pre-fire briefing tone. "Two blocks south and one west. The Top Pub."

Gordon managed to find a clock. It was straight up noon…at least he assumed it wasn't midnight by the sunshine still leaking around the curtain's edges.

"You hear me?"

"No."

"No you don't hear me?" Mark was doing his amused-with-the-world thing that always pissed off Gordon.

"No, as in I've had less than three hours sleep and I need more."

"Yes," Mark replied, "as in you need to get up and stay up until at least eight p.m. if you're going to make the time zone switch. Be there in twenty-nine minutes." Then he paused for a long moment. "I remember dropping you at your door five hours ago. You must have gotten five hours sleep…or you owe me another fifty bucks. And that's US, not this Australian crap."

Once again Mark Henderson was riding his ass. "Yeah, sure, whatever." He hung up on Mark before Henderson could do the same to him.

He rolled back over, careful not to clip Ripley again. "Gotta go," he shook her lightly.

"Have fun," she pulled the covers more tightly over her head, her back to him.

"No. We gotta go."

"Give me one good reason," might have been her response. Through the covers it was hard to tell.

He didn't have one, not until his hand found her hip. Then he thought of several reasons not to go. He started by slipping his hand around her waist and cupping a soft warm breast.

"Oh no you don't," she pulled away. "You're not going to entice me back awake with sex."

Gordon slid closer and stroked his hand over her again. "God damn but you feel glorious as you look, *woman*."

"Well, I am *wonder*ful, at least you said so," she scooted to the very edge of the bed. "And it's only skin."

"No, it's not."

She glared at him over her shoulder.

"It's—" but he didn't know where to go with it.

"Is that why you're with me? Never bedded a black woman and wanted to give it a try?"

"There are guys who actually do that?" Gordon could think of some jerks who needed a quick punch to the nuts.

Ripley studied him a moment, "Okay, so you're not one of those."

He shook his head.

"Then what?"

"It goes deeper than that. Like a vibrant strength that shines from somewhere deep inside." Waxing eloquent had never been his style, but she made him want to.

"Meaning what, Gordon? I'm just a girl from Oklahoma."

He could hear her rising irritation.

"You're just so goddamn beautiful, Ripley."

"Says the man who slept with Vanessa."

"She's awfully pretty, I grant you." Gordon was amused by her tone. That anyone could ever be jealous of anything he'd ever done was funny. "Also so shy that I never actually saw her unclothed with the lights on."

He was about to turn it into a tease, but Ripley's deepening frown warned him off.

"But you're in a whole other league, Ripley. Even discounting your skin color," he ran a hand from the curve of her breast down the wonderful lines to her hip, "you are a complete and total knockout."

She looked down at his hand resting on her hip. "Whereas I look at you and I wonder to myself, how did I end up in bed with a pasty-skinned white guy?" Her smile gave her away.

"Just luck I guess," he slid against her hoping to ease her back into bed with him. "I also think that you're soft, warm, luscious—"

She slipped off the edge of the bed and dodged his grab for her. He tumbled to the floor in his attempt. The terra cotta tile was neither soft, warm, nor luscious.

* * *

Ripley was stumbling by the time they reached the restaurant. They threaded their way beneath towering palm and banana trees. Massive pots of orchids bloomed wildly on porches like they hung fuchsia baskets in Oregon. Every building had deep verandahs for hot sunny days like today…like most days in Far North Queensland.

It wasn't the heat or the humidity, which were both high but not obscenely so, that had her stumbling over herself. It was Gordon. There had been men who pleased her. And there'd certainly been plenty who had disappointed her. Her skin color had often been an issue with both.

Yet Gordon seemed fascinated solely by the "contrasting color values of their complexions" (his phrase not hers, yet it had sounded stupidly charming to her…still did). To make his point, he had stood her in front of the mirror—never a comfortable place to be for any woman. Then he'd moved behind her and slid his arms around her, one up between her breasts to hold the opposite shoulder, the other around her waist. Of their own volition her hands had slid to cover his. His bigger arms had made it look as if hers were outlined in white against her own skin. It was an intimate image rather than one in which she was left to judge her breast and hip size. When he had planted a kiss upon her neck, she had watched their reflection in fascination. His eyes closing as he planted the kiss. The happy smile as he bent forward enough to rest his cheek against hers.

She'd never been so aware of her own color before, and yet less self-conscious of it. Gordon was her lover because he wanted to be, but he wasn't thinking of her as anything other than who she was.

I see you as you are and I see beauty.

It wasn't Shakespeare, but it was one of the nicest things ever said to her.

She wanted to protest that there was ugliness inside her…but there really wasn't. Over her years in the Navy she'd bunked with them all: tough babes, nasty bitches, weak women and strong. The only dark place she knew of was actually one of light, of her constant hope for achieving the unattainable.

So she'd looked at the two of them in the mirror and felt a strange inner fear for the first time. There was a hint—just a hint, *no more than that* she promised herself—that she'd somehow found even a small piece of the wonderful relationship shared by her parents. Their example had always humbled her. That was why she saw no future like that for herself; how could she ever achieve what her parents had?

Now she was walking down the streets of Cooktown holding hands with Gordon "Tweety Bird" Finchley. And she felt as if she was floating.

The Top Pub also bore a big sign declaring it had been The Cooktown Hotel as well as several other names in the years since founding in 1873. It was a grand two-story building with a wraparound verandah on both floors. It looked like what it was, a local institution.

As they wandered through, they were greeted cheerily by any number of locals.

"You Yanks must be the pilots. Others said you were coming along. Imagine Cooktown with an Aircrane visiting here. Hoo's flyin' her?"

And then Gordon pointed at her with his free hand.

"The Sheila?" "Nah!" "Really?" "Good on ya!" The last delivered more like one word than three, "G'don'ya."

"We on fire?" At that last call from the crowd that the whole group of them twisted to see if the main street was on fire right outside the door.

Gordon assured them it was all clear.

They turned to her as if they needed her to translate. She'd forgotten that Gordon hadn't ever been Down Under.

"No worries, mates," she called out and the crowd's sudden anxiety instantly dissipated. She only wished her own would as well.

By the time they'd run the gauntlet of the pool table ("Only table in town! Free on Sundays!"), the bar (almost invisible against the kaleidoscopic swirl of beer stickers and signs stuck on every available surface), the dining area (over half full of locals, which was a good sign), and out the back door to where they found the others in the beer garden, Ripley had entirely forgotten how to walk. She'd have embarrassed herself completely if Gordon hadn't pulled out a chair for her to collapse into.

Janet must have arrived close behind them because she slapped Ripley on the arm, "The Sheila pilot! Whoot!"

Brad and Janet did a little Michael Jackson *Smooth Criminal* dance that they'd been working on. It earned them a round of applause and everyone squeezed together to make more room for them.

Beer and pizza were soon rolling out. Ripley's attempt to warn Gordon off Cooper's Extra Stout was in vain. She'd tried it…once. It was so dark that even holding it up to the sun, no light passed through the glass. For some reason she'd assumed he was a pale ale sort of person, but he declared he'd found a new love in his life as he tasted it.

There was the briefest pause after he said it, and he covered it with a laugh.

But Ripley heard it go by. Felt it in their still-clasped hands.

He was *not* thinking that.

There wasn't a chance in *hell* that he was thinking that!

She must have misread him.

No one else at the table was looking at him. Not a single one of her hyper-sensitive new friends were looking at him strangely or in alarm…except Vanessa. She was studying Gordon as if she didn't recognize him at all. When Vanessa's gaze slid to Ripley's face, Ripley gave an infinitesimal head shake. Vanessa tipped her head uncertainly and then let Vern distract her with some question.

That's it. Ripley was overthinking everything. It was alarming enough to be feeling new things. If love was somehow a possibility here, she'd catch the next Antonov back to the States.

Then Gordon leaned over and kissed her on the temple.

Which was charming.

"Sorry about that," he whispered softly into her hair before leaning back to sip more of his beer.

Which ruined the charm and kicked her right back toward panic. She was absolutely not, under no circumstances, falling for a schizoid guy who couldn't decide if he was the sweetheart everyone had declared him to be or the rampant alpha male she kept finding in her arms.

The buzz and chatter eased somewhere deep in the second slice of pizza. She didn't remember eating more than the one in her hand, but she could see a crust on her plate. Then Gordon snagged the crust and muttered something about leaving the best part behind. She felt full enough that maybe this was her third piece. She put it down carefully and sipped at her XXXX Pale Ale. Its high-alcohol content was no less of a mule-kick than any other Aussie beer, but at least she could see through it.

"Tomorrow we go dry," Mark announced. The first words he said instantly silenced the table. Even in the shaded beer garden he wore his mirrored glasses.

She pulled down her own to match him, but couldn't see a thing because they were smeared with fingerprints she hadn't cleaned off. Ripley shoved them back up onto her forehead in disgust.

"Dry?" Janet asked, making a joke of it. "New firefighting technology with no water?"

Mark smiled tolerantly, then tapped his beer glass against one of the pitchers on the table. "Twenty-four hours bottle to throttle from here on out."

"Twenty-four?" Gordon sounded puzzled.

"So you guys actually do that?" Ripley asked. FAA rules were eight hours from your last drink to sitting in the pilot's seat. Most of the military followed the same rule. But rumor said that Mark's old outfit, the Night Stalkers, lived to a different standard…which shouldn't be surprising.

Mark simply aimed his mirrored gaze at her in response.

To hell with being able to see. She pulled down her own dark shades. Next pair she'd buy them mirrored too.

Again that infinitesimal smile before he continued.

"FNQ, that's Far North Queensland, which we're sitting in the middle of, is like Oregon in reverse, only much more severe. Ocean to the east," he tipped his beer toward the waterfront that had been visible from their hotel room window. "Steep front range escarpment less than a dozen kilometers to the west. Hot and dry interior. I want to work on some new tactics. Let's see what we can do to fully integrate the Aircrane into the company."

Ripley opened her mouth, but closed it again. She sensed that even though Mark was turning as if facing them all, it was her he was watching from behind those mirrored lenses. She'd thought that they'd integrated the *Diana Prince* smoothly over the first two fires. But Major Mark Henderson (retired) of the 160th SOAR had lived to a different standard. Rumor had said that Emily was a better pilot, but Mark had been her unit commander. So, Ripley would shut up and see what she could learn.

Mark handed around credit cards, "Good for up to a thousand Australian each. If you lost more than that in the base fire, we'll have to file a claim. Your personal vehicles are already listed and you'll be getting replacement vouchers. Denise, your Fiat Spyder, don't know if we can replace that. We can do a used one plus an upgrade allowance, but making it as cherry as your old one…" Mark just shrugged.

"That's okay. With the kid on the way, I need a four-seater anyway," Denise turned to Vern. "How do you feel about a 1964 first-year classic Porsche 911, honey?" She batted her eyelashes and Ripley could see that Vern was a goner.

Would she have that kind of power over Gordon someday? Or he over her? And why in the world was she thinking about such things?

She tried to hand back the card that came to her, as did Brad and Janet. "All I lost was a sneaker." Her copilot and mechanic hadn't even lost that much.

Mark waved them off. "Gift from the owner, then."

Nobody gave out thousand-dollar gifts to people they'd hired forty-eight hours earlier. Forty-eight hours and a continent ago. What the hell had she landed in the middle of? If anything was proof that she was in way over her head, it was the little piece of plastic in her hand.

Gordon leaned in and asked if she was done.

"Uh, sure." Done in… Done for… What was he talking about?

He snagged the half-finished slice of pizza off her plate and began eating it.

* * *

It was a week later and Gordon didn't know what was happening to him.

It had started in Cairns when Mark had dragged him across the airfield within minutes of landing. They had strolled through the cool dawn to a remote hanger a half-mile walk from the Antonovs—which were so damn big that they didn't seem to shrink with distance. A Beech King Air had been waiting for them: an older version of the twin-engine spotter aircraft that Mark flew in Oregon.

"You have your fixed-wing ticket?" Fixed-wing airplane rather than rotorcraft.

Gordon had picked it up a couple of seasons ago. It was before he'd landed the job with Mount Hood Aviation and wanted to have his options open. "I got my instrument rating and have everything I need for my commercial, except air time."

"Multi-engine rating?"

Gordon could only shake his head. Did Henderson think he was made out of money? Multi-engine training time cost a lot per hour. The same reason he didn't have his commercial ticket yet… two hundred and fifty hours of flight time for that was a big chunk of change. Mark took the operations manual out of the seat pocket as they prepped the plane and dropped it in his lap. "Learn it."

Gordon had sat in the cockpit and read as Mark prepped the plane. He'd barely noticed when the helicopters had taken off—wouldn't have if the Antonovs hadn't bugged out first, each with their four massive D-18T Progress turbofans at full roar.

Once Mark was ready, they'd flown the King Air up to Cooktown, with Gordon nearly crapping his pants at the controls and Mark only telling him what to do.

"We need to get you some more airtime in this."

No kidding.

At five hundred kilometers an hour, Cooktown was only twenty minutes away. But even in that short time Gordon could appreciate why this was such an exceptional spotter plane for firefighting. It had great visibility out the window. With a stall speed of only a hundred and forty kilometers an hour, he could practically hover over a fire. At five hundred, he could outrace any helicopter, match any smokejumper plane, and even act as a guide for air tanker jets when the heavy armor had to be called in. As long as someone else was picking up the tab, he was glad to learn to fly it.

The week since the pizza gathering had been spent flying to bushfires all across the northeastern peninsula that was Far North Queensland. Most of the fires were too small to justify the might of Mount Hood Aviation, but they flew anyway. When there was no fire, they flew training scenarios, putting in long days in remote areas. Mark never touched the controls...not even the radios.

He left it to Gordon to learn to handle all of the air-to-air and air-to-ground traffic. Then he layered in resource management of aircraft and fuel times, drop capacities, and fire tactics. The last Gordon had thought he knew, but he'd been right—the ICA had a very different worldview high up over the firefight.

At night, he'd curl up with Ripley. They'd practically set up housekeeping together. There were days he was too exhausted to do more than hold her as he fell asleep and she took that in stride. Thankfully there were other days.

She didn't push or demand. They were in a comfortably neutral state. He had the most *Wonderful Woman* in his bed and for the low price of remembering to tell her that often, they were simply enjoying each other.

"You know what's happening, don't you?" Ripley asked him one night when he'd managed to stay awake long enough to enjoy dinner out on the hotel's verandah overlooking the ocean.

The Great Barrier Reef, which lay less than twenty kilometers offshore, moderated the waves into easy ripples against the pristine beach. Beautiful as they were, the beaches were closed to swimming due to the deadly box jellyfish that surrounded northern Australia for half the year.

Gordon couldn't imagine. He was barely able to handle each day. In a week he'd added over eighty hours to his pilot's log book. Multi-engine certification had been a quick flight to Cairns for a flight check ride with a Civil Aviation Safety Authority tester. He watched the light shift as it set over the escarpment to the west.

Ripley's skin no longer surprised him as much, but he was still fascinated with how she changed with the light. It was as if the night accepted and welcomed her, hiding and protecting her from view far sooner than himself. Yet the sunrise was equally kind, revealing the wonder of her dark eyes and shining smile like a new gift each day.

"Mark is grooming you."

"He is?" Then Gordon jolted and sat up. Actually, that explained a lot of his past week. "He is. But why and for what?"

Ripley's shrug almost distracted him. Even the simplicity of the shifting curve of her shoulder to neckline in the summer-weight blouse nearly sent his thoughts spiraling off in a new direction.

"But I can't…" Lead? Where did Incident Commander-Airs come from? They weren't born that way. Mark had years of military service behind him. Gordon had…years of flying to fire in helicopters. Could he be? No. It didn't make sense.

Ripley rested a soothing hand on his arm. "You understood my *Diana Prince* and what she could do while you were still in shock after crashing, didn't you?"

"I've watched you a lot since, too." He tried to put some suave tone on it because he wasn't comfortable with this whole conversation. And he'd certainly enjoyed watching her unravel in sexual climax any number of times this week…an event that was always new and astonishing.

"Be yourself, Gordon."

He nodded, it was good advice.

Before she could think of something else to say to make his head hurt, Gordon decided to follow that advice. He stood, scooped her into his arms, and carried her through the balcony doorway to make love to her on the bed washed with cool evening air by the whispering fan.

Chapter 12

*P*ack it up. We're gone. Ten minutes out front."

Ripley stared at the phone in her hand as Mark's voice was replaced by the blaring hyperactive-cricket dial tone of Australian phone systems.

She reached over to tease Gordon awake, but she was the only one in the bed. She pulled on a long-tailed shirt and stumbled about. His packed bag sat close beside the door—how had he done that without waking her? Gordon himself…she finally found on the balcony.

He was slouched in the same chair he had been last night, except now it was coming up dawn.

"Mark said ten minutes. More like eight or nine now."

He nodded without looking at her. But his hand reached out to slide up the back of her leg and up under her loose shirt. "You feel incredible in the morning."

"Not incredible enough to wake up next to?" She teased him.

"But I did wake up next to you and that, Ripley, is an amazing gift."

Girly was not something she ever did, had ever done. But with his hand absentmindedly stroking up and down the curve of her behind, some part of her wanted to gush. To be so comfortable, him with her and her with him, *was* an amazing gift.

She almost teased with, "Be careful. Do more of what you're doing and I just might keep you." But caught herself in time. She'd just be setting herself up for some Shakespearean tragedy. Star-crossed lovers, dead in the fire's flames. One thing she'd learned was that she wasn't the settling down type. Restless as a kid, the same in the Navy, and now a fire gypsy. She'd take the man now, sharing what they did, and leave it at that. Time to cast off the Shakespearian drama with all of its ever-after or unto-death plots, and replace it with…the frivolous cotton candy of Gilbert and Sullivan operettas.

Ripley leaned down, took a long kiss that did more to wake her up than any phone call, then went in to pack. She walked away with a swinging sashay of her hips—another thing she never did—just to make Gordon crazy. But a last-second glance as she stepped inside revealed that he hadn't noticed. He'd returned to his sullen study of the distant horizon.

It was ridiculous to feel piqued, but she did anyway.

Seven minutes later when he held the front door open for her, she didn't offer him a hip sashay. Not even a little one. And he didn't appear to notice that either.

* * *

Gordon watched silently as the Australian coast slipped away beneath the Beech King Air. Another five minutes and his first-ever glimpse of the Great Barrier Reef was slipping by as well.

Someday he'd have to come back here, because the image of Ripley diving in a clinging neoprene wetsuit was one he wanted to take from fantasy to reality as soon as possible. The small arced slices of sand that rose shining white above the turquoise water made him consider the advantages of taking her snorkeling in a bikini as well. He'd never swum in anything bigger than a water tank, but with her…

He glanced again to check on "his" flight—Mark hadn't touched the King Air's controls once since their arrival Down Under. Three Firehawks, Mickey in his 212, Vanessa's MD 530, and Ripley lumbering along in her Aircrane like the friendly giant—slow but so powerful. He stayed high and a little behind so that he could see them all easily.

Beyond them lay nothing but blank horizon. They passed over the last island and entered a uniquely dangerous world of flight. A helicopter was often called "ten thousand parts that just happen to be flying in formation." The smallest failure of any one of those parts could down the aircraft…and there was no way to land any of these aircraft gracefully on the water. None of these were an old Coast Guard HH-3 Pelican especially rigged so that they could float. And his Beech was the worst of all. A high-wing aircraft might have some chance to land and bleed speed before catching a wing tip in the long, rolling waves, but the Beech was a low-wing. The first thing to catch would be a wing tip. First his aircraft would tumble and shatter…then it would sink. With both pilots aboard.

"What are we doing out here, Mark?"

"Maintain your bearing."

An hour later, Gordon could feel the whole flight sort of hesitating. They didn't slow or change course, yet still they… hesitated. Vanessa started flying a little higher. Vern veered slightly as he and Mickey probably exchanged silent looks.

"We're reaching the point of no return for several of the aircraft," Gordon found it hard to speak into Mark's waiting silence.

Mark opened his mouth and Gordon cut him off.

"Yeah, I know: maintain heading."

Mark nodded.

Gordon keyed the mic for the first time since calling clear of Cooktown airspace. "Keep it sharp, people. Don't want anyone getting their feet wet."

"Okay if I pee my pants?" Mickey earned a round of laughs, mostly silent ones shown by the rocking of helicopter rotors side to side.

Fifteen minutes later they crossed the point of no return for the Erickson Aircrane to return to Australia. In another five minutes, they were beyond any ability to reach even a Great Barrier Reef island. Vanessa's MD 530 tripped over that fateful limitation only moments later.

"Mark?"

"Uh-huh?"

"So where…" and then Gordon figured it out, "…is this aircraft carrier we're headed for?" Nothing else would be big enough to receive their entire flight. "Wait a minute! Don't you need special training to land on one of those?"

"Uh-huh."

Gordon was gonna pop him a good one in the "Uh-huh." Mark must have figured that out.

"This," he patted the King Air's console, "is the aircraft they train in before they get to land in a jet."

"You're not expecting me to learn how to—"

But Mark was shaking his head no. "They made me go through special retraining a couple weeks ago. They'd never trust a civilian to not mess up one of their precious aircraft carriers."

"That's a relief."

"Good thing it's such nice weather, or they wouldn't let me or our helo pilots try it. Then we'd have to come up with a different solution because you can't delay a full carrier group on the move. We need to arrive relatively quietly—which puts the Antonovs out of the question—in Ho Chi Minh City, Vietnam, as quickly as possible. They've got a brutal fire and aren't at all prepared to fight it."

That wasn't the itch that had woken Gordon in the night. He'd like to say that it was some sort of pre-cognitive knowledge that their training sojourn in Australia was done. But that wasn't it.

It had been nerves. Nerves he couldn't get past.

He and Ripley had made love last night. Not sex, not amazing sex, not even "made love." They'd made *love*.

Some part of him had packed his bags before he caught himself. The part that said, "This is scary as shit!" He'd gotten control of himself with the hand on the door knob. He wasn't a guy who ran away, but he'd rather crash a helicopter upside down into a lake any day. Refusing to leave, but unable to stay in the room, he'd opted for the balcony and watched the Southern Cross constellation kiss the ocean to the south and then climb back up into the eastern sky.

For hours he'd sat there above the Coral Sea, listening to the soft surf, the winging sounds of the occasional fruit bat, and the echoing silence of the night. Had Mickey been afraid when he met Robin? Hard to imagine. Vern and Denise? Maybe, though Vern was generally so laid back that it would be hard to tell.

"Did Emily scare the shit out of you before you two got together?" The question slid out and landed like a dead fish in the cockpit. Gordon couldn't think of how to pick it back up or nudge it out the door with the toe of his boot.

"Emily?" Mark scoffed.

Once again, Gordon should have kept his mouth shut.

"You've got no idea at all how scary as hell that woman was back then. And since then. Hell, still is."

Gordon had never seen Mark flustered. "But you two get along, don't you? Sure looks like you do."

"Sure. She's the queen of confidence, and I'm quaking in mortal terror most days."

Gordon laughed. That was an image that just wouldn't stick. Especially not with the way Mark was smiling as he looked northeast, as if he could see her across the Pacific.

"Seriously. First I thought she was dating the President…had to get halfway around the world to figure out what was up with that. Then she made it clear she was dumping my ass. By the time she said yes I don't know which of us was more surprised."

Gordon eyed the empty ocean and the woman flying down and

to his left. He could just make her out through the broad curving windshield of the Aircrane. "Yeah, the surprised part I get."

And the way he'd greeted her this morning. Without thought, without hesitation, his hand had trailed up her leg and under her shirt with such easy familiarity as if there'd never been a question.

"I guess it's too bad about the blind panic part of it," Gordon managed a fairly good *Mr. Avatar* tone.

"You get over that, if she's the right one."

Gordon's spin to face Mark actually twitched the flight controls hard enough for Mark to reach for them.

"What?" He asked after Gordon had regained control.

"The 'right one'? Don't know if I'm ready to be thinking about that." Actually there was no question in Gordon's mind—he wasn't ready for that.

"Buddy, if you aren't, then you're a lot dumber than I think you are."

"*That* I have no trouble at all believing."

Mark's laugh was cut off when a radio that had remained silent until this moment squawked to life. "Flight presently one-five-oh kilometers east of Cooktown, Australia, identify." The voice brooked no nonsense.

In moments Mark was chatting back and forth with them like it was old home week. They'd just crossed the hundred-mile perimeter to the aircraft carrier. Inside that line you were either a friendly or an immediate missile target.

* * *

Ripley didn't need to see the massive white "74" painted on the side of the USS *John C. Stennis* Nimitz-class supercarrier's conning tower to know that she'd turn around right now if she had enough fuel to reach shore.

"Someone up there hates me." Maybe she'd turn around anyway.

"Who?" Janet asked.

A glance up and she could see the Beech King Air cruising a thousand or so feet above her. "Got some candidates."

"I thought Gordon dug you?" Janet's slang was a wildly unpredictable commodity ranging back and forth across decades.

"Yeah, babe," Ripley did her best to respond in kind. "He digs me, if you know what I mean."

"If you get where I'm at," Janet corrected.

"Doesn't mean he's innocent," Ripley gave it up just as she usually did.

"If he's innocent around a hot number like you, then he's a total doofus."

She recalled just how amazing he'd been in bed last night. He'd hadn't sought new heights. Instead, he'd been so impossibly gentle while making love. He'd been…tender, not something she typically engendered in a man who'd gotten her out of her clothes. She'd felt heavenly, then appreciated, and ultimately cherished. He'd spent more time tracing the shape of her face than he had the curves of her breasts.

Even the memory of it had her pulse racing.

Or maybe that was the fast approaching carrier.

"This is Petty Officer Second Class Jones to Erickson Aircrane," the call came in on the short range radio they'd been using with the ground crews. The signal wouldn't carry more than a few dozen kilometers from the carrier group.

"Hey, Jones. Ripley Vaughan here."

"Rip!" He sounded genuinely pleased to hear from her. "You traitor!"

So much for pleased, though his tone remained merry. She'd left the Navy…and now her old shipmates were going to make her pay for it.

"You know the tricks. Show the rest of your flight how it's done. Heli-pad three."

"Roger."

Jones still gave her turn by turn directions. The Mini Boss up in Pri-Fly—Primary Flight perched high atop the conning tower, which was the airport control tower for an aircraft carrier—would be watching her like a hawk. It made her terribly self-conscious as she was years out of practice on carrier landing. Thankfully, the Air Boss himself would be too busy with the jets launching off the catapult to maintain the group's over-the-horizon security.

"Vaughan," the Mini Boss came on, she knew Jim Harding's voice. "Don't you be messing up my deck."

"Yes, sir." Operations must be slow if he had the leisure to give her crap.

"Did I hear you giving me the finger in that salute?"

"No, sir. If only because it takes two hands to fly a helicopter."

It earned her a chuckle as she lined up on the "green"—the green-vested airman in charge of giving her landing directions with his two red wands. In a carrier landing, you never watched the deck, only the Landing Signals Enlisted crewman. He guided her down…closer, closer…

Her wheels slammed into the deck, hard enough to earn her the sharp clang of a shock absorber hitting its end stop.

All around this end of the deck, people spun around to see what had gone wrong and if something was on its way to kill them. When they saw what it was, most turned away.

What had gone wrong was that the deck was several feet closer than the "green" had indicated. Then she focused on who it was—Petty Officer First Class Weasel Williams! If she still wore her sidearm, she'd shoot him right through the windshield and damn the consequences.

A glance at the Landing Signals Officer revealed him holding up two fingers, a score of gross but still safe deviations from a best possible five points for her landing.

She recognized him and held up one finger.

She could see him laugh, then he flipped up a third finger before turning back to other duties. She hadn't earned only a three since her third-ever landing on a carrier, which had been another rip-off due to the tropical storm they were steaming through at the time.

"Hey, Rip," Weasel greeted her with a sassy grin as she climbed down among the green-vested maintenance personnel who were swarming her machine. In moments they were working with Janet to remove the main rotor blades.

"Hey, Weasel," she stepped up to him and let him know exactly what she thought of him. It was extremely satisfying.

The next Petty Officer, who replaced Weasel while he went to tend with his bloody and hopefully broken nose, was much more respectful.

A glance up at Pri-Fly revealed the Mini Boss in his bright green t-shirt, leaning on the outer rail and looking down. The Air Boss was there in his commanding yellow as well—immaculately clean compared to the deck hands bearing random stains of grease and soot from hot jet exhaust on their gear. She shot him a sharp salute and he sent a lazy one back. Five stories up she couldn't tell whether or not he was smiling. She hoped so—because she'd just spilled blood on his nice clean deck and didn't regret it for a second.

The man standing next to him, Rear Admiral James Parker, who was partly responsible for her being in this mess, she was less sure of. She wondered if she'd have a chance to meet with him during however long they were aboard. *Don't punch* him *in the nose,* she told herself. A good reminder.

The other helicopters all landed much more cleanly than she had, despite their lack of familiarity with carrier landings. Punching Weasel was not even close to sufficient retribution.

The task of removing the six ten-meter-long rotor blades that had taken Janet and Denise an hour last week was accomplished in minutes by the deck crew, even though they were unfamiliar with her aircraft. They had the blades dismounted and in a cart. She had to grab her duffel bag quickly before they towed her bird away to the elevator that lowered it into the hangar bay. Not used to aircraft carrier operations, Janet was on the verge of a meltdown with it happening so fast.

Ripley hooked an arm through Brad's and Janet's to keep

them in place until a handler came to escort them safely across the deck. Her crew were each wearing heavy earmuffs issued by the deck crew as they climbed down. The handlers escorted one helicopter crew after another, all toting brand new duffels or knapsacks. Soon there was a fair collection of them who'd been led across the deck, through the sound-deadening double doors, and were now waiting in the pilot's ready room.

Most moved to windows overlooking the rest of the carrier strike group. A trio of *Arleigh Burke* destroyers, a *Ticonderoga*-class cruiser, and a half dozen other ships made quite a display. No one would notice the two *Los Angeles*-class fast attack submarines that were circling somewhere below the ocean's surface fore and aft of the surface ships. They were in friendly waters, so there was only a thin cloud of jets and helos in the air.

A couple of people hit the soda machine. After a two-hour flight without time for breakfast, the sugar and caffeine were going to make for some interesting group dynamics.

Ripley stood by the window to the flight deck and watched the King Air come down. Its descent was slow and clean. Full flaps, just above stall speed, it looked to be standing still. Because the carrier was also steaming ahead at—she checked the waves below—about twenty-five knots, the King Air was gaining ground at barely eighty kilometers an hour. It touched down neatly and picked up the Three Wire as its engines burst to life. If it had missed all four of the pickup wires, it would need the speed to not fall into the ocean at the other end of the ship's short runway. Because they caught the wire, they were jerked to a halt, then Mark eased the engines down immediately.

Ripley glanced astern as the LSO held up five fingers. It pissed her off that Henderson rated a five and she'd earned a lousy three because of Weasel. After she busted his nose, she should have kicked his ass over the side and let him swim to Australia.

She could feel herself radiating sick fury. As intense as the moment she'd caught him humping their wedding caterer. She was the one who had lost so much. Wedding, self-respect, career. Why was he the one still in the Navy? She didn't miss the bureaucracy or the crazy pressure, but she missed the flying.

Flying to fire was good. Except for the occasional drone disaster, it was a safe enough job. Yes, she'd take flying to fire any day…as long as she had the chance to string Petty Officer First Class Weasel Williams up by his balls until he—

"Who pissed you off?" Gordon startled her.

"You don't want to know."

Gordon lifted her hand and inspected her bloody knuckles.

She yanked her hand away and tried not to hiss at the sudden pain. "His face was harder than I thought it was."

"Who? I'll take him down for you."

"Have you ever hit a man?"

"Can't think of one." Then that smile of his that she had so little defense against. "Might have punched Mickey in the arm a time or two."

Overhearing the last, Mickey stepped up beside Gordon and slugged him hard enough on the arm to knock him into her. She pushed him back hard enough to send the two of them stumbling together.

"Just paying you back, Tweety Bird," Mickey was all smiles.

Gordon gave him the finger, but between them, they'd broken her dark mood and she appreciated that.

"Vaughan," a voice snapped from close beside her.

Mini Boss Jim Harding stepped up beside her.

"Sir!" Old habits died hard and she was most of the way to a salute before she noticed, but finished it anyway.

* * *

Gordon watched the spectacle of Ripley saluting. A change ran through her. Her amazing posture was suddenly incredible.

"You were in the Navy?" She hadn't given even a hint.

She ignored him and paid attention to the ticked-off officer standing in front of her. He was wearing a bright green t-shirt with the words "Mini Boss" across it in six-inch-high letters. Despite his t-shirt's message, he was a big guy and Gordon hoped this wasn't the guy he'd just offered to take down.

"I want an incident report on my desk by end of day today, Vaughan."

"Not in the service anymore, sir." Despite her claim, she dropped into something that Gordon guessed was parade rest with her hands folded neatly at the small of her back and her feet planted wide. It looked awfully good on her.

"I have two safety violation reports on my desk and a Petty Officer Williams with a broken nose confined to quarters pending investigation. You will give me a report."

"You punched an officer?" Gordon hadn't even known she was in the military just a moment ago. Was she still? "Isn't that bad? Can you get in trouble for that?"

"Asshole deserved it, sir. A petty officer isn't an officer, Gordon. And yes, I punched him."

"Hey, Cuz," Mark Henderson slapped a hand down on the Mini Boss' shoulder.

"Hey, Mark," the greeting was suddenly cheery. The two of them were clearly friends in addition to being related. The Mini Boss nodded toward Ripley. "She one of yours?"

Which Gordon figured was pretty damned obvious. He assumed that they were the only group of civilians landing on a US aircraft carrier in the middle of the Coral Sea today.

"Might be. What did she do?"

Gordon stepped in. "Damn straight she is. So is she in trouble or not?"

The Mini Boss looked at him for a long moment, then busted out laughing.

Gordon suddenly understood Ripley's urge to land a punch.

"The day Ripley Vaughan does something without just cause will be the day I quit this Navy. Seriously, Rip. Report. Written. My desk."

"What went down?" Mark wasn't looking so jovial any more.

"An LSE," Ripley explained between clenched teeth. "That's a Landing Signals Enlisted Personnel, decided to see if he could damage my Aircrane by mis-signaling a landing."

"Why the hell would he do that?"

"He was my ex."

"You have an ex? You were married?" Gordon couldn't make sense of it. Twenty minutes ago he'd been talking to Mark about whether Ripley was the "right one," whatever in the world that was. And now he was facing a woman who saluted and had a past he knew nothing about. Funny parents and firefighting. That was all he knew of her past...until now.

"I was not married," her voice had gone dark and nasty.

This was beyond temper; she sounded mean.

"Caught him screwing the caterer two days before the wedding," she bit it off. Looked pissed that he'd dragged the words out of her.

"He's why you resigned?" The Mini Boss pointed toward the depths of the ship. "To marry that piece of shit?"

Ripley's nod was sharp and hurt.

Gordon wanted to move in and console her. Offer a supporting arm...but he didn't even know this furious woman standing in such a stiff military posture.

He looked around the circle of people. Heard Janet's laughter from the crowd over by the window. She had friends. Good ones. Was an exceptional pilot, based on what he'd seen but based on the Mini Boss' anger as well.

No! He did know Ripley. Whatever else he didn't know about her, he did know...*her*. He didn't have a better word for it, but he knew her.

Gordon could feel her anger become his own. Felt what it would take to make him want to hurt another. Not a flash of confused anger at Mark's teasing, but rather a heat moving to his face. It wasn't a blush of embarrassment, he knew that feeling well enough. No, it was a cold flush of blood that cleared away all other thoughts.

* * *

Ripley had watched Gordon's expression change as her past was revealed.

Bewildered.

Confused.

Hurt.

That was the worst. She didn't want to remember that past. Had blocked it out of her life. Even her parents didn't know the final ugly truth and how confused it had made her, losing everything she'd thought she was. And having to start over.

But that she could hurt Gordon through that omission was something she'd never considered.

In that instant, Ripley began to understand quite how much she stood to lose. Not merely a magnificent lover, but the best man she'd ever been with. Perhaps the best she'd ever known.

She began to reach for him. To prepare herself to lay her pain out on the deck for all to see. There had to be some way to make him listen to her long enough for her to explain why she'd—

However, the man standing beside her was no longer the easy-going Gordon Finchley. He changed. Changed in a way she'd never fully seen.

Her alpha lover was one thing.

The man beside her radiated anger like a physical force. It pushed her partially extended hand back. It made her want to cower and hide.

It was all over. The truth landed far harder than the blow she'd planted in "Weasel's" face. Once again he'd found a way to take and destroy another piece of her.

No one as angry as Gordon could every forgive her. Somehow, once again, she'd lost everything.

But he turned from looking at Ripley and faced Jim Harding, the Mini Boss.

"Introduce me to this bastard," his voice was dark and dangerous. "So that I can pound his goddamn face in."

Somehow Gordon had swallowed her lies—well, her evasions—and decided that he was her champion defender. He was up on his toes, his big hands balled into massive fists.

"Remember," Mickey spoke up, "the part where you've never hit anyone?"

"I'll learn!" Gordon's snarl had even the affable Mickey stepping back, finally realizing just how close he'd come to tangling with a primal force.

"Ripley," Mark said in a calm voice. "Why don't you take Gordon for a walk? Somewhere quiet."

"Try 03-75-4-L," the Mini Boss told her. Deck-frame-compartment-L for Living quarters. "We've got a little space in officer country at the moment due to a medical emergency. You're only aboard for four days, so we'll give it to you. You know the way."

Ripley nodded. She remembered. Her own quarters hadn't been far away.

"Meanwhile," Jim Harding slapped Mark on the back almost as hard as she'd punched Weasel in the face. Mark barely wavered. "I'm gonna bunk my cousin-in-law in a special spot as a thanks for introducing me to his screamingly cute cousin and making my days eternally happy. You," another friendly blow, "are headed for deck 4 frame 25."

Ripley managed to suppress a laugh. Picturing Night Stalker Mark Henderson in with the ordinary seamen and engine swabbies bunking sixty to a room was almost worth waiting around to see.

But then she glanced at Gordon. His expression was still dark and dangerous. He jolted only slightly when she slipped an arm through his, but he followed her docilely enough.

As soon as they were down the first ladderway and away from the rest of MHA, she stopped. There was never peace and quiet on an aircraft carrier nor any place that was truly out of the way. Especially during active flight operations…which typically lasted only twenty-four hours a day. But there was a small space to the side of a firefighting station where the ship's architects had somehow not managed to cram yet one more piece of gear. It was out of the way and only visible on a direct inspection, as it was half under the stairs.

Gordon was still in near automaton mode and Ripley could feel the fear bubbling back into her.

As much to calm herself as him, she lay a hand upon his chest. It felt so good, so right, that she lay her head there as well.

She listened to his heart a long time. It wasn't racing. No. It was rock steady. She wanted to hide there and not face whatever came next. Not a fire, not Weasel Williams, not the old haunts that had been her home for so much of her four years in the service.

Please, she prayed to no one in particular. *Please don't let me have screwed this up. Please. Please. Please.*

Like some benediction, Gordon finally moved to place his hands upon her waist.

"I'm so sorry, Gordon. I should have told you."

He shrugged.

"No, really. It's just…" Ripley pulled back and looked up at his face, still harsh in the fluorescent lighting. And again the fear prickled through her that she'd screwed up something important. Really important. Perhaps—

"Do. Not." He managed his first deep breath since they'd left the group. "Do *not* let me near that fucker. Okay?" His voice was so harsh that she didn't even recognize it.

"Okay."

Gordon nodded once to himself, firmly.

His eyes slowly cleared; somehow their bright blue had gone so dark as to be impenetrable, but the blue was slowly returning.

Ripley tried to read his opinion of her that lay behind those eyes, but couldn't read him when he was like this.

Other members of MHA came thudding down the ladder. She could tell each one by their footsteps. The steady military strides of Vern and Mark with the slightly lighter ones by Robin. The rapid steps of Brenna, the slower ones of Denise, and Vanessa's own light tread. The others continued by over their heads, along with their escorts to make sure they ended up in the right place.

They were long gone before his eyes finally focused on her, for perhaps the first time since last night.

"Anything else you want to tell me?"

Ripley tried to think. Were there any other dark secrets she'd kept hidden? Maybe not only from Gordon, but from herself?

He waited. The gentle man waited, though she could still feel the hard one beneath the palms of her hands.

"I can only think of one thing."

He tipped his head.

"It would be easier if you were really holding me."

"Tough requirement," he slid his arms around her and held her close. So close she could barely breath. "Go ahead."

"Scary and hidden? Yeah, one more secret. It'll be a surprise for both of us."

"Waiting."

Ripley closed her eyes to steel herself to say it, but Gordon flexed his arms in a nudge to make her open them again.

"I'll be right here when you're done. Just say it, Ripley." Well, that certainly did it.

"I'm crazy about you, Gordon Finchley. I know it's fast, stupid, awkward, and probably the last thing you wanted to hear right after learning about my past. But it's—"

"Something I spent most of last night thinking about too."

"Really?" It came out in some small, little-girl voice. A voice of hope.

"Scared the shit out of me."

"Uh…is that why you were all packed before I woke up? Were you about to leave me?" She considered getting angry, but after the events of the last hour didn't have it in her.

"Thought about it some," then he kissed her forehead. "Stopped before I did anything that stupid."

"Thank god!" She'd have melted to the deck plates if he hadn't held her up.

"You aren't angry?" Gordon's voice was a whisper against her ear.

"I don't seem to be," Ripley checked in with herself. *Nope!* "I must admit that I thought about running a couple times myself, but figured that having signed a contract and all, that might be bad form. Still scares the shit out of me, though. I was afraid it was just me."

"Not a chance, Wonder Woman." She could feel the chuckle deep in his chest. "You're doing a fine job of freaking me out as well."

He squeezed her for a moment longer, then took in a deep breath.

"What's that smell?"

"Aircraft carrier," she'd noticed the instant she'd gotten aboard. "Sweat, dirt, hydraulic fluid, Jet-A fuel, unwashed bodies, maybe some mold because everything is always damp. You should smell it when the cooks really burn something, not like searing a steak but a real screw up-and-scorch. The carbon stink lasts for days. Smells like home to me. Jim said we'd be aboard for three or four days; you won't notice it by then."

"Huh. Not what I was noticing, but it is kind of rank."

"What were you noticing?"

He buried his nose in her hair and breathed in.

There was no question that he was referring to her.

"The best smell in the world."

Chapter 13

*T*hey all had accommodations close enough together that the Navy assigned a bathroom for their dedicated use. It wasn't much: three toilets, two showers, and a couple sinks, but it was theirs. And as the compartments were four- and six-up with narrow bunk beds in which it was physically impossible for two people to sleep together...or do much of anything even if the other occupants were decent enough to leave the room, other locations had to be found for more than the most basic cuddling.

Gordon would have thought that was a trivial task on a ship a thousand feet long, two-fifty wide, and a dozen or so stories tall. But with six thousand people and over ninety jets and helicopters, it was a wonder the MHA team and aircraft fit aboard at all.

With space for privacy being such an issue, by the third day it went out the window between the members of MHA. The old Navy joke that two people could shower twice as long together was a paltry one, extending two minutes of water to four: wet down, soap up (without water running), rinse off. Of course, without the water running, there was no real time limit on the soaping up portion of a shared shower.

Ripley had ruined the effect by giggling nearly hysterically the entire time.

"I keep thinking someone's going to catch me and kick me out of the Navy."

Others had better luck. And it had become accepted that there were times when loud humming or singing was appropriate while shaving or performing other bathroom tasks.

However, Gordon didn't know what to think when he was washing his hands and happened to look up in the mirror as Brenna and Vanessa came out of a shower stall together. The two of them were…glowing. Happy and laughing as they walked by behind him, their wet hair slicked back and holding hands.

He stood there staring blankly at the mirror long after their reflections followed them out of the room.

"What the hell?"

Ripley came up to wash her face. " 'What the hell' what?"

"What the hell Brenna and Vanessa?"

"They make a cute couple: Asian and Italian."

"Yeah, but—"

"Hello!" Ripley turned to face him. "Black and white," she pointed back and forth between them. "You don't have an issue with that."

"But I do," he leaned in to nuzzle her neck. "Can't seem to get enough of it."

"Cut it out, you two," Henderson called out from the doorway.

"Go away," Ripley called without turning. "My man is about to kiss me in a Navy bathroom that smells of soap and steam."

"You're both with me. Come on." And Henderson held the door.

"Your man?" Gordon couldn't help but whisper. Now he was the one who was going to laugh hysterically. Over the last few days they'd switched from not talking about the past to talking about little else. Childhoods, love affairs, flying, they delved into it all. Oddly, it had meant that they didn't talk at all about the present.

"You bet your cute ass," and Ripley slapped it as Henderson rolled his eyes.

"What?" Gordon asked him. "You never slap Emily's ass?"

"Are you kidding me? If you were married to Major Emily Beale, would you try it?"

Gordon considered…not a chance, and kept his mouth shut.

They climbed ladderway upon ladderway. It took Gordon a moment to realize that they must be above the height of the hangar and the flight deck, and still they were climbing an interior stairway. He glanced down a corridor that had a longline of closed doors and an armed guard at the far end watching him carefully. The nearest door stated Communications and the one beside it Fire Control.

"Do they really have that many fires?" He kept his voice to a whisper.

"Fire control as in firing defensive missiles," Mark and Ripley answered almost in unison.

"Oh, okay," as if he needed another excuse to feel completely out of his depth.

Three more stories of narrow hallways and closed doors went by.

"How high are we going?"

"This high," Mark turned out of the stairwell.

Ripley stumbled to a halt; Gordon ran into her back and had to grab her shoulders to keep them both upright. He followed her gaze but didn't see anything usual, except that the steel decking was covered in blue flooring tiles with stars on them.

"What?"

She pointed down. "Blue is officer country. The star is admiral country."

Ripley began tugging at her clothes, not that there was all that much to tug at. She wore a t-shirt, jeans, and boots, just as he did.

"Do you have any boot polish?" Her voice came out as something of a squeak.

"Ripley. Civilian now," he gave her a little shake by the shoulder.

"You don't get it. Just because you're a civilian, if you were meeting someone like the Vice President on his home turf, wouldn't you dress up for it?"

"Actually," Mark was waiting patiently, looking amused by the whole situation. "President Peter Matthews' home turf might be Washington, D.C., but Zack's is Colorado. He's an Air Force Academy brat, but leans toward cowboy boots and jeans himself."

"You're on first name terms with the Vice President turned President-elect as well?" Gordon didn't know why he was surprised.

"Sure," Mark shrugged as if it was no big thing. "But not Rear Admiral James Parker. I don't think even Emily enjoys that privilege. Come on. We're keeping him waiting."

When Ripley didn't move to follow, Gordon gave her a little push. Finally he gave her a bigger one and she stumbled into action.

* * *

"So these are the two you were telling me about," the admiral asked Mark even as he shook their hands.

Ripley had never been on the Flag Bridge before. From here the admiral could command the entire Strike Group without interfering with the Captain's operation of the aircraft carrier from the bridge one deck higher. He in turn was generally isolated from Pri-Fly on the top deck of the ship's superstructure, so that they could stay focused on the flight operations.

The view was astonishing. Glass windows provided a sweeping view of everywhere except dead astern by simply swiveling the massive armchair that commanded the space. Astern was visible on any of a half dozen screens as were local and distant ships.

"You," he pointed at her as he sat back into his big chair and left them all standing.

Mark leaned against a console, but Ripley went for parade rest, even though it felt wrong while wearing civvies.

"I should court-martial you for abandoning your post and leaving the Navy. Speaking of courts-martial, I have recommended that Petty Officer First Class Williams be tried under Sections 909 and 933 of the Uniform Code. Section 908, willful intent to damage government property, wouldn't stick as neither you nor that peculiar machine that you call a helicopter are technically government property, however 909 non-military property definitely applies. Also, 933 active dereliction of duties as a safety officer is conduct unbecoming an officer and a gentlemen. I'm recommending a Bad Conduct Discharge."

She gasped at the scale of the hammer landing on Weasel Williams' head for a single act of malice. "That seems a bit harsh, sir."

"Why the hell are you defending him?" Gordon burst out.

"Watch your language, Gordon," she hissed at him as softly as she could.

"The problem isn't his language, Ms. Vaughan. The problem, as he points out, is why are you defending a man who placed you and your crew in danger?"

She didn't have a good answer, so she didn't try to provide one.

"His service record indicates a history of marginal conduct, never enough to remove him—until now—but there is a reason he has been passed over for promotion three times. Now let it go."

Ripley nodded and resisted the urge to kiss his feet. There was some sort of freedom that permeated through her. Unwilling to reveal quite how thoroughly she was touched, she turned to watch a pair of fighters launching off the catapults. The massive thunder of the jet engines was no more than a muted background through the thick windows of the Flag Bridge.

"Now, you," the admiral's attention swung to Gordon. "Mark said that he sees something in you. When the best commander outside the Navy—not officer," he turned on Mark, "she married you, though god alone knows why—but the best commander." He swung back to Gordon before Mark could respond. "Well, I figured I needed to meet that man."

"In that case, sir," Gordon answered with impressive composure, "I would say that Mark has been feeding you a bunch of hooey."

"Wouldn't be the first time," Admiral Parker somehow grinned as he glared at Mark. "If you think I don't know what went on aboard my own ship six years ago, you'd best think again, mister."

Mark grimaced, but the admiral had already looked away in that roving attention he appeared to have.

"For a short while, Ms. Vaughan, your esteemed leader couldn't land a helicopter on a clear day aboard my carrier without bouncing it a dozen feet back into the air. Never saw a man so frustrated by a woman." Then the admiral was back to Gordon, but his finger remained aimed at Ripley. "This woman frustrating the hell out of you, Mr. Finchley?"

Gordon grinned at her, "Frustrate me? No. Scare the shit out of me? Absolutely, sir."

The admiral nodded. "Good man. Then you already understand a woman's role in your life." Again that attention back to her. "Keep it up, Vaughan. I'm hearing good things about you, despite abandoning the service. 'Weasel' Williams," he barked out a laugh. "Saw that in the safety officer's report. Good one. Now get off my bridge. We're headed into the Spratly Islands in the next few hours—going to scare the crap out of the Chinese who built them. We'll be getting shut of you sometime tonight under cover of darkness." He signaled over an aide who had just arrived.

The three of them were halfway out through the door when the rear admiral called out once more without looking up from the information the aide had handed him.

"Going to be an interesting view on Vultures Row here in

about ten or twelve minutes," then he turned away, clearly done with them this time.

She led the way down the hall, doing her best to step lightly on the stars in the blue floor tiles.

* * *

"Do you have anything in your pockets?"

Gordon checked. And then held out what he found: wallet, phone, keys. Then he looked at the keys. One for his MD 530 helicopter that they'd recovered but would never fly again, a second for his pickup truck, blown to shreds halfway up a mountain in the Oregon wilderness, and a third for his door in the bunkhouse that had burned to the ground.

He tossed the keys in a handy trashcan. That was so two weeks ago.

As was not having Ripley in his life. He'd count that as a major trade up.

At Ripley's nod, he stuffed the wallet and phone back in his pockets. She handed him a set of ear plugs as well as hearing protection ear muffs.

"Why is it called Vultures Row?" The door well down the hall from the Admiral's Flag Bridge, past the end of the blue tile, was labeled with several large warning signs. "And what's all this?"

FOD Free Zone.

Remove Covers.

No Flash Photography.

Hazardous Noise.

"You'll see. FOD is foreign object debris. That's why I had you check your pockets. A bolt sucked up by a jet engine—"

"Been there. Done that." Gordon could still hear the grinding as his helicopter's engine had inhaled that drone. "Once is enough. But I don't have a cover, I'm not a book."

"Navy for hat," Mark told him as he donned his own hearing

protection. "They're a strange lot; seem to need a special word for everything."

Then he pulled aside a heavy steel door and they were outside. Outside and a half dozen stories above the Flight Deck. A narrow walkway ran along most of the side of the island and there were a half dozen other people leaning on the railing and watching the operations going on below. Following Ripley's pointed finger, he leaned out and could see that Vultures Row was actually three rows, but the vulture was accurate. He wondered how many hours crewmembers spent here watching the spectacular chess game going on below them.

Even as he watched, a jet landed, slamming to a halt as it caught a wire at the same moment another was being fired off the catapult. Both were operating within narrow corridors between jets and helicopters parked to either side. Here, if you didn't land on the centerline, you'd go careening into a half dozen other aircraft. Space was the true premium on this floating world.

The more he watched, the more bewildering it became. A hundred or more men and women, each in their specifically-colored vests, performed a complex choreography that he expected had even more order and purpose than he could see.

Hand signals flashed back and forth, everyone always seemed to be looking at the right person at the right moment... but they'd have to be. Hearing anything would be impossible. Despite the heavy doubled hearing protection, the roar of the next jet launching off the catapult pounded into his chest and ears. Watching *Top Gun* a half dozen times had done nothing to prepare him for the raw impact of the full Sensurround, live experience.

Ripley tapped his arm and pointed into the sky off the stern. Two tiny black dots against the blue sky. More jets coming in to land.

Then an air-shattering alarm, painful despite the hearing protection, sounded throughout the ship. Oddly, no one on the deck stopped their elaborate dance.

And the people along Vultures Row were all pulling out their cameras or cell phones.

Gordon copied them, though he wasn't sure why.

He went to video instead of photos.

Ripley indicated that he should be sure to grip the phone tightly. He glanced down at the steel deck fifty feet below and decided that was good advice.

Gordon started recording.

The dots grew rapidly, but there was something odd. They appeared to be side by side rather than in a line. And Gordon had seen enough landings already to know that they usually came in higher up, then descended to land—one at a time.

These two aircraft were coming straight in and low to the water.

He glanced at Mark and Ripley. Both had knuckle white clenches on the railing. A glance below showed that all motion on the deck had stopped.

The dots were growing very fast, though he couldn't hear them.

They resolved to have wings, then engines.

Two other jets moved in close behind them, but they had different configurations.

Straight in.

Straight in.

Just shy of the carrier's stern, one of the pair of jets peeled off to pass on the other side of the superstructure. The ones he could see were so close it felt as if he could reach out and touch them.

Then the slap of a sonic boom slammed him back against the steel hull. It was a good thing Ripley had warned him to clutch the phone tightly or he'd have lost it.

He couldn't have just seen… It had been too fast to be sure.

Gordon stopped the video and scrolled back until he had a clear image of the aircraft that had flown directly over the aircraft carrier's deck, actually below his position on Vultures Row. The Chinese red star was clear on its twin tailfins. The nose of an American jet could be seen flying close behind its tail, probably ready to shoot down the Chinese at a moment's notice.

He turned it so that Ripley and Mark could see.

"Chengdu J-20 Black Eagle," Mark shouted loud enough to be heard through their hearing protection. "Those aren't even supposed to be operational yet."

"Is that bad?" Gordon yelled back.

One look at Mark's and Ripley's faces told him that it wasn't merely bad, it was very bad.

As he watched the two Chinese jets peel away with the pair of American jets hard on their tails, Gordon considered the situation: loaded on Antonovs at what had seemed a moment's notice, a very odd week of training in the remote wilderness of the Australian Outback, a civilian firefighting team traveling on an aircraft carrier, and a meeting with a rear admiral in charge of an entire carrier strike group.

Gordon didn't know what it added up to, but he didn't need to be a genius to add in the Chinese jets and Mark and Ripley's reaction to them.

The carrier deck operations were slowly restarting, but they were still quiet and subdued.

"Well," he shouted to his two teammates standing with him on Vultures Row. "Thank god we're only here to fight forest fires."

Mark looked at him like he was an idiot, but Ripley's laugh showed that she understood the absolute absurdity of the situation.

Her laugh always made him feel better, smarter, stronger... even sexier, which was never an adjective he'd thought of attaching to himself.

He could really get used to having that in his life.

Chapter 14

It was four a.m. before the MHA flight was cleared off the deck. The Chinese had made three more passes, or tried to.

And with each one, Ripley had felt smaller and more afraid. She knew it wasn't unusual for foreign militaries to test themselves against American forces. She'd seen Iran and Russia both run jets close by American destroyers in the Persian Gulf. But three years out of the service, she'd lost that sense of assumed superiority that others around her showed. And the Chinese weren't playing chicken with a destroyer, they were harassing an aircraft carrier, a ship so well protected that it never traveled anywhere without an entire destroyer group and air wing escort.

She held tight onto Gordon's hand the entire time that they sat below decks watching the video feeds. She noticed the others crowding tightly together and didn't begrudge Vanessa arranging it so that she was sandwiched between Gordon and Brenna as they all watched the unfolding events.

On the second pass, two American F-18 Super Hornets crowded each Chengdu J-20, forcing the Chengdus to use their higher speed to get clear. The J-20s were fast, but they weren't agile. The F-18s were so maneuverable that they could keep the Chinese aircraft inside easy firing range on anything except a full-power straightaway escape.

On the third, she, like everyone else aboard, sat riveted to channel 14TV as the American pilots crowded so close to the Chengdus that the J-20s' only option was to swing wide of the carrier.

The fourth test came at night. The feed showed in night-vision green with an overlaid tactical display. The Chinese were chased away out at the twenty-mile marker by a brilliantly bright stream of 20mm tracer fire—warning shots from all four of the escorting F-18s' M61 Vulcan rotary cannons, simultaneously.

The Chinese were apparently wise enough to know that on the fifth attempt they'd lose one or both of their newest aircraft to missiles fired by twenty-year-old aircraft of the US military. There was only so far that patience could be pushed.

In response, the USS *John C. Stennis* did what only an American aircraft supercarrier could do. Ten thousand miles from home, they sent sixteen fully armed jets flying over the Chinese airfield on Fiery Cross Reef in the Spratly Islands. They did it at twenty feet above the runway, moving one-and-a-half times the speed of sound in four-jet formations tighter than the two Chinese jets had managed.

The message was clear, "If you touch us, we can *destroy* you. Even out here in the South China Sea."

Everyone aboard had cheered at that video sent back by a ScanEagle drone positioned to circle high above. They knew that the world press, the Chinese media spin doctors, and the United Nations would be wrangling this out for weeks or until the next big news story, whichever came first. But the victory had already gone to the Americans and the Chinese damn well knew it.

Minutes later, Mount Hood Aviation was called to the Flight Deck.

Rear Admiral Parker stepped into the ready room while jets were recovered from operations and MHA waited for their helicopters to be brought back on deck and reassembled. At his signal, Ripley joined him out in the hall.

"How are the nerves, Vaughan?"

Ripley didn't like the question. As if she'd lost some edge since leaving the Navy. Maybe she had, but she'd be damned if she'd show it.

"Good."

She hoped that it was her determination and not her doubts that he could see.

Gordon stepped over as well, though Mark didn't. He appeared to be so deep in conversation with Vern and Mickey that he didn't notice...but Ripley had already learned that Mark noticed everything. For some reason, he was leaving this to her and Gordon.

"Slight change of plan: we're pushing north to the Paracel Islands, another site where the Chinese have built up islands by dredging onto reefs and installing military bases. Closest we can get you to land is going to be at your fuel limit to Nha Trang. They know you're coming. With the recent lifting of the US arms export embargo to Vietnam, they are now full allies."

"Which," Gordon nodded, "has got to be pissing off the Chinese."

"Exactly. So the Chinese are bringing pressure to bear in any way they can, like that stupid-ass demonstration with their J-20s. We flew heavy surveillance birds during their forays. We know far more about the J-20's capabilities now than we ever did: radar capability, acceleration, maneuvering, communications. All of it. We now know how to jam their onboard systems and could drop them into the ocean without a single shot."

Ripley glanced at Gordon. She'd have to make sure he understood quite how unusual it was that civilians were being told this information. Unusual? Strange as hell was more like it. But she didn't have time to make sense of it.

"I don't want to be running my full Strike Group into Vietnamese territorial waters. It would just tick the Chinese off even more and I don't want to be adding that pressure to Vietnam. However, a US firefighting team is a nice, friendly glove for the hand to be inside of."

"That's our only assignment?" Ripley wondered just how high the political maneuvering went. At least that explained why the aircraft carrier had been so willing to take them for a quick ride.

"You're all civilians, Vaughan. It is not the policy of the US military to place civilians in harm's way. You'll have a fighter escort most of the way to the beach to be sure that you remain safe. You are here to fight a forest fire that is chewing up one of our newest and most strategically located military ally's World Heritage Sites. That's the media report that has already gone out. End of story."

"Got it, sir."

Gordon nodded in easy agreement as well.

"However," Parker leaned in, "I'm not saying that you shouldn't keep your eyes open and be smart about it." He nodded to each of them, then walked away down the hall, various crewmembers snapping to attention and saluting as he walked by.

"What was that about?" Gordon asked her softly.

She'd thought that Gordon had simply accepted Admiral Parker's statement.

As for herself, she'd been momentarily overwhelmed at being singled out by the Rear Admiral. Now she wasn't so sure of herself.

"Maybe he wants us to trust him for some reason," Ripley gazed after the admiral. But before she could pursue the thought further, yellow-vested handlers came in and began gathering up the MHA crews.

In the sudden exodus, Gordon only had a moment to brush a hand over her shoulder and down her arm before they separated. Touching had never been a standard part of her relationships. Yet with Gordon it was rare for them to be together and not be in some form of contact.

And she was liking it, which was also a surprise.

"It must be a plot," she told Janet as soon as they were safely back inside the *Diana Prince.*

"What?"

"Gordon. He's always wanting to hold my hand or something. It's like he's trying to undermine my natural defense mechanisms."

"Is it working?"

She sighed. It was.

"I think," Janet spoke up enough to be easily heard over the noise of the engines now at full roar. "It's like one of those entries in the *Nice Guy's Secret Handbook to Making Women Melt.*"

"Is that true, Brad?"

Her copilot wisely kept his thoughts to himself, but offered her a shrug and smile. He too was always holding Janet's hand.

The "blues" cleared the chocks and chains, the "whites" inspected that everything was clear, and a "green" (who wasn't Weasel) waved them aloft when the Air Boss called them clear.

She lifted into the darkness and watched as the others climbed aloft with her. Rigged for night operations, the aircraft carrier was outlined by only a few running lights. The soft glow of the deck lights, bright enough for deck crew safety but dim enough to not interfere with a pilot's night vision, rapidly faded from view.

A crucial part of her life was rapidly falling astern and all that lay ahead past the last circling destroyer was three hundred kilometers of darkness.

Ripley tried to fathom how long this contract would last. How long she and Gordon could possibly remain together. But that wasn't how the firefighting world worked. The contract would be up and she'd move on. And for the first time in her life, she hated that thought.

Exit quietly stage left, but for the first time since forever, she really wanted to see what Act Three had in store for her.

Chapter 15

The Cam Ranh Naval Base in Nha Trang was a quiet regional strip which had only a single terminal building with two Jetways. There were four passenger jets on a parking apron that could accommodate twenty. But the people who rushed out to greet them, though it was barely dawn, were so excited that Gordon could hardly credit it.

"I am Minh. You come to fight the fire?" One of the men asked in quite passable English.

"I'm Gordon. Uh, yes." Gordon glanced around. Perhaps it was because he climbed out of the plane first that they decided he was in charge. *The fire? Singular? Must be one hell of a fire.*

Others were rushing to fuel the helicopters. It looked as if every truck on the base had come over…there was one for every helicopter.

"Have you had breakfast, Gordon?"

"No, I—" Before he could say more, a string of Vietnamese was shouted out and several people hustled away.

"We don't want to delay you from fire. We bring you a very

nice breakfast, then they wait for you in Da Nang. Your biggest helicopter, we are told, can only fly four hundred kilometers. Da Nang will be good. From there Dong Ha then to Dong Hoi and the fire."

Gordon nodded his head and tried to remember the names, but the sounds were so unfamiliar. He'd never seen such a cohesive people. He was far taller than any of them and the men and women were all fine-boned, fair-featured, with straight black hair.

When Ripley and Denise walked up together, the statuesque black and the pregnant blonde, all of the Vietnamese's attention shifted sideways. The two women appeared unaware of the sensation they were creating.

The juxtaposition was creating a sensation for him as well. For just a moment he pictured Denise's pregnancy on Ripley and his legs almost went out from under him. He'd always wanted family. But until this moment he hadn't really connected the possibility of it being with Wonder Woman Ripley Vaughan. It was ludicrous, a mere mirage, but one that he couldn't shake out of his head though he tried.

"What's with the wet dog act?" Mark asked from close beside him.

"Picturing her," he nodded toward Ripley, "looking like that," he nodded toward the pregnant Denise and the circle of people who wanted to touch her waist-length blond hair.

"Just wait until it really happens," Mark said softly. "That's the day you know why you were put on this planet to begin with." There was no questioning the sincerity—it ran soul-deep in Mark's voice.

Several bicycles pulled up with small foot carts in tow.

"*Xoi cha.* Very good. Very good," Minh the interpreter repeated as he led Gordon first of all to the cart. Again, apparently he was the leader. Others were practicing snatches of English on the members of MHA with varying success.

In moments he was served a pristine white dinner plate

piled high with sticky rice, fried meat rolls cut into bite-size pieces, and a small bowl of sweet dipping sauce. He nodded his thanks many times and tried not to wince at the sight of chopsticks.

Ripley was soon served and came to stand beside him. She was eating easily.

"How can you do that?" he asked her quietly.

"I'm from Oklahoma, not the moon."

"I'm from Wyoming. I think we have three Chinese restaurants in the whole state."

"Wimp," she kept eating and his stomach growled loudly.

The interpreter noticed and with little fuss managed to find one of those porcelain soup spoons and hand it over with an indulgent smile. Gordon felt like a heathen for the rest of the meal…which was good, even if it was lightly flavored with the odor of the kerosene in the Jet-A fuel being pumped into their helicopters.

The interpreter was back. "When are you and your wife to have your child?"

Gordon looked at Ripley and then back at Minh.

Ripley snorted out a laugh.

"She isn't my wife."

"He means you and Denise," Ripley was still laughing. "Our two token blonds now that Emily isn't with us."

"Oh," Gordon looked over at Denise and Vern. "They," he pointed with his soup spoon, "are expecting their first child in three months."

The interpreter looked at Denise in surprise and then back at Gordon, his gaze traveling briefly to Gordon's hair.

"No," Gordon pointed his spoon at Ripley, "this is my—" And he stopped unsure of his next noun.

Minh looked very surprised, but not half as surprised as Ripley.

"You did *not* just go there," her voice was low and stern.

Minh, with the tact of a good interpreter and the wisdom of a smart man, abandoned him.

"Gordon Finchley! You had better tell me *now* that you didn't just go there."

He opened his mouth, but couldn't find the denial she was after. He had *gone there*. And he had rather liked the way the thought, however premature, was sitting.

"Gor...don..."

He raised his soup spoon, "My name is George Washington and I cannot tell a lie."

"Your name is Gordon Finchley and you had *better* be lying about this. Don't you ever lie to me about something like that."

The logic of that one defeated him, so he kept his spoon raised, "My name is George Washington and I cannot tell a lie."

"Gor. Don!"

"I went there," he admitted, then scooped up some more rice with his spoon like the heathen he was and smiled at Ripley as he ate it.

"Not *no*," Ripley stated carefully. "More like *never!*"

"Never?" He made it a joke.

"Never." Her tone made it clear that she wasn't joking.

He used his fingers to pick up a meat roll and dip it into the sweet sauce.

"And I refuse to launch into a Gilbert and Sullivan skit here."

He puzzled at the reference while he chewed the spicy meat and decided that maybe he should learn to use chopsticks because this food was really good. Ripley was dipping little clumps of sticky rice into the sauce, but he'd tried that and it didn't work very well with the spoon.

"It's from the operetta *H.M.S. Pinafore*," she explained as if that meant something to him. "The sailing ship's captain protests that he 'never' does various bad things and the crew responds with 'What, never?' and he..." she groaned in frustration. "Never mind."

"What, never?"

She aimed the points of her chopsticks at his nose and he took a judicious step back.

"Okay, why never?"

"Just..." Ripley fumed down at her innocent rice for a long moment. "Just trust me on that. Sex, sure. But the rest of that isn't going to happen, so get over it."

Gordon went for another piece of meat roll. "That's really too bad."

"Tough."

"No, I mean the part about you *thinking* never."

"Oh? And why is that too bad?"

"Because I didn't think there was a single thing that I'd ever change about you. Now I'm just going to have to convince you of ever." He stuffed the entire piece of meat roll into his mouth, dribbling sauce down his chin and ending his side of the conversation.

She opened her mouth to continue her side of the argument, but he'd anticipated that. He quickly dipped another piece of meat roll and stuffed it into her open mouth.

Ripley grunted a protest around the blockade.

He left a sticky kiss on her nose and went to check up on the refueling.

* * *

The flight to Da Nang passed in a blur.

Ripley didn't need this. She didn't want this.

Sure, Gordon was the best lover she'd ever had. He made her want to melt into a little puddle of Ripley every time he touched her. That's what someone who was the best lover ever should be able to do.

She liked him too, which was a major bonus.

But permanent men were not a part of her life. Not in any manner, shape, or form.

For the first time, she wished she had someone to discuss it with but didn't want to have Brad be a part of that. Wanted to discuss what was going on with Gordon, but also didn't. Because that would make him even more important than he already was.

Both Denise and Janet already had the "happily married" bias. That wouldn't be any help. And Vanessa and Brenna were so self-involved at the moment that she almost didn't recognize them. The shy Vanessa now talked almost as much as Brenna did, at least when she was talking to Brenna. Was that what she looked like when she was with Gordon, head over heels goofy? She sure as hell hoped not.

"China Beach," Brad announced over the intercom.

"What?" Ripley couldn't comprehend what those two words could possibly have to do with the turmoil that was going on in her head.

"China Beach," he pointed at the coastline they were flying over. "Dad used to tell me about it. It was like *the* R&R spot for the entire US military during the Vietnam War. Awesome surfing. Food. USO and other entertainments. It was a place for the guys to renormalize after they were out in the jungle for too long. He said the TV show was actually pretty good, other than being so cleaned up."

"The TV show?"

"*China Beach.*"

"Oh."

"You okay, Ripley?"

So not. "I'm fine." Sure she was. She was flying over China Beach in Vietnam on her way to fight a forest fire with her lover. "Just fine," she was protesting too much but couldn't stop herself. "Seriously, I'm good. No need to worry about me."

"Uh-huh," Janet chimed in. "Now we *are* worried."

"Don't be. Let's just watch the beach go by in happy peace and silence." And she tried to do just that. China Beach was a thirty-mile-long curve of pristine sand. Headlands to the north and south focused the waves, and the early morning light showed that the waves rolling in were good sized. It probably was good surfing, not that she knew a thing about that. Maybe she and Gordon could try—

No. Erase that thought. *Crap!* Couldn't he leave well enough alone. Awesome sex and call it good? Maybe she was glad to have a short-term contract after all.

"What's up, Rip?"

"Nothing, Brad."

"Seriously," Janet made it a demand.

"Dammit, Janet!" Ripley felt as if she nailed the intonation; just the way it sounded in *The Rocky Horror Picture Show*. It should have been enough to distract Brad and Janet into singing the song from the movie.

"Nuh-uh. Try again, sister."

Dammit! Apparently not.

She managed to concentrate on the beach housing and occasional massive seaside resort until they reached the sprawl of Da Nang. Gordon pulled ahead in the King Air and led them into the airfield.

It might not be an escape, but at least it was a temporary reprieve.

Except they were wheels up out of both Da Nang and Dong Ha in record time. The last hour and a quarter flight up to Dong Hoi should have been fun, pointing out the sights as they flew over rice paddies, sand dunes, beach, and river. Instead, an awkward silence reigned.

"Sorry," was all she could think to say as they descended into Dong Hoi.

"No worries," Janet had latched onto the Aussie-ism.

"We're just worried about you," Brad agreed.

"I mean we know it has to do with, you know, some guy."

"Yeah, some guy," Ripley would be tearing her hair out if she wasn't wearing a helmet.

"But seriously, Rip. You gotta get your shit together, girl."

"Thanks, Janet. I didn't know that." Ripley once again followed the Beech King Air into the airport. Was she going to be stuck following in Gordon's wake all day? Forever? *No way!* But her protest sounded lame even to her own ears.

San bay Dong Hoi was a small airport. A single concrete strip with a small terminal building and a parking apron that could handle only two regional jets at a time. A second parking apron had been built, but had nothing around it except for low grassy fields, perfect for their operation.

Unlike the relatively leisurely pace at the previous airports, Mount Hood Aviation slammed into full gear the moment they hit the ground.

Firehawk *Oh-two* had the container of Denise and Brenna's service shop set at the edge of the apron and in moments they and Janet were thoroughly checking over each aircraft.

Firehawk *Oh-one* set down the launch-and-recovery trailer for the small drone and Ripley made sure she was there to see what was going on.

Steve and Carly worked together with the efficient unison of long practice. MHA must have owned this setup for a while for them to get so smooth. In moments they had the trailer's stabilizers down. From *Oh-one's* cargo bay they carried over a black case eighteen inches square and four feet long. Sure enough, it was a disassembled ScanEagle drone.

She'd seen them on the aircraft carrier, but never up close like this. It was a sleek package, like a fat mailing tube with a pointed nose. Within minutes, they'd bolted on a pair of five-foot wings, a tail section, and a two-bladed propeller the length of her forearm attached to its tiny engine. In the payload bay, Steve inserted a pair of cameras, daylight and infrared, and a communications module the size of Ripley's hand. A gallon of fuel and then the tiny engine buzzed to life. After warning everyone back, Steve shot the drone aloft with a sharp snap and hiss of compressed air from the launcher.

"Fifteen minutes to the fire. I'll have images for you then," Steve announced in general as he climbed back into *Oh-one's* cargo bay. He had a console there of three screens, a keyboard, and a set of flight controls.

Ripley was shocked when she saw the billowing smoke that was revealed as soon as he had the ScanEagle turned and headed inland. What state had her brain been in that she hadn't seen that coming in? This was the narrowest part of the country, just fifty kilometers from the beach to the Laotian border. The ScanEagle only flew at a hundred-and-forty kilometers an hour but it was already sending back images that told her one thing: this fire was a bad one.

"People!" Mark called out and soon everyone except Steve and the three mechanics were huddled around a topography map covered in markings.

There was also a Vietnamese woman there. She was as short as Denise and as slender as Vanessa.

"This is Vo Thi Chau Tham. She will be our liaison for this fire. Ms. Vo is the assistant supervisor of the Provincial Fire District."

She wasn't what Ripley had expected, though she wasn't sure why. The supervisor wore work boots, fitted jeans, and a silk blouse that she wore like everyday wear but was gloriously colored in an ornate orange and gold floral pattern. Her straight black hair fell halfway down her back in a neat ponytail. She looked beautiful and delicate and when she spoke, her voice was very light.

"Please simply call me Tham Chau. That is my first and second middle name and it will be easiest for all of you. It is how a friend would call to me," Tham Chau said in perfect, unaccented English with just the slight sing-song of her native tongue that might be soft, but it was pure business. "This is a UNESCO World Heritage Site, Phong Nha-Ke Bang National Park. There is a small airport here by the park, Khe Gat Airfield, that would have been ideal for your use, except that it is currently on fire. Over a thousand hectares have burned."

That earned her some low whistles of surprise. Twenty thousand acres, thirty square miles. This was a monster.

"It is accelerating not slowing," Tham Chau continued. "It is not contained on any side and it is beyond our capabilities. These marks on the map are our army personnel, these the firefighting teams. We have five hundred people on the fire.

More are coming. And this is the burned area." Even as she indicated the perimeter, a man with a handheld radio rushed up and expanded the line adding another hundred acres or so.

There were several gentle coughs and grim expressions around the circle. There were a half-dozen helicopters on a fire that would normally call for two dozen plus air tankers and a couple thousand strong, professional ground crew.

"We have very little experience with wildfire in our country," Tham Chau concluded sadly.

* * *

And right there Gordon knew he was in trouble.

The Vietnamese didn't just need someone to coordinate the helicopters…they needed someone to coordinate the firefight. Someone to choose where to risk ground teams and how to cut off a blaze of this scale. But how had MHA known, or whoever was pulling the strings on Mount Hood Aviation…like perhaps the US military or the State Department…ah! How had they known to move the team here?

"We," Tham Chau continued, "have had many small fires over these last weeks. Finally, five days ago, this one escaped from us and we could not stop it."

That at least explained the timing. Or rather the last part of the timing. Four days ago they had been awakened at dawn to leave Cooktown, Australia. How much happenstance was it that the Carrier Strike Group had been passing at that moment? And that MHA was practicing fire tactics in FNQ rather than central Oregon for the week before that? Which begged the question of just how deep was the shit he was standing in?

"Have you determined the origin of the fires?" Ripley was obviously wondering at the timeline as well. No. She was asking about the multiple fires.

"Munitions."

All attention riveted on Tham Chau.

"Most of our fires are started by old bombs. A farmer digs them up to reclaim the metal, or he starts a small fire to clear land and it ignites an old bomb, and it is now a big fire."

Gordon wasn't the only one to look uncomfortably aloft. What must it have been like to have flights of B-52s sweeping by overhead and laying down massive carpets of destruction.

"It did not work," Tham Chau said, misreading Gordon's thoughts. "Many attempts were made by your air force to start forest fires during the Second Indochina War, but they failed against the rich moisture of our jungles. But now, we are in our worst drought in a century and have broken many temperature records this year. Humidity is at a record low and this is also taking moisture from our trees. That is why the fire is so out of season."

Steve brought over a large tablet screen and laid it down beside the map. It was a live feed from the ScanEagle drone. Dense jungle, thick smoke, and an overlaid heat map. The fire was progressing on every front, though most rapidly toward the north.

"Tell me about the terrain," Gordon turned back to the liaison, only at that moment realizing that Mark was there but not saying a word. He was leaving Gordon to take the lead…a pattern he really had to ask about soon.

"It is very rugged and there are very few roads. There are two great rivers," Tham Chau traced the lines with a delicate hand, "and over three hundred caves. Our Son Doong Cave is the largest in the world. It can only be reached by a two-day hike. Most of the hike must be upon, sorry, *in* the river. There are more than twenty peaks that reach over a thousand meters. The valleys are very narrow and deep."

"So, basically an absolute nightmare for firefighting," Vern commented.

"Worst that *I've* ever seen," Mickey agreed. As he was the longest-term heli-aviation firefighter on the team, the only one with more years than Gordon, that was not a good sign.

Gordon studied the map, then tapped his finger at the marked point of origin.

"We start here. Robin's and Jeannie's Firehawks on the right flank with Mickey's little 212 flying cleanup."

"Hey!" Mickey protested and Gordon ignored him and kept his smile to himself. *Score one for the home team.*

"Vern, Ripley, and Vanessa…"

"Her helicopter is smaller than mine."

Gordon kept ignoring him. "…you're working the left flank."

"You are ignoring the main fire?" Tham Chau sounded worried.

"Yes, for now," he reassured her before she could protest. "The flanks are expanding sideways. If we try to tackle the head, the flanks will overrun us. If we can contain the flanks, then we can start narrowing the head. Until then, simply tell your people up near the head to stay out of harm's way. Every hand who can get there, help us defend the flanks."

Tham Chau watched him for a long moment. He couldn't read her eyes, narrowed to thin slits. Then she looked at the other waiting pilots.

Finally she nodded.

"It seems that these people trust you. For now I will do the same," she rested a fine hand on his arm to reinforce her statement. "I will fly with you so that I may interpret on the radio."

"Thank you. I'm sure that will be very helpful," Gordon nodded. Then he called out, "Denise? We good to go?"

"All birds fueled and checked."

"Good. Janet," Gordon called over to her. "You're grounded. You and Brenna are my lead mechanics. I want record speed on turnovers for every helicopter and full safety checks every time they rotate back here for refuel." He pointed at Denise. "Feel free to tie her down if that's what it takes to keep her off her feet as much as possible."

"Hey!"

But it was easy to ignore Denise's protest when he saw the relief on Vern's face.

"Think of yourself as one of those white-vested types on the aircraft carrier in charge of safety. You can check your team all you want, but you pick up so much as a socket wrench and I *will* have them tie you down."

Denise planted fists on her hips, but the baby must have kicked because a moment later her hands were on her belly and all the protest slipped out of her face. The soft look that replaced it was a wonder to behold.

"Let's go, people."

All of the pilots ran for their aircraft, except Ripley. Instead she ran up to him and pulled him into a kiss hotter than any he'd received since Australia, maybe hotter than he'd ever received. It fired through him in a flash of heat that could melt a path through a Wyoming blizzard.

"What was that for?" He managed when it ended as abruptly as it started.

"I'm not the possessive type, so this will sound weird. I just want you to be sure you remember which one of us belongs in your bed."

"Which one of who?" Would he ever understand women?

"The lovely Ms. Tham Chau."

"What about her?" He looked around and spotted her climbing aboard the Beechcraft with Mark. She was very attractive; he simply hadn't thought about it.

"You didn't notice her coming on to you?"

"Was she?"

"Oh, god," Ripley brushed her lips over his. "You really are too sweet for words." Then she turned him and gave him a hard shove toward his plane before she ran over to the Aircrane.

Gordon just shook his head as he climbed aboard and pulled up the stairway that turned into the door.

He knew exactly who belonged in his bed. He was a little surprised at Ripley though, after all of her protests of "No, never."

Definitely a good sign that at least some part of her psyche was on his side of the question. Now he just needed to tip over the rest of her.

Chapter 16

The battle of the fire flanks was mostly won by nightfall. Vanessa's MD and Mickey's 212 weren't night-drop certified, but the other four helicopters were and kept right on going.

Gordon had them run another two hours, but he knew they were tiring. So he'd stationed Vanessa, Mickey, and Mark on the three Firehawks and climbed aboard the *Diana Prince* himself, taking the observer's seat. He figured that the fresh blood and on-board conversations would get him another couple of hours of useful flight time before everyone was too ragged to be safe. It was hard to believe that twenty-four hours ago they'd still been on the aircraft carrier for a long, sleepless night while being harassed by the Chinese Chengdus.

Being back in the firefight felt good, familiar. He could forget all of his concerns about why they were here and what Mark was trying to do with him. Flying above the fire was beginning to feel familiar, enough so that it was a relief from the other worries. But even sitting in the *Diana Prince* reminded him of who he really was. He was a heli-pilot first.

Steve had set him up with the tablet, and Gordon was frequently conferring with him and Carly as their Fire Behavior Analyst. But for this stage of the firefight, very little guidance was needed. With a second tactical display, he might not even need the Beech King Air. Mounting a couple more radios and keeping Steve's drone aloft would make this an ideal control location.

Tham Chau had been formally polite, even pleasant, but Ripley's "declaration" must have worked. Tham Chau had been very helpful, but politely distant throughout the day.

During the day, MHA and the Vietnamese ground teams had gotten it down to the point where the need for radio communication was minimal. And for the nighttime work, he'd told Tham Chau to have them all pull back to a safe distance and get some sleep.

Tomorrow, they would return to the routine they'd worked out. The helicopters would fly over and douse the fire enough to knock it out of the crowns of the lush Indian mahogany, the towering *Hopea,* and the mid-story guava crape myrtle. The ground teams—just like the US teams, armed primarily with saws, shovels, and flails—would cut out the laurel, camellia, and wild rose undergrowth, then bury and beat the fire to death. When the helos hit the next section, the ground teams would follow along.

Small teams, mostly those flagging from the exhaustion from the long days they'd already been on the fire, were intentionally left behind. They worked along at a slower pace as the mop-up crew. The helos also worked back and forth across the middle of The Black between the two flanks, killing hotspots so that the fire hopefully wouldn't reignite behind them.

"It seems like we're making progress."

Gordon could hear the weariness in Ripley's voice over the intercom and didn't want to disappoint her. But he was looking at the feed Steve was still running from his drone. The ScanEagle had a twenty-four hour loiter time on a single tank of fuel, so it was acting as their infrared nighttime eye in the sky.

"That bad, huh?" She prompted again, trying to make it funny, which he appreciated.

"We're doing well against the flanks."

"Victory!" Ripley crowed it out with far more energy than he could muster. "Hey, at this point I'll celebrate any little thing."

Looking out the observer's large window, Gordon contemplated the fire. Even more than back in his poor dead MD, the view here was astonishing. There was no console at all blocking his view, just a small set of flight controls placed conveniently by his right hand that would allow very fine control of any hoisting operation. For fire operation, he looked up into the front end of the water tank. Looking down, everything below was wide open to view, racing away from him at a hundred miles an hour.

The darkness of the night jungle was complete. Phong Na and the other small villages near the southeast side of the park had been evacuated. Not a single light showed in the night. Their chances of saving the villages were miniscule, but at least no lives were at risk there. Out of the intense darkness, the first fire in this area would show up. Because his observer's seat faced backward, each appearance was a surprise when the Aircrane rushed over it and each fire appeared suddenly.

A small one popped into view. Then another. A third to the right and a fourth directly below. He could see a ground team tackling the last, the humans garishly lit by the flame's glow. Once a fire escaped its first few acres, hand-to-fire combat—with a lot of air support—was the only true solution. The final battle was always fought on the ground.

The head fire still had him stumped. It was climbing into the three hundred square miles of Phong Nha-Ke Bang National Park. He, Mark, and Tham Chau had flown low over that country. It was beautiful, immensely wild, and many of the evergreens that defined the majority of this section of jungle were wilting; some even had browning leaves. The tops of the conifers were drooping. The wet season hadn't arrived on schedule, and the summer heat wasn't easing. The gentle

October fall was baking more like a country that…well, was too close to the equator.

But the fire wasn't…right.

He couldn't identify the itch. Maybe it was because these species burned differently, but that didn't feel right. Perhaps there was weaker Coriolis effect this close to the equator, making the fire smoke move wrong. But it was more than that. No matter how Gordon studied the fire—from the air, on Steve's data feeds, or on the ground reports combined on Tham Chau's maps—something wasn't making sense.

None of the other pilots felt it. Mark had tried to act as a sounding board, but hadn't been any help. Carly was too involved with the active fire's behavior to see past that. And he was reluctant to approach more of them, not even Ripley, for fear he was quietly losing it. Perhaps he'd just gotten his brain rattled when he crashed.

The more he worried at it, the less he could see; but he somehow knew it was there. If only he could find it.

* * *

Ripley didn't like feeling helpless; it wasn't a skill she'd spent a lot of time practicing. But how to help Gordon was beyond her.

He staggered off the *Diana Prince* like a man wounded or in shell shock. He might well have wandered off aimlessly into the dark of Dong Hoi Airport never to be seen again if she'd let him.

Tham Chau had minivans waiting for them and they were soon at a luxurious hotel. No question of checking in; each team was whisked onto waiting elevators and escorted to their rooms.

"Half an hour to sunrise, breakfast downstairs," Gordon roused himself enough to inform the group before they went their separate ways.

She hadn't known what to expect, but the room they were led to was shocking. It might be the nicest hotel she'd ever stayed in. The spacious room's entryway was white marble inlaid into dark stone. Ahead was a luxurious looking king-sized bed—though at the moment, any bed would look luxurious. Tasteful soft brown-and-white décor was accented with panels of exotically-grained wood of a golden luster and ornate gilded metal dividers that were more design than substance, yet made the room appear even larger. One wall was all glass and looked out over a large swimming pool, the beach, and the dark sea beyond.

The only real oddity, which she didn't notice until after their guide had deposited their duffels, handed over their room's keycard, and departed with a bow, was the bathroom. The dark stone flooring of the hallway continued sideways into the space and all of the fixtures were modern, even elegant…but the walls dividing it from the bedroom were floor-to-ceiling glass.

She'd served four years on carriers. Clambering into the small steel boxes of the *John C. Stennis'* shower stalls was comfortable and familiar; well, until Gordon had joined her there. It had invoked unstoppable fits of un-Ripley-like giggles. They attacked her each time a naked firefighter followed her so eagerly into a four-minute shower.

She supposed that the hotel room's glass walls made both the bedroom and bathroom feel bigger, but it was still odd to her American sensibilities.

Gordon was out of it. She guided him to bed. Stripping him down wasn't as fun as it should have been. His body barely reacted as she got him naked and then tucked him in. It looked as if he was out before he hit the pillow. She shut off the bedroom lights, but the subdued bathroom lighting still lit the bedroom softly.

He might be too out of it, but Ripley desperately needed a shower.

She stood for a long moment staring at the glass walls, then finally decided to stop wasting time or she'd pass out standing up and Gordon would find her in a little heap on the cool tile in the morning. The shower was hot, but the fan was strong enough to keep the windows from steaming up. She ducked into the hard spray and let the water wash off…the days.

The first day of the firefight rinsed down the drain. The shampoo washed away the tension of the Chinese Chengdu J-20s flying so aggressively at the American ships. The soap finally cleared away the general grime from returning to an aircraft carrier and seeing Weasel for please god the last time ever. But the long, soaking heat did nothing to wash away her feelings for Gordon.

She leaned her forehead against the window, mostly to stay upright as the hot water pounded against her shoulders, and studied the dim outline Gordon made on the bed.

Telling herself she was not in love with the man wasn't going to work much longer.

Then what the hell would she do?

* * *

Gordon floated in the bed, so numb with exhaustion that he could barely feel the clean sheets.

The fire was a disaster...and somehow, *he* was supposed to fix it. Even Henderson had been at a loss as they had flown the King Air back and forth over the fire earlier in the day.

"Steve and his drone can tell you what the fire is doing," Mark had spoken softly. "Carly can tell you what the fire is going to do. Jeannie, Vern, Mickey, Robin, and Vanessa are some of the best firefighting heli-pilots you'll find anywhere."

"But none of them can tell me *what* to do," Gordon made it a statement.

"Exactly," Mark agreed sadly. "Regrettably, on this one, I've got nothing you don't."

"Would Emily?" Mark's sigh made Gordon wish he hadn't brought her up. "Sorry, you must miss her."

"It shouldn't be possible to miss a woman this much—I saw her just last week—but it is. And no, Emily wouldn't be any help. She's a consummate team builder and an incredible tactician. You give her a plan and she can execute it better than anyone, anywhere. But getting her head up into the plan isn't her forte. That's why we always made a good team."

In between guiding the firefight, Gordon had spent much of the afternoon since that conversation thinking about those teams. And just because he was lying in a comfortable bed watching his gorgeous lover shower, those thoughts didn't stop.

Carly and Steve made perfect sense as a couple—the fire behavior analyst and the man who could feed her the data.

Jeannie the pilot and Cal the photographer. She was the best trained person on fire behavior other than Carly…and she flew with Cal—the nation's leading wildfire photographer. Somehow he'd been recruited to the MHA team. Because…? Details. Nobody saw details the way Cal did. Origins, terrain anomalies, tortured winds—he often spotted all of those before anyone else.

Vern and Denise. A straight-ahead fantastic pilot and an ace mechanic. Both major assets.

Mickey and Robin. MHA's most seasoned flier and their newest one—a tough lady from a US National Guard background. Gordon recalled Mark chewing out Robin for not looking after her team first of all. And he'd seen her learn that lesson. Almost in that moment, Robin had become the den mother of Mount Hood Aviation. Not the nurturing type you went to and cried on her shoulder—more the kind who'd kick your ass, with all the love in her heart, if you performed one iota less than your best.

Even Vanessa and Brenna somehow made sense together in the same way Vern and Denise did—another great pilot/mechanic pairing.

"Was it intentional?" He'd asked Mark.

"Was what intentional?"

But Gordon hadn't bothered to repeat the question because even as he asked it, he knew the real answer. Just as Mark had said, it wasn't him who had built the Mount Hood Aviation team. Emily Beale was the one who tested, hired, and trained pilot after pilot. MHA was as much her creation over the last three years as it had been the founders like TJ, Chutes, and Carly's father three decades before.

And yet Emily had stayed on the ground rather than flying on this trip.

Now, as he floated on the edge of sleep, Gordon watched Ripley showering. Watched the white suds slide over that luscious dark skin. Watched her lean against the glass, her eyes too shadowed to see, but he could feel them closing as she gave herself to the sensations of the hot water streaming over her.

Now, to round out the MHA team, there were he and Ripley. Brad and Janet were also a good addition, but he and Ripley were the next key to Emily's MHA team.

No. They were the final key. That's why Emily hadn't needed to come along. Ripley was a fantastic pilot and her aircraft was an amazing complement to the team.

Was it intentional?

Perhaps some parts of it and not others. He and Vanessa should have been predictable, plannable. But they weren't. So, Emily had gone to the next step.

Consciously or just by feel and intuition?

Gordon decided he didn't even care if it was a complete and total setup. Had Emily chosen a fantastic pilot in a hugely powerful aircraft, or had she specifically chosen a woman who she thought Gordon would like? Would fall head over heels for?

Again, didn't care.

Whether chance or Major Emily Beale (retired) had brought them together, didn't matter. Gordon was smart enough to know that he'd never find another woman like the one currently toweling down on the other side of the glass.

When she slid into bed beside him, he was just awake enough to roll over and pull her tightly against him. He wasn't going to mention his Emily Beale theory. It would probably freak Ripley out and send her running the other way.

Instead he was simply going to hold onto her so tightly that she could never escape. He'd take her soft hum of contentment as a good sign when he buried his face in her ever-so-fresh hair the moment before sleep finally crashed in on him.

Chapter 17

W*hat the hell is* up with this fire?" Steve stabbed his chopsticks into his breakfast rice, apparently just to poke holes in it rather than eat any.

Nobody, least of all Ripley, was going to argue with Steve's sentiment. Especially since his tablet offered him the only view of what was happening this morning. After two full days containing the flanks, MHA and the Vietnamese forces had worked for four straight days attacking the fire's head. It had grown, twisted, shifted, and burned afresh in unlikely—and worse, unpredictable—ways.

"Did Vietnam develop some kind of a *smart* forest fire?" Robin growled in exasperation.

"Maybe we just don't understand how the plants burn here," Mickey stared down at his morning tea.

"That's not it," Jeannie poked at her *xoi nep than* black rice a few times, then threw her chopsticks down with a loud clatter. "Before I came to the US, I fought several jungle fires Down Under and some in Papua New Guinea. Jungle burns just like any other fire—hotter in the hardwoods, faster in the conifers. None of that explains this."

"Well," Steve dropped his tablet on the table. "Day Four report: we lost half of yesterday's gains." No one bothered picking it up to double-check his terse summary.

The heavy silence descended over their group again.

It was still dark outside the dining room's sweeping windows. Today not even the nicely restrained beauty of the white-and-black stone floor and the high ceilings with more of the golden wood that Ripley was definitely going to decorate her home with (if she ever had a home) was able to cheer them up.

She looked around the table. Everyone was glaring at their breakfast or staring up at the ceiling in dismay. The broad buffet table set with both Vietnamese and European dishes—though some were slightly odd for breakfast, like this morning's Irish stew—had been barely touched by the MHA crew. Half hadn't gotten food at all. They weren't even all sitting as couples anymore. Vanessa and Brenna were several seats apart and Gordon was across the table from her, though she refused to read anything into that.

Except Gordon didn't look sullen. His expression was puzzled. He was looking around as if he'd missed something.

"What?" Ripley mouthed at him when his glance slid her way.

He shrugged like an itch was—

"Robin!" It shot out of Ripley suddenly enough to startle everyone at the table. She wasn't sure why she'd said it. "Repeat your last comment."

Robin narrowed her eyes at Ripley, "I don't even remember what I said."

"I do," Mickey nodded. "You said, 'Did Vietnam develop some kind of a smart forest fire?' Word for word I think."

"How did you do that?"

"I remember everything you ever say, my love," and Mickey leaned forward to plant a big mushy kiss on her.

Robin placed a hand over his face and pushed him back

into the chair. "He's full of crap, but it sounds like something I might have said. Why?"

Ripley didn't answer, but was looking at Gordon, who had jolted upright in his seat just as Tham Chau came in to fetch them.

"Tham Chau!" This time it was Gordon who spoke loudly enough to make everyone jolt.

The few other early morning Vietnamese diners, who had been so quiet as to be invisible, jumped and twisted as well to see what was happening.

"You said that old munitions started this fire. Old bombs. How do you know?"

"There is a crater, a very big one."

"Larger than usual?"

"This one, it may be the biggest ever. Over ten meters in radius."

Ripley gasped. She'd done some ferrying for effectiveness teams on Naval bombing ranges. She'd fly a team of scientists from ship to beach to inspect the effectiveness of the latest five-hundred-pounder JDAM bomb dropped by an FA-18 Super Hornet. By those standards, a three-meter radius was a massive hole. The damage range would be much broader, but blowing a hole in soil took an immense amount of energy. To jump from an eighteen-foot diameter hole to a sixty-foot one was an enormous energy factor.

"I'm guessing that's big?" Gordon asked.

Ripley could only nod.

"That can't be some random bomb drop that never went off. Someone had to collect a lot of munitions together to cause that," Mark confirmed grimly.

But Gordon wasn't looking at him. Instead he was up on the edge of his seat.

"Steve, can you run me everything you've got from the last six days. Start with the moment we arrived and give me the whole fire, as much as you can."

Steve tapped away at his tablet for a minute, mumbling about how much easier it would be to do on the Firehawk with the full console. "There. I've set it to do a thermal gradient. Straight visual won't show you what's really going on. But this will show the fire from blue ambient temperature, rising in gradients of a hundred degrees Celsius, about one-eighty Fahrenheit. To dark red over two thousand degrees Fahrenheit. The smoke plume will cause irregular variations and the resolution may miss spot fires that—"

"Just run it," Carly cut off her husband.

He frowned, but hit the play. "It's at a factor of three thousand time compression," he had to finish.

"Three thousand?"

Steve obviously felt he was getting a little of his own back when he said, "Six days. A hundred and fifty hours in just under three minutes."

Ripley didn't listen as the crew teased him about going from a lead smokejumper to a geek. Ripley hadn't known that about his past—lead smokies were very tough guys. She wondered how his bad limp played into that career change.

On the display, the fire head grew as it chewed its way into Phong Nha-Ke Bang National Park. Within fifteen seconds the results of Gordon's opening strategy of attacking the flanks could be seen. Over the next thirty seconds—a full day—the fire collapsed in scale, shrinking in size by two-thirds as the flank, tail, and finally the spot fires in The Black were all beaten down and killed in the next thirty-second day.

"I did not think it was so dramatic," Tham Chau said softly. "You were right Gordon, to do that first. It also gave us hope and new energy."

Every thirty seconds the background image swung from day to night and back. But the thermal overlay showed the constant deep red of the head fire. It was several kilometers wide and moving steadily.

Then it jumped during one of the nights.

"Wait." "Did something happen?" "Go back."

"No!" Gordon ordered. "Let it run."

Twice more the fire jumped significantly. Each time it was close by the head of the fire, but not quite in the fire.

"Give me a tight view on each of those three events."

Gordon's voice had gone deep and dangerous. What did he know? She was afraid to ask. With that tone of voice, apparently so was everyone else. They all waited in silence, breakfast forgotten and shoved aside. Helpful waiters attempted to clear some of the plates but were merely snarled at by the MHA members crowded so close together that they formed a solid wall around the table.

"Here we go," Steve was less officious about it this time, simply hitting play.

The display took about three seconds, flashing like a strobe light.

"Wait, sorry. Have to slow it down." He ran it again.

The sequence took thirty seconds to play, but still the flashes were extremely brief.

He trimmed off the chaff and ran it again, even slower. He cut it off after the first flash. "Shit! Give me a sec."

Nobody interrupted his deft alterations to the playback settings.

"Weird," he kept tinkering. "Okay…here are the three fire jumps in real time."

The leading edge of the fire was a range of deep oranges and bright reds, indicating eight hundred to a thousand degrees. The darker reds of fifteen hundred degrees in the central fire would be off the edge of the screen.

In less than a second, the first fire-jump transitioned from the pale blue of ambient air temperature to black.

"What's black?" Ripley asked, afraid that she already knew.

"That's what's weird. That's at least three thousand degrees, perhaps four. And the time cycle is strange. A bomb should be a single hot flash, not like this."

It flared hard black for over thirty seconds. And when it faded away, the area turned into deepest red of very active fire, which the main blaze engulfed moments later. Also, it didn't burn in one spot, but rather in a longline.

While the screen repeated the pattern a second and then a third time, she glanced around the group. It took her a moment to sort out those with puzzled expressions versus those with grim ones—civilian versus ex-military.

Mark, Robin, and Vern (she hadn't known that about Vern) all recognized a thermite flare when they saw one.

No wonder the wildfire wouldn't die.

* * *

Gordon had known he was close when he'd seen Ripley's surprise at the size of the ignition crater that had started the whole fire. And when she unerringly exchanged looks with Mark, Robin, and Vern, he didn't need to turn to see their expressions.

"What is it? What burns so hot?"

"Thermite," Ripley whispered softly. "Rust and aluminum powder. In the military we use thermite grenades when we really need to melt through something: destroy a weapons cache, burn into a bunker, something like that. When we left Afghanistan, there were thousands of vehicles too disabled to bring home, but we didn't want anyone else using them. Thermite grenade on the engine block will melt straight through in seconds. Needs a strip of magnesium to ignite it, but any fire can do that."

He faced Tham Chau, "Someone wishes your park to burn. Not nature. Not old bombs. That may have started it, but this is malicious. Find out who." He half expected her to go running from the room to find out. Instead, he could see her jaw clench tightly as she puzzled at it herself.

While she did, he turned to Steve.

"Look within the body of the fire for—Ripley, what temperature does thermite burn at?"

"Four thousand Fahrenheit."

"Steve, look for that."

"What are you thinking?" Ripley tried to follow where Gordon had gone. Very few people made her feel slow, but mild-mannered Gordon was moving in a direction she couldn't follow.

"Those three jumps aren't enough to explain this fire's erratic behavior. What if there are thermite booby traps spread throughout the forest? Those three were probably sparked off by embers traveling just ahead of the fire. Normally, the fire would roll over the thermite and the ignition and flare-up would be masked by the flames themselves."

"Got 'em," Steve called out. "Holy shit! It has been going on all along. I have over a dozen of these."

Gordon was just nodding. "And if you map the trail of them, they're leading straight into the heart of Phong Nha-Ke Bang Park." He didn't make it a question.

"Yes," Steve confirmed. "That's why the bulk of it is continuing due north despite the easterly winds blowing it toward Laos."

Tham Chau jolted at the last word.

Gordon didn't need to know what she was thinking to know that the threat was real—humans rather than nature were at work here.

He began barking out orders as he strode out of the dining room, Tham Chau racing along beside him. They all hurried after the two of them, breakfast abandoned without a thought. Even Mark had to scramble to keep up. Though Ripley was unsure why he was so happy—it seemed an odd moment to be grinning like an idiot.

The few diners watched them go with looks of alarm. The dawn light was only now illuminating the palm trees and beach beyond the windows and most people at the resort were probably still asleep.

She spotted several looks of surprise as the rest of the team raced after Gordon. They kept looking at Mark in surprise, even though he was no longer smiling.

Mark had been the strategist to the team's tacticians, especially his wife.

Now it seemed Gordon was the master strategist to the team's tacticians, especially—

Ripley caught her boot hard on the threshold as she raced out the door to the waiting vans.

Especially her?

A glance back revealed that there wasn't any threshold marring the smooth floor.

Chapter 18

*W*e're changing it up," Gordon announced at the airfield. "Tham Chau, you're with Vanessa. I want the two of you hunting the thermite traps. Their placement through the jungle is very linear and the spacing is relatively predictable. Tham Chau, get your ground teams ahead of the fire and track those down. I want them disabled, cleaned up. Use encrypted radios only. I don't want whoever is out there doing this to know we're onto them."

They rushed off together.

"Mark, you're with Vern; you're the oversight and protection for them. Fight the fire where you can, but your top priority is their safety."

Mark thumped Gordon once hard on the shoulder. No words were necessary. Gordon could feel that he finally had a lead on this fire, one that even Mark hadn't seen—though there was no doubt that Mark was no more than seconds behind him.

What was strange was that none of the others had seen it. It was as if he'd pulled a magic rabbit out of the hat. Not

Mickey with all of his experience or Vern with his military background.

Not even Ripley, which was particularly interesting. She'd followed along quickly enough when he led the way, but she was...she was the military half of Emily's latest pairing. Gordon could see the big picture, but she was the one that the rear admiral had treated with such respect.

Ripley was the one who knew about thermite.

Ripley was also the team builder. He could see how the women had embraced her. After just a few weeks she was already as close to them as Gordon was to the guys he'd worked with for years. He didn't doubt that she'd have them all swooning around her as well given a little time—and it wasn't just her looks.

"I'm going up with Ripley and Brad," he continued doling out the changes. Partly because he just flat wanted to, but mostly because he didn't want to be stuck flying a fixed-wing aircraft above the fray if this got down and dirty. "Steve, rig me a couple of screens at the observer's seat on the *Diana Prince*: visual, infrared, and get a drone up there with radio surveillance. Can you do that?"

"An EM package? Sure, but why?"

"EM?" Now it was his turn to be confused.

"Electro-magnetic surveillance package. I can pick up radio, cell phone, most anything you want," he began unpacking a second drone as he spoke.

"What the hell?" Ripley had come over and looked down into the black crate Steve had opened.

"Great, huh?" Steve rapped a knuckle on the drone's skin. Rather than a bright ring of aluminum, there was a dull thump of composite material.

Ripley dragged Gordon aside. He used it as an excuse to sweep her into his arms and kiss her. He ignored the fist thump against his shoulder and just pulled her in closer. For six days he'd done little more than hold her while he slept. Occasionally they managed to stay awake long enough to shower together, but over the last few days even that had become more about getting clean than playing together. Had they even had sex in the last few days? He didn't think so and at the moment couldn't imagine how he'd done that.

Right now he felt supercharged. Ripley leaning so hard against him that he was pinned against the clear acrylic bubble of the Aircrane's observer's window made him wish they could take each other down this second. Here. Now! Just bury himself in the glory that was Wonder Woman Ripley Vaughan. She made him feel more alive than he had ever imagined possible.

When she finally broke the kiss but continued to lie against him, they were both gasping for air.

"Do you," Ripley managed between desperate breaths that were heaving her chest against his, "have any idea…how sexy it is…to watch you think?"

Gordon burst out laughing, "As good as watching you fly?"

"Better!" She leaned back enough to smile up at him.

"Not a chance!" That got them both laughing.

Then she sobered abruptly in that I'm-now-all-business way she did—a transition which was also sexy as hell. It made him want to push and see just how much he would have to do to break that military shell, that mighty shield she wore against her past. What would it take to make Lieutenant Vaughan groan with that sound his lover Ripley made the moment before sexual release slammed into her?

"Gordon, seriously," and there was his Lieutenant Ripley in full force.

Because now wasn't the time, he kissed her on the tip of the nose, wondering how a woman could be so powerful and so cute at the same time.

"Mount Hood Aviation has a stealth drone?"

Gordon shrugged. He knew it was stealth. "It's part of the non-disclosure agreement we signed. *You shall not discuss MHA's drone capabilities with any other party.* I assume that's the bird they're talking about."

There was the sharp hiss and clang of the launcher as Steve got the stealth version of the ScanEagle aloft.

"We didn't even have one of those on the *John C. Stennis!* That's top-tier, and probably very secret military gear. You are…a civilian outfit."

And there it was. *You.* MHA was something other than Ripley Vaughan and even in the heat of frustration, she didn't let go of that. Well, he took some courage from the thought that no one had ever said it would be easy to lasso Wonder Woman.

"Well?"

"Well what? We don't have time for this now," he squeezed her lovely taut behind as a tease.

This time the protesting fist thump slammed into his shoulder hard enough to hurt.

"Get your helicopter ready," he told her.

As if in answer, the APU screamed to life right over their heads. In seconds, the Aircrane's main engines were clawing to life and the big rotor began turning.

She kissed him on the nose with the same light tease he'd just done to her. Then she squeezed his ass before stepping aside and climbing the ladder up into *Diana Prince's* cockpit.

The entire flight was aloft in minutes.

* * *

Ripley flew the firefight.

She wished she could turn around and see what Gordon was doing. She couldn't hear what he was saying most of the time. He, Steve, Vanessa, and Mark had set up a dedicated radio link, an encrypted one.

Civilian Mount Hood Aviation. Stealth drones and encryption-capable radios. Gordon even had Vanessa drop one to the ground team sent ahead to look for the thermite traps. Everyone else had been instructed to discuss nothing except the fire itself over the air.

Maybe it was just as well. She'd almost said far more than she was comfortable with. *You are…a civilian outfit*, had only been a last-moment recovery.

It was obvious that MHA was heavily equipped and supported by the military. Whoever heard of a firefighting team getting a ride on an aircraft carrier? But the line was clear. MHA was technically a hundred percent civilian. Not some military contractor like Blackwater (now called Academi), G4S Risk Management, Triple Canopy (now also part of Academi), and all the others. MHA were like special firefighting consultants.

Now that they knew where the fire was headed and how it was behaving, they could tackle it rationally. The head was over five kilometers wide, but the thermite trap line was only a half-kilometer path up the east side of the fire. So they hit the west side hard and began the process of narrowing the fire.

By focusing all of their forces, the ground team cleared a fireline through the trees a half kilometer long and twenty meters wide in just a matter of hours. The fire slammed against the firebreak full force, but between the clean fireline and the helicopters dumping water on it, they were able to hold it at bay. Embers sparked and spit, but once they pulled off the teams from the now-beaten flank fires, they had enough people to battle flying embers. It was a pitched battle to hold that section of the fire in place until it had burned all its fuel or been soaked down. But it was working.

But protests about MHA's role and equipment hadn't been what almost slipped out: *You are…killing me here, Gordon.* Despite the stresses and exhaustion of the fire, he had proven different from any male she'd ever met.

He was more interested in holding her than screwing her. Even when he was past exhaustion, every night he had pulled her back against him until it seemed they were one body. And when they did have sex, he still wasn't "screwing" her. She could feel the need in him sometimes, that hot, frantic frustration desperately seeking release. Somehow, somewhere inside him, he always managed to turn it. At times he was gentle, at times desperate, but he never failed to recall that there were two of them and she wasn't just some soft and warm vessel waiting for a male to empty himself into.

And she hadn't been kidding. Watching Gordon take threads she couldn't even see and weave them into a tapestry of the obvious had been incredible to watch. And there was more there. Ripley could see that, even if there hadn't been time to ask what it was.

Yet even in that moment, he'd given. A kiss that wasn't amused, triumphant, or condescending. It was a kiss of welcome.

Gods! He really was killing her.

Fire. She understood fire. That's what she'd focus on.

She was able to run the sea snorkel in long, swooping re-tankings along the Son River. She even flew close enough to the end of the river to see where it disappeared into the Phong Na Cave. There it ran twenty kilometers underground before reappearing on the other side of the mountains. Phong Na had been the record-holding cave in the world prior to the 2009 discovery of Son Doong Cave, now the biggest in the world by far.

She'd like to see that. There weren't a lot of caves in Oklahoma and even fewer on aircraft carriers. Actually, except for members of the deck crew and air wing, a carrier pretty much was a steel cave with no windows, but it still didn't count. She'd only ever been in one natural cave, the one-hour tour of the Oregon Caves not far from Erickson Air-Crane's operations base in Medford. Son Doong must really be something.

* * *

"We found one," Tham Chau reported, her voice going even higher than normal in her excitement.

Gordon sagged with relief. Good! He wasn't going crazy. "Describe it."

Tham Chau relayed the ground team's description in bits and pieces. "Approximately twenty liters of powder."

That made his head spin. A five gallon paint bucket's worth of powder and Ripley had told him that a thermite grenade held perhaps a cup.

"Spread in a line three meters long. With magnesium strips every half meter. A spark on any one of them would be enough to light the entire mass."

"Where would whoever did this get so much thermite?"

"I do not know."

"Ripley," Gordon turned up the volume on the intercom. He had enjoyed having her voice in the background even during the moments when he couldn't be paying attention to the fire itself.

"Here, Gordon," her voice was deeply sultry enough to have Brad laughing.

He felt it like a punch below the belt. He'd never needed anyone the way he needed her. It was strange to sit here, back to back, unable to see her.

"Did you need something?"

"Yes, to get my breath back. And that's a loaded question."

Ripley's happy giggle tickled down his spine. Gordon had twisted enough that he could see Brad's startled expression as he turned to look at Ripley in shock. Gordon would take that as a good sign.

"They found about five gallons of thermite in a pile. How hard would that be to make?"

"Five gallons?" Ripley nearly choked on her own surprise. "Uh, rust is everywhere. Aluminum powder needs only soda drink cans and a very good blender. Magnesium strip is also very easy. Good thermite mostly takes more effort, but only a little more technology. Pretty common ingredients. There are some common additives, but they aren't needed to be effective."

Gordon sighed. No help tracing the culprit there. He turned his attention back to his encrypted radio link to Tham Chau.

"Have them load it into buckets. Vanessa can carry them back to the base for your people to deal with. Get the mess cleared up and have your people search for the next one."

"Now that we know what to look for, we will be much faster."

"Good news. We need that on this fire." He looked at the terrain ahead and knew they needed more than that. They were headed into the more rugged mountains. The ground crews would soon have to be part goat to navigate the terrain.

They would also have to be very careful about deploying the teams in such a harsh landscape. Steep slopes would slow down a ground crew—but not the fire. They'd have to be very careful to not let any personnel become trapped. It was a safe bet they didn't each have their own individual five-hundred-dollar foil fire shelter. A burnover event here was guaranteed to be fatal.

He could shift the fire battle to the east side and trust that the investigation team didn't miss any thermite surprises. Then at least they could start squeezing the fire away from the most precious sections of the park.

Some instinct stopped Gordon's hand halfway to the radio. Maybe they should leave that side of the fire alone…or was he just being paranoid?

*　*　*

"Hey, Ripley?"

She concentrated on scooping the last five hundred gallons out of the Son River and into her tanks.

"Two thousand," Brad called out. "Two-two. Two-three. Two-four. Twenty-five hundred," he announced as she retracted the sea snorkel and pulled aloft.

"Yes, Gordon." It was such a lovely view, the jungle crowded tight to either edge of the river. Up ahead, the massive cliff face with the dark cave's mouth that the river poured into. Tham Chau had said that normally tourist boats would be lined up at the cave entrance. Phong Na cave was much more accessible and Son Doong—a hard day's hike over rough country even though they were less than ten kilometers apart by air…or fire. Two days for tourists.

"I need a reality check."

"You're an *awesome* lover. You have no concerns in that department." It came out as a tease but Ripley couldn't believe she'd just said that. *Lover?* Who the hell was she kidding? Ripley Vaughan never took lovers, at least not any more. It was a word that had been stricken from her vocabulary by the Weasel. Even then she hadn't used *that* word.

"That isn't what I was asking," Gordon sounded as if he suddenly was doubting himself.

Ripley peeked at Brad. He was keeping his attention carefully out the right-side window, though if his face was as red as his neck below the edge of the helmet, then he was actively glowing with embarrassment.

"Well, you shouldn't be asking about it," the tease slipped out despite her rapidly escalating horror at what was happening inside her. "You rock my world every time, lover." She could practically feel the heat radiating off Brad's face. Teasing two men for the price of one made it a good day in any girl's book.

And it was true. He did. Every single time. But for the price of a tease she had spoken…truth? Well it was no goddamn truth that she wanted to know about.

"I meant about the fire."

"Spoilsport," she managed to keep her tone even as she climbed up over the new fireline the ground team was cutting and worked spot fire control for the newly-narrowed flank.

"I'll make up for it later."

"You better or I'll tell everyone what a welcher you are."

"Well, I never," he sounded indignant rather than Gilbert and Sullivan-esque. She really needed to take him to a show of *H.M.S. Pinafore.* She'd let it slide for the moment and give him an A for effort.

Though she was looking forward to the way Gordon might be making things up to her. Even better than teasing two men at once. But the thought of them hot and sweaty in bed together looped back to calling him "lover" and that was seriously freaking her out. Who the *hell* was this Ripley Vaughan person who would have a lover?

"A military question?"

"Man oh man, talk about a mood killer." Ripley was, however, thrilled with the subject change, but she had to get Brad back for his silence. "What do you think, Brad, should I even listen to him?"

"Please leave me out of this," he sounded like he was begging in earnest like the bad baronet in *Ruddigore*.

"I bet you're taking notes to tell Janet later."

"Sure," Brad cheered up. "It's just gonna kill her that she wasn't here for this."

"Hear that, Gordon? I think we should go back to the subject of our sex life."

"I'd love to, honey, when I'm in a position to do something about it."

Honey? Gads! Could she like being called that? What was wrong with her?

"If you were conducting an active fire campaign against someone, or a military campaign, would you just *leave* your booby traps? Or would you be monitoring to make sure that everything was running on track?"

"Absolutely stay, if there was a risk to civilians—"

"What if you didn't care about the civilians?"

That question sent a chill up her spine as she dumped the last spot fire's worth of water out of her tank and turned back for the river.

"I'd..." she swallowed hard, remembering her training. Major, critical US military operations were frequently aborted on the mere possibility of harming a civilian. "I'd... The US military would absolutely have a forward observer there. A forest fire can't ignite thermite by itself and—"

"Why not?"

"It isn't hot enough."

"A wildfire isn't hot enough to burn thermite?"

"Not really. That's why they use the magnesium ribbon. A cigarette lighter can ignite magnesium, which burns around three thousand degrees. That in turn is hot enough to start the thermite reaction."

Gordon was silent at that. Long enough for her to reload her tank along the river. Her trip from river to fire had been growing shorter throughout the day.

"Anyway. What I was saying is that an in-place observer could shut down thermite booby traps by just pulling the magnesium wicks."

"Or set up another one."

"Right. Easy-peasy."

"We can't fight the eastern fire. We need to let it burn convincingly."

Now that Ripley knew where the conversation was going, her mood did evaporate like a water dump made too high above a hot fire. They could turn it aside if they shifted all of their forces to the eastern side…but they couldn't let the bad guys know they were onto them.

"Tham Chau," Gordon called on the open firefighter frequency.

"I am here, Gordon."

Ripley wondered that Gordon didn't simply swoon at the sound. Despite her job, she was so delicate and feminine with no issues like herself. *Holy crap! Jealous?* She was being jealous? It was a miracle that her hands stayed steady on the controls.

"We will keep narrowing the fire from the west," Gordon transmitted calmly as if Ripley's own world wasn't shattering into a thousand pieces in this moment. "But I want to start a team, whatever few you can spare, far ahead of the fire on the eastern leg. Send a team close beside the main caves to start cutting a new line. We can't control this fire, but maybe we can salvage something if we're lucky."

"But you said—"

Ripley thumbed her mike transmit and held it down. The doubled transmission would cause nothing but a high squeal of interference to anyone listening. Gordon must have told Tham Chau something on the encrypted radio that she was about to repeat over clear air.

After ten seconds, Ripley let off the transmit key, ready to slam the key back down if Tham Chau was still transmitting.

She wasn't. Then their liaison started again.

"I understand," Tham Chau's voice was now softly sad like a fallen leaf. "We must salvage what we can."

"I'm glad you *understand*," Gordon transmitted back.

The silence in the helicopter was a solid wall through her entire next drop and re-tanking.

"Ripley," Gordon's voice was low and angry by the time she was once more back to the west side of the fire. "You kill this fucking fire. You hear me? Kill it dead."

"All by my lonesome?" She did her best to make it light. "Or is it okay if the others help me, too?"

It earned her a growled, "Just kill it."

Chapter 19

*G**ot a hit!"*

The call jolted Gordon out of his lethargy. Over the last forty-eight hours they had narrowed the fire by half. The teams knew their roles so well that managing the fire was almost easy. MHA's pilots were all so experienced that they only required the vaguest of directions to mount an attack. And the ground teams must be killing themselves for the miracles they pulled off. Hundreds of reinforcements had been sent in, but still Gordon hadn't dared to let them tackle the eastern fire.

At least that side of the fire was distinctly less vigorous. So far, the forward team had found all except two of the thermite booby traps. Now that they knew what to look for, Steve's drone easily picked out the two hard flare-ups that had relaunched that side of the fire. But over a dozen others were now contained in a stack of heavily guarded buckets back at Dong Hoi Airport. Hopefully the bad guys hadn't noticed the eastern flank was slowly losing power.

The bad guys.

He had lain in bed last night thinking about them after he and Ripley had spent their bodies upon each other. For once, they had both desperately needed the release of sex. It had been fast, hard, and amazing. They had used each other, but since there was no question that's what they were doing, neither had minded. When he had flopped down on her, rather than easing down or catching himself on his elbows, Ripley had merely huffed out a breath. Her arms didn't come up around him, but neither did her legs unlock from about his hips, keeping him pressed hard against her.

He'd finally managed to roll his weight off her.

Hardly pausing after he was off her, she had gone to the shower. On the second day they'd found the blinds that could be lowered over the bathroom windows, but neither of them could be bothered. She didn't this time either.

Ripley's drying ritual never varied. Up one side of her body, down the other, then a hard squeeze of hair in towel, then the hair dryer. "Militarily efficient" he had accused her and she hadn't denied it.

He should have gotten up with her. Soaped, scrubbed, and dried her himself—a truly fun process he'd only had the opportunity to do a few times. He loved the way she looked, the way she felt, who she was.

She had come back to bed, showing no regrets. Curled up beside him and gone to sleep.

And he had been left to stare into the darkened bathroom where his heart had just been standing.

And then he'd thought about the bad guys.

Tham Chau had no doubt of who was behind it, he'd been able to see that in her face over that breakfast two days ago. It had made her furious.

He had tried getting it out of her and she had refused. "It is too horrible. I do not want to be wrong."

But it didn't take much asking around to understand. If ever there was a country doing their best to piss off Vietnam, it was

Laos. All buddy-buddy on the surface, but underneath there were riots in Laos, even witch hunts leading to the murder of illegal Vietnamese residents—at least supposedly illegal. Vietnam had allied with the US and Laos with China, another area of contention, as if they needed one. The several back-and-forth invasions between Laos, China, Cambodia, and Vietnam were called the Third Indochina War; the Vietnam War was called the Second. Laos was also going out of their way to sabotage every Vietnamese initiative at the international level.

He was sure that neither side of the conflict were innocent; they never were. But Gordon didn't care about the details. He was here to stop a fire and someone was trying to stop him. Probably Laos, but again, didn't care.

When he'd rolled over, Ripley had shifted. So…not asleep.

"I'm sorry for—" *how I just used you.* But the words wouldn't come.

"I'm not. Like I said, Gordon. Sex with you is great." Then she'd rolled over ending the conversation. Somehow, that single round of pure sex had let her pull her shields back up around her.

He'd have cursed himself if it would have helped. Instead, it was all part of the higher-level problems that were clogging his every thought.

Day eight of the fire—day two after removing most of the thermite traps—they were still narrowing the left flank and Gordon was having trouble focusing.

In the morning, Ripley wanted a quick "wakeup fuck." She'd managed to get her walls up higher than any time since they'd met. He'd tried to slow down, to take an extra moment that they didn't really have.

Instead she'd pushed him down in one of the hotel's comfortable chairs, sheathed him, straddled him, and taken him. He knew by her shudders that she found release, as did he, but it had nothing in common with making love to her. He'd barely been done before she'd climbed off his lap and taken a quick shower before dressing and heading downstairs for breakfast ahead of him.

The only thing he'd been able to think was how much he still wanted her.

And then, after a long day aloft, broken by only the most sporadic need for instructions, Steve's call had come in on the encrypted radio.

"Got a hit!"

* * *

Ripley had flown the entire day and into the afternoon in chilly silence, not sure who she was angrier at, herself or…herself.

She'd been doing her normal Ripley routine, at least normal before Gordon. Sure, let the guy have what he wanted, then he was happy and you were done having to deal with him until the next time. Guys were insatiable, wanting sex day after day, but they were also easy. Give them what they want and they're done until the next time, content in their self-image of all-conquering stud.

Twice now she'd practically forced Gordon to simply use her. To fit into that safely familiar place of a man needing to fuck a woman and be done with her.

Except it had never been that between them and she hated it. No matter how hard she scrubbed in the shower, she couldn't wash away Gordon's empty expression as he had still slouched in the chair, naked, sheathed, and limp as she headed out the door.

She didn't want to remember the man whose merest touch electrified her body. There was no place in her life for a permanent man who made her feel so feminine and so strong at the same time. Ripley Vaughan the Firefighting Gypsy. That was her.

Wonder Woman would be really, really pissed at her. Diana Prince always told the truth. As if to prove her point, the Aircrane's left engine lost ten-percent of its power. She could feel the jolt of it, right down to her unsatisfied core.

Since when had she wanted more than sexual release from anyone?

Engine temperature was steady. Fuel was still standing at a third of capacity.

Since Gordon.

"What's happening, Brad?"

He had been wise enough to sense the chilly atmosphere. But he'd felt the change as well and was working through the status screens. "Nothing. Some dirty fuel? Overworked oil? We've been pushing her awfully hard…especially today." Brad offered the last very carefully.

Pushing awfully hard? She always took care of her aircraft first. Who the hell was he telling her how to fly her Aircrane? *Shit!*

"Gordon?" She might as well bite the bullet.

"Busy," was all he said back.

"I have to return to base. Engine trouble."

"Then do it," this time it was a hard snap.

Well, Ripley. You finally did it. You got to be the one who destroyed the relationship. How does that feel?

She called ahead to Janet to warn her about the problem… the helicopter's problem.

As to the relationship problem? She certainly wasn't going anywhere near Wonder Woman's lasso of truth.

Halfway back to the Dong Hoi Airport, the other engine began losing power as well.

＊ ＊ ＊

Gordon looked up and out the window and tried to make sense of where he was. An area of pavement hung less than ten feet below his observer's window. Where? Oh. The helicopter was settling down on the airport's paved parking area.

"What are we doing here?" The bird hit the pavement hard enough that he could see the rear shocks fighting to take the hit. That wasn't like her at all. He turned enough to see that Brad's hands weren't on the controls, so it had to be Ripley.

"Issue with the engines," Ripley informed him tersely.

"Really?"

She stopped by his seat, had to so that she could open the rear door and prepare to climb down. "Damn Gordon, where's your head at?"

It should have been funny. He remembered her saying something earlier, but he'd been too busy on the encrypted radio to pay much attention.

But it didn't come out funny. Instead, her face looked like some crazy cross between the ice of Ripley gone behind her shields, and a slice of anguished pain that he couldn't lend credence to.

Then she was gone and talking to the mechanics on the ground. A fuel truck moved in from the other side.

He couldn't even focus on Ripley at the moment, because his head was too busy trying to make sense of what Steve had finally uncovered after two full days of keeping both drones aloft. The day-and-night camera package was too big and heavy to be flown on the same bird as the full EM surveillance suite. So Steve had opted to keep both birds up as much as possible.

And after two days, they'd caught a transmission.

Steve had taped the call and was working on locating both ends of the transmission. They'd looped in Tham Chau for a translation.

"Thermite is gone, location R-17."

"Gone?"

"Scooped up. No thermite. No magnesium ignition ribbon. Nothing but Mung boot prints."

Gordon had to ask for an interpretation of Mung. Tham Chau had explained that it was a slur from the Vietnam War to describe Vietnamese who had moved to America. The speaker on the radio, she guessed, had been referring to the increasingly close ties between Vietnam and the US, thereby disparaging all Vietnamese people.

"Return to base," had been the instruction on the radio. "Tonight we will show them what we mean."

And the call had ended.

The call had been by radio, so Steve's drone was only able to localize the conversation. A cell phone he could have pinned down and tracked easily. Instead he was having to work with how far the drone had traveled during the brief conversation and attempt to triangulate the shifting angle of drone to transmission points.

They needed to…

Gordon looked up again.

Three or four hours to sunset. If they were going to stop these people, it had to be soon.

Looking around, he finally spotted his pilot.

He couldn't hear Ripley over the dying whine of the Aircrane's engines, but he could see that she was standing nose-to-nose with Janet and Brad—he hadn't even noticed Brad climbing down. Ripley had one finger jabbing angrily up toward the engine; her face set in lines of dark fury.

Gordon wrestled with the unfamiliar harness release, and only remembered at the last moment that his helmet was wired in and would try to throttle him if he leapt to his feet. He dumped it and scrambled down the short ladder.

There was no point in trying to intervene with a soothing tone and a joking word. She was throwing a full-on tantrum. About to—

He made a grab for Ripley's arm…and missed.

Her punch clipped Brad on the chin. He didn't struggle, or shake it off. He simply folded up and collapsed to the concrete. His head hit hard. He lay like a rag doll, the two impacts had knocked him out cold.

Janet cried out and knelt over him.

Ripley's face contorted as it shifted from fury to horror. She too tried to kneel, but Gordon simply grabbed her arm and dragged her away. Over his shoulder, he called back.

"Brenna. Find out why Engine One is having problems. I need to get back aloft."

Ripley struggled, but he didn't let go. He dragged her along, stumbling in his wake until they were out of sight behind the service pod. Then he shoved her against the side of the container and let go as her back slammed into the corrugated steel.

She pushed back off and he shoved her again.

"I have to go see Brad."

He didn't even bother to comment.

"I…oh shit!" Ripley's back slid down the steel until she was sitting on the pavement.

Gordon squatted down to face her and waited.

* * *

"You should can my ass," Ripley couldn't even bring herself to look at Gordon.

"Not today."

"Does it count in my favor that it was a clean punch?"

"Not this time, Ripley."

"So much for laughter curing a multitude of ills."

"Another Shakespeare quote? Or Gilbert and whoever?"

"Audrey Hepburn." She shook out her hand. It didn't hurt… much. Less than the nose breaker she'd fired at Weasel Williams. That one had felt clean and good. This one felt awful. "I can't believe I did that."

"How many men have you hit in your life? Is this a pattern I should know about?"

She pulled up her knees under folded arms and hid her face. "Two. Ever. I didn't even hit Weasel for screwing the caterer. It took him trying to damage my helicopter for me to go after him."

"You must really love that helicopter. Making me jealous there, Ripley."

"Don't be. I love you way more than that."

And the world went strangely silent. Like that slow motion moment that occurred during the split second before an accident. The words had come out of her mouth. As she slowly raised her head to gauge Gordon's reaction, she saw small blades of fresh mown grass tumbling slowly across the pavement, driven by an afternoon breeze so light she hadn't noticed it on landing. At the distant terminal she could see one of the rare passenger planes taxiing up to the terminal—she could practically see each beat of its propellers—but she didn't hear a thing louder than her own indrawn breath and the pounding of her heart.

Gordon's face changed even as she focused on it. There hadn't been anger there, which she had totally deserved. Instead, there had been a thoughtful expression as if she were an intriguing puzzle.

Then, a smile formed slowly. One that started simultaneously on lips, cheeks, and crinkling at the corners of his blue eyes richer than the sunlit sky.

"More than your helicopter. Wow! That's a good thing, right?"

Ripley could only nod, her hair swooping slowly back and forth, her brain still turning everything into slow motion.

"I'm glad we got that straightened out." He waved a hand back toward Brad and her helicopter, "Then what was all that?"

If she could answer that...

She went to put her face back down on her arms, but Gordon reached out and caught her chin, forcing her to continue looking at him. But he didn't speak. He just waited. Waited and smiled when he should be screaming at her for unprofessional and dangerous conduct.

"I do love you." It was less surprising the second time she said it. And the world snapped back into focus. Normal speed. The thrumming of the passenger plane's propellers as it reached the terminal and wound down. The groan of someone...

"Brad!" Ripley jolted to her feet and raced back to the scene of her crime.

Brad was sitting up, blinking hard, and rubbing the back of his head.

"Oh, god!" Ripley knelt beside him. "I'm so sorry. I can't believe that I did that."

"I can't either," Janet didn't sound too angry. "Do you really love Gordon so much that you had to punch Brad?"

"Do I *what?*" Yet she'd said it to him just moments ago. It simply hadn't sunk in yet.

Janet rolled her eyes.

"I'd roll my eyes at you," Brad said softly. "But it would hurt too much."

"How can I ever make it up to you?"

"First, never do that again," he hissed sharply as Ripley ran gentle fingers on the lump at the back of his head. It was a big one, but her fingers didn't come away with blood on them.

"I swear. Oh god, I absolutely swear."

"Second," Janet actually had the decency to smile at her, "we'll come up with something really juicy and totally embarrassing later."

"More embarrassing than knowing all the steps to the *Rocky Horror* 'The Time Warp' dance?"

"Way!" Brad and Janet said in unison.

"Water in the aft tank," Brenna announced as she walked up. "Who checked the fuel this morning?"

Ripley bowed her head. She'd done the pre-flight on the helicopter to avoid dealing with Gordon.

"Janet," Brenna said harshly enough to have Ripley looking up at her in shock. "Didn't your maintenance instructor ever tell you to never, ever, under any circumstances let a pilot touch your aircraft?"

"Totally my bad," Janet agreed.

"Crap," was the only response Ripley could think of.

"I checked everything else," Brenna said in a more kindly voice. "Looks good. Fuel truck is done. Boss man is itching to go."

Ripley looked around and saw that Gordon was already back in the observer's seat, working the encrypted radio channel.

"What do you say, Brad?" Ripley asked as gently as she could. "Still willing to fly with the bitch?"

"You mean the one with the sucker punch?"

"That would be me."

"Sure." He started to his feet, then sat back down on the pavement abruptly and winced his eyes closed. "Or maybe not so much."

Ripley felt worse than awful as she and Janet helped him slowly to his feet. They each took an arm and led him over to where a water cooler, Denise, and a couple of extra chairs had been placed under an awning.

He groaned as he settled. Brenna handed him two aspirin, a bottle of water, and an ice pack.

Ripley stood there for a moment, feeling completely helpless. She needed another pilot. Technically, one pilot could fly an Aircrane, it was that gentle an aircraft, but the bird was neither certified or advisable for solo flight. Especially not with the busy radio work over a forest fire.

She looked at the three women hovering around the disabled pilot. There was only one other choice for a pilot.

"Sorry," she whispered to Brad as she kissed him on the head.

"Maybe once the aspirin kicks in," he said softly.

Ripley decided that was one of the nicest things that anyone had ever said to her. Despite her momentary irrationality, he was still willing to fly with her. She looked up at Janet over Brad's bowed head.

"You've got a good man here."

Janet was suddenly all teary and nodded fiercely. "So do you," she whispered. "Now go."

Ripley went.

"Front seat, Gordon," Ripley nudged his shoulder to rouse him out of his intense focus after she latched the door.

"What?"

"Brad's down. You're up. Let's go!" She didn't wait, but climbed into the front right seat and began working down the "Warm Start" checklist while Gordon moved.

Not having Brad beside her was strange.

But having Gordon beside her was so right. Which shouldn't be possible, but it was. Somewhere between calling him "lover" and punching out poor Brad's lights, Ripley had changed. Had changed so much that being with Gordon they way they'd been now made perfect sense. Perfect sense? No, she wanted…more. Wasn't that a shocker.

* * *

Gordon managed to get settled in the seat about the same time Ripley had it ready for takeoff. It took him a few moments to figure out how to patch the encrypted radio into the selectable radio feed. He couldn't find a place for the tablet that Steve had given him to monitor the drone's feed.

Ripley snatched it from his hand and stuffed it into a door pocket. Then she leaned over across the middle console until she was practically in his lap. She tapped the controls around one of the big LCD screens mounted in the main console dashboard. Steve's drone feed appeared on the screen.

But his attention was on the line of her shoulder and neck. And the smell of her. Her scent was so unique that he'd never been able to classify it, had never thought to. She simply smelled like Ripley.

"I love you," he whispered over the intercom.

"You smoothie. You never said that before," she sat back up, her voice once again a tease as she exchanged hand signals with Brenna.

Hadn't he told Ripley that he loved her? It felt as if he had.

Gordon looked around in time to see Janet climbing up the ladder on the side of the hull close beside his seat. It was one of the strange parts of starting an Aircrane. On every engine start, a mechanic climbed a dozen feet up until their head was just a foot or two from the massive rotor whirling above. From there they performed a final visual check, which was very effective because the engines were uncowled—their workings visible for all to see.

"You certainly showed me enough times, though," Ripley said softly. "I'm sorry that I was so slow to pick up on that."

"You'll get better with practice," Gordon was finding that himself. At first thinking about being in love with Ripley had been a deep shock, but he was now to the point where he couldn't imagine not loving her. Not even when she was in a pissed-off stupid mood like a few minutes ago.

"I thought we were already pretty good, but I'll practice with you anytime you want...lover."

There was a strange pause before the final word that he wasn't going to try to analyze. As if she was tasting it for the first time. No, he absolutely wasn't going to ask what she was thinking.

Ripley waved at Janet's thumbs-up from safely to the side and then lifted off to head back to the fire. Firehawk *Oh-three* was inbound for refueling and Ripley waggled *Diana Prince's* rotor in a friendly wave.

"Not quite the kind of practice I meant," Gordon figured that was a safe enough reply. Then he pictured her with her back against the glass of the bathroom wall and her eyes closed as he took her in the shower. "But that's a date."

To stop the conversation before it ran completely our of hand, Gordon switched the encrypted radio into the shared circuit.

* * *

"I have his location," Steve said over the radio. "What he called R-17 is our T-15. That means that there must have been two more thermite reactions back in the fire that we missed. Probably from before our arrival."

Ripley didn't need to be a genius to figure out what they were talking about. Steve had numbered each thermite booby trap as it led away from the fire's point of origin. Someone else had a different numbering system. That meant they'd overheard a bad guy.

"Vanessa is closest."

"Vanessa," Gordon called over the radio. "Make a pass or two over the area Steve identified. Make it look as if you're carrying water back and forth. See if you can spot this guy."

"Roger."

"Steve, can you get me the other end? Where he's headed?"

"Still working on it. I figured to focus on the mobile element first."

"Good call. Now hurry it up. Sunset isn't that far off."

Ripley had reached the Son River. She lined up and lowered the snorkel to refill the tanks. "Why is sunset important?"

"The transmission Steve intercepted said that 'they'd really show the Vietnamese scum tonight.' Or words like that. Tonight is ninety minutes off."

Ripley came in close behind the two Firehawks. They flew side by side along the latest firebreak, knocking a double-wide swath of fire out of the crown. She went for a lighter coverage intended to cool the whole area farther. Ripley made four separate runs dumping twenty-five percent of her load each time.

"I do like this aircraft," Gordon kept turning around to watch the results of the drop out the observer's window wall.

"She's such a neat little, sweet little craft. Never mind, you still don't know Gilbert and Sullivan."

"Same show, or a different one? Are there more than one?"

"There are over a dozen, but that's the same one."

"What's it about?" Gordon sounded genuinely interested.

"How do you do that?"

"Do what?"

"Do what!" Ripley could only shake her head as she returned to the river. The two Firehawks, with Mickey's 212 in formation this time, were already headed back to the fire. "How do you segment your emotions like that?"

"Segment them from what?" He was poking at the damn screen, changing colors and zoom factors. Was he even paying attention?

"I need to decide whether or not to get a new pair of boots and what color dress to wear to thc ball." She loaded up another twenty-five hundred gallons of water and turned back for the fire.

"Red," he said in a gravelly voice. "You, in a slinky red dress? Oh yeah, now we're talking."

"You heard that?" She glanced over but he hadn't looked up from the screen. "Are you really listening to me?"

"Not any more. I'm still back on the slinky red dress. Do you tango?"

"No!"

"Me neither. Too bad. Bet we'd look good together. Well you would; no one would notice me. Not with you around."

She would. He was the sort of man she'd never have noticed before, and couldn't help noticing now. He left far more of an impression than an alpha like Mark or everybody's buddy Mickey. He was...

Ripley had no idea how to finish that sentence. Why did that happen every single time she tried to describe Gordon to herself?

Asking the question didn't help her find the answer.

Chapter 20

*T*he *rugged landscape broke* the firefight into several pieces.

A long sideways leg of wind-driven fire had sliced to the west.

The eastern branch that he hadn't dared touch, for fear of revealing their knowledge to the arsonists armed with thermite, was now open for the battle. Thank goodness. There were a half-dozen villages under immediate threat.

He now unleashed everything MHA and Tham Chau could bring to bear on the eastern flank. They slammed into the flank like a juggernaut; nothing was going to stop them until it was killed dead.

A third head, a nasty burn punching into the center of the massive park, climbed up the middle between the two other fronts.

Fighting the center of a fire was typically a fool's errand. Every effort would be in constant risk of being flanked to either side. A wind shift, or even an unexpected fire jump across the uneven terrain, could trap and kill a ground team.

"Stay on the east," Gordon told Mickey and the three Firehawks. It was where the Vietnamese ground teams were concentrated anyway.

Tham Chau had protested, but Gordon was forced to ignore that. He couldn't win the central firefight without any assistance on the ground.

Yet Steve had localized the other end of the arsonists' radio communication as being in the general vicinity of this middle fork of the fire.

With everyone fighting the eastern front, the chances of tripping another thermite booby trap was significantly lowered. Besides, they had cleared them all the way up to the villages that clustered near the center of the park. Hundreds of homes, thousands of residents whose homes might now be saved.

But if the one traveling arsonist was returning to base…he'd be somewhere near the central head.

Publicly he re-tasked Vanessa to "fight" the central fire; and privately on the encrypted radio he kept her after their elusive quarry.

Steve sent the conventional drone over the eastern fire and Gordon used his data feed to keep an eye on that fire. He assigned whole sections of the firefight to Robin, Mickey, Jeannie, and Vern aloft with Mark.

Gordon wanted these bad guys. And he wanted them badly. He would fly oversight on the central head.

"Work with Vanessa," he told Ripley.

"Against that?" She nodded toward the middle fire burning fast and hot along the steep slopes. "*Diana Prince* and an MD 530 against a hellcat wildfire. Sounds like my kind of impossible challenge."

"Go for it, Wonder Woman."

And she did.

Ripley never ceased to amaze him. He had just given her an impossible task that could never succeed, and she'd made it a joke and taken it in stride.

It made her outburst at the airport all the more surprising… outburst and a fine right punch. Her attack on Weasel Williams had been justified, even the admiral agreed. Though it still rankled deep inside that she was the one to deck him and not Gordon. It also really bothered him that she had slept with… that. He didn't expect her to be a twenty-nine-year-old virgin. Or a thirty-two-year-old one or…he didn't even know when her birthday was. But knowing that Slime-ball Navy Boy had ever had his hands on her incredible body just pissed him off.

Then he connected the pieces and he laughed.

"What?" Ripley asked.

Nope! There was no way he was explaining that one to her.

Gordon himself had never struck at anyone, except the most dangerous man he'd ever met. What idiot would ever think of attempting to punch Mark Henderson? His kind of idiot. One who thought he was about to lose Ripley Vaughan just two days after he met her.

Ripley had taken on a much less dangerous target, poor Brad.

But now Gordon understood that she'd done it for the same reason he had. She'd "used" him sexually, trying to prove that her walls were as high as the average male's. And for just a moment, it had worked. She'd convinced herself that she'd scared him off. And it had taken Janet to see through it.

"Do you really love Gordon so much that you had to punch Brad?"

He had overheard Janet's question and scooted for the safety of the Aircrane's cockpit while he tried to figure that out for himself. He'd just realized that he'd felt that way since the moment he met Ripley Vaughan.

No. He definitely wouldn't be explaining himself any time soon.

* * *

Ripley led a two-woman attack on a kilometer-long fire front. Worse, per Gordon's instructions, Vanessa was traveling several minutes extra each way for water so that she could continue her search for the roving arsonist. Because the area was between the central and eastern head, it wasn't safe for a ground team to search for him, even if they could have crossed the rugged terrain. The risk of them getting caught between the fires was unacceptable.

Gordon remained focused on the eastern fire, coordinating everything from refueling breaks to attack plans and ground efforts. She eavesdropped as he conferred with Mark.

Those were fascinating conversations. Despite Mark's Night Stalker Major (retired) personality, he was an exceptional—if brusque—trainer. He never told Gordon what to do, but let him use Mark as a sounding board to test his ideas.

At first she was a little piqued that he didn't ask her first, but she got over that quickly enough listening to them as she and Vanessa did what little they could to narrow the central fire. Gordon and Mark were no longer talking about fire tactics.

In her Seahawk, she'd been noted as a top tactician, able to execute any order flawlessly.

They were talking *strategy,* which was almost another language.

"If we can crowd the fire up against this slope, we can defeat it when it tries to cross the ridgeline."

"This firebreak would be more effective if we shifted it two hundred meters south. It will take the load off Ground Team Four until reinforcements can reach them—those guys have been at the center of the fight for the last forty-eight hours and must be hammered."

Carly talked about burn behavior as if wildfire was a conscious thinking force capable of choosing which type of tree, undergrowth, and terrain burned the best. Any of the species that Carly didn't know, Jeannie could backfill.

Rather than making her feel incompetent, it made her feel included. With each passing moment she gained a better understanding of how she fit into a firefight, even if the one she was battling mostly by herself was by and large pointless.

They weren't merely knocking crown fires down within reach of ground teams. The Firehawks and the 212 were double-, even triple-overlapping their loads to fully extinguish hard-to-reach areas, forcing the fire into more accessible terrain. Twice there were medivacs of injured firefighters and several times they switched to helitack—picking up a crew of a dozen per Firehawk—and repositioning the teams at tactical weak spots during critical fights.

And still she circled from the Son River to the ever-nearing Son Doong Cave.

The countryside here was astonishingly beautiful. She wanted to share it with Gordon, but he was too busy, not even looking up when she had to return to the airport to refuel—not a moment she'd been looking forward to.

"He's asleep," Janet informed her.

"Is that safe?" Ripley was having trouble meeting Janet's eyes.

"Tham Chau had a top doctor from the local hospital come out to see him. He's the one who suggested sleep."

"That's good, I guess." She kicked the pavement. She ought to be kicking herself.

"Ripley."

She inspected her boots some more.

"Ripley," Janet ducked down and twisted so that her face was directly in Ripley's field of view and looked her right in the eyes.

As she stood, Ripley was forced to look up as well.

"We get that wasn't you when you hit Brad."

"How do you know?"

Inexplicably Janet hugged her. "Why do you think we requested every assignment we could get with you? And we had to sign contracts with Mount Hood Aviation as well. We both know you, Ripley. You're the best."

"Yet I punched Brad."

"He'll recover."

Ripley couldn't help herself and smiled at Janet. "He may. Question is, will I?"

"From being in love? *God*, I hope not! It's the best thing ever, Ripley. Now go. They've got you refueled."

Brenna passed by giving her two *Banh Mi* sandwiches, two Chuong Duong orange sodas, and a thumbs-up.

She handed a soda and sandwich to Gordon as she reboarded. Once he finished his, he took over long enough for her to eat as well, showing he wasn't completely unaware of her. At least as a pilot.

"How is this monster so light on the controls?"

"*Diana Prince* is not a monster."

"Okay, to quote your Gilbert and whoever, 'she's a neat little sweet little craft.' Just like her pilot."

"Sweet? What drugs are you taking?"

"Ripley Vaughan. Straight up. Undiluted."

Ripley took back the flight controls. "Go play with your fire."

"Don't really need to. They've got a good handle on it. That head will be trapped inside the hour. If all goes well, they'll have it fully contained this evening and dead by the morning. Then we can really tackle this head. Until then, I'm just going to sit here and think about you in a slinky red dress."

"Dream on!"

"Oh, I will. While I'm dreaming about that I can also fantasize about how you're going to make it up to me for punching Brad."

"I'm what? You think that I'm going to give you awesome and amazing make-up sex because I punched my copilot?"

"Guilt has its uses," Gordon agreed happily. "I'm really looking forward to it."

Ripley couldn't believe this was Gordon. No, she could. This was almost the guy who had accused her of being "serious eye candy." Now that she looked back, she could see that he'd been trying to be the guy who "fit in" rather than being himself. But he'd also thought that about her from the very beginning. He saw her as beautiful. He also saw her so strong. And Janet said that Ripley loved him, just in case she didn't know that herself. Well, she did now.

And, dammit, he was right—the make-up sex was going to be awesome.

* * *

Gordon gasped in surprise as they crossed the ridge.

There'd been no sign, no warning.

One moment they'd been in clear and level flight.

The next a tailwind completely cut the lift out from under them.

He'd been riding his hands on the controls, liking the connection with Ripley through the shared movements. Suddenly she was heaving up on the collective, feeding every horsepower the Aircrane could deliver into the rotor.

Downdraft and turbulent winds were common on the backside of a ridge, but helicopters by their nature were much less susceptible to such issues.

A few hundred meters in either direction were thick with smoke flowing smoothly over the ridge. They were in a pocket of clear air.

Even the massive climbing power of the big Aircrane barely slowed their descent. If they were in a fixed-wing air tanker, they'd be crashed into the trees already.

It was the same problem the stealth helicopter had in the bin Laden compound before it crashed. The air trapped by the compound's high walls became so turbulent that there was nothing for the rotor blades to bite on and create lift.

The smoke to either side was now rolling toward them.

"Two hundred meters down," he called out, knowing Ripley would be too busy flying to look down at the flight instruments. "Three hundred."

So far the land had fallen away at the same rate they were descending, but they were going to run out of steep, descending hillside in moments. The jungle of the valley floor was fast approaching.

The smoke closed over them like the slamming of a door. The heat in the cabin rose sharply as the view completely disappeared.

It was suddenly so dark in the cabin that Gordon flipped on the console lights. The big landing lights did little more than glare off the smoke.

"I saw something," Ripley grunted out. "Not sure." She twisted the Aircrane to the west, higher into the narrow mountain valley rather than lower.

"Down four hundred. Rate of descent slowing," Gordon managed. He trusted Ripley's instincts and *Diana Prince* was recovering better than any MD 530 or Firehawk could have.

"I always like good news with my morning blackout."

"More of a gray out." The landing lights revealed that the gray smoke was thick with dark ash. "Outside temp crossing upward of one-fifty." Which meant that they'd have even less lift due to the thinning of the air as it became hotter.

"I'm not sure that the air conditioning was made for that," Ripley managed as she slalomed around the first tree to stick its head through the smoke. "This is good. I was rusty on panic."

Gordon was glad that he wasn't the only one who quoted from bad firefighting movies when he was stressed. Of course she'd quoted Richard Dreyfuss, who had far more macho in *Always* than Gordon's John Goodman.

The next tree came close enough that it might have passed between the rear wheels as Ripley slewed sideways.

"Not exactly agile here." The big Aircrane could be precise, but for agile they needed his MD hel—

"Bank right!" Gordon called out.

Ripley followed his call without hesitation. The smoke had a current here and it curved abruptly upward—he'd take any updraft they could find, even in a cloud of superheated smoke. They punched through the wall of it and arrived in clear air. In the calmer air she was able to stabilize their flight and ease them into a hover.

Gordon's heart rate was running faster than the rotor's spin, not that he'd noticed it until this moment. If Ripley had been one tiny bit less of a pilot, they'd be dead by now.

After flipping into the Oregon lake, he'd said that crashing and burning once in a lifetime was enough for anyone. He decided that this last thirty seconds of flight was something else he could say a grateful farewell to, as in *never again*.

The outside temperature gauge plummeted, first back into October-in-Vietnam normal temperatures and then ten degrees cooler. The lowest he'd seen since leaving Oregon.

"Look at that."

Gordon glanced up. They were in a great circle of smoke, no, a solid dome shape. He could dimly see the wall climbing to all sides, passing directly over their bubble of clear air.

"No, down."

What he saw didn't make sense at first. The jungle around the edges of gray dome was actually slightly above them. Their refuge was over a hundred yards across—at least four times the diameter of their own rotor. But the jungle below them lay the same distance below. It was like someone had taken a giant cookie cutter and punched a hole in the earth. They hovered in the center of the opening. The little bit of light that penetrated the swirling smoke revealed a vast cavity in the earth.

"It's a doline into the Son Doong Caves," Ripley voice was a gasp of wonder.

"A who into the what?" Though he certainly couldn't question the wonder. It was one of the most dramatic settings he'd ever seen. The inverse of the time he'd taken his father's ranch helicopter and landed it on the very top of the Red Butte that gave Red Butte, Wyoming its name—a stunt his father had thrashed him soundly for, for wasting time and fuel and making a spectacle of himself.

There he'd been perched over a vast expanse of arid land, the iron red soil turned almost bloody by the setting sun. Here, they were hovering over a lush jungle that filled the great circular cutout below them. Even in the dim, smoke-shrouded light, the color was vibrantly alive with green growth.

"Doline, a giant sinkhole. It's from the collapse of a cave's roof."

"This was a cave?" He could see the curves that indicated this indeed had once been a domed roof, the upper walls arching inward. Down below, the space expanded to two football fields in size, maybe three. It would be enough room to park a half-dozen Aircranes without any problem. Even the Antonov An-124 transport would fit in here easily. The jungle wasn't as thick as it was above the rim, it grew on the rough-and-tumble rock of the collapsed roof—an entire underground fairy world now open to the sky. "There's no way that all of this was once underground."

"The Son Doong Cave is nine kilometers long and they only discovered it in 2009. Tham Chau told us about it, the largest cave in the world. This isn't even the biggest chamber." Ripley began descending toward the cave's floor.

"I'm not sure this is the smartest idea."

"You want to fly back into that?" She nodded upward.

Gordon looked up at the heavy swirls of smoke being kept aloft by some strange current that was pumping cool air upward out of the caves.

"Not my first choice."

She eased over to a clear perch, a flat-topped hill that rose fifty feet above the jungle growing on the floor of the ancient cave-in. Unlike Red Butte, with the sharp escarpment of its limestone cap, this hill looked like a stack of decreasing-sized pancakes. Actually, "It kind of looks like a giant had diarrhea and pooped out layers of rock."

"It's called a stalagmite. I've never seen one so big. Haven't you ever been in a cave?"

"Sure," Gordon replied as she settled the Aircrane atop the stalagmite. There was just room for all three wheels to be safely on the flat top.

Ripley locked the wheel brakes so that they didn't roll off, and eased the engines down to idle. "We should let the madness up above stabilize a bit."

"Calling *Diana Prince*," Steve's voice squawked over the radio.

"This is Ripley," she called back.

"Where are you?" His signal faded out at the end. The drone must have passed directly over the doline for them to be heard. Anything else would block their radio signal.

Ripley made a long transmission, repeatedly describing their situation to give Steve a chance to discover when he had a drone directly over them enough to keep a clear signal.

"You guys okay?"

"Happy as two hogs in a waller," Ripley told him. "Just going to let that turbulence settle for a few minutes."

Gordon snorted out a laugh that the mic picked up before she let go of the transmit switch.

"What?"

"Just picturing wrestling with you in the mud. Not quite what I imagined, but I could get into it."

"Finchley! You're not getting me in a bikini for some mud wrestling."

"How about a bikini in general? Or are you more of a one-piece gal?"

"I," she climbed out of her seat, "am going to stretch my legs since we're here for a few minutes. Because it's completely clear where your mind has gone."

Gordon supposed it was.

There wasn't room in the pilot's seat, so he rose close behind her and followed. As soon as she stopped to open the cockpit door, he dropped into the more spacious aft-facing pilot's seat and yanked her into his lap.

He covered her initial protest with a kiss.

She sighed against his kiss and then leaned harder into it, running a hand up around his neck. As he worked his way from her mouth down her neck, she lay her head back against the top of the radio console. With the tip of his nose he could feel her pulse quickening at the base of her neck.

He unzipped the front of her flightsuit and buried his face between her breasts, only the thin cotton of her t-shirt separating him from heaven.

"A man could lose himself right here forever and die happy."

"In my cleavage?" Ripley's laugh rippled against his face.

"Can you tell me a better place to be?"

In response she wrapped her arms about his head and he was overwhelmed with the sensation of being held—of being precisely where he belonged—lost in a deep, dark… "Hey!"

"Hey what?" Ripley voice was smooth and languid as she kissed the top of his head.

"Lost in the deep…"

"…cleavage of a dark Wonder Woman."

"No," he struggled to sit up and she finally let him.

Her expression was deeply puzzled by his abrupt change of mood. "No?"

"Well," he looked down at her cleavage where his face had just been. Where one of his hands was still full of the finest breast he'd ever held. "Well, yes. But no."

He could see Ripley getting irritated at the sudden change, but some thought had occurred to him. He was halfway back down to nuzzling her chest, when the rest of the non-Ripley thought came back.

"Lost in the deep, dark—"

"Which is what you're supposed to be doing at this moment," she growled. "Or letting go of my breast and letting me off your lap."

"It's an awfully nice breast. I would hate to let go." He rubbed a thumb over the tip earning him a sharp hiss of frustration. "You have really amazing breasts, Ripley."

"My best feature, I'm sure. Are you going to do something about it?"

"No," Gordon looked out the tall aft-facing window. Directly behind the Aircrane, the side of the towering stalagmite sloped down to the jungle floor. But it didn't stop there. Just beyond the base of the hill was a vast, deep opening. An entrance to the cave.

He took his hand off Ripley's breast, which was hard to do because it really was such a very nice one, and grabbed the handheld microphone hooked at the aft pilot's position.

"Steve, they're in a cave. That's why you're having trouble finding them."

"Huh!" Gordon could feel Steve thinking about it. "That would certainly change their signal pattern. Give me a minute."

"Take all the time you need," Gordon hung up the mic and placed his hand and face right back where they had been a moment before.

* * *

"Goddamn you, Finchley!" But no matter how much he was ticking her off, Ripley couldn't help but arch up against his mouth where he had buried it against her breast.

His hand wandered down the inside of her flightsuit, inside her shorts, and cupped her hard.

She couldn't find enough leverage lying in his lap to press against all the parts of him that she wanted to press. But Gordon didn't make her wait. The analyst who thought about caves and radio transmitters was gone. This was her deeply sexual man, the one who she wanted to take her apart. She clamped her arms around his head to make sure he didn't go astray this time and prepared herself for an incredible ride.

This wasn't going to be some short, fast shot at ecstasy. Actually, it would be, but somehow it was totally different from what she had done to him this morning. This morning she had used him, as if it somehow had been a smart idea to drive him away.

But Gordon wasn't doing this for himself, to her. Just the opposite, he was doing it to her and yet for her. Somehow he was able to forgive her idiocy and just—

All thought blurred away for a moment as he found some wild new connection within her body.

And even as she strained against his mouth and hands, she knew how he had done it. How he'd forgiven her.

It was because he'd never felt there was anything to forgive. It was because he loved her.

"Too simple," she murmured to herself. It was too simple that this is what love felt like. It felt like belonging.

It felt like rising up.

It felt like arching into—

"Mayday! Mayday! Mayday!"

It felt like that, but not in Vanessa's voice.

"*Merda!*" Vanessa swore over the radio. "I found the mobile agent. But he has got me."

Ripley considered warning her that the FCC wasn't a big fan of profanity over the radio. But since the curse was in Italian, the FCC was in the US, and they were in Vietnam, she decided to leave well enough alone.

She also considered turning off the radio until Gordon had finished driving her completely mad with need and release.

"*Sto sparato!*" Vanessa's curse was emphatic.

"Vanessa?" Gordon grabbed the microphone with the hand that had been cradling Ripley's head a moment before. His other hand was still deep down inside her flightsuit. She was frozen in mid-arch against his palm.

"We are, I am shot. No, not me. My helicopter. It is shot. At least that is what Tham Chau says. Several times. I know that we are still flying, but my hydraulics are very bad."

Gordon pulled his other hand free.

Absurdly, Ripley had been so close that his final gesture tipped her over the edge and her body shook and shuddered with her release as she struggled to sit upright.

Gordon wrapped his arm about her waist for a second and just held her tightly against his chest. She rested her forehead on his strong shoulder, giving herself a few seconds. Hardly daring to believe that she had found a man so thoughtful.

"Talk to me," Gordon said.

For a moment she was wondering if Gordon had lost his mind and was too thoughtful, but then she heard the click as he released the transmit switch.

Ripley pulled herself together. Grabbing the back of the two pilot chairs, she hauled herself up out of his lap and managed to collapse into her seat and pull on her helmet.

She cycled up *Diana Prince's* engines and looked up at the sky. The gray dome of hot smoke still danced across the surface of the cool wind rising out of the cave. Well, she was about to show it just what a pair of Wonder Women could do.

Gordon climbed into the seat beside her and donned his helmet. He continued talking to Vanessa through the drone's link. Keeping the conversation steady and calm.

Just as she was finishing the last of the pre-takeoff checks, Gordon reached out and ran a hand along her cheek. He smiled despite what was happening, despite the fear she had felt jolt through him just as strongly as the pleasure he'd given her. His smile said a thousand things.

It said just how much he had enjoyed doing what he had done to her.

It also had a softness. The alpha might revel in the sex, but the man loved her. And that was more than she had ever imagined to be possible, because she loved him back. Their situation was utterly ridiculous at the moment, but she finally knew that one thing—all the way down to her still-shaky core.

Ripley heaved up on the collective, put the nose down, and drove straight up. This is what the Erickson did better than any other helicopter made—it climbed like a demon. It held the world record for the fastest time to reach altitudes of three, six, and nine kilometers and also the record for highest level flight by any helicopter at eleven kilometers—one of the few helos able to even climb over thirty-five thousand feet.

A single ember had started a fire in the jungle on the cave's floor.

She circled closer to the wall, flicked the water-release setting to salvo, and hit the release on her cyclic. Twenty-five hundred gallons of water blasted the fire out of existence. In seconds she was ten tons lighter and taking the escalator straight up.

Even as the small fire below died in a shroud of steam, they slammed into the smoky dome above. The ride was rough, but they had enough vertical speed that it took less than thirty seconds to punch through into clear air.

Gordon slashed a hand toward the northeast and Ripley raced in that direction. A final glance back revealed that their temporary haven was indeed lost beneath the seething ocean of smoke, but it was there. Deep inside her, for the first time ever, she knew that there was a perfectly safe, perfectly clear space. A space where Gordon's love would always reside.

Three kilometers and less than a minute later, they cleared a ridge and could see her. Vanessa was easy to spot, the smudge of burning hydraulic fluid created a black plume behind her. Even with the smoke of the approaching fire filling the valley, the burning black trail stood out.

There was nowhere to land except in the trees. No river. Not even a clearing.

She was racing down the valley toward them, trying to get clear before losing altitude or control. The other problem was that she was racing directly toward the face of the oncoming fire.

"Vanessa. Gordon here. Ease down. The hydraulic system on the MD 530 is only about vibration dampening. You should still have control; it's an all-mechanical control linkage." His voice was good, soothing.

Ripley's reaction to a partial loss of engine power had been to punch her copilot. Gordon's reaction to having one of his closest friends shot at was to talk her down. Yet something else she had to learn from him. Or was it another reason that this could never work between them? Just how much did love conquer? She had no real experience to judge by, because what she'd felt after a year with Petty Officer Williams paled in comparison to what she felt after two weeks with Gordon Finchley.

"It is not only my hydraulics," Vanessa answered back and continued to race in their direction.

Ripley used her altitude and position ahead of Vanessa to survey the area at the mouth of the valley. No clearing, but there was a river. She slewed the *Diana Prince* over for a look and could see the rocky bottom. It looked fast, but not deep.

"First possible landing is directly below me," she moved to hover over the area of a relatively calm pool. Ripley wondered why the other MHA helicopters weren't responding. Then she saw that she and Vanessa were still on the encrypted radio. No one else except Steve would know what was going on.

"Water?" Vanessa groaned. "Like Gordon, I must crash in water? That is not fun."

Ripley moved farther aloft to get a wider view. Over a small hill she spotted a cleared area that might have been a farm. "Swing wide around this hill below me. There is a clearing on the other side." Fire was fast approaching the area, but there should be enough time for a rescue.

"Thank you, Ripley. I will try."

Vanessa carved a turn around the hill and Ripley could see the MD 530 appear to stumble in the air.

Gordon cried out as the little helicopter tumbled viciously onto its side in mid-flight.

By some miracle Vanessa forced it back into level flight, though now she was flying more sideways than forward.

The next fifteen seconds she and Gordon could do nothing but lean forward and watch. The MD made another near fatal twist toward the trees, but finally settled on its skids with a hard thump at one edge of the clearing. One of the skids buckled, tipping the helicopter halfway over, and the rotor shredded itself as it beat on the field. It almost flipped the helicopter, but finally it stayed upright and the now bladeless rotor began to slow.

Despite the destruction of her rotor blades, the small clearing didn't seem big enough for both helicopters to land. But with some creative thinking, it was. The top of the MD's broken rotor stood barely ten feet above the tilled soil and the Aircrane's rotor blades spun at over fifteen feet. Ripley was able to land with the crippled MD parked *under* the canopy of *Diana Prince's* spinning rotor.

Ripley tried not to feel bad about settling in the middle of someone's neatly-arranged vegetable garden. It was a home that the residents must have evacuated just ahead of the oncoming fire. Of course, in minutes the fire would be here and the loss would be far more than the damage of having a couple of helicopters parked in their garden.

"Keep it running," Gordon commanded before racing out of the Aircrane.

When he opened the door, the stink and heat of wood smoke swirled into the cabin. The smoke was thick enough that she could see it veiling Vanessa's crashed helicopter though its crumpled remains were barely thirty feet away.

In moments, Gordon was helping both women out of the crashed MD. He and Vanessa embraced tightly, the hug of two good friends. She could see that now. Besides, if she couldn't trust Gordon, who could she?

There was a good joke. She'd never trusted a man, not even Weasel back before he earned his nickname. That's what had sent her searching for him that day. If she'd been more trusting, he could have had his caterer and her as well.

How was it that she'd learned to never trust? Her parents were completely trust wor—

"Gordon?" Steve called on the radio.

"This is Ripley, he's out helping Tham Chau and Vanessa. They're okay."

"That's great, but we have another problem."

"More important than the forest fire that's about overrun us? Excellent. I need a distraction." Just because this wasn't the main leg of the fire, didn't mean that it couldn't kill them.

Steve paused for a long moment. He always took a moment to digest her statements like that. It was as if he was always searching for a comeback, but was too straightforward a guy to think one up. Gordon never missed her sense of humor.

"I found their base. I was able to follow the shooter with one of the drone's infrared cameras. He's warmer than the jungle by just enough and he led me right there. I'd never have seen him if he hadn't shot Vanessa's helicopter."

"Great! Send in the Army."

"There is no one in that area; you landed in the area that Gordon said to keep clear. And they're fortified inside a small cave. I guess with over three hundred caves in the park, that's no surprise. But I mean fortified. They built a wall across the front. Sunset is in half an hour and we can't lose them."

Ripley looked up trying to see the long shadows, but it was already mostly dark down here in the shadowed valley. And that was without the smoke.

The smell abruptly intensified when the cockpit door was opened again and first Tham Chau, then Vanessa stumbled into the cockpit.

Tham Chau collapsed into the aft-facing pilot's seat, cradling her arm carefully.

Vanessa leaned forward and hugged Ripley, partly around the shoulder and partly around the helmet. She planted a kiss on the top of the latter.

"Your guidance was very timely. Thank you." Then she too collapsed to sit on the floor facing backward with her feet in the stairwell.

Gordon began clambering over Vanessa to get to his seat. "The MD is a total loss. Get us out of here."

"No!" Vanessa wrapped her arms about one of his legs to keep him in place. "We have over fifty gallons of thermite powder and magnesium ribbons on my MD in five gallon buckets. If that much burns, then this fire will never stop."

Gordon grunted and remained still for a moment, one hand on the back of his seat and Vanessa's arms still wrapped around one of his legs. There wasn't room in the cockpit for four people and all those buckets. She didn't even want them on her aircraft.

"Ripley? Can you lift the Little Bird?"

"Easily, if I dropped the tank and hooked up a hoist. That would take me about two hours, if I had the right equipment.

I'll get right on it, though the fire is about five minutes away. So you might think about a different plan."

"How about those mounting holes beside the tank…and some rope or wire?"

"That's…" she hadn't thought about that. "Brilliant! She's not certified for it, but each of those loops can carry the MD's entire weight a couple times over. Rig it to both sides so that I'm balanced and there shouldn't be a problem. Check the locker by the base of the ladder for some line."

He turned to go and Ripley stopped him and told him what Steve had found. For a moment Gordon grimaced, looking toward the conflicting priorities of the imminent fire, the crippled MD, and the location of the fire-wielding terrorists soon to be lost in the night. If she was them, she'd be on the move at the moment of nightfall, untraceable under the jungle's canopy.

Then Gordon smiled brilliantly, grabbed Ripley by the chin strap, and kissed her hard. Hard enough to make her lips hurt and her head spin, though so briefly that she didn't have a moment to do more than groan against the kiss. He grabbed Vanessa and was out of the cockpit.

* * *

Gordon scrabbled through the locker Ripley had indicated and found the rope he needed. The first problem was that the loops on the frame that he needed to thread the rope through were ten feet in the air.

He squatted in front of Vanessa. "Up on my shoulders."

"You are serious?"

"Yes. Now." Gingerly she placed a leg over either shoulder and he rose carefully to his feet. "Here," he handed her one end of the rope. "Run it through that loop," he indicated the heavy bracket mounted on the side of the Erickson's spine above the water tank. It must be for mounting some other piece of equipment.

She looped it through and pulled an extra ten feet.

"Same thing on the other side. Watch your head," and he walked around the end of the water tank hanging down. She didn't have to duck to be clear of the high spine of the Aircrane.

Through the open door at the rear of the cockpit he could see Tham Chau watching him from the aft pilot's seat and Ripley twisted around to see what was happening. He shot her a teasing grin and patted his hands where they were holding onto Vanessa's thighs.

Ripley shot him a thumbs-up.

They had the rope looped through the other side in moments. Then he eased Vanessa back down to the ground. He quickly tied a loop around the crippled MD 530's rotor head.

He had to stare at the line for about thirty seconds, with Vanessa fidgeting beside him and watching the thickening smoke, before he figured out how to make the knots do what he needed. If there was one thing he'd learned riding after cattle on a Wyoming ranch, it was that if you just thought hard enough about it, you could make a good piece of rope and the right knots do almost anything.

Gordon tied everything off, but didn't have quite enough slack to run the loose ends back into the cabin. He wasn't exactly sure what he had planned to do with them, but he'd expected to figure that out once he got there.

But they were too short. The red glow running toward them through the trees told him that he didn't have time to retie them.

Those ends had to be held, tightly.

That's when he spotted the open doors on the firefighting water tank. At the bottom edge of the big orange tank were two, twenty foot long, steel louvers. They were hinged down their length so that they could swing open and release the water. If they were strong enough to hold back ten tons of water, they were strong enough to hold his two ropes.

He held the two ends side by side and yelled for Ripley to close the drop doors. They snapped shut abruptly enough to make him jump. He tugged on each rope. Secure as could be.

Now for the tricky part.

* * *

"You're going to do what?" Ripley yelled at Gordon.

"Don't have time for this, Rip," Gordon nodded toward the trees.

The fire was close enough that she could feel the air temperature rising.

Trying to tease her with a beautiful woman on his shoulders had been a cute joke.

Using the rope harness and the drop tank's louvered door to lift the entire broken helicopter—once she understood what he was trying to do—was brilliant.

But this next part was utter lunacy.

"If you have a better solution, Ripley, I'm listening." But he wasn't stopping. He continued tying knots every two feet down another length of rope.

If she had a better idea, she wouldn't be so upset.

She glared at the little helicopter. A dozen plastic buckets of thermite powder and a lucky thirteenth, with dozens of section of magnesium ribbons to ignite them. And Gordon was proposing riding in the towed helicopter to set them all off.

"If you die doing this stunt, I'm gonna track you down and kill you."

"Deal."

The gaps in the jungle had resolved from red glow to active flame.

"Gordon…" But she couldn't find the words. There was too much to say. Too much she wanted to share. Not that she'd ever been big on sharing, but with Gordon she wanted to experiment with changing that.

"Trust me." He stepped into a rescue harness, pulled the straps over his shoulders—she flipped a twist out of one of them and used it as an excuse to brush a hand down his shoulder—and buckled himself in. He tied the end of the rope to the big D-ring on the front of the harness.

"Not giving me a lot of choice."

He gave her one of those charming smiles. "I am sorry about that. All the choices you want—after this is over."

"Promise?" She didn't know quite what promise she was asking for.

"Promise! Now get along." He turned her toward the cockpit and slapped her butt like she was some cow to shoo along.

If it was to be their last contact ever, she didn't want it to be a slap on her butt. She took an extra moment to turn back to him.

"Remember. Return or I kill you."

"Got it."

She dropped a kiss on his cheek and then they both rushed aboard their separate helicopters.

In moments he called "Ready" over the radio and she fed power into her rotor with a raised collective. The fire had reached the jungle wall and she could feel the heat radiating through her windshield as she pulled aloft.

"Vanessa, call it out."

"Call what out?"

"Slack on the line."

"Oh, of course. I am sorry. I still cannot believe you are letting him do this."

As if Ripley had a choice. Maybe she did. Maybe if she'd told him not to do this, he wouldn't have. But she also knew that his solution was so far out of the box that even with a week of thinking, she wouldn't find a better one.

"Forty feet," Vanessa called out. "Thirty, twenty…"

Ripley slowed her ascent so that she didn't jolt the lines as they took the weight of the MD helicopter. She could barely feel it when *Diana Prince* picked up the light load.

"You should climb quickly now," Vanessa called out. "The flames are very close to him."

Giving it all the power she dared, they were soon above the clearing, then the flames…and wallowing in blackout smoke.

"Vanessa, get up here. Right seat. I need some help."

One pilot could fly an Aircrane by herself…if she had six extra hands.

"Get on the radar and keep me from running into any mountains." Then she hit the radio. "Steve, I need the coordinates of their hideout."

Their location flashed up on the heat map that Steve had linked to the cockpit.

If Ripley ever needed to know how to act after a crash, she'd behave like Gordon or Vanessa. It still didn't seem right that they weren't together. But if they were, she wouldn't be with Gordon, so she wasn't complaining.

It took forever to claw their way clear of the smoke. Even straight up altitude didn't break them free, they were over the heart of the fire and the smoke column had reached tens of thousands of feet up into the jet stream.

Finally clear of the smoke, she could see that twilight was already upon them.

Chapter 21

Ripley raced the Aircrane toward the barricaded cave and tried not to think about Gordon sitting in the MD helo dangling on the ropes beneath her.

"Do you have eyes on him, Tham Chau?"

"Yes, two of them. An odd way to ask."

Ripley didn't take time to explain the military idiom.

"He is in the pilot's seat. I have waved," she hissed in pain. "But my injured arm wishes I hadn't done that. I think it is broken. But he has waved back."

Even Tham Chau was more polite than herself. She was the wild beast who punched her copilot because…what was it Janet had said? *Do you really love Gordon that much?*

Ripley laughed. She couldn't help herself. It was so obvious that everyone except her could see it. Well, she did now. And all they had to do was survive to see what else there might be.

"Along that river," Vanessa pointed.

This was not one of the big open stretches of the Son River. They were following the winding course of a narrow tributary of the Chay as it twisted between hillsides. Tall trees reached out from either side as if hoping to ensnare her rotors, crash her, and end this whole fiasco.

She wanted to keep low, but she had a man and a helicopter dangling seventy feet below her. At each turn she had to be careful of the amount of swing the MD helicopter took. It was a pendulum at the other end of her line. Slewing him sideways into a tree was a real possibility.

It was getting so close to full dark that she had Vanessa take the controls for a moment.

"Do *not* hit the hoist release on the cyclic," Ripley warned her. "That will open the tank doors and release the MD."

"I will not lose him for you," Vanessa answered the real reason for the order.

Ripley pulled out the night-vision goggles and clipped them onto the front of her helmet. Clicking them on turned the world into brilliant green relief. There was still plenty of ambient light for the image intensifiers to enhance. Ripley had used them for night drops any number of times, but she had never tried to fly up the gut of a narrow river valley using them.

Ripley turned off the running lights before she took back the flight controls. If the bad guys didn't have night vision, she would be invisible. The bullet holes in the MD helicopter had been instructive.

Whoever lurked in that cave had wanted to be close to the fire. The main leg, the one they had egged along with their thermite booby traps, would pass close above their hideout. The bulk of the fire that still burned to the west of that had entered the park itself. The fire's head had been beaten back and narrowed to several times smaller than its original area, but the front was still a kilometer-wide behemoth eating a path through the jungle.

They swung around the final curve in the river and she could see it. An unnatural amount of heat clarified the image all the more in her goggles.

A great wall had been built across the mouth of this secluded cave. Big enough to cover the twenty-foot high entrance. Now to hope that it wasn't strong enough to resist their battering ram.

"Now, Gordon," she transmitted over the encrypted link.

"Already on it."

Ripley waited, wishing she could remove a hand from the controls to wipe the sweat off her palms.

"Fuses lit," he announced.

At a hundred miles an hour, this was going to be a brutal maneuver. The timing was trickier than any water drop on a wildfire. She tried juggling all of the unpredictable factors in her head, but couldn't.

The river flowed close by the cave itself; several boats were tied up near the entrance. The jungle-covered cliffs rose to either side. She was aimed directly at the massive stone wall above the cave entrance.

"You better be climbing fast," she told Gordon, not daring to distract herself with the radio button.

Three hundred feet.

Two hundred.

One fifty.

At just a hundred feet from the cave wall, she let her instincts take over. She watched, like a passive observer, as all of her years of experience took control of *Diana Prince*.

Hard up on the collective—maximum power.

Full back on the cyclic—tipping the Aircrane's nose high in the air. It was like slamming on the brakes full force.

Looking down between her feet—out the part of her lower windshield not obscured by knees and rudder pedals—she could see Vanessa's ruined MD 530 helicopter swinging forward at the end of its rope. Their precious pendulum.

Just above it, she could see Gordon swinging on the end of his own knotted rope like a Cirque du Soleil trapeze artist. At least he was out of the MD.

The moment before both man and helicopter reached the peak of their arc, she pressed the tank release button.

For a moment it seemed as if nothing happened. She feared that it had all gone wrong. A single snag in the lines holding the helicopter would be fatal at this moment. Failure of their attack, and probably their flight as well.

But the MD continued its swinging arc, taking one last flight toward the false wall across the cave's entrance.

With its release, *Diana Prince* decelerated even faster, backward and away from the cliff face—now no more than a dozen meters from her wheels.

As she backed up and away, she continued to watch through her night-vision goggles. The crystal-green view showed the heat radiating out all the doors and windows of the MD helicopter—the magnesium ribbons that Gordon had lit fired off. The thermite in each of the stacked buckets began to burn in a brilliant white-red conflagration.

Gouts of flame shot through the hull just moments before it completed its arc and slammed into the cave's front wall.

Fifteen hundred pounds of MD helicopter and thermite reaction smashed through the door. It blew inward. As the burning helicopter tumbled deeper into the cave, it spewed and scattered unquenchable fire in all directions. Deep in the cave the fuel tank burned through; an explosion turned the helo into a thousand pieces of burning shrapnel.

A dozen or more people raced out of the cave, heading for the boats.

The conflagration grew as more and more of the thermite reaction took hold. Soon the cave entrance was blindingly bright and she had to look away.

A thousand meters back and five hundred up from the burning cave, she slowed to a hover. Now the fear slammed into her.

"Is he—"

"He is alive," Tham Chau assured her as she opened the back door and let in the roar of the two engines and the heavy rotor.

"You sure?" Gordon's familiar voice asked.

At first Ripley didn't cry. It just wasn't in her, never had been, except that one time in Gordon's arms.

But hearing Gordon ask the same question as when they'd rescued him from an Oregon lake, she couldn't help herself. Tears and laughter spilled from her simultaneously and she couldn't stop them.

When his strong hand rested on her shoulder, she pinned it there with the side of her helmet.

"Well," and she managed to say the *Galaxy Quest* line in unison with him this time. "That was a hell of a thing." His nervous laugh reassured her more than anything else. The mighty hero who had just shattered the bad guys' hideout in the middle of a Vietnamese jungle was still the same man she'd first met.

He swung over the jump seat and sat down between the two pilot's seats. Again the connection of his hand on her shoulder. She didn't begrudge him for a second placing a hand on Vanessa's shoulder as well. Her face too was tear-tracked.

* * *

"Did it work?" Gordon asked and peered forward.

"You did not see?" Vanessa handed him a set of NVGs.

"I was a little busy trying not to get tossed along with the helicopter."

He clicked the NVGs into place and turned them on.

The front wall across the cave mouth must have been only for show, cloth painted like rock. Vanessa's MD 530 had tumbled far into the cave, spewing fire in every direction as it went.

The people from the cave, at least any survivors, had piled into a trio of speedboats and were racing down along the river.

"How do we stop them?"

"We must capture them," Tham Chau spoke up.

Gordon didn't know how four people in an unarmed helicopter were going to capture three boatloads of bad guys. Someone was bound to have a weapon and probably a lot nastier than the handgun they'd used on the ranch to put down the occasional injured cow.

"This one is mine," Ripley announced as she rolled *Diana Prince* to fly downstream and began giving orders for Tham Chau to pass on to her army troops.

Less than a mile downstream, at a wide spot in the river, Ripley again turned to face sharply upstream. There was a long, straight stretch here and she flew down to ten feet above the water and lowered the sea snorkel.

Gordon watched as she swept up fifteen hundred gallons of water before the first boat appeared from the jungle-shrouded upper stretch of the river.

She continued flying as if she didn't see them.

"Look out!" Gordon couldn't believe she didn't see it. "You're going to—"

But it was too late!

The long strut of the sea snorkel impacted the first boat solidly in the square bow. There was hardly a jolt as the wide dive plane at the base of the strut tore the boat apart, then sheared itself off (exactly as Ripley had told him it was designed to do if it hit a log).

Above the second boat, Ripley released her load of water in a massive salvo of her entire load. Six tons of water crashed down on the small boat, sinking it instantly.

The third boat tried to swing wide.

As calmly as could be, Ripley veered to match their new course.

He barely saw the gesture as she released the pond snorkel. Unlike the sea snorkel strut that was gently lowered, then raised for each usage, the pond snorkel could only be released once per flight; after that it was simply down.

He looked back in time to see the latch let go of the pump at the end of the twenty-foot-long, ten-inch-across reinforced hose. The five-hundred-pound pump head swung down and shattered the third boat with a bullseye strike.

"Oopsie!" Ripley said softly as she eased up on the collective to observe her handiwork.

The survivors—probably shell-shocked into near paralysis—floated along helplessly in the current.

Around the next bend, the river widened, shoaled, and slowed. One of Tham Chau's firefighting teams dragged the arsonists one by one out of the water. If they'd had their boats and guns, they might have raced through and managed to disappear somewhere downstream; but not one of them escaped the firefighters who had fought the fire for two weeks. Especially not after they'd been told exactly who was floating downriver toward them. They had been told not to kill the perpetrators, but he did wonder quite how battered they would be by the time they reached interrogation.

Oddly, he didn't feel any pity.

Chapter 22

*K*new you still had some tricks up your sleeve!"

Despite his being dressed in casual slacks and a plain men's shirt, Ripley resisted the desire to do something unkind to Rear Admiral Parker. They were all squatting in the back of Firehawk *Oh-one* reviewing the footage that Steve had captured on the drone's night-vision cameras. Ripley wasn't going to admit anything out loud, but she was pretty damned pleased with herself.

It had taken two more days to beat the fire, but without someone egging it along, it hadn't taken long to kill off the last heads of the wildfire.

She'd personally made a point of checking on the doline jungle of Son Doong Cave several times during the firefight and found one other fire there that she nipped quickly enough. Not having a replacement wing foil for the strut of the sea snorkel, she'd been relegated to the slower suction of the pond snorkel—which hadn't even been dented as it destroyed the arsonists' third boat.

Her most surreal memory of the last days of that firefight was putting out that doline fire. The tank of water she'd been carrying hadn't been quite enough to quench it. So, she'd flown into the massive opening in the side of the cavern, actually hovering inside the cave over a broad underground pond complete with a sand beach. There she'd pumped up another tankload to finish off the fire.

Brad had been flying beside her.

Gordon had been aboard Mickey's 212.

But she wished he'd been there. Wished she had a bikini so that they could have swum together in that underground pool and made love on the sandy beach inside a cave in the middle of the Vietnamese jungle.

There was a precious quality to their victory as a team that Admiral Parker's overly-pleased manner was rubbing the wrong way. He acted as if he had arranged everything and that the firefighting miracle that MHA had achieved was none of their doing. Not Vanessa being shot at, not Gordon's insightful choices and impossible bravery, and not her use of an Erickson Aircrane as a weapon of war.

For that's what this was...or rather had been. It was an act of war by Laos against Vietnam. If it had been her country that was crisscrossed with great slashes of black char, she'd have invaded the bastards. Jungle wasn't like the US and Australian forests. Wildfire was not a part of the natural plant life cycle. It might take generations for these scars on the landscape to heal.

But the Vietnamese had proven why they were the diplomats and she wasn't. They had obtained confessions of high military ranks and uncovered proof of the approval by a deputy prime minister and several cabinet members of the socialist party's leadership—and turned the whole thing over to the ASEAN and UN tribunals.

"Glad to have been of service, sir," Gordon said, saving Ripley from achieving personal disgrace by chewing out a rear admiral for his arrogance.

"It's good to know who I can count on." He shook Gordon's hand, then gave her a sharp salute. "Lieutenant."

Parker then earned Ripley's respect by ignoring Mark Henderson's outstretched hand and instead punching him on the arm and saying, "Hug Emily for me." A moment later he was gone. The last words she could hear as Parker walked away in the company of Tham Chau were, "So, Major General Vo. What's your analysis of…"

Ripley glanced at Gordon, but he hadn't heard it. That meant that Tham Chau, with her arm still in a sling, was the Vietnamese Army equivalent of a rear admiral. Now there was a shocker.

Dong Hoi Airport was quiet now. No passenger planes stood at the small terminal.

The five remaining helicopters were parked neatly around the paved apron. The drone was down and packed, even the service container was closed up.

"What now?" Ripley asked as Gordon slipped his hand into hers.

"Don't really know."

"Now," Mark said. "Now we go home."

Chapter 23

The quiet start to the Australian fire season had continued while they were chasing arsonists through the Vietnamese jungle. There was no need for them to return. Gordon wondered if there'd ever been a reason for them to go.

The only interesting part of the whole journey home had been while the helicopters were being reloaded onto the Antonov An-124s at Noi Bai International Airport. They'd flown up to Hanoi that morning because Dong Hoi's runway wasn't rated for the heavy wheel load of the massive jets.

He'd been sitting with Ripley on the edge of the front ramp of the Antonov, trying to escape the tropical sun. The massive curve of the raised nose cone to allow access to the aircraft's cargo hold made the most ridiculous sun parasol Gordon had ever seen: twenty feet across and two stories above them. In its shade, they'd been quietly discussing what was going to happen to them once they were back in the US. Would her contract be terminated? If so, which direction would she go? Would he go? Would they only be together off-season? The questions had pointlessly whirled and snarled for lack of information. Or—

A man in his fifties walked straight up her. He wasn't tall or heavy, but he was solid. His neat white beard framed his tan face, which revealed nothing about what he was thinking. He gave the impression that he was about to have a truly serious talk with someone and it wasn't going to turn out well for whoever he was addressing.

Ripley jolted to her feet.

"Randy?" Ripley took a hesitant step toward the man. "What are you doing here?"

She'd mentioned her boss' name at Erickson on occasion. This must be him.

"Me?" He sounded pissed as hell. "Came into Hanoi on a passenger jet. I'm transiting to Australia. Two of Erickson's Aircranes, *Elvis* and *The Incredible Hulk,* are contracted Down Under this season. But apparently I'm here because some idiot borrowed a Beechcraft King Air a couple weeks ago and the Australians want it back. I have no idea why it's up to me to get it back to them, but it is. You know how I hate fixed-wing aircraft. Besides, I'm supposed to talk with you."

"With me?"

Gordon was amazed at the squeak of surprise in Ripley's voice. She'd never struck him as a woman who squeaked.

"At least I think so. I can't make heads or tails of this paperwork, I just know that it requires your signature. Here," he shoved it at her.

Gordon rose to his feet to look over Ripley's shoulder while she puzzled at it.

"Are you as much trouble as she is?" The man asked sourly.

"I'm afraid so, sir."

"Good!" He snapped it out. "She needs someone like that. Wouldn't want her settling for anything less. And don't be *sir-ing* me. I'm a civilian now and so are you."

"Yes, sir," Gordon tried offering a wink.

Randy winked back, grinned for a moment, then quickly resumed scowling at Ripley sorting through the paperwork.

"This is a purchase agreement."

"Uh-huh!"

Gordon decided that it was just his kind of cruel to play along with Randy, because whatever his game was, Gordon bet it would be fun. "What are you buying, honey?"

"Don't *honey* me. Not buying, selling. No! Not that either. Not me anyway," she riffled back and forth through the pages, then sat down abruptly. If Gordon hadn't pulled her back a quick step as her knees let go, she'd have sat on the pavement rather than the edge of the ramp.

"Erickson is selling my *Diana Prince*."

"Really?" He eyed Randy, wondering what his game was. He could see the guy was practically bursting at the seams, but it sure as hell sounded like bad news to him. If they were selling the Aircrane, was Ripley out of a job? Maybe there'd be some way to make a place for her at MHA. He liked the sound of that idea a lot.

Then he caught the edge of that smile that Randy couldn't seem to keep in check. So, this couldn't be bad news. He looked like the kind of guy Gordon would like. If this was a setup, he wasn't going to resist.

"Who would want the ugly bug beast?"

He barely caught Ripley's elbow before it slammed into his side.

"I would, you jerk!"

"You have a spare twenty million? Clearly I'm hanging out with the right woman."

"No, I don't, double jerk. She's being sold to…" she went back and forth through the pages once more. "It doesn't say."

"It doesn't?" Mark came over and snatched the pages from her hands. "Let me see that." He didn't bother to raise his mirrored shades. "Oh, I see the problem. Anybody have a pen?"

Randy pulled one out and handed it over.

Mark filled out something on the form, but from where Gordon sat beside Ripley, he couldn't see what it was.

"That should take care of it," Mark nodded, returned the pen to Randy, and then dropped the stack of paper back into Ripley's lap.

Her body brushed against his as they both leaned in to read it. He could feel the nerves vibrating through her.

He spotted the change first and glanced up to see Randy and Mark were grinning like mad commanders of the Queen's Navy. He'd finally caught up with an online video of *HMS Pinafore* last night and couldn't stop laughing.

"Mount Hood Aviation is buying *Diana Prince?*" Ripley's voice was as small as he'd ever heard it.

"Well, it needs another signature," Mark drawled out.

"I guess it does," Randy agreed drily. "If we're going to get technical about it."

Ripley flipped through the pages again, "I don't see anywhere to sign."

"What? Oh!" Randy patted all of his pockets before "happening" to find the missing page folded up in his back pocket.

"Sign here," and he handed the page to Ripley.

She read it over, "It says that the purchase is only valid if I'm the pilot."

"Does it?" Randy said in a tone he might use to discuss the weather on a clear day.

"Really?" This time Gordon could feel his own voice squeaking. Ripley being attached permanently to MHA was a possibility that neither of them had ever considered.

"What? Is that some kind of problem?" Randy scowled at him. But Gordon could see the smile that was his natural condition.

"No, *sir!*"

"I told you to stop doing that," Randy growled happily. "You, Ripley? Brad and Janet already agreed to it. You got a problem with your new assignment?"

Ripley looked at Gordon for a long, heart-stopping moment

before replying very softly without turning to look at Randy, "No, sir."

"This guy giving you problems, Ripley? Let me know. I bet I can still kick your ass, young man."

Gordon certainly wasn't going to argue the point…the guy looked a little dangerous despite that smile that kept slipping out.

"He *is* giving me problems, Randy," Ripley replied as her dark eyes inspected him from just inches away. "But not that kind." Then she leaned in to kiss him.

The fact that they'd be together at MHA still hadn't sunk in. It meant they'd have time to…figure out what was next. That alone was worth kissing her for.

After a bit, Randy growled. "Ripley! Just sign the damned thing, I have a flight to catch. Fire waits on no man."

"Or woman!" And she took the pen and signed.

* * *

Ripley was too numb for any of it to sink in on the flight home. Instead, she'd sat there wired awake for the entire first leg of the flight. Gordon had been the same, sitting beside her, holding her hand for most of it.

They didn't speak, to each other or anyone else.

Someone served up food, but she didn't remember what it was or if she'd eaten any.

She should have been passed out from exhaustion; they'd only finished the fire last night and then stayed up to watch *Pinafore*. Or she might be beyond ecstatic, but that didn't sink in either. She couldn't even look at Gordon, but it was as if his hand was the only thing anchoring her from disappearing into the sky.

Something had shifted while the plane was refueling in Tokyo, and she'd collapsed into a dreamless sleep.

It was midafternoon when they landed and unloaded at the Portland, Oregon, airport.

"Just a short hop," Mark had announced. "Form up on me,"

and then he climbed into MHA's own Beech King Air that had been parked in this corner of the airport since they'd left just a month before.

Rather than joining Mark, Gordon chose to sit just behind Ripley and Brad in the jump seat. Janet was down in her usual aft-facing spot.

"His heading's wrong."

"Wrong for what?" Gordon leaned forward to stare out the window.

It was the first words they'd actually spoken since Randy's revelation and they were so mundane that Ripley had to fight off a sudden bout of the giggles. Their lives had just changed, but neither of them could deal with it.

"We're headed southeast to Mount Hood."

"But Jernstedt Field is that way," Ripley nodded to the east. "Is there any other field around Mount Hood?"

"No," Gordon said it slowly. "Only… Oh shit!"

"He's taking us back to the burned-out airfield at MHA's base," Ripley knew it as soon as she heard Gordon's curse.

The numb silence between them now turned grim. For the balance of the thirty-minute flight, Ripley couldn't think of what to say to Gordon. He'd lost the only home he had. His parents' Wyoming ranch certainly had never been a real home as he'd described it.

Home. That word jostled about in her mind, but it didn't really land anywhere. She hadn't had a home of her own. Not really. She even lived in a company apartment between jobs because she was so itinerant it was never worth renting anywhere.

But Henderson forcing the whole crew back to the burned-out MHA field was a cruelty, especially after the long firefight and the long flight home.

Home. There was that word again.

They rounded the south flank of the mountain, flew over Timberline Lodge, and then flew into The Black of the burn. The whole hillside was a wasteland.

No…it wasn't.

Little patches of green, as so often happened even in the harshest wildfires, still existed. A dozen trees here. A patch of scrub brush there. Without rhyme or reason, the patches of hope and new life remained.

They crested the ridge and it looked as if Mickey's helicopter stumbled in the sky. Then all three of the Firehawks hesitated.

She'd been lagging behind, wanting to protect Gordon, but they couldn't help arriving.

And when they did, Ripley saw why the other four helos had jerked to a confused hover, as disarrayed as they'd been after the fire.

* * *

Gordon looked down too, unable to believe what he was seeing.

The devastation of the bunkhouse, parachute loft, and dining hall had been scraped away. The burned-out skeletons of their vehicles had been hauled off as well.

The area beside the runway that had been MHA's base had been scraped clean as if it had never been there. Even the control tower was gone.

But in the tower's place, several dozen new logs had been planted into the soil, bolted and lashed together. The second-story platform was complete, though only a single finished wall of the central cab stood on the platform.

"Foundation forms for new concrete footings," Brad pointed to the perimeter of the old bunkhouse.

"They're expanding it," Gordon couldn't get over the shock. It was almost as big as Ripley not flying out of his life the moment they landed on US soil. He'd spent the whole flight holding on to her tightly and praying that it was true and not some cosmic joke. And now this.

"Tents," Ripley twisted *Diana Prince* to face toward a small patch of unburned trees at the far end of the runway. An entire tent village had been set up their shade.

One by one, the pilots shook it off and landed their aircraft. Ripley's Aircrane filled the entire area where his and Vanessa's MD 530s were usually parked. Mark brought down the King Air last of all.

Like a group of vagabonds, they all drifted over to the base. There were stacks of lumber, a crew shack, piles of rebar. This wasn't a small operation. A big construction crew had been working on this hard during their absence.

Mount Hood Aviation was going to continue. And they'd purchased the *Diana Prince*, so Ripley would continue with them. Surely, somehow he and Vanessa would have a place as well. She came up beside him and the three of them held hands for comfort for a moment as others looked around.

A brand new quad-cab Ford pickup rolled up the road and turned into the empty parking lot. It was a cheery robin's egg blue. It was towing a large trailer.

"Damned woman," Mark grumbled from close beside Gordon. "Never let the woman buy the pickup, Gordon. Trust me on that. Now I'm going to have to get it repainted black." Then he hurried ahead to sweep Emily into his arms as she climbed down.

"I wish him luck with that," Vanessa whispered.

They shared a laugh and a hand squeeze.

"You hitting on my girl, Finchley?" Brenna asked as she moved up beside them.

"Absolutely!" He tried to slip his arm around Vanessa's waist as a tease, but she walked right out of it as if he'd ceased to exist.

"I know what's under that tarp," Vanessa's voice was soft with wonder.

Gordon hadn't been paying attention to what Emily had been towing, but as soon as he looked, he too knew what it was.

In seconds she and Brenna stripped the tarp. There on the trailer stood a brand new MD 530, already painted with the MHA gloss-black-and-flames. It even had Vanessa's name painted in small letters on the pilot's door.

Vanessa and Brenna clutched each other tightly. Gordon could see Brenna's face…and she was weeping. With joy, granted, but he'd never known that the tough mechanic was even capable of that.

Ripley slipped a hand around his waist and he hugged her tightly. Everyone had their place now…everyone except him.

"Come along, you two. Let's go for a walk," Mark and Emily stood close behind them.

Gordon did what he could to hold his nerves in check and held on to Ripley tightly in hopes that he'd still be around tomorrow. Mark and Emily led them up onto the lookout platform. The timber railing wasn't in place yet, but a temporary railing of two-by-fours wrapped all the way around.

For a while they just looked out at the line of helicopters parked and silent along the tree line. There was no underbrush, and the trees were badly blackened, but Gordon would guess a third of them would survive. Next spring Mark would have to arrange for the rest to be cut.

From the other side, they looked down over the camp. The sun was low in the west, brilliantly lighting the glaciers atop Mount Hood. The rest of the crew was gathered around Vanessa's new helicopter.

"The transformation of this team, you two," Gordon addressed Mark and Emily. "You've done an amazing thing. In the three years I've been here, you've really turned MHA into a world-class outfit. And Emily, doing the cleanup, starting the rebuild, and the new MD, that was just a miracle of a much more immediate nature."

"Thanks. Now just keep it that way."

"What do you mean?"

"Here," Mark handed him a set of keys.

* * *

Ripley recognized them. They were the keys to the King Air spotter plane.

"You should get yourself a pilot," Mark was telling him. "That way you can concentrate on the radios and the fire, but your instincts are exceptional."

There was a distant round of cheers from the other pilots.

A van had pulled up beside Mark and Emily's new truck. She didn't need to see Amy's red hair or Gerald's silent bulk to know that The Doghouse had brought dinner. They had a big barbeque grill on a trailer, which told her all she needed to know. They'd be eating well tonight.

"He's staying?" Ripley couldn't quite believe that everything was coming together. It was too much! It was too fast!

That stopped her, but instead of a cold chill, she felt a warm happiness surge over her. Gordon would be here. Flying that spotter plane to—

"Wait a sec!"

"What?" All three of them turned to face her.

Gordon looked puzzled but not by the miracle that had just happened to him. He held the keys as if he'd already taken ownership of them, flipping the ring around one fingertip, catching them, and then flipping them again. With each spin and catch he looked taller, more powerful, more utterly her alpha male with each passing moment as the new truth sank in that he was now Mount Hood Aviation's Incident Commander-Air.

Mark looked smug, all tall and male behind his mirrored shades.

Emily looked at her…as if waiting for the obvious question.

So Ripley asked it, "Where are you two going?"

"Wait!" Gordon stopped playing with his keys. "What? Where is who going?"

"Us," Mark pointed toward the east. "Montana. My dad has this gorgeous ranch out on the Montana Front Range, strangely enough called Henderson's Ranch. You two should think about getting married out there."

Gordon made a spluttering sound of surprise that Ripley

didn't even deign to respond to. Of course they were getting married. She didn't have to be the Monarch of the Queen's Navy to see that simple truth. Though kids, perhaps two kids like Mark and Emily had, *that* she'd have to consider. No, not even that. If they were Gordon's, no question. Definitely two kids.

"Sounds gr—"

"You're leaving?" Gordon's shout exploded out, silencing everyone in the camp.

They all looked up at the tower.

"You're leaving?" he said a little more quietly after everyone's attention had shifted to the cooler of beer that Gerald unearthed from the back of his truck.

"We've done everything we wanted to do here," Emily confirmed what Ripley already knew, but still Gordon's jaw dropped.

He might be her out-of-the-box genius and the best lover that there'd ever been, but there were times that he was a little slow on the uptake.

"Here," Emily handed a small package to Ripley.

Mark's cell phone rang.

He fished it out of his pocket and handed it to Gordon. He didn't even look to see who was the caller.

In moments, Gordon was *uh-huh-ing* into the phone. "A fire in Idaho? This time of year?" He said "uh-huh" a few more times. "Well, we're on the ground in Oregon right now. Can't fly tonight, but if you need us after midday tomorrow…"

Ripley stopped listening. If there was anything she needed to know, he'd tell her.

She watched Mark and Emily descending the stairs hand in hand to join the celebrating crowd.

Ripley leaned on the rail, once more facing out over the helicopters and the sleeping forest that would grow again.

"Going to need a paint job, girl," she whispered to *Diana Price*. Ripley could imagine her hard-hitting lady with the black-and-flame paint job and her name in flaming letters. "I'll make sure you get the golden W-shaped breast plate as well."

This worked for her. For the first time in her life she could see a great vista before her. Not one measured in fire seasons or even years, but rather in lives…two lives.

She unwrapped Emily's present.

Ripley didn't laugh when she saw them, because they were too perfect for that. But they sure made her smile.

She slipped off her own sunglasses and put on the mirrored Ray-Ban aviator sunglasses and just knew that everything was going to turn out wonderfully.

And when Gordon finished his call, he slipped up behind her and slid his hands around her waist; Ripley knew that she'd been absolutely right about that.

About the Author

M. *L. Buchman has* over 50 novels and 40 short stories in print. Military romantic suspense titles from both his Night Stalker and Firehawks series have been named Booklist "Top 10 of the Year," placing two titles on their "Top 101 Romances of the Last 10 Years" list. His Delta Force series opener, Target Engaged, was a 2016 RITA nominee. In addition to romance, he also writes thrillers, fantasy, and science fiction.

In among his career as a corporate project manager he has: rebuilt and single-handed a fifty-foot sailboat, both flown and jumped out of airplanes, and designed and built two houses. Somewhere along the way he also bicycled solo around the world.

He is now making his living as a full-time writer on the Oregon Coast with his beloved wife and is constantly amazed at what you can do with a degree in Geophysics. You may keep up with his writing and receive a free 4-novel starter e-library by subscribing to his newsletter at: www.mlbuchman.com.

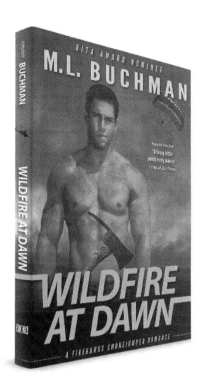

If you enjoyed this title, you might also enjoy:

Wildfire at Dawn

*M*ount Hood Aviation's lead smokejumper Johnny Akbar Jepps rolled out of his lower bunk careful not to bang his head on the upper. Well, he tried to roll out, but every muscle fought him, making it more a crawl than a roll. He checked the clock on his phone. Late morning.

He'd slept twenty of the last twenty-four hours and his body felt as if he'd spent the entire time in one position. The coarse plank flooring had been worn smooth by thousands of feet hitting exactly this same spot year in and year out for decades. He managed to stand upright…then he felt it, his shoulders and legs screamed.

Oh, right.

The New Tillamook Burn. Just about the nastiest damn blaze he'd fought in a decade of jumping wildfires. Two hundred thousand acres—over three hundred square miles—of rugged Pacific Coast Range forest, poof! The worst forest fire in a decade for the Pacific Northwest, but they'd killed it off without a single fatality or losing a single town. There'd been a few bigger ones, out in the flatter eastern part of Oregon state. But that much area—mostly on terrain too steep to climb even when it wasn't on fire—had been a horror.

Akbar opened the blackout curtain and winced against the summer brightness of blue sky and towering trees that lined the firefighter's camp. Tim was gone from the upper bunk, without kicking Akbar on his way out. He must have been as hazed out as Akbar felt.

He did a couple of side stretches and could feel every single minute of the eight straight days on the wildfire to contain the bastard, then the excruciating nine days more to convince it that it was dead enough to hand off to a Type II incident mop-up crew. Not since his beginning days on a hotshot crew had he spent seventeen days on a single fire.

And in all that time nothing more than catnaps in the acrid safety of the "black"—the burned-over section of a fire, black with char and stark with no hint of green foliage. The mop-up crews would be out there for weeks before it was dead past restarting, but at least it was truly done in. That fire wasn't merely contained; they'd killed it bad.

Yesterday morning, after demobilizing, his team of smokies had pitched into their bunks. No wonder he was so damned sore. His stretches worked out the worst of the kinks but he still must be looking like an old man stumbling about.

He looked down at the sheets. Damn it. They'd been fresh before he went to the fire, now he'd have to wash them again. He'd been too exhausted to shower before sleeping and they were all smeared with the dirt and soot that he could still feel caking his skin. Two-Tall Tim, his number two man and as tall as two of Akbar, kinda, wasn't in his bunk. His towel was missing from the hook.

Shower. Shower would be good. He grabbed his own towel and headed down the dark, narrow hall to the far end of the bunk house. Every one of the dozen doors of his smoke teams were still closed, smokies still sacked out. A glance down another corridor and he could see that at least a couple of the Mount Hood Aviation helicopter crews were up, but most still had closed doors with no hint of light from open curtains sliding under them. All of MHA had gone above and beyond on this one.

"Hey, Tim." Sure enough, the tall Eurasian was in one of the shower stalls, propped up against the back wall letting the hot water stream over him.

"Akbar the Great lives," Two-Tall sounded half asleep.

"Mostly. Doghouse?" Akbar stripped down and hit the next stall. The old plywood dividers were flimsy with age and gray with too many showers. The Mount Hood Aviation firefighters' Hoodie One base camp had been a kids' summer camp for decades. Long since defunct, MHA had taken it over and converted the playfields into landing areas for their helicopters, and regraded the main road into a decent airstrip for the spotter and jump planes.

"Doghouse? Hell, yeah. I'm like ten thousand calories short." Two-Tall found some energy in his voice at the idea of a trip into town.

The Doghouse Inn was in the nearest town. Hood River lay about a half hour down the mountain and had exactly what they needed: smokejumper-sized portions and a very high ratio of awesomely fit young women come to windsurf the Columbia Gorge. The Gorge, which formed the Washington and Oregon border, provided a fantastically target-rich environment for a smokejumper too long in the woods.

"You're too tall to be short of anything," Akbar knew he was being a little slow to reply, but he'd only been awake for minutes.

"You're like a hundred thousand calories short of being even a halfway decent size," Tim was obviously recovering faster than he was.

"Just because my parents loved me instead of tying me to a rack every night ain't my problem, buddy."

He scrubbed and soaped and scrubbed some more until he felt mostly clean.

"I'm telling you, Two-Tall. Whoever invented the hot shower, that's the dude we should give the Nobel prize to."

"You say that every time."

"You arguing?"

He heard Tim give a satisfied groan as some muscle finally let go under the steamy hot water. "Not for a second."

Akbar stepped out and walked over to the line of sinks, smearing a hand back and forth to wipe the condensation from the sheet of stainless steel screwed to the wall. His hazy reflection still sported several smears of char.

"You so purdy, Akbar."

"Purdier than you, Two-Tall." He headed back into the shower to get the last of it.

"So not. You're jealous."

Akbar wasn't the least bit jealous. Yes, despite his lean height, Tim was handsome enough to sweep up any ladies he wanted.

But on his own, Akbar did pretty damn well himself. What he didn't have in height, he made up for with a proper smokejumper's muscled build. Mixed with his tan-dark Indian complexion, he did fine.

The real fun, of course, was when the two of them went cruising together. The women never knew what to make of the two of them side by side. The contrast kept them off balance enough to open even more doors.

He smiled as he toweled down. It also didn't hurt that their opening answer to "what do you do" was "I jump out of planes to fight forest fires."

Worked every damn time. God he loved this job.

* * *

The small town of Hood River, a winding half-an-hour down the mountain from the MHA base camp, was hopping. Mid-June, colleges letting out. Students and the younger set of professors high-tailing it to the Gorge. They packed the bars and breweries and sidewalk cafes. Suddenly every other car on the street had a windsurfing board tied on the roof. The snooty rich folks were up at the historic Timberline Lodge on Mount Hood itself, not far in the other direction from MHA. Down here it was a younger, thrill seeker set and you could feel the energy.

There were other restaurants in town that might have better pickings, but the Doghouse Inn was MHA tradition and it was a good luck charm—no smokie in his right mind messed with that. This was the bar where all of the MHA crew hung out. It didn't look like much from the outside, just a worn old brick building beaten by the Gorge's violent weather. Aged before its time, which had been long ago.

But inside was awesome.

A long wooden bar stretched down one side with a half-jillion microbrew taps and a small but well-stocked kitchen at the far end. The dark wood paneling, even on the ceiling, was barely visible beneath thousands of pictures of doghouses sent from patrons all over the world.

Miniature dachshunds in ornately decorated shoeboxes, massive Newfoundlands in backyard mansions that could easily house hundreds of their smaller kin, and everything in between. A gigantic Snoopy atop his doghouse in full Red Baron fighting gear dominated the far wall. Rumor said Shulz himself had been here two owners before and drawn it.

Tables were grouped close together, some for standing and drinking, others for sitting and eating.

"Amy, sweetheart!" Two-Tall called out as they entered the bar. The perky redhead came out from behind the bar to receive a hug from Tim. Akbar got one in turn, so he wasn't complaining. Cute as could be and about his height; her hugs were better than taking most women to bed. Of course, Gerald the cook and the bar's co-owner was big enough and strong enough to squish either Tim or Akbar if they got even a tiny step out of line with his wife. Gerald was one amazingly lucky man.

Akbar grabbed a Walking Man stout and turned to assess the crowd. A couple of the air jocks were in. Carly and Steve were at a little table for two in the corner, obviously not interested in anyone's company but each others. Damn, that had happened fast. New guy on the base swept up one of the most beautiful women on the planet. One of these days he'd have to ask Steve how he'd done that. Or maybe not. It looked like they were settling in for the long haul; the big "M" was so not his own first choice.

Carly was also one of the best FBANs in the business. Akbar was a good Fire Behavior Analyst, had to be or he wouldn't have made it to first stick—lead smokie of the whole MHA crew. But Carly was something else again. He'd always found the Flame Witch, as she was often called, daunting and a bit scary besides; she knew the fire better than it did itself. Steve had latched on to one seriously driven lady. More power to him.

The selection of female tourists was especially good today, but no other smokies in yet. They'd be in soon enough…most of them had groaned awake and said they were coming as he and Two-Tall kicked their hallway doors, but not until they'd been on their way out—he and Tim had first pick. Actually some of the smokies were coming, others had told them quite succinctly where they could go—but hey, jumping into fiery hell is what they did for a living anyway, so no big change there.

A couple of the chopper pilots had nailed down a big table

right in the middle of the bustling seating area: Jeannie, Mickey, and Vern. Good "field of fire" in the immediate area.

He and Tim headed over, but Akbar managed to snag the chair closest to the really hot lady with down-her-back curling dark-auburn hair at the next table over—set just right to see her profile easily. Hard shot, sitting there with her parents, but damn she was amazing. And if that was her mom, it said the woman would be good looking for a long time to come.

Two-Tall grimaced at him and Akbar offered his most comfortable "beat out your ass" grin. But this one didn't feel like that. Maybe it was the whole parental thing. He sat back and kept his mouth shut.

He made sure that Two-Tall could see his interest. That made Tim honor bound to try and cut Akbar out of the running.

* * *

Laura Jenson had spotted them coming into the restaurant. Her dad was only moments behind.

"Those two are walking like they just climbed off their first-ever horseback ride."

She had to laugh, they did. So stiff and awkward they barely managed to move upright. They didn't look like first-time windsurfers, aching from the unexpected workout. They'd also walked in like they thought they were two gifts to god, which was even funnier. She turned away to avoid laughing in their faces. Guys who thought like that rarely appreciated getting a reality check.

A couple minutes later, at a nod from her dad, she did a careful sideways glance. Sure enough, they'd joined in with a group of friends who were seated at the next table behind her. The short one, shorter than she was by four or five inches, sat to one side. He was doing the old stare without staring routine, as if she were so naïve as to not recognize it. His ridiculously tall companion sat around the next turn of the table to her other side.

Then the tall one raised his voice enough to be heard easily over her dad's story about the latest goings-on at the local drone manufacturer. His company was the first one to be certified by the FAA for limited testing on wildfire and search-and-rescue overflights. She wanted to hear about it, but the tall guy had a deep voice that carried as if he were barrel-chested rather than pencil thin.

"Hell of fire, wasn't it? Where do you think we'll be jumping next?"

Smokies. Well, maybe they had some right to arrogance, but it didn't gain any ground with her.

"Please make it a small one," a woman who Laura couldn't see right behind her chimed in. "I wouldn't mind getting to sleep at least a couple times this summer if I'm gonna be flying you guys around."

Laura tried to listen to her dad, but the patter behind her was picking up speed.

Another guy, "Yeah, know what you mean, Jeannie. I caught myself flying along trying to figure out how to fit crows and Stellar jays with little belly tanks to douse the flames. Maybe get a turkey vulture with a Type I heavy load classification."

"At least you weren't knocked down," Jeannie again. Laura liked her voice; she sounded fun. "Damn tree took out my rotor. They got it aloft, but maintenance hasn't signed it off for fire yet. They better have it done before the next call." A woman who knew no fear—or at least knew about getting back up on the horse.

A woman who flew choppers; that was kind of cool actually. Laura had thought about smokejumping, but not very hard. She enjoyed being down in the forest too much. She'd been born and bred to be a guide. And her job at Timberline Lodge let her do a lot of that.

Dad was working on the search-and-rescue testing. Said they could find a human body heat signature, even in deep trees.

"Hey," Laura finally managed to drag her attention wholly

back to her parents. "If you guys need somewhere to test them, I'd love to play. As the Lodge's activities director, I'm down rivers, out on lakes, and leading mountain hikes on most days. All with tourists. And you know how much trouble they get into."

Mom laughed, she knew exactly what her daughter meant. Laura had come by the trade right down the matrilineal line. Grandma had been a fishing and hunting tour guide out of Nome, Alaska back when a woman had to go to Alaska to do more than be a teacher or nurse. Mom had done the same until she met a man from the lower forty-eight who promised they could ride horses almost year-round in Oregon. Laura had practically grown up on horseback, leading group rides deep into the Oregon Wilderness first with her mom and, by the time she was in her mid-teens, on her own.

They chatted about the newest drone technology for a while.

The guy with the big, deep voice finally faded away, one less guy to worry about hitting on her. But out of her peripheral vision, she could still see the other guy, the short one with the tan-dark skin, tight curly black hair, and shoulders like Atlas.

He'd teased the tall guy as they sat down and then gone silent. Not quite watching her; the same way she was not quite watching him.

Her dad missed what was going on, but her mom's smile was definitely giving her shit about it.

Other works by M. L. Buchman:

Firehawks

MAIN FLIGHT
Pure Heat
Full Blaze
Hot Point
Flash of Fire
Wild Fire

SMOKEJUMPERS
Wildfire at Dawn
Wildfire at Larch Creek
Wildfire on the Skagit

The Night Stalkers

MAIN FLIGHT
The Night Is Mine
I Own the Dawn
Wait Until Dark
Take Over at Midnight
Light Up the Night
Bring On the Dusk
By Break of Day

WHITE HOUSE HOLIDAY
Daniel's Christmas
Frank's Independence Day
Peter's Christmas
Zachary's Christmas
Roy's Independence Day
Cornelia's Christmas

AND THE NAVY
Christmas at Steel Beach
Christmas at Peleliu Cove

5E
Target of the Heart
Target Lock on Love
Target of Mine

Delta Force
Target Engaged
Heart Strike

Deities Anonymous
Cookbook from Hell: Reheated
Saviors 101

Dead Chef Thrillers
Swap Out!
One Chef!
Two Chef!

Angelo's Hearth
Where Dreams are Born
Where Dreams Reside
Maria's Christmas Table
Where Dreams Unfold
Where Dreams Are Written

Eagle Cove
Return to Eagle Cove
Recipe for Eagle Cove
Longing for Eagle Cove
Keepsake for Eagle Cove

SF/F Titles
Nara
Monk's Maze
the Me and Elsie Chronicles

Made in the USA
Columbia, SC
13 May 2018